THE
HIDING
GAME

J.E. Irvin

**The New
Atlantian Library**

Habent Sua Fata Libelli

The New Atlantian Library

Manhanset House
Shelter Island Hts., New York 11965-0342

bricktower@aol.com • tech@absolutelyamazingebooks.com
• absolutelyamazingebooks.com

Library of Congress Cataloging-in-Publication Data
Irvin, J.E.
The Hiding Game
p. cm.

1. FICTION / Thrillers / Psychological. 2. FICTION / Romance / Suspense. 3. FICTION / Mystery & Detective / International Mystery & Crime Fiction, I. Title.
ISBN: 978-1-955036-79-5, Trade Paper

January 2025

THE HIDING GAME

J.E. Irvin

Oh what a tangled web we weave
When first we practice to deceive

—Sir Walter Scott, *Marmion*

The truth must dazzle gradually
Or every man be blind

—Emily Dickinson, *Tell all the Truth, but tell it slant*

Other books by J.E. Irvin

The Dark End of the Rainbow
Hopewell 1

The Rules of the Game
Hopewell 2

The Strange Disappearance of Rose Stone
Hopewell 3

A Principle of Light

Broken
Love and Murder in the Adirondacks 1

Betrayed
Love and Murder in the Adirondacks 2

Carrion
A Byrd & Crowe Mystery

Vero

The daddy-long-legs crouched in the corner had spun a new web overnight. Veronica Simon poked a strand with one enameled fingernail, sending the arachnid scurrying into the crack between the display window and the sash. She intended to capture and dispose of it, but so far, the wily spider had eluded every attempt. Frustrated, she wiped the sticky mess on a tissue, leaned a shoulder against the wall, and stared at the raindrops splashing over the awning above the front door. Across the road, the waters of Lake Kalamazoo rippled, while outside the shop, the SIMON's JEWELERS sign rattled against the wrought iron brace from which it hung, reminding Vero of the forecast for strong winds and flooding on the roadways. The stranger loitering in the parking lot across the street had left, driven off by the encroaching cold front. Anxious to reach the hospital before visiting hours ended, she checked the grandfather clock in the corner. Ten till six. Close enough. Flipping the *Open* sign to *Closed*, she collected the necklace rack and the bracelets from the front case and carried them to the counter along the back wall. She had just settled the gold chains in the vault when the door, aided by a gust of wind, banged open. A man wearing an expensive tailored suit, a gray overcoat, and a frown stepped in. He brushed a hand through his wet hair and glared at her.

"It isn't six for ten more minutes. You can't close yet." The stern rebuke filled the empty store, raising goosebumps along Vero's arms. Dominance echoed in the words and the arrogant belief that whatever his demands, they would be met without question. Rising to her full five feet, eight inches plus stilettos, she took a deep breath and raised her head to confront the stranger, her green eyes unblinking at the dark gaze with which he regarded her. "You advertise personal service."

"We do," she said, "and I'll be glad to provide that. Tomorrow."

"Too late. I need your help today." He cocked an eyebrow to forestall her reply. "I've been to every jewelry store from here to Grand Rapids. Not one has a ring to satisfy my fiancée. You advertise one-of-a-kind designs. I'd like to see them. Now."

What an ass. Vero gritted her teeth to keep from uttering the words aloud. Instead, she decided to appeal to whatever counted as a conscience in the stranger, who stood well over six feet, broad-shouldered, with the cheekbones of a rock star and a stare that accepted no excuses. "I'm sorry, but my grandmother is in the hospital, and I need to visit her this evening. With the storm coming, it's imperative that I close now."

The man rested one hand on the counter and raised the other in warning. Vero noticed things like hands. His were large, well-tended, with callouses visible on the long fingers. A musician, perhaps, but unlikely with his well-groomed look. A businessman, then, wearing a Rolex and no wedding band. Well, duh, he did mention a fiancée. "Show me what you have. If nothing looks promising, I'll leave."

"Really, *sir*," she said, heavy on the sarcasm, "I'd be happy to show you all our offerings. Tomorrow."

He narrowed his eyes, his smile predatory. "Do you want me to report you to the Better Business Bureau and the Chamber of Commerce?"

Not an ass, then, but a giant, entitled prick. Before she said something she couldn't take back, Vero brushed away the curls that had escaped her scrunchie and pointed to the diamond solitaires beneath the glass. "We carry all the name brands."

He shook his head. "I've seen all those. Show me the ones this shop advertises as originals."

Not the shop, asshole, me. Vero reached for the tray of her original creations. Each ring nested in a black velvet pouch shaped like the petal of a rose. She couldn't disguise the pride that crept into her voice as she gazed at the gold and silver bands she had designed and crafted herself. "We use only the finest materials. Each stone is personally selected by our jeweler. Then, a ring is designed around the gem, which is cut, polished, and set here at the store. A Simon ring is one of a kind. You won't find another like it anywhere else in the world."

The man bent to examine the selection, his dark hair falling forward, the faint smell of aftershave drifting over her. "This is exactly what I'm looking for."

"Prices range from—"

He cut Vero off again. "Price doesn't matter. I just need to find something the woman will like." He pronounced the words with a sigh. When he looked up, Vero detected a hint of despair in his eyes. She didn't want to feel sorry for him, but, in that moment, she did.

"Any woman would be thrilled with one of these."

The man drummed his fingers on the glass, then raised his dark chocolate eyes to hers. "Which one would you pick?"

Vero knew the answer before he asked. To irritate him, she traced a finger over each one before stopping at a wide gold band. It bore a cushion-cut diamond set within prongs that mimicked the leaves of a rosebud. "If it were up to me," she plucked the ring from its velvet perch, "I would choose this one."

When he reached for it, his fingers grazed her knuckles, sending an electric charge up her arm. His eyes widened at the contact, then shifted as he held the band up to catch the light.

"I need to see it on a woman's hand." Before Vero could protest, he slid the ring onto her finger. The diamond sparked, sending out a shaft of iridescence. "Beautiful."

Flushed and shaking, she pulled her hand away. The clock chimed the quarter hour. *Twenty-five minutes gone already.* She tugged off the selection and prepared to return it to the case.

"Don't. I'll take it." He reached into an inside pocket, pulled out a business card and a credit card, and offered both to her. "Unless you'll take a check."

Vero blinked at the name printed above a sketch of a house on a lake. *Calderón A. Castro.* It looked familiar, but she couldn't think why. "Don't you want to know how much it costs?"

"Doesn't matter if she finally accepts the damn thing. In case she doesn't, what's your return policy?"

Vero worried her lower lip with her teeth. Favorite ring or not, she dared not consider it being rejected. This single sale would keep the store solvent for at least one more month. She fingered the card, looked up, caught him staring. "It's a gorgeous ring, Mr. Castro. Any woman would be honored to wear it. However, if there's a problem, our standard return policy is ten days. We will also," she took a breath, "adjust the sizing, if necessary."

"Right." Castro didn't look away. "And thank your jeweler for me."

"My jeweler?" Vero set the card beside the register and keyed in the sale amount. $14,500 plus tax.

"Yes. He's an excellent craftsman."

"Oh, but—" Vero swallowed her response. This man didn't, wouldn't care that she designed the ring. He might even decide not to purchase it if he knew a woman had crafted it. *An asshole, a prick, and a misogynist. And drop-dead gorgeous.*

"How much do I owe you?" Castro said.

She choked out the amount, calculated the cost if he used credit, and decided a check would work. Castro didn't blink as he wrote out the numbers and slid the check in front of her. "I'd like a signed receipt in case I have to bring it back and you're not here."

"Of course, and I've entered the sale into our records. We also have a video record," she added, waving at the camera mounted in the corner. Ignoring the keen sense of loss coursing through her, she flipped the tablet so he could sign for the purchase. She had created that ring for herself, spent nights imagining a lover placing it on her hand. *Then,* she thought, *you shouldn't have put it on display, Vero Simon. Stop being a romantic fool.* When Castro handed back the stylus, she tapped the screen again. "Do you want your receipt emailed, printed, or both?"

Once more, he cut her off. "Printed. And box and wrap the ring."

Egotistical, self-centered jackass. Vero was surprised bolts of fire weren't shooting from her eyes. While Castro fiddled with his phone, probably checking his investments, she slipped the store copy of the sale and the check into a pouch containing the day's receipts and stashed it beneath the change tray. She could drop by the bank on her way home from the hospital or early tomorrow morning. She turned to the back shelf for paper and ribbon to assemble the gift box. The clock chimed the half hour, and she remembered who he was. Calderón Castro, the reigning king of real estate in Allegan County. She should have recognized him immediately from the TV ads and the billboards plastered around town. Heir to the family business, a playboy extraordinaire who, rumor had it, planned to merge the Castro interests with those of a rival firm by marrying one of the twin daughters of land mogul Harold Townsend. And then Vero remembered the girls, too, from high school. Cerise, of the quick wit and the sharp tongue. And Gisele, also a spoiled brat, who had become a successful broker in her own right, one who didn't care who she had to intimidate to make a deal. One of them was the woman who would wear Vero's prized creation. She wanted to weep, except that at that moment, as she slipped the ring into the box and taped the black and gold foil signature paper around it, she wanted even more to slap Mr. Arrogant. She placed the gift in a SIMON's bag, shoved his copy of the receipt in with it, and looked up. Cal Castro stood a mere foot away, staring at her with a puzzled look on his handsome ass of a face. She handed over the ring, rounded the counter to take him by the elbow, and pushed him toward the door, startled once more by the jolt that contact with him produced.

"Thank you, Mr. Castro. Let me know how Miss Townsend likes the ring. Good night." Before he could reply, she opened the door, escorted him out, and slammed it shut. She set the locks, checked that the sign still read CLOSED, and hurried to empty the other display window, almost sobbing as she realized she'd never reach the hospital in time.

Cal

Hustled out of the store into the rain-soaked afternoon, Cal Castro hunched his shoulders against the wind and waited for his driver to open the door to the company car. Slipping inside, he settled the gift bag on the seat and peered through the tinted window at the jewelry store. The CLOSED sign glowered in the dying October light. Inside, the woman with sea-glass eyes and long, shapely legs moved back and forth from the display window to the counter, her high-necked crimson blouse and black pencil skirt barely visible, her perfume a whisper in the air around the bag resting beside him. Roses and something else, something indefinable and somehow familiar. Should he know her? He shook off the odd sense that he did and tapped his driver's shoulder. "Thanks for getting here so quickly, Brad."

"Everything all right, Mr. C.?" Brad Hanson eased the Escalade away from the curb, the car's wipers slashing at the windshield. He paused to check for traffic, then sped up, heading toward the country club and the celebratory dinner Cal's parents were hosting to announce the intended merger with the Townsends. That's all this engagement was, a business decision, arrived at under duress. Forget about what he wanted. Or needed.

Music drifted from the radio, Brad's coffeehouse channel filling the air with eighties harmonies. Cal's fingers twitched, mirroring the chords of the acoustic guitar backing the female singer. He missed it, the once-smoky bars, the stale beer smell, the way the crowd quieted when he began to play. All, for the most part, in the past now that he'd been coerced into joining the family company. He scrubbed a hand over his face, his unsettling encounter with the salesclerk and the earlier argument with Gisele coloring his mood. Gigi had refused to explain her involvement with the developer who purchased those sixties-era apartments on Francis Street. The man, Eric Bergeron out of Chicago, was also angling to buy up property on Goshorn, a small, quiet lake ten miles out of Saugatuck. Cal had questioned her about the proposed deal. Gisele told him to mind his own business. That didn't sound like a partner-to-be. It sounded like a competitor.

Cal twisted to look back at the jewelry store, aware he had acted like a bully with the saleswoman. Her calm demeanor in the face of his demands belied the fire in her gaze, challenging him every time their eyes met. A few years ago, he would have been all over that, flirting, teasing a smile and perhaps more from those sassy lips. Today, he'd played the overbearing macho male, interrupting, insisting. Damn it. His attempts to placate Gisele and protect his parents were turning him into an asshole. His mother, God bless her, believed a man in his thirties needed to settle down. His father insisted that a marriage between two wealthy families had long-term advantages. Gigi presented a more ominous argument: blackmail. Cal groaned. His life resembled the plot of a Victorian romance novel. Or a Shakespeare play.

Brad glanced over his shoulder. "Cal?"

"I'm here, aren't I, Brad? Doing my duty." Brad returned his attention to the road. Cal stared out at the water in the bay. Could he go through with this sham of a marriage to keep his family safe? He rubbed a thumb over his lips, ticked off the pros and cons. Gisele was beautiful, and she knew her real estate. And yes, her family had local connections to balance his immigrant roots. The sex, when they had it, was passable for an ice queen, if a bit weird. His bride-to-be liked role-playing, a lot. But Cal was tired of pretending to be a bad guy or a spy to make her come. And this business about the ring sounded a warning. He'd purchased no fewer than four previous diamonds. She had rejected each one, claiming some fault or other, from not expensive enough to not big enough. He wasn't confident she would approve of this one either, although it looked perfect on the saleswoman's finger. He patted the bag resting on the seat and shook his head. Two could play the cat and mouse game. Maybe he wouldn't offer this ring to Gisele just yet.

"Big sigh, boss." Brad caught Cal's eye in the rearview mirror. "What's up?"

"Nothing a stiff drink won't cure. Swing by Gisele's office, Brad. I told her we'd pick her up."

"Not necessary, Mr. Castro. The lady called to say she had some work to finish up. Said she'd meet you at the club."

Cal leaned against the seatback. If Gisele didn't want him to pick her up, she must still be furious about their argument. So, no ring tonight. Cal closed his eyes, taking advantage of the twenty minutes of quiet time to savor the shock and brief shiver of desire on the green-eyed shopgirl's face when he took her hand.

Vero

The antique clock chimed twice more before Veronica locked the shop. Coat over her shoulders, purse clutched under her arm, she hurried into her aging Subaru and pulled out from behind the building. Grains of sand and stray leaves, tossed by the wind, spattered the windshield. She pressed on the gas, ignoring the speed limit signs. Visiting hours ended at 7:30, and she had promised Nana Verna to be there tonight. Her grandmother had insisted, and from experience, Vero knew that when Verna Simon ordered you to show up, she had something important to say. Come hell or high water, you had better be there to hear it.

By the time she found a space in the last row of the visitor lot, a nasty mix of rain and snow flung itself at the ground. Pulling up the hood of her coat, she trudged through the puddles and dripped her way through the automatic doors. The oncology ward was quiet, the silence broken only by the hum of machines measuring heartbeats and blood pressure, and the occasional whoosh as an oxygen tube was adjusted. The door to Room 320 stood open. Vero glimpsed her mother's plump backside bent over her grandmother's bed. Her dad sprawled in the only comfortable chair in the room. Raising her head, Nana gestured weakly with the hand not bearing an IV tube.

"Oh, Veronica." Her mother turned to hug her, then moved aside so Vero could reach her grandmother. "Nana's been asking for you."

"Before you and my mother start one of your marathon chats," her father rose from the chair, "give me a hug. Then your mom and I are out of here. It's been an eventful day."

Vero returned his embrace, disturbed by the things he wasn't saying. No mention of improving health. No plan to take Nana back to the house on Goshorn Lake, the place her grandmother had declared her forever home. "Did Sonny and Dave stop by?"

"Yes." Her mother gathered her belongings and took her father's hand. "Your brothers both came by earlier. Sonny wanted to speak to Grandma's doctor. Call me when you get home, hmmm?"

With a nod and another quick hug, Vero watched them leave. It was good that her brothers had shown up. Jason, better known as Sonny, played his medical card as often as possible. Usually, she was grateful, although sometimes the know-it-all big brother act grated. His specialty was pediatrics, but his familiarity with the tests Nana had endured did help them understand what was happening. Her brother Dave, a car nut, owned an auto parts store on the edge of Saugatuck. Neither one had any interest in the jewelry shop that had been in the Simon family, along with the house on Goshorn, for a hundred years.

A century of ancestral stories, some of dubious merit, some factual, resided inside Nana Verna's head, but Vero was the only one of the grandchildren who cared about keeping those memories alive. Vero loved the jewelry business, and lately, it was her designs that attracted customers, both locals and tourists, and her innovative ideas that had kept the shop going through the pandemic. Offering the inventory online helped them stay afloat, but it was foot traffic that made a profit. Owning the building outright was a plus, although taxes and insurance kept rising. SIMON's remained Vero's artistic lifeline, but her grandmother was the soul of the shop. Her illness over the last few months had drained their rainy-day fund. What would happen to the family legacy if Vero couldn't keep the store going? Dropping onto the chair beside the bed, she squeezed her grandmother's hand.

"You have to get better, Nana. I can't manage SIMON's without you."

"Sweet girl." Her grandmother squeezed back, but her grip was weak. "Are they gone yet?"

Vero looked toward the door, which had swung closed as her parents left. "Yes. Now tell me how you really are."

Her grandmother pushed the button to elevate the head of the bed. When she could look Vero in the eye, she sighed. "I thought we'd have more time, but my pancreas doesn't agree. I'm not going back to the lake house, Veronica, and I won't be returning to the shop."

"No, Nana. I can't do this without you."

"You can, Veronica, and you will. I'm leaving the store in your very capable hands. And I'm counting on you moving to the cabin. You love Goshorn as much as I do. No." Nana Verna held up a hand. "Don't you dare cry, sweet girl. No tears and no arguments."

"I can't move into the lake house, Nana. I agreed to share the lease with Ellie until next August."

Nana closed her eyes. "Some things can't be helped, Veronica. Death comes for us all."

"Don't." Vero held her breath, released it slowly. "Don't talk like that."

Nana's eyes, the same green as Vero's, sparked. "I'm not afraid, and I know you'll work it out. You always do. But there is so much more you need to know."

"Tell me, Nana. I'm listening."

"I want to, Vero." Nana, restless, pressed a hand to her abdomen. "Tomorrow. Only, promise me one thing, that you won't let the family bully you into selling. Not the shop and not the lake house. Promise me."

Alarmed by the beeping of the blood pressure machine, Vero wrapped her arms around her grandmother. "You have my word, Nana."

"Good." Her grandmother sighed and leaned back against the pillows. "Now, what happened today to put that fire in your eyes?"

Veronica shook her head, wondering how the woman knew her so well, although it wasn't really a mystery. Nana Verna had been a solid presence in her life since forever, welcoming Vero at the shop after school on days when her parents were still at work, teaching her to crochet, to play pinochle and poker, entertaining her when her brothers insisted she was too young and too weak to tag along. Vero twisted a stray curl before deciding how to explain her mood.

"A very annoying man came in ten minutes before closing and demanded to look at engagement rings."

Nana sat up, groaning as she did so. The blood pressure cuff beeped again, reminding her to straighten her arm. She pressed the button administering the morphine and closed her eyes. "Did he buy one?"

"He did." Vero failed to keep the dismay from her voice. "Paid fourteen thousand five hundred dollars plus tax and never blinked once."

Her grandmother fixed her with her signature stare. "What's so bad about that?"

"He bought the ring I wanted for my own engagement, as improbable as that seems at the moment."

"Don't give up just yet. Your princeling is coming, granddaughter."

"Princeling?" Vero snorted, and they both laughed.

Before Nana could explain, a nurse bustled in, checked the tubes attached to her, and reset the monitors. She recorded all the vital statistics on a chart and laid a hand over Nana's. "Can I get you anything, Ms. Simon? Water? Juice?"

Her grandmother shook her head. The nurse retreated, but not before fixing Vero with a sad smile. "Visiting hours are over now, hon. You'll have to go."

"I'll only be a few more minutes, I promise." Vero waited for the door to close again. "You might as well know, Nana, that Bobby and I broke up, months ago actually, so I am officially on the market. Again."

"Listen, Veronica, Robert Austen was never the one for you, so no loss there. Now, the store is yours. I put it in the will, and the lake house, too, I think." Nana Verna stared at the wall, frowning.

"What does that mean?"

"I'm tired, sweetie. It's hard to remember everything I've done. Go home and rest. And don't worry about the ring. Things we love have a habit of coming back to us in unexpected ways."

Vero straightened the tangled sheets and blankets, kissed her grandmother's forehead, and dimmed the lights. She stopped at the nursing station to request that any updates be shared with her, then hurried to the car.

The rain-snow mix continued to fall, obscuring visibility. Vero peered into the darkness, unable to imagine life without her proud, determined grandmother. Nor could she see herself living, as Nana had done for two years now, so far out of town. The setting was to die for, but no neighbors lived close by. The place was secluded and remote, especially in the off-season. Well, that wasn't her concern. She and her roommate had a good relationship. Their apartment was well-situated between their jobs and nearby restaurants and shopping. She set aside her grandmother's cryptic remarks about secrets and the lake property, focusing her ire on the inconsiderate Calderón Castro, who kept her at work past closing time and then bought her favorite ring for his society girlfriend. She didn't stop to puzzle out why that bothered her.

Cal

The sleet fell harder as Brad pulled the car up to the front entrance of the Saugatuck Country Club. Light spilled from the arched windows overlooking the driveway and fanned out behind the structure, illuminating the lawn area and the putting green beyond. Couples dressed for dinner made their way up the limestone steps to the canopied entrance. Cal's parents would be stationed inside to welcome guests and proclaim their excitement over the expected engagement.

Umbrella in one hand, keys in the other, Brad opened Cal's door. "I'll pull around back," he said. "Might leave to run an errand or two, but I'll be in the kitchen later if you need me."

"Understood," Cal said. He didn't mind Brad taking care of personal business while he waited. In fact, he wished he were going with him. About to dash for cover, Cal remembered the bag from SIMON's. He hefted the package in one hand, then held it out.

"Lock this in the glove compartment, will you? I won't be needing it tonight." Without waiting for a reply, he darted up the steps and into the club, heading for the men's locker room, where he kept a spare shirt and where fresh towels were always available for members. Dried off and once more presentable, he took the stairs to the private dining room on the second floor. The Townsends' small entourage of fellow realtors and the Castro family, all twenty-seven aunts, uncles, cousins, and grandchildren, greeted him as he entered. He thought he spotted Gisele, her blonde hair arranged in a chignon, among the women congregating at the far end of the bar.

"There you are," his father announced. "Everyone, here's my son, realtor of the year in Allegan County."

Harold Townsend stepped next to Antonio Castro and raised his glass. "Cal. A well-deserved honor, the man of the evening. And soon to be joined with my beautiful and talented daughter, Gisele Townsend, who gave him a run for the realtor award."

Congratulations echoed around the room. The blonde at the bar glanced up, then made a beeline for Cal, her face a mask of calm fury. Frowning, he raised his glass. It wasn't Gisele but her twin, Cerise, who glided over, one eyebrow raised, imperious and cool as a queen among her subjects. If it weren't for the tiny freckle under her right eye, she and her sister would be absolutely identical. A diamond choker ringed Cerise's neck above an aubergine sheath that complemented her violet eyes. In heels, she stood as tall as Cal. She took his arm, pecked his cheek, and smiled at the crowd. "Gisele's a lucky woman, right?"

"No need for claws tonight, Ceri. I'm not looking for a fight."

"Maybe not, but you're going to get one. Where's my sister, Cal?"

"She isn't here yet?"

"She insisted you were picking her up."

Cal shook his head. "I thought so, too, but no. She told my driver she'd meet me here."

"Strange," Cerise tapped a fingernail against her champagne flute. "Gigi didn't say anything to me about a change of plans. Where have you been, anyway? Why so late to your own party?"

"I had some unfinished business to take care of. The meeting ran long."

"Of course, it did. Always work before pleasure, right?" Cerise handed her empty glass to a passing waiter and helped herself to a full one from the tray. "Tell me, soon-to-be-brother-in-law, did you find my sister a ring yet?"

Cal blinked, opened his mouth, closed it. He didn't intend to be taken to task again, especially not in front of all these people. The previous aborted attempts to propose had left him skittish about trying one more time in public.

"That's a very personal question, Ceri. Jealous, are you?"

"Of you and Gisele? Spare me. Although I did enjoy our summer hook-up after university." She glanced over the room, nodded at a broker Cal didn't recognize, and lowered her eyes. "Just answer the question, Cal. Inquiring minds want to know."

"I'm working on it."

"Good to know. Gisele told me she's not announcing anything until that ring is on her finger. So, unless you have a surprise for us tonight, my father is going to be quite disappointed."

"He'll get over it." Cal swallowed back the bitterness threatening to explode.

"FYI. Too bad you chose Gisele. I would have said yes the first time you asked." Cerise slipped her arm through his. "Come on. Let's get you another drink. My sister loves a grand entrance. I'm sure she'll be here any moment."

"Hold off on the drinks. Looks like dinner is about to be served." Cal propelled Cerise into the dining room, unable to shake the feeling that he was the main course.

Vero

The Scottish, a yellow brick, two-story apartment building, blazed with light. Despite the storm, residents stood outside under umbrellas, arguing with each other. Vero pulled into the designated parking space, gathered her belongings, and hustled inside before anyone could drag her into whatever hot-button issue had them all standing in the sleeting rain. She liked her neighbors, but they were a contentious lot, mounting protests over anything and everything: rent raises, missed garbage pickups, tardy repairs to broken fixtures. Angry voices drifted toward her as she slipped into the foyer and took the stairs to the second floor. *Unconscionable. Unforgiveable. Sue!* Struggling to insert the key, she fell forward into the tiled entry when her roommate jerked the door open. Ellie caught her and pulled her upright.

"Thank God you're home, Vero. I'm, like, going crazy." Ellie dragged her toward the kitchen, the panic in her voice settling into a dull resignation. Vero dropped her jacket and purse on a chair and wrapped her arms around her friend until the woman stopped shaking.

"Does this have anything to do with the crowd gathered outside?"

"Everyone's upset." Wiping her eyes on the hem of her *Lake people make waves* tee, Ellie plucked an envelope from the breakfast bar and shoved it at Vero. "The landlord's selling the building, like the entire block, actually, to a developer, some rich dude from Chicago who's also, according to Mr.

Porky in one B, trying to buy land on our lakes. Like the one where your family has that house. Whatever. We have to get out. Like now!"

Ellie took a deep breath while Vero skimmed the letter, pausing at the offer of a full refund of their deposits and compensation of $2000 per tenant. "Isn't this illegal?"

"Probably. Maybe. Like, I don't know, but it stinks." Ellie poured tequila into shot glasses and offered one to Vero. "Which calls for a drink. Or ten."

"I need salt and citrus and advice from someone who knows the law." Vero rummaged through the fruit drawer in the refrigerator until she found a container of lemon wedges.

"I already called Ray." Her roommate sprinkled salt on her hand, threw back the tequila, and reached for a lemon. "He asked if I read the lease agreement before I moved in."

"Did you?"

Ellie rolled the empty shot glass in her hand. Vero repeated the question. "When you asked me to share the apartment, you told me everything was fine. What's in the lease?"

"If the property is sold for a new development, our landlord has the right to kick us out."

"It does not say that."

"Not exactly, but close enough. Here." Ellie handed over the agreement she had signed when she first rented the place. Vero sighed. After spending two post-college years in her parents' house, she had been eager to move in with her friend. Giddy, even. As much as she loved her family, she needed to be on her own. The arrangement had worked fine until now. Sliding onto a stool, Vero smoothed out the two-page agreement and read it line for line, something that had not occurred to her to do before. When she finished, she drummed her fingers on the counter and groaned. Despite all the supposed protections for renters, the language was unequivocal. She and Ellie were officially homeless.

"When do we start looking for a new place?" Vero folded the contract and handed it back. Ellie shoved it in a drawer, her pale face now flushed a deep red.

"The thing is," she poured a second shot and downed it, "Ray, um, asked me to move in with him, and I accepted."

Veronica dropped her head in her hands, foreboding tickling a path up her spine. With Nana Verna too ill to return to the store and now losing

18

the apartment, she felt adrift. The image of Cal Castro intruded. The man was the most successful realtor in the area. Maybe he would know of a house she could rent or buy. No, her finances were stretched too thin to take on a mortgage. Another apartment? Unlikely. Rentals in the downtown Saugatuck area were expensive and hard to find, especially ones within walking distance of SIMON's. She only drove her older model Subaru, a venerable vehicle with almost two hundred thousand miles on it, when the weather was bad or she had to go to Holland or beyond. What options did she have? Go home? No way. She would not move back in with her parents. Ask Calderón Castro for help? Absolutely not. She refused to ask that arrogant man for anything. She would find a place on her own...but how?

"Vero?" Ellie said. "Are you okay?"

"How long before we have to be out?"

Ellie set a plate of cheese and crackers on the counter and eased onto the other stool. "I'm sorry, Vero. You know I had planned to move in with Ray eventually. This just, like, changes the timetable, but you'll find something. I mean, your parents—"

"No. I'm not crawling back home." They ate in silence, the rain dripping down the window a counterpoint to their sadness.

"I'm really sorry." Ellie got up to refill the plate with slices of oranges and apples. "And I forgot to ask. How's your grandmother? You went to see her tonight, didn't you?"

"She's not doing well. They're transferring her to a nursing home, and she won't be returning to the store." Speaking of Nana, Vero recalled her grandmother's insistence that she move into the lake home. She did want to be on her own, but not that alone. Scooting the empty plate toward the sink, she rinsed the glasses and put them in the dishwasher. Her mind skittered from problem to problem, landing back on the eviction letter. Two weeks and a consolation payoff to keep the residents from going to court. Great.

Ellie attempted conversation, but Vero barely managed to respond. Gathering her mail, she kicked off her shoes and shuffled toward her bedroom, wondering what further bombshells awaited in the handful of envelopes and mailers. After changing into sweatpants and a fleece pullover, she made a quick bathroom stop, then sat at the desk to wade through the bills and brochures. Most of the letters were addressed to

Verna Simon from sellers of gems, none of whom seemed familiar. Over the years, her grandmother had been the sole procurer of inventory, and Nana kept the sources to herself. Now Vero, tasked with that additional responsibility, regretted not pressing for more information. Unless her grandmother shared her contacts, Vero would have to establish new connections. She sorted through the mailings again, concentrating on those with known reputations and discarding the offers from unknown sources. She used the store checkbook to pay October's utility and insurance bills. The ring sale today certainly increased the bottom line for the month, but she couldn't shake the sense of hopelessness. Why had she shown Castro that specific design? When she created that ring, it spoke to her, inspiring the hope that someone she loved would give it to her one day. Well, that fantasy was gone. *No more whining.*

She straightened her shoulders and picked up an oversized postcard to stare at the stunning blonde beckoning readers to find their dream home with her. Gisele Townsend, Realtor, followed by five acronyms touting her expertise. A wheeler and dealer and master manipulator even in high school. Wait. Local gossip mentioned the Townsend women almost daily, something to do with dynasties and realtor awards and backstabbing... especially Gisele. No. No, no, no. Vero's ring, the one she had created, gracing the finger of Gigi Townsend, the queen bitch of Saugatuck? Was it for this that she had spent all those late nights crafting such a beautiful work of art? She laid her head down and covered it with her hands, the voice of Darth Vader echoing in her head. *Now, my triumph is complete.*

Cal

The dinner service concluded, guests drifted off to the restrooms or the open bar. Cerise wandered back to the gaggle of females from Gisele's office, using her status as legal counsel for the Townsend firm to speculate on the upcoming election and who would throw a hat in the race a year from now. Cal suspected Ceri had political aspirations, ones she intended to further with his help. What raging hormonal fantasy had possessed him to date both her and her sister after college? To revel in their competitive nature while he enjoyed the attention and pursued his music, playing gigs at local bars and summer festivals? He'd dropped Ceri and the dual dating game, planned to book gigs in neighboring states only to be hauled back in when Gisele threatened to commit suicide. He'd resisted her manipulation until she promised to reveal what she knew about his mother, and just like that, he was hooked. Four years of her playing the blackmail card. Cal was sick of it.

Eager to escape the press of well-wishers asking when they could expect a formal announcement, Cal headed toward the game room. His mother intercepted him in the hall.

"*Mijo*," Isabel Castro stretched her petite frame to kiss his cheek, "my son, you seem distracted. Are you unhappy with the dinner or the service? I can ask the manager to adjust his fees."

"No, *mamá*, everything was fine tonight. I'm just wondering where Gisele is." He looked at his phone. "I've tried calling. No answer."

"Ah, that one. Just like her to keep us all wondering. I know your father has his sights set on a merger with her family, and I agree there are advantages to joining our two families, but she's not as warm as I would like your wife and my future daughter-in-law to be. But you have dated her for a long time now. Tell me, do you have doubts?"

Cal leaned over to kiss her cheek. "I've bought her four engagement rings. She didn't approve any of them, so tonight, I made another purchase, trying to please her."

"Did she reject that one, too?"

"She isn't here to ask, is she? So, no, I haven't offered it to her yet."

His mother stepped back, placed her hands on her hips, and shook her head. "And why is that, *cariño*?"

He wasn't sure if she was referring to Gisele's rejections or his hesitancy. "Gigi is a difficult woman to please."

"Well, perhaps this woman is not right for you after all." She patted his cheek. "Take your time, *mijo*. I know you will make the right decision. Now, go be with your friends."

Cal didn't remind her that he was thirty and didn't need his mother to tell him what to do. He kissed the top of her head. "I think I'll take a walk."

"It's storming outside. Do not get struck by lightning."

Cal slipped through the patio doors to stroll along the canopied terrace. The darkened golf course angled off to the left, trees obscuring the cart paths beyond the first tee. He replayed Cerise's dinner conversation, her breathy invitation to stop by her place later to continue the discussion. Once, he might have flirted back, then laughed it off, certain Cerise wasn't serious, but tonight, everything felt off. Maybe it was the lack of communication from Gisele after their fight over the lake development deal. Maybe it was his father's insistence that he, not the Townsends, land the contract. Or perhaps it was this whole arranged marriage, how both families had cornered him into it with promises and threats. Cal didn't feel much like catering to anyone's plans for him tonight. He rested his hands on the low stone wall that bordered the walkway and stared into the night, wondering what to do about the ring he'd purchased. Veronica Simon's face rose to mind, those alluring green eyes shimmering with challenge and a touch of sadness as she handed over the ring. He thought he remembered a younger, shyer, high-school version of the woman with the same banked fire. What would happen, he wondered, if someone lit that spark?

A deer broke cover along the cart path at the eighteenth green, stilled at the noise spilling from the club, then vanished into the woods. Cal spent a moment wishing he were escaping with it. He contemplated leaving. Brad wouldn't mind getting home early, and Cal needed to set up several new listings. He startled when an emergency vehicle, accompanied by a police car, roared down the driveway, bypassed the front of the club, and continued on to the service entrance in the rear. He pulled out his phone to check with the driver when his mother stepped onto the terrace.

"Calderón, *hijo*? Are you out here?"

"Sí, *mamá*. What's wrong?" As Cal started toward her, shouts erupted from inside the Club.

"Your father needs you. Now." Grabbing his arm, she tugged him inside and over to the guests clustered around Antonio Castro and Harold Townsend.

"That was the police." Townsend held his phone in the air, glaring at Cal as he approached. "Something has happened to Gisele."

Vero

The fierce whine of emergency sirens brought Vero back to the window. She twitched aside the curtain to scan the parking lot. The neighbors remained below, still huddled under umbrellas as they wandered like ants displaced from their hill. The first police car passed the entrance to the apartments and raced toward the downtown district three blocks away. An ambulance followed, then more police and fire vehicles. Vero twisted to peer as far down the road as she could, but no flames raged against the rain. She spotted no smoke either. Perhaps a car accident, a bad one, was responsible for the outsized local response.

Returning to her desk, Vero scrolled through the listing of real estate offices in and around Saugatuck. She immediately dismissed the Townsend firm and didn't even pause when the Castro Group appeared on screen. No way was she asking them for help. Then she recognized another name from her past, Lincoln Storey, a high school friend of her brother Dave. She doubted he would remember her, but it was worth a shot. She tapped the contact button, composed an email, and pressed send before she could re-think her decision. Only two weeks remained to find a new place. Nothing like pressure to kick off a migraine.

The sound of her roommate rattling pans reminded Vero she hadn't eaten anything substantial since noon. She slid into the well-worn corduroy slippers Nana had gifted her when she left for college and joined Ellie in the kitchen.

"Sorry for being such a bitch, El. It's not your fault we're being evicted and that you have a generous and loving boyfriend who wants you for his snuggle buddy every night."

Ellie shot her a sheepish grin, then held up a jar of homemade chicken noodle soup from her mother's stash. "Want some?"

"How can I turn down Mama Manzo's special cure-all? Of course, I want some."

"Honestly, I feel terrible, Vero. When I asked you to move in, I, like, had no idea the landlord planned to sell. And I'm sorry I didn't read the contract. If I had…"

"If you had," Vero interrupted, "we wouldn't have had the chance to become friends. Right?"

Tears rolled down Ellie's cheeks. "What a shitty end to a shitty day."

"What happened to you?"

"Remember I had an appointment with the gyno doctor?"

Vero rooted in the dishwasher for clean bowls and spoons and set the table. "Yeah. Did she figure out what's wrong?"

"My endometriosis is back. I have to have surgery. Again."

"Oh, Ellie, now I really feel like a horrible person." She hurried over to hug her friend. What was the loss of a favorite ring compared to the recurrence of the disease Ellie had struggled with since puberty? This would be the third operation to remove excess tissue growth and improve the chances of conceiving a baby one day. Ellie refused to set a wedding date unless she could assure her boyfriend they'd be parents. Ray didn't care, but for the Manzo family, parenthood was everything. Thinking about kids reminded Vero of her childhood, those days she and her brothers had spent paddle boarding on Lake Goshorn. She missed the way they were before grown-up problems changed everything. "What can I do to help?"

Ellie pushed away with a sigh. "Be my friend, like you've always been. Now, let's have some soup, drink too much, and find some sliver of happy in this sad mess we call life."

"You got it, girlfriend." Vero placed a candle in the middle of the table, filled the wine glasses, and waited for her roommate to join her.

Ellie ladled soup into bowls, squeezed Vero's hand, and plopped into her chair. "Your turn. Tell me about your shitty day."

Vero shook her head. "Can't compare to yours. Listen, I have some work to do after we eat, but can we watch a movie later?"

Ellie pressed her hands against her belly. "Not tonight, roomie. I'm going to take two powerful painkillers and try to forget all my woman troubles. I'll see you in the morning, okay?"

Back in her bedroom, Vero finished paying bills, the feeling that she'd forgotten something nagging like an itch she couldn't quite scratch, and thought about the day's strange ending. Cal Castro had paid for the ring without blinking, then demanded to know the refund policy. Snooty and rich, the worst kind of man, and handsome enough to charm snakes. After one final check of her personal account, she closed the laptop and dialed Sonny's number.

"You saw Nana." Sonny's abrupt statement grated. Where was his self-proclaimed winning bedside manner?

"Hi, Sonny. It's Veronica. I'm fine, thanks. How are you?"

"No time for pleasantries, Ironica. I'm on call tonight. What's up?"

The use of the childhood nickname raised her blood pressure, but she was determined to stay calm. "I'm about to be homeless. Do you know of any apartments for rent close to the shop?"

"What did you do?"

Vero clenched her fist. "I didn't do anything. The owner is selling the building to an out-of-town developer who, Ellie thinks, may also be interested in properties on Lake Goshorn."

"Oh, right. Someone's going to make out like a bandit there." Sonny chuckled. "Might as well be us."

"Wait. What do you mean, us?"

Her brother paused. "I'm not getting into that with you tonight. How are things at the shop?"

"We're hanging in there." Now would be the time to tell him about the ring, how the sale would keep SIMON's solvent for another month, but she knew he'd be dismissive of her news. Sonny thought designing jewelry wasn't a legitimate career. The arts, in his opinion, were nothing more than hobbies. "Grandma wants me to have the shop, Sonny, and I want it."

"That's a big commitment, little sister, and an expensive one."

"You think I'm going to fail, don't you?"

Sonny blew out an exasperated breath. "You don't even have a place to live. You think you can keep a business going? Ask Mom and Dad—"

"I'm not moving back home, and before you say anything else, I'm not moving in with you and Yuki and the kids or with Dave. End of discussion. Now, tell me. How bad is Nana Verna?"

The silence stretched out before her brother spoke again, his professional voice overriding the familiar snarky tone. "She's not good, Vero. In addition to the cancer, Tom Cullen, her cardiologist, believes her heart has reached the end of its useful life."

"No. I can't lose her." Vero covered her mouth, stifled a sob. Her brother sighed.

"Look, I'm on call tonight, and there's one coming in. We'll talk tomorrow, okay?"

"Sure. Thanks for the update." She hung up, then checked her email for the twentieth time to see if, against all possibility, Lincoln Storey had contacted her. Nothing. After a quick check that the apartment door was locked, she huddled beneath the covers, unable to forget Calderón Castro slipping the ring on her finger and the heat that swept through her when his palm grazed her hand. She roused from sleep to the ping of her cell phone. Desperate to orient herself in the pre-dawn darkness, Vero reached for the bedside lamp, tumbled forward, and banged her head on the nightstand. She scrambled to her feet, listened to her mother's brief statement about Nana, and struggled into jeans and a sweater. "I'll be there as soon as I can," she promised.

"Hurry, honey," her mother urged. "Grandma hasn't got much time."

Cal

At the urging of Gisele's father, the guests departed for the bar area. After the last straggler cleared the room, the Townsends joined the Castros in the private dining room, anger replacing worry when Cal strode in. Sensing their resentment, Isabel placed a hand on her son's arm and hissed a warning. "*Cuidado,* Calderón. Be careful." Harold Townsend advanced on Cal, the man's bulldog jowls quivering with rage.

"What did you do to my daughter, Castro?"

Cal shoved past the man's outstretched arm. Isabel intervened, her calm voice tamping down the growing animosity. "Please, Harold, my son is as much in the dark as you are. We are all worried about Gisele's safety."

Townsend clutched Cal's arm. "You were supposed to bring her here tonight. Why didn't you?"

"Because," Cal ran a hand through his hair and glanced around the room, "she told my driver that she'd meet me here instead."

Cerise, standing beside her father, raised an eyebrow and smirked. While they were debating the point, two men entered from the hall. The first wore a rumpled gray suit, while the other, in a University of Chicago sweatshirt and jeans, rested a hand on the gun at his waist as he checked out the room. The man in the suit flashed a badge. "Detective Dick Norsuch. Please, everyone, take a seat." Mr. Townsend pushed his way toward the cop.

"Where's my daughter? Where's Gisele? Have you found her?"

"Mr. Townsend." Norsuch extended a hand and re-introduced himself. "We met at the Policemen's Benefit in Holland last year. This is my partner, Duane Harry. We're as anxious to find Miss Townsend as you are, sir. To do that, we need your cooperation, so again, please calm down. You may have information helpful to our investigation. Where are the other guests?"

"Waiting in the bar," Townsend replied. Norsuch spoke to a patrolman in the hall, then returned to the Townsend and Castro families.

"While the officer gets their particulars, Detective Harry will come around to gather some basic information." Norsuch waited for quiet. Cal leaned against the wall, hands in pockets, and inspected the group. Cerise met his stare and winked, causing Cal to shake his head. What the hell was wrong with her? Harry prowled the room, pausing to write down names and establish each person's relationship to the missing woman. When the detective reached Gisele's twin, he leaned closer, peered at her face, and shook his head.

"You're not seeing double," Cerise said. "My sister and I are identical twins, and we're very close, so tell me, do you have any idea where Gisele is?"

Harry deferred to Norsuch, who raised a hand to request everyone's attention. "Mr. and Mrs. Townsend, Miss Townsend, will you please come with me?"

Cerise and her mother followed Norsuch from the room. Harold stopped to point at Cal. "You should ask Calderón Castro to explain where my daughter is. He was supposed to bring her here tonight, yet when he arrived late, he was alone. If anything's happened to my daughter, he's responsible."

Norsuch turned back to separate the two. "I assure you, Mr. Townsend, we will speak with Mr. Castro. Now, if you'll come with me."

Cal moved to follow. Harry placed a hand on his chest. "My partner will deal with you when he finishes with the family. Do you have your cell phone on you, Castro?"

Pulling the phone from his pocket, Cal held it up. "Why? Do you need it?"

"You and Miss Townsend were dating, right?" The detective cocked an eyebrow. "And you were at the realty office around noon today?"

"Is there a problem, officer?" Antonio Castro joined Cal. Isabel rose to stand beside them. "Does my son need a lawyer?"

Harry scratched his chin. "Let's wait to see what my partner says after he talks to the family of the missing—"

"Missing?" Isabel wrung her hands. "What does that mean, missing? She had plans to be with us this evening."

Cal wrapped an arm around his mother, spoke to her, then stepped toward Harry. His father shook his head and pulled Cal back. "We have nothing further to say, Detective, until you explain what is going on." He herded his wife and son away from the policeman. A waiter appeared, carrying a tray of glasses and a carafe of water. She circled the room, serving those who requested it, while Cal paced. Forty minutes passed before the Townsends hurried from the adjoining room. Harold glared Castro's way, then hustled his family down the hall toward the exit.

"Mr. Castro?" Detective Norsuch hooked a finger at Cal. "You can join me now." Mr. and Mrs. Castro followed their son. Harry cut them off. He motioned to a second patrolman in the hall to keep an eye on them, then followed Norsuch into the office they were using for interviews. Cal's mother folded herself against his father, tears glistening on her cheeks. This was every immigrant's nightmare, being accused of crimes because of their background. But Cal had been born here. He should be safe from persecution.

"Have a seat, Mr. Castro. Calderón." Norsuch dropped a notepad onto the leather and mahogany desk, clicked the pen he carried, and settled into a high-backed chair. "All right if I call you Cal? Let's see if I understand things so far. You and Gisele Townsend are an item. You intended to announce your engagement this evening, but you didn't."

Cal remained standing. Duane Harry leaned against the bookshelves lining the far wall. "Gisele and I have been dating for several years. Our families believe we would be a good match, and," Cal hesitated, "several weeks ago, I did offer to marry her. She made her acceptance conditional."

"Conditional? Doesn't sound like a love match, does it, Duane?"

Harry shook his head. Cal buried his hands in his pockets. "Gisele Townsend is a hard woman to please, especially when it comes to jewelry. She likes big, shiny, and expensive. Over the past month, I've offered her four rings. She didn't find any of them acceptable."

"Is that what you fought about at lunchtime today?"

"We didn't fight."

Norsuch opened his notebook to flip through the pages. "A secretary, Nancy Janowski, at Townsend's firm, Saugatuck-Douglas Realty, describes hearing raised voices coming from Miss Townsend's office at approximately 12:10. You were with Miss Townsend at that time, weren't you?"

Cal balled his hands into fists. "We had a disagreement about the dinner tonight."

"Did you threaten Gisele?"

"I did not."

The detective flipped to another page. "According to Cerise Townsend, her sister told her you were so angry you punched the wall."

Cal snorted. "Cerise would say anything to make me look bad."

"Did you punch the wall?" Duane Harry said.

Cal took his hands from his pockets and held them out. "Do you see any evidence of that?"

Harry examined Cal's knuckles. "Mind if I take a photograph?"

"Be my guest," Cal said. "And when you're done interrogating me, maybe you'll tell me what the hell is going on with my girlfriend."

The detectives exchanged glances. Harry returned to the bookshelves. Norsuch folded his hands on top of the notes. "According to the secretary, when she left work at five, Miss Townsend was working the phones from her private office. Gisele informed her that you and your driver were picking her up at six. Nancy was almost to the gym for her yoga class when she realized she had left her exercise mat and clothes at the office. She returned to the building at five-forty. The door to Gisele's office was closed, but Nancy heard voices, a man's and a woman's. She left without disturbing whoever was there. When the regular cleaning crew arrived at eight-thirty, they found all the lights on. They started emptying wastebaskets in the main office. When they reached Miss Townsend's room, they noticed blood on the floor and smears on the wall leading to the back door, which was unlocked. Mr. Feijoa called the emergency hotline at eight-fifty-five. The police arrived at three minutes after nine. So, Mr. Castro, our question to you is this: where is Gisele Townsend?"

Cal dropped into a chair, resting his elbows on his knees. "I have no idea. Am I a suspect?"

"At the moment, you are a person of interest. You have a documented, contentious relationship with your girlfriend, a fight the same day she goes missing, and witnesses who place you at the building around the time the secretary heard voices in the inner office. So, we're asking you. What happened in that building, and where is your girlfriend?"

"There are no witnesses placing me at her office. I didn't go there tonight. I was running an errand." Cal didn't want to reveal his desperate last-ditch attempt to soothe Gisele's anger by buying a new ring. And he had an alibi, that testy saleswoman at the jewelry store. *Por Dios*, she'd probably refuse to alibi him, but he had the receipt, except that it was in the bag with the ring. "I had business to take care of, which made me late for the dinner. Brad, my driver, said Gisele called to say she'd meet us here at the Country Club."

"Your driver, Brad Hanson?"

"Yes, he can back me up."

"That's interesting, Castro, because Brad Hanson is in the hospital with a life-threatening head injury."

"That's ridiculous." Cal bounced to his feet. "He was here at the Club, having dinner with the other drivers."

"Well, apparently, somebody decided to bash his head in with a golf club. The man is unconscious and unavailable to provide you with a cover story. And we understand you were out strolling the grounds about the same time Mr. Hanson was attacked."

Thunder rumbled. The lights flickered three times as lightning crackled, illuminating the golf course. Cal took a deep breath, wondering what spider had woven the web in which he found himself caught. An enemy had laid a trap, one he had fallen into without warning, and only one woman could get him out.

Vero

Morning staff bustled in as the night shift nurses completed their chores and headed home. The Simon family huddled in the hospital foyer, waiting by the ambulance for the gurney carrying Nana Verna to roll toward them. Hospice had been alerted, a social worker had spoken with Vero's parents, and her brothers had departed for their day jobs with a promise to visit after Nana was settled in.

"Mom? Dad?" Vero wrapped an arm around each of her parents. "I can go with Nana. I'll close the shop and—"

"No, Veronica. Mom and I will stay with her today. You take care of business at the store. Besides, you'll have to close for the funeral and—" Her father dropped his head into his hands and sobbed. Shaken by the sight of her father weeping and desperate to fend off her own tears, Vero busied herself scrolling through her emails, hoping for a reply from Lincoln Storey.

"Your father's right." Her mother clutched her elbow. "You need to stay open as much as possible, reduce your inventory, and then consider holding a going-out-of-business sale."

"What are you talking about?"

Her mother exchanged a look with her father. He shook his head, and she waved off Vero's question. "No need to discuss that now. How about you stay with Nana Verna tonight?"

"Don't change the subject, Mom. I'm not closing anything. Nana made me promise to keep the shop and our place on Goshorn Lake."

"Vero, honey. You're barely making ends meet now. Without your grandmother's expertise, it will only get harder. And the land, Nana's land, is worth a great deal."

"Angela. Veronica." Her father's warning rumbled through the atrium. "Not now. We'll discuss this later."

When her father used that tone, Vero knew better than to push the issue. She walked away, disappointment and anger clouding her vision. Her whole family expected her to fail, everyone except Nana, and she was leaving just when Vero needed her most. Sadness replaced the rage. Shoving her phone in her purse, she waited until an orderly wheeled her grandmother toward the exit and the transport idling there. "I'll be there tonight," she announced and, facing into the wind, headed for the car. SIMON's needed her. At least there, she felt in control, competent, respected. Along with the house on the lake, the shop remained her happy place, one she wasn't giving up no matter what it cost her.

Last night's storm had scoured most of the leaves from the trees lining the approach to Saugatuck, opening the route to a view of the bay. Her spirits lifted when she spotted the waters that led to Lake Michigan. She must be a true Aquarius if even a glimpse of a shoreline had her thinking about strolling the path from the back porch to Lake Goshorn, the caress of summer breezes through the pines that lined the uncleared tracts of land, the ruffle of the water beneath her paddle. Vero came alive at the lake. That reminded her of Nana's suggestion that she move there permanently. She had dismissed the idea as untenable, but maybe she shouldn't be so quick to discount it. And why did her mother say that about the land's value? Surely her parents weren't thinking about selling. The Simon family and the house on the lake were inseparable. Vero refused to consider relinquishing her heritage. But first things first. At the stop light, she checked her phone for messages. If Storey could find her an affordable apartment in town, she wouldn't have to consider the more extreme option.

Vero pulled onto Lake Street, intending to slip down the alley and park behind the store, when movement at the front of the shop caught her attention. A man paced the sidewalk, one hand in his pocket, the other thumbing his phone. His tall form and dark hair reminded her of Cal

Castro, but that couldn't be right. That arrogant ass wouldn't dare return to SIMON's today, would he? Except he had. The longer she stared, the surer she became that it was him. A thought struck her so forcefully that she doubled over. He wanted to return the ring. Vero experienced a moment of elation followed by panic. With Nana so ill, the burden of shepherding the store through the looming financial crisis fell on Veronica. Like it or not, the sale of her favorite creation meant breathing room, a chance to figure out a long-term solution.

The man rattled the doorknob, slapped a hand against the jamb, and headed toward the intersection of Culver and Allegan, stopping to peer into the window of the music shop two doors down the street. The fingers of his left hand tapped against his pant leg, playing chords on an imaginary instrument. Vero kept her gaze on Castro until the car behind her honked twice. The noise drew Cal's attention. He looked her way and frowned. She ignored him and drove on.

Pulling into one of the two spaces in the alley behind the shop, Vero entered through the rear and turned off the alarm. She hurried to open the front door and stepped out. The sidewalk stood empty. Cal Castro was gone.

Cal

"Where is she?" Cal read the placard listing the shop hours for the tenth time, then returned to his phone. Glenn Canard, his father's legal counsel, had sent another text. MEET ME AT THE POLICE STATION NOW! Reluctant to leave without speaking to the woman in SIMON's, Cal considered ignoring Glenn's command. He needed her to back up his alibi. Was she the same girl he vaguely remembered from high school art class? Those green eyes. That olive skin. Those long, supple fingers, capable of playing piano or caressing a man with sensual finesse. *Don't go there, Calderón. This issue is too important to screw up.* Judging by the antagonism and disdain radiating off her yesterday after he mishandled the purchase, she would be challenging to persuade. What if she refused to speak up on his behalf? Cal didn't want to think where that left him. If only he had the bag with the ring and the receipt she had stuffed inside. That would prove his innocence. Except the police might not believe he was the one who made the purchase. They could claim Brad bought it, and the driver was in no condition to disprove that theory. *¡Qué lío!* What a mess! Muttering every profanity he could recall in Spanish, Cal headed to the Cadillac he'd borrowed from the office. He pulled away, passing an older model Subaru with a canoe carrier on the top. He glanced briefly at the driver but made out no more than a mass of dark hair before the car passed him. Shrugging away the possibility that Ms. Snobby Green Eyes had finally shown up to work, he made his way to the state police station on the Blue Star Highway.

Glenn Canard stood near the flagpole, his navy suit, white shirt, and conservative tie screaming legal competence. Cal felt as rumpled as he looked. Sleep had not come at all last night as he and his family waited for updates on the whereabouts of Gisele. Once or twice, he thought of contacting the Townsends, but his mother persuaded him to wait. For the moment, Gigi's parents were blaming him for their daughter's disappearance. "No need," Isabel claimed, "to stir the pot."

Canard escorted Cal in, then had the desk inform the investigating detectives of their arrival. A uniformed officer showed them to an interrogation room and offered coffee, which Cal accepted. He waited until he and the lawyer were alone before asking about Gisele.

"No further information has been provided. A forensic team is still collecting evidence, and we are interviewing anyone and everyone with cameras in and around the vicinity." Canard set his briefcase on the table and extracted a folder before stowing the case at his feet. "Listen to me, Cal. When they ask you a question, answer only after I indicate it is safe to do so. Do not, I repeat, do not offer any additional information, especially with regard to something they don't yet know."

"I didn't harm Gisele, Glenn. You need to know that upfront."

The lawyer patted Cal's arm. "I believe you, Calderón, but intimate partners, married or not, are always considered the primary suspects until evidence proves they aren't."

"I have an alibi—"

Before Cal could explain further, three men and a woman swept into the room. The representative of the State Patrol took the seat at the head of the table. The female uniformed officer from the Saugatuck-Douglas Police Department sat next to him. Detectives Norsuch and Harry followed, unshaven and wearing the clothes they'd had on last night. The odors of coffee and donuts drifted around the room. Cal's stomach growled.

The group settled themselves, exchanged glances, and began the interrogation with introductions and the notification of date, time, and place for the recording in progress. Norsuch asked Cal to account for his movements from early yesterday morning until the noontime meeting with Gisele at the Townsend Realty office. To that point, the atmosphere, though strained, was polite and respectful. Then Duane Harry took over, and everything changed. He inquired about the argument Nancy and Cerise claimed to have overheard.

"What exactly did you fight about?" Harry said.

Cal steepled his hands to peer at the detective. He glanced at Glenn, who leaned close to caution him again.

"Several things," Cal said.

"What were they?" Harry prodded. Cal narrowed his eyes.

"Private matters, very personal, of concern only to Gisele and me."

"Now is not the time to play knight-in-shining-armor, Castro. What did you fight about?"

Resting his hands flat on the table, Cal pursed his lips. "Our relationship has always been contentious, so to answer your question," he looked at Glenn, who nodded but narrowed his eyes. Cal got the message. Keep it simple. "Everything. The celebratory dinner. The menu my family selected. Gigi wanted to change it at the last minute. The realtor of the year award. I won. She expected to win, and when she didn't, she accused me of playing the diversity card."

"Huh. Because you're...what? Male?"

"Hispanic."

Duane Harry snorted but didn't say anything. Norsuch made a get-on-with-it motion with his index finger. "What else?" Norsuch said.

Cal sat back. "Gisele had her mind set on a special engagement ring, one that nobody else would have, and it had to be expensive. I had already purchased and offered her four. She rejected every one of them. Yesterday, she insisted I find yet another ring, a perfect one, and present it to her at the dinner, or there would be no engagement."

"And you were okay with that?" Norsuch said.

"I was sick of trying to please her, which is why I went—"

Norsuch interrupted him. "Is that why you went back later, to tell her you were through as a couple?"

"No."

"And why you hit her hard enough to knock her out or kill her?"

Cal bristled at the suggestion. Glenn placed a warning hand on his arm. "No. I've never hit a woman, and I never will."

"Did you argue about anything else yesterday?" Harry fiddled with the pen in his hand.

"We did."

Everyone looked at Cal. He shrugged. "Maybe you heard about Eric Bergeron, that developer from Chicago who's buying old apartment buildings and tearing them down so he can put in new, more expensive properties? Apparently, his company is also interested in acquiring land around our local lakes. I have been approached to represent EB Investments."

"The person or firm that secures these acquisition deals for Bergeron stands to make a lot of money, right?" Norsuch said.

Cal acknowledged the jab. "It's no secret there is money in land, especially in and around resort towns. I know several people itching to sell to the EB company right now."

"So, you fought about money," Harry said.

"I asked her to stop trying to poach my client. She declined."

"Cal." The lawyer's warning did not go unnoticed by the investigators. Norsuch smirked.

"Mr. Castro, if there's anything else you want to tell us, now would be the time to do so. Should forensics yield evidence linking you to the attack and abduction, your ass will be in very hot water."

"And I'm telling you again," Cal stood to lean into Norsuch. "I did not harm Gisele Townsend. But here's a tip. Check into her background. You'll find plenty of men with more motive than me." Glenn Canard stood, too. He escorted his client from the room, but not before Harry called Cal's name.

"We're not done, Castro. We'll be in touch."

Vero

Although Vero longed to be at Nana's side, her parents were right. She couldn't afford to close the shop too often, because return patrons and occasional browsers might discover a jewelry store in Holland. Between customers entering and leaving, she dusted shelves and updated inventory needs for the coming holiday season, now only weeks away. Small business Saturday, coming as it did so soon after Thanksgiving, had established itself as an essential addition to the Black-Friday tradition. She examined the tray of specialty rings, sketching a few new designs on the drawing pad she kept by the register. She thought about recreating the ring Cal Castro had bought but dismissed that idea as soon as it crossed her mind. SIMON's advertised each piece of their jewelry as one of a kind. If she backed away from that promise, it would compromise the shop's integrity and appeal.

Despite the blustery weather, foot traffic remained steady throughout the day. A couple looking for a 'promise' ring spent a solid hour trying on and commenting about the difference between commercial offerings and her more artistic creations, then opted for a thin silver circlet with a small opal set into the band. The woman had an October birthday, so the ring suited her, she crowed. After the couple left, Vero returned to checking her messages, hoping for updates on Nana. She also texted her parents, reiterating her intention to spend the night and the day tomorrow at the Hospice Center. She responded to a message from Agatha Wiggins, the retired assistant manager, who agreed to work Sunday so Vero could sit with her dying grandmother.

Vero opened a cup of key lime yogurt and settled on a stool to eat when the phone rang, identifying the number as *unlisted*. She let the call go to voicemail. "If they don't leave a message," she muttered to the temporarily empty shop, "I'll know it's spam." A minute later, the distinctive chime of a recording proved that whoever called had indeed wanted to speak to her. She opened the screen and pushed the transcription key.

"This is Cal Castro. I bought a ring in your shop yesterday. If you're the woman who sold it to me, call me back. It's urgent." Wow! The man expected her to return his call without so much as a please and thank you. *Jerk.* She moved to erase the call and message, then hesitated. Had it been Castro outside the shop this morning? Did he want his money back? Shrugging off the chill racing up her arms, Vero returned to her yogurt and worrying about Nana.

At ten to four, she ignored her scruples and closed early. With luck, she could change at the apartment, grab her overnight bag and laptop, and be by Nana's bedside by half past five. She had begun to empty the left display window when a shadow fell over the beveled glass that graced the antique front door. She looked up and into the smiling face of a man with tousled, sand-colored hair and dark blue eyes. He had his hands buried in the pockets of a camel-colored overcoat. A tartan plaid scarf completed the image of a confident man inclined to take charge of every situation. Expecting a repeat of yesterday's late, overbearing customer, Vero groaned. Laying the bracelets back in the window, she reached for the closed sign a fraction too late. The door opened, and the stranger swept in, stamping leaves off his shoes.

"Well, it's officially not summer anymore," he said, his voice filling the space. "You must be Veronica Simon. I sat behind you in Art class, and I remember that gorgeous hair. Lincoln Storey."

Caught off guard by the reference to high school, Vero accepted his outstretched hand. "You remember me?"

"I do, but I don't blame you for forgetting me." Storey rubbed his hands together and looked around the shop. "I was a senior jerk taking art to fill up my schedule, and you were a genius freshman."

"Ah!" Her memory dredged up images of her shy teenage self. She begged the blush threatening her cheeks to stay away. "And you sell real estate now."

"I do. And you, I understand, are looking for an apartment near your store. Thanks for the email, by the way. It made my day."

Vero returned to the display window to gather the contents and carry them to the counter. She did not intend to be late again. "I am, but you didn't have to come down here. We could talk on the phone, unless you have something to show me, or you're shopping for a gift for a wife or girlfriend."

"Not many rentals available this time of year in the price range you mentioned." He cocked his head and swept his gaze over her.

Uncomfortable with his frank appraisal, Vero continued to ferry items to the safe. "Then why are you here?"

"I happened to be in the area and wanted to see you."

He paused to finger a strand of pearls hanging from a display rack. When he turned her way, he smiled, displaying a dimple in his cheek. "No wife. No girlfriend. You?"

Vero responded to his smile with one of her own. "No wife. No girlfriend."

"Good to know." Storey reached into his pocket for a business card, which he laid on the counter. He rubbed his thumb across his chin.

"Listen, Veronica, can I call you Veronica?" His grin widened, revealing an identical dimple in the other cheek. "How about I keep looking for a place for you? I'll call you tomorrow. Okay?"

"That'll work, Mr. Storey."

He held out his hand again, waited for her to take it. "Lincoln or, better yet, Link. I'm glad we reconnected, Veronica. I'll be in touch." Then he was gone, the door banging closed behind him and his dimples. Vero narrowed her eyebrows. Who would believe that the most storied baseball player in Saugatuck High history would remember her shy teenage self? Despite his friendship with her brother, the two rarely hung out at the Simon home. And why did his focused attention leave her half-giddy and half-suspicious? Link Storey. Maybe Ellie would know some recent gossip about him that would jog Vero's memory. At least he had the grace to come and go without ordering her around. Shaking off the blatant sexual attraction of the man, she hurried to lock away the merchandise and set the alarm. Nana Verna came first. The insufferable Cal Castro and sexy Lincoln Storey would have to wait.

Cal

At eight o'clock Sunday morning, Glenn Canard escorted Cal back to the room where the detectives had interrogated him yesterday. Showered and caffeinated, Cal felt more at ease in jeans and a blazer. He checked his phone to see if the Simon woman had returned his call, then set the *Do Not Disturb* button.

Norsuch and Harry had also changed clothes, but evidence of another long day and night lingered. Dark circles marked the skin beneath the portly detective's eyes. Harry kept rubbing a hand over his close-cropped hair. Neither man had shaved. Cal went on the offensive.

"What do you know about the assault on my driver, Brad Hanson? And have you found the ring I entrusted to him?"

Norsuch shook his head. "Until we know if Gisele Townsend's disappearance and Mr. Hanson's attack are connected, the department is treating them as separate incidents. Detective Harry and I are focused solely on Miss Townsend's case. So, let's go over the timeline once more, starting with your arrival at TCF Bank at 9:30." He turned on the recorder and began the interview by stating the time, the date, and the names of all present. "Why were you and Miss Townsend at the bank?"

"We had a closing. Gisele represented the seller, and I, the buyer. TCF handled the finances and facilitated the paperwork and transfer of funds."

"So, you and Miss Townsend didn't spend the night before together?" Norsuch paused, letting the statement hang in the air.

"No. We're a little old for sleepovers, Detective."

"You're planning to get married, and you're not having sex." Duane Harry snorted.

Cal blinked. Canard tugged his tie. "Cal," he murmured.

"It's no secret, Glenn. They'll find out soon enough." Cal turned back to Norsuch. "Our proposed marriage is more of a financial transaction. Our fathers have been pushing us toward this for some time. Gisele agrees with them."

"But you don't." Duane Harry said.

"I have reservations, Detective. I suspect most people do before making such a commitment."

"Hmmm," Norsuch said. "Did you and Miss Townsend argue about that, too?"

"Not really."

"At any point, did you threaten her?" Norsuch asked.

"No."

"You didn't grab her or slap her or shake her?"

"I don't do that to women."

Harry opened a folder in front of him. "But you do that to men, right? Six months ago, you assaulted a man, Kurt Givens, at the Country Club."

"It wasn't an assault. No charges were filed."

"You're a big guy, Castro. You work out regularly." Harry tapped the folder. "The guy you punched –"

"Gigi, my mother, and I were having lunch when Blevins came over to our table. He had clearly been drinking. He spotted us on the terrace, charged over, and insisted that Gisele leave with him. Kept telling my mother and me to go back to our own country and leave white women alone. When he grabbed Gisele's arm, I asked him to back off. He told me to go fuck myself."

"Did you know this man?"

"No, but Gisele did."

"Blevin's assault was a clear case of harassment, bordering on racial profiling and discrimination," Glenn added. "I urged Mr. Castro to pursue the matter. He declined."

"Out of the goodness of his heart," Norsuch said. His partner smirked.

"Well, you only got in one punch," Harry feigned a jab, "and you broke the guy's jaw."

Cal folded his hands on the table. "I paid his medical bills."

Harry raised his eyebrows. "No mention of that in the report."

"It's easy to check," Cal said.

"Do you have anything to add to your statement?"

Cal and Canard exchanged a glance. Did his transfer of cash from his savings to his checking after the closing constitute a material fact? Glenn considered it irrelevant and motioned Cal to continue. "I wasn't the only one Gisele argued with Friday."

That caught their attention. Harry leaned forward, interest and expectation clear on his face. "Who else?"

"After we agreed to disagree, I left Gisele's office to chat with Nancy about another closing scheduled for," Cal checked the calendar on his watch, "next Tuesday in Holland. That's when Cerise came out of her office. She had papers in her hand and a scowl on her face. I don't think she saw me. When she went in to see her sister, she didn't close the door."

"What did they argue about?"

Cal shook his head. "I'm not sure. When Ceri realized the door was open, she slammed it shut, but not before I heard one thing."

"And what was that one thing?" Norsuch narrowed his gaze.

"Gisele shouted it was her idea, and she'd handle it her way. And Cerise said, 'I'll see you in hell before I let you do this.'"

"As you can see," Canard said, tugging his shirt cuff, "the missing woman apparently had issues with others besides my client. Now, if there's nothing else?"

Harry exchanged a glance with Norsuch. Cal's phone vibrated. Maybe the Simon woman had listened to his message and was returning the call, but he couldn't answer now. Instead, he turned to the lawyer. "Glenn, with your permission, I have some details to add to yesterday's statement regarding where I was between 5:45 and 6:55."

"If it's relevant, Cal. Just remember what we discussed earlier."

Norsuch nodded. Duane Harry settled back in his chair. "Let's hear it."

"Before the dinner at the Country Club, I decided to try one more place to find Gisele a ring she would accept. Brad Hanson drove me from my office to SIMON's Jewelers. We arrived about five-fifty. The woman who waited on me in the shop can attest to my presence. I was there for at least half an hour, maybe longer."

"Did you purchase a ring?" Norsuch fought to hide the skepticism threatening to break free.

"I did."

"Where is this ring now?"

"I gave it to my driver before I went into the club. I expected him to lock it in the glove compartment."

"So, you didn't take it inside to give to Miss Townsend?" Harry sat up straighter. "Is that because you knew she wouldn't be there?"

Cal felt cornered. They were determined to blame him for whatever happened to Gisele. Glenn shook his head, but Cal continued to speak.

"I don't know why I didn't take it inside. Maybe I didn't want to be humiliated again."

"Humiliated?" Norsuch repeated.

"I'm guessing you've never had a run-in with anyone in the Townsend family. Gisele's a master of put-downs and enjoys embarrassing people in front of others."

"Sounds formidable," Harry said. He toyed with his pen. "You have a receipt for this purchase, right?"

"It's in the bag with the ring."

"Did you use a credit card?" Norsuch doodled on the edge of his folder.

"I wrote a check."

"And when you, Detective, speak to the woman at the jewelry store," Canard added, "she will verify the transaction. So will Mr. Castro's bank since he transferred money to cover a potential purchase that very morning."

"That's interesting." Norsuch again. "How you knew to withdraw funds. Must have been pretty sure you'd find that elusive ring."

Cal bristled. "SIMON's has a reputation for unique pieces. I should have gone there first."

"Why didn't you?" Harry said.

"I don't know, Harry, but believe me when I say I wish I had."

Glenn rested a hand on his arm. "Thank you, Cal. This has all been very informative for the detectives. Now, if there is nothing further, we're going to leave and allow you to get on with your search for Miss Townsend. Mr. Castro has been more than cooperative."

Norsuch held up a hand. "Before you go, I'd like you to look at a video recovered from the building across the street from Townsend Realty. Maybe you can help us identify someone."

Glenn Canard objected. "This is highly unusual, Detectives, and smells of entrapment. My client was nowhere near that office."

"Settle down, Councilor. The video has been released to the media. We're asking for everyone's help on this. Perhaps Mr. Castro hasn't seen it yet." Norsuch cued up a segment of camera footage on his tablet and turned the screen toward Cal and the lawyer. "Take a good look and tell me who you think this is."

In grainy black and white footage, a camera opposite the Townsend Building had recorded the traffic passing down Water Street between Francis and Mary. The wind and rain from last night's storm rattled the device, blurring the images. A time graphic scrolled across the top right corner of the recording. At five minutes to six, a vehicle pulled to a stop in front of the realty office, angled so the license plate was indistinguishable. "Looks like a Cadillac Escalade to me," Harry murmured. "Just like the one you arrived in last night at the Country Club."

"My client's firm isn't the only one with access to this type of vehicle."

"Keep watching." A person wearing a ball cap and a dark jacket exited the passenger side of the car and entered through the front door. The car drove off. Twenty minutes later, Nancy, returning for her gym bag, pulled up to the curb and ran inside. She spent no more than five minutes in the building. Norsuch pushed the fast-forward button, and the video spooled on. He stopped it again at seven o'clock. "Notice that no one else arrived or left during that hour and a half."

"How is that possible?" Cal said. "If no one came out, where's Gisele?"

"We'd like to know the answer to that question, too, Mr. Castro." Harry reached for the tablet, scooted it to his seat, and rewound the recording to the moment the unknown visitor arrived. Turning the screen again toward Cal, he tapped a finger on the now-paused image. "Thing is," Harry said, "from this angle, our mystery man, tall, muscular, looks an awful lot like you."

Vero

The Allegan County Hospice Center sat halfway up the hill past the Chain Ferry. The rooms faced north toward Mt. Baldhead State Park or south to Lake Kalamazoo. Oblivious to the view, Vero hoisted the overnight bag to her shoulder, locked the car, and pushed the intercom button. After she held her driver's license up to the viewing screen, the buzzer sounded, and the door clicked open. A soothing palette of cream and blue walls and tan furnishings added to the calming nature of the facility. The receptionist waved and directed her to a nurse who led the way to Nana Verna's room. Her parents rose as she slipped in and went to her grandmother's bedside.

"Thanks for being here tonight, honey." Her dad wrapped his arms around her. "Your mom and I are grateful for your help."

Vero felt the tension in his arms, heard the sadness in his voice. He was losing his mother, and they could do nothing to change that. After a few murmured words of support and more hugs, they left. Vero smoothed Nana's blankets, kissed her, then settled into a padded chair next to a low desk under the window. She set up the laptop and opened the store's spreadsheet. Engrossed in the debits and credits from the past three months, Vero didn't sense her grandmother waking until movement caught her eye. Abandoning the work screen, she dragged the chair closer to adjust the yellow turban covering Nana's once-thick hair. Her grandmother stared up at her, eyes wide in her gaunt face. How could so much have changed in such a short time? They sat in silence, hands clasped, as evening crept over the stand of pines outside the window. Fingers of wind rattled the branches of a weeping willow that spread its leafless branches over the koi pond in the memory garden behind the Center. Breathing heavily, her grandmother struggled to sit up.

"Wait, Nana. Let me adjust the bed." Vero fiddled with the controls until the bed rose slowly. She waited for her grandmother to nod before stopping it.

"Veronica." Nana's voice bled out in whispers. She grasped Vero's hand to pull her closer. "The lake house belongs to you now. You must move there. It's the only way."

The words made no sense to Vero. The way to what? Perhaps her grandmother was hallucinating, but her eyes remained clear and alert despite the medication dulling the pain. "No, Nana. I need to be close to the shop. I'm going to find an apartment."

"What's wrong with your current one?"

"The landlord's selling it to a developer. But there's a realtor, Lincoln Storey, who's helping me look for a new place. I don't suppose you remember him. We went to school together. He was a senior when I was a freshman, and he barely acknowledged me then."

A smile flirted at the corners of Nana's mouth. "I'll bet," her grandmother licked her lips, "he's interested now. Water. Please."

"Nana, I'm not looking for a relationship with some flirt I barely knew in high school." Vero steadied the straw as her grandmother drank.

"Oh, so he's already flirting with you?" Nana paused for breath, clenching her jaw. Pain flickered across her face. "But that's not what's important. Listen, Veronica. You must move into the cabin. Find the hiding place. Find the truth about our past."

"I don't understand, Grandma." Vero took both of her grandmother's hands in hers. "What truth do I need to find?"

But Verna Simon's clarity had reached its limit. Her grandmother collapsed back against the pillow, her pulse uneven, her life force ticking away. Vero made no effort to stem the tears coursing down her cheeks. Whatever else Nana wanted to tell her was lost for now.

At seven, the nurse who had shown her to the room brought a supper tray. Vero was surprised to find she was hungry. The tomato soup, fresh-baked roll, and chocolate chip cookies revived her. She remained by the bed at shift change, waited as the nurse listened to Nana's heart and tucked the bedsheet tighter. Sonny showed up at eleven, grumpy and exhausted, giving her a chance to get up and move around.

The family lounge was empty when she wandered in, but the chapel next to it held several people, their muffled sobs and whispered prayers reminding her that she wasn't the only one grieving the last moments of a loved one. She pushed through a door that led onto a patio overlooking the pond. Trees with memorial plaques at their roots ringed the walkway. Flowerbeds, donated by families whose members had spent their final days at the Center, lay withered in the dying, late-autumn light. The night stretched cold and inscrutable around her, the sky clear and filled with a sweep of stars that took her breath away. Nana was the one who had taught her about constellations. They had spent many evenings at the cabin hunting favorites, the Pleiades, Taurus, Orion the Hunter and his bow. She would give a great deal to have more times like those with her grandmother. *If you move to the cabin*, an inner voice whispered, *you can have those nights again.* Yeah, but alone and lonely, with no lover of star formations to point out the patterns. Her cell pinged in her coat pocket, reminding her she hadn't checked her phone in hours. Drawing it out, she read messages of support from Ellie and Aunt Agatha, and one from her brother Dave, who promised to relieve her tomorrow so she could open the store. She had almost finished scrolling through the Facebook posts when she noticed the dot beside voicemail. Five calls from the same number. The unknown caller was certainly persistent. She punched **Answer** when the cell rang again. Maybe she could relieve her stress by reaming them out for bugging her.

"Veronica Simon." The deep voice on the other end sent a shiver up her spine. Her thumb hovered above the **Dismiss** button.

"Don't hang up, Miss Simon. I need your help."

Damn! The only man she knew with a voice as sexy and domineering as this was the insufferable Cal Castro, and she didn't want to talk to him. Her hand shook. "I don't know how I can help you, Mr. Castro. If you wish to return the ring—"

"This isn't about the ring. Well, yes, it is, but I don't want to return it, not yet."

She touched the button to cut him off, then paused. The nerve. Still, she couldn't ignore the desperate tone of his words, nor could she discount the unexpected reaction of her body to his hand holding hers as he slipped the ring, her ring, onto her finger. *What the hell is wrong with me?* "I can't talk to you right now, Mr. Castro." Ending the call, she tugged the handle of the French door that opened into the lounge when the phone rang again. Despite misgivings, she answered.

"Don't hang up, Verónica." A woman's voice this time, older, softer, rich with the accent of her native Spanish. "My son needs to talk to you. I ask you to hear him out. Please."

"Who is this?"

"Isabel Castro Del Valle. I am Calderón's mother. Here is my son."

"Miss Simon? Don't hang up until you hear me out." He sounded almost contrite and more than a little stressed. "*Por favor*. Please."

Vero counted to ten twice, but she didn't hang up. "Miss Simon?"

"I'm listening. You have five minutes, then I need to get back to my grandmother."

His voice dropped as though he were trying not to be overheard. "Is something wrong, Miss Simon?"

"My grandmother is in Hospice, Mr. Castro. She's dying, so you can see why your petty concerns about the ring I sold you are less important to me now."

A deep breath. A long, silent moment. "You are right, Miss Simon. Family is the most important thing. Those we love should always come first, and I swear to you that if it weren't a matter of life or death, I would never intrude at such a difficult time."

Every skeptical bone in her body screamed *He's playing you, Vero*. Her rational brain urged her to hang up, but a kernel of doubt kept her on the line. "Whose life are you talking about?"

Another pause during which she overheard his mother ask to speak to her. "No, *Mamá*," he said, "let me handle this."

Vero clutched the phone tighter, hugging herself against the cold. "Whose life, Castro?"

"Mine, Veronica. You're the only one who can save me."

Cal

He could almost hear Veronica Simon thinking. His statement wasn't hyperbole. The police had already grilled him twice, and Norsuch hinted at a third interview the following day. Several clients had called to request a hiatus in their search for a new home, and one of his sellers had withdrawn his listing. Strangely, not one word from the development company about the lake property deal. Bergeron must not be worried, or maybe the news hadn't leaked as far as Chicago yet. Cal rubbed the calluses on his left hand, wishing he were anywhere but here. Should he push Veronica Simon harder? His desire to be exonerated argued yes, but her grandmother was dying. He understood familial loyalty. If his *abuela* were in Hospice, he wouldn't take any calls either. Her willingness to defend that right revealed something about the Simon woman he hadn't considered. Decency. Compassion. Maybe she wasn't a stone-cold ice queen after all. At the other end of the phone, Veronica Simon cleared her throat.

"All right, Mr. Castro." A frustrated sigh escaped, followed by a fake cough to cover her capitulation. "Meet me at the shop tomorrow morning. If you're there by eleven, we can discuss your situation."

Cal closed his fist and pumped the air, relief flooding him with adrenaline. "I'll see you then, and thank you, Veronica."

"Vero," she said faintly.

"What?"

"Call me Vero. Everyone does. Don't be late, or I might change my mind." She hung up. Cal stared at the phone. The woman had let down her guard. Maybe that signaled she'd be willing to talk to the police and support his version of events the night Gisele disappeared. Moving to the bar off the dining room of his parent's home, Cal poured a shot of tequila and rolled the glass in his hand. He mulled over Friday night's events, convinced that Gisele's disappearance and Brad's attack weren't random acts. They had to be connected in some weird way. *What a shitshow.* He stared at the Realtor award his mother had brought home, the one Gisele wanted. Why had he ever hooked up with her? He had never intended either Townsend to be more than a casual date, arm candy for the many social functions he was expected to attend. He should have learned his lesson from Cerise's fake pregnancy tantrum. When he insisted on a test, she had recanted. Angry at being manipulated, he broke off the relationship with one twin, drank too much, played too hard. Then one night after a great set, slightly drunk and horny, he'd agreed to Gisele's offer of casual, on-going fringe benefits without thinking it through. By then he was already working part-time for the firm, pleasing his father at the expense of his own dreams. He'd cut down on the drinking, abandoned his music, and allowed their arrangement to continue without thought. Until Gigi's ultimatum six months ago. He swallowed the Cuervo and poured another.

"Calderón, *mijo*," his mother entered from the kitchen, hands dusted with flour.

"*Mamá*. It's late for you to be baking."

"I can't sleep, especially when my son is so unhappy," she said. "Did you get what you needed from the woman on the phone?"

Cal dipped his chin. "She agreed to meet me tomorrow."

"Good. Now, go to bed. You can stay in your old room. I changed the sheets and put fresh towels in your bathroom."

Finishing his drink, Cal swept his keys off the counter as he shook his head. "No, *Mamá*, I'm too old to sleep at my parents' house. I have a very nice condo with a water view that I haven't visited much the past three days, which means I'm paying the pet sitter a ton of money to take care of the dogs. I miss them, and I need some space, some alone time."

"Calderón Jesús Santiago Castro." She reached for his hand. "You don't have to marry the Townsend woman. If your father and I made you think so, I apologize, and I release you from such a commitment."

"You don't understand." He touched her cheek. "When she returns, if she returns, I'll have no choice."

"You always have a choice."

Cal stepped away, shaking his head. How could he bring it up to her, reveal all he knew, crack open the protective casing around the lie that was the Castro family? "I'll be fine, *Mamá*, don't you worry. *No te preocupes*."

"You shouldn't be alone."

Planting a kiss on her brow, Cal let himself out. "I'll call you tomorrow. I'll be fine." The falsehood accompanied him all the way home. He observed the speed limit, convinced he was being followed by police in an unmarked car. His paranoia didn't disappear when the garage door came down, shutting away the vehicle's headlights and the suspicions crowding around him. When he opened the door into the kitchen, Amigo barked hello and nosed Cal's legs until he stooped to pet the chocolate lab, then knelt to wrap his arms around the rescued two-year-old. Choco, Amigo's litter sister, sidled up, stumpy tail wagging, and insinuated herself into the embrace.

"Looks like Bob has taken good care of you." Amigo licked Cal's ear, then settled back on his haunches. Choco followed him as Cal rose to read the notes the dog sitter always left behind. "You've been walked and brushed and treated like royalty. No more food for you guys tonight, but you can each have a chewy."

The dogs carried their treats to the doggie beds in the corner of the family room. Choco curled up immediately. Amigo circled until he found his comfort spot. Cal debated whether to pour another drink as he flipped through the accumulated mail on the counter. A cable bill, three political flyers, and a credit card offer. Tucked between the pages of an outdoor furniture catalog, he found an envelope bearing an official Northern Michigan Insurance Company logo. Convinced it was yet another solicitation, he considered tossing it unread, but something about the address, hand-written rather than printed, stayed his hand. He slit the seal and pulled out a letter.

"Dear Mr. Castro,

My name is Elgin Barkley, and I represent the Northern Michigan Insurance Company in the Investigative Claims Department. I have information of a sensitive nature to share with you concerning a policy for Miss Gisele Townsend purchased in August of this year. Please contact me at the number below at your earliest convenience.

Sincerely,

Elgin Barkley, Sr. Accounts Manager

Cal checked his watch. Midnight. Too late for anything but worry. He would contact this Barkley guy tomorrow, but first, he intended to meet with Veronica Simon and convince her to stand by him. Why he found the prospect intriguing was as mysterious as the thrum of pleasure that settled in his chest when she suggested he call her Vero.

Vero

Another restless night spent alone had Vero awake before the alarm sounded. The apartment whispered of the laughter once shared, the confidences exchanged. Since the eviction letter, Ellie spent all her free time with her fiancé, and, in fact, had moved most of her personal belongings to Ray's place. Sad and lonely, Vero burrowed deeper under the covers. But the morning demanded commitment. She tunneled out from under the sheets and stretched, debating the wisdom of a morning run. The arrangement to meet Cal Castro at the store later intruded. No run, then, only yoga. She unrolled the mat and spent an hour moving through poses, then showered and grabbed a toaster waffle. Tying her hair back, she dressed, stuffed her stilettos in a tote bag, and laced her tennis shoes. She filled a thermos with a double dose of French roast and, scarf and then hat secured against the wind off the water, made her way downtown, choosing to walk the ten blocks to SIMON's rather than take the car. A chill breeze stirred the few tenacious leaves remaining on the trees and tugged at the collar of her quilted jacket. *Go, Blue!* signs decorated shop windows, anticipating next Saturday's football clash with Big Ten opponent Indiana. She wished she could share in that excitement, but the fact of Nana dying overshadowed everything, even the anticipated meeting with the overbearing Cal Castro. Why had she agreed to meet him before business hours? Being alone with him the first time had irritated every nerve. Despite that initial encounter, she couldn't ignore the sincerity of his request and his mother's gentle but forceful plea. *You can't afford sentimentality, Vero, so don't let him intimidate you. SIMON's is more important than the ring, and with Nana dying, you are the only one who can save the shop.* Which reminded her of the pressing need to hire another full-time salesperson. Agatha Wiggins was a dear soul and Nana's long-time friend who had worked for them for years, but she was well into her eighties now and slow to complete every task.

Setting the search for an assistant temporarily aside, Vero hurried past the café on the corner of Griffith and Culver and glanced at the clothing boutique next door, admiring the cocktail dress in the window. Out of her price range. Besides, she had no fancy parties scheduled for October, none for the rest of the year, maybe forever. Shaking her head, she paused to stare at the vintage guitars in the window of Ponte's Music, the business two doors from SIMON's, convinced that the man pacing the sidewalk yesterday had been Cal Castro. He had stopped in this very spot. Which of the instruments had caught his eye? Recalling the callouses on his fingertips, she bet it was one of the collectibles. Acoustic or electric? With his voice, he didn't need amplification to be heard. Definitely acoustic. As if it mattered. Vero hurried on, anxious to settle the matter of Cal Castro and the ring. Afterward, she could immerse herself in preparing the shop for customers. Fretting over the business's financial health would distract her from thinking about Nana Verna, at least for a little while, and that niggling feeling that she had forgotten something important returned.

The grandfather clock in the corner struck ten forty-five just as she unlocked the display window, displacing the tenacious spider again. She was arranging the rings in the front case when a car drove down Culver, alerting her to Castro's arrival. Five minutes after it passed the shop, he knocked, then braced his shoulders as though he expected to be upbraided for his early arrival. Vero bit her lip to hide a smile. She smoothed down the sleeves of her black silk blouse and made her way to the front entry, heels clicking on the wooden floorboards.

"Mr. Castro." She stood aside, aware that, as tall as she was, she still had to look up to meet his eyes. He slipped inside, one hand in the pocket of his dress slacks, the other twirling a set of car keys, which he stashed in his coat as she closed and locked the door behind him.

"Thank you for agreeing to meet me, Miss Simon." She dipped her chin. He smiled and kept going. "Miss Veronica Simon, a descendant of Sebastian Simon, one of the early prominent citizens of Allegan County. 2012 graduate of Saugatuck High. Art student and holder of an MBA from U of M."

Vero ignored the tentative smile he sent her way. "You've done some digging, Mr. Castro. Why is that, I wonder?"

"I like to know who and what I'm dealing with. Pleased to officially meet you again, Vero." He strode to the counter, pausing to inspect the display of original rings beneath the glass. "I misspoke when I told you to thank Mr. Simon the other day. I realize now that I should have applauded your grandmother for her fine work."

Vero rolled her eyes but, again, chose not to correct him. The secret behind the current SIMON creative designs would stay that way. His digging into her past hadn't uncovered everything about her. She accepted his hand, shook it, and stepped back. "Why are you here, Mr. Castro?"

"To apologize for my behavior Friday." He rested a hand on the counter, fingers tapping nervously on the glass.

Now, I'll have to polish that again. Vero blushed. Castro wouldn't be the only customer to leave fingerprints as they shopped. She crossed her arms, aware as she did so that the movement pressed her breasts against the fabric of her blouse. She dropped her hands to her side. "What exactly do you want, Mr. Castro?"

"Cal. Please." He took a deep breath. "You must have heard that Gisele Townsend is missing. The police believe she may have been abducted and is possibly a victim of foul play. And they think I had something to do with her disappearance."

Vero's stomach clenched, but she kept her gaze level. "How does that concern me?"

"I was here, in your shop, when Gisele disappeared. You are my alibi."

"Me?" Vero moved then, heels tapping her way to the register. "I don't see the problem. Just show them the receipt."

"I...can't."

"Why not?" Vero folded her hands to keep them from shaking. She might be alone and vulnerable in a room with a violent man. "Wait, is the Townsend woman wearing my...the ring?"

"No, she wasn't wearing it."

"She wasn't wearing it?" *I sound like a parrot.* Vero blushed again.

Cal ran a hand through his dark hair. "I never gave it to her. I handed it to my driver to keep it safe."

Vero threw up her hands. "Well, duh. Just have him turn it over to the police."

"He can't. He's in the hospital unconscious. While he was waiting for me at the country club, someone attacked him."

"Oh, no." Vero lifted a hand to her mouth. She shouldn't be more concerned for the jewelry than the man, but she couldn't help herself. "Did they steal the ring?"

Cal placed his hands on the counter and leaned toward her, their noses almost touching. "I don't know, which means the only way I can prove I had nothing to do with Gisele's disappearance is your word that I was here with you. Will you help me?"

The grandfather clock chimed the hour, each stroke a hammer blow in the silence that followed. Vero continued to stare at Cal, weighing his words, allowing conjecture and possibility to push aside other concerns. Whatever else the man was, arrogant, smug, self-serving, he didn't act like a criminal, did he? She shifted her gaze from Castro to the clock to the tray of rings below the glass counter. Her instinct to help warred with the desire to remain uninvolved. Compassion won out. "All right. Stop giving me those puppy-dog eyes. I'll tell the police where you were Friday night from five-fifty until six-twenty-three. Before or after that, you're on your own."

Cal's shoulders lifted. He grabbed her hand, turned it over, and kissed the inside of her wrist, a gesture as old-world as vampires, then looked up. "Thank you. And if you think I have puppy-dog eyes, wait until you meet Amigo and Choco."

The smell of his aftershave drifted over her. Vero caught her breath. *Who was this man?* "Amigo? Choco?"

"Chocolate."

"Choco-latte?"

"Cho-co-la-te...Spanish for chocolate. You might not like me, Miss Simon, but you'll love my dogs."

"I'm more of a cat person," she stammered.

"We'll see. When can you go to the police station and give a statement?"

Vero hadn't thought about that, the need to speak to the police, to offer her testimony. Maybe this was a mistake. On the shelf behind her, the phone chirped. Spell broken, she turned away, checked the number, and pressed the button to take the call.

"Vero." Her brother Sonny's voice sputtered down the line. "Come now. Nana's worse. The Hospice nurse thinks it might be time."

"Vero?" Castro moved behind the counter and rested a hand on her shoulder. "What's wrong?"

"You need to leave. I'll have to close the shop today. But I can't afford to do that." She brushed away tears, but they returned. "I need to call an Uber. My grandmother's dying at the Hospice Center, and I don't have my car."

Plucking the keys from his pocket, Cal grabbed her hand. "I'll drive you there."

Cal

Shaken by the news of her grandmother, the Simon woman hyperventilated. Cal rubbed his thumb over Vero's hand and waited for her to decide between her conflicting obligations. He expected her to pull away. Instead, she turned her hand to lace their fingers. He kept his grip light but firm, hoping to anchor her in the moment.

"Tell me what you need," he said. "Prioritize."

"I have to think," Vero said, her face ashen. Afraid she might faint, Cal slipped his arm around her waist, using his body to brace hers, keeping her upright. Her dark hair slipped free when she shook her head, brushing against his cheek. She took another deep breath. "Okay, okay. What do I need to do? Call Agatha Wiggins. Maybe she can come now instead of waiting until three. I should, um, what else? What else?"

Tightening his grip, Cal guided her to the stool behind the counter. He waited for her to sit, then lifted her chin to cup her face in his hand. "Breathe, Vero, breathe. Slow. Easy. Better?"

"Yes." She wrapped her fingers around his wrist. "Why are you being so nice to me?"

Cal ignored the question. "Give me your phone."

She handed it to him. He brought up her contacts, searched for the name she had mentioned, and handed it back. "Call the woman."

While she dialed, he disappeared into the rear of the shop, emerging with a glass of water and the coat she'd hung by the back door. When Vero ended the call, Cal raised an eyebrow. She nodded.

"Agatha's coming over. She only lives five minutes away." Vero gulped back a sob. "She's struggling with Nana's illness, too. They've been best friends for more than forty years."

Cal tapped the glass in her hand. Vero took small sips, then texted her brother Dave and Ellie. Frantic with worry, she thumbed through her texts, exclaiming at one.

"What's wrong, Veronica?"

"I—nothing, just a reminder of a payment due the end of the month."

"Is that all?"

She dropped her head into her hand and sighed. "It's been a shitty few days. Along with everything else, I'm being evicted from my apartment. I contacted a realtor. Lincoln Storey. He texted, too, to say he hasn't found anything yet."

Cal frowned. Link Storey working with her? No fucking way that asshole was coming anywhere near Veronica. He gritted his teeth. If he helped the Simon woman with her grandmother, maybe she'd be more inclined to help him with his alibi. And he was a realtor, after all. He could find her a place to live. "Does Storey want to talk now?"

"He did. I told him we'd meet later this week, maybe for coffee. I sent the bank a message, too." She turned off the phone and shoved it in her purse. Cal returned the glass before checking his cell. Glenn had left a reminder of the next scheduled interview with Norsuch and Harry. Vero busied herself rearranging the ring display while he wandered the showroom, neither comfortable breaking the silence. Ten minutes later, Agatha hurried in, dragging a small, wheeled suitcase behind her. She rushed to Vero. When she noticed Cal, her eyes narrowed.

"Who are you, young man, and why are you here? The shop is currently closed."

Vero escorted the older woman behind the register before slipping into the coat Cal held out. "Mr. Castro is," Vero hesitated, "Cal's a friend, Miss Agatha. He's taking me to see Nana. Are you sure you'll be all right here for the day?"

"Of course, dear. I've got everything I need in my carryall." She cut her eyes at Cal, then leaned closer to tap Vero's cheek with one arthritic finger. "You take care, dear. That man's trouble with a capital T."

Cal recognized the Music Man reference. So did Vero, who giggled despite the sadness pressing at her. "Oh, Miss Agatha, you always know how to make me smile."

"Give my love to Verna," Agatha said, "and tell her I said goodbye."

Collecting her purse, Vero moved toward the exit, barely aware of Cal's arm at her elbow until they reached the door. Agatha watched them leave, head bobbing back and forth like a metronome. Castro led the way down Culver, then across to the parking lot at Coghlin Park. "How are you feeling?" Cal asked.

Vero clutched her purse. "Empty. Confused. Lost. It's not like I haven't known this day was coming. We all did, but now that it's here, I can't bear it."

Cal helped her into the car. "The two of you are close?"

"More than you know." Cal leaned over to buckle her in. "Oh, you smell good."

"Probably because I showered this morning." He leaned a hand against the door jamb, his face close to hers. She blushed, dropped her eyes, and bit her lip, then latched onto his arm. "Oh, no, the police. I need to tell them about you and the ring."

Cal shook his head. "Not today, Vero. You have more important things to take care of."

"I promised."

"And I'll hold you to it. But not today." He detached her fingers from his sleeve, moved around to the driver's side, and buckled his seatbelt. The SUV rolled down Lake, heading around the inlet toward the Hospice Center. Cal kept one eye on the road and the other on Vero, who closed her eyes, holding back the tears. Moved by her sadness, he hummed a few bars of "Stairway to Heaven," then sang the opening lines. She shifted to stare at him.

"You have a beautiful voice. Did you ever think about being a singer?"

Cal focused on the road, wondering how to answer that question. Before he could, they reached the Center.

Sonny Simon waited at the entrance, his shoulders hunched inside his coat. Cal opened Vero's door and stepped aside, the fingers of his left hand tapping on his thigh. Vero shoved her phone at him. "Give me your number. Please. I'll call as soon as I can, and we'll go to the police together."

Cal entered the number of his new cell phone. The police had confiscated the old one with his permission. His lawyer agreed with the decision, confident that cooperating worked better than antagonizing the detectives.

"Go be with your grandmother, Miss Simon. We'll talk later." He stared into her eyes, opened his mouth to speak again, and closed it. When Vero reached the entryway, Cal got back in the car and drove away, warmed by the grateful tears in those sea-green eyes.

Vero

Sonny escorted Vero in and hustled her toward Nana Verna's room. He glanced back several times as though he expected Cal to follow them. "Who was that? Why were you riding with him?"

"You should recognize Cal Castro," Vero offered. "The realtor. I'm helping him with a situation."

Sonny yanked her to a stop so abruptly she almost toppled over. "Rumor has it that's the guy who harmed Gisele Townsend."

"Yes. No. He didn't."

Her brother started walking again, his grip tight on her elbow. "You shouldn't be anywhere near that man."

Vero bristled and pulled away. "Stop ordering me around, Sonny. I happen to know the man is innocent."

Sonny huffed. "You can't know that."

"And you can't know he's guilty. No one even knows if Gisele is missing. The woman I remember from high school would disappear just for the drama."

Her brother slowed his pace. "Wait. You knew Townsend from school?"

"I did. Gisele and her sister bullied or seduced everyone they could. Didn't you date one of them?"

"Maybe Dave, not me. I was too busy studying."

Vero rolled her eyes. "You weren't always such a nerd, Sonny. You may have forgotten, but I haven't. You used to know how to relax. Nana would want you to, you know. Enjoy life more and stress less."

"Some of us have bills to pay, little sister. Student loans. Mortgages. Which I do, on time, every month."

Vero tried to ignore the dig, but it hurt. She had no student debt, thanks to scholarships. She didn't have a mortgage because she didn't own a house. Of course, there was the loan on SIMON's. But her brothers had never given her credit for what she had done to pull the shop through the pandemic years. Instead, they spent their time criticizing her for what she didn't have: a stable relationship, a steady income, a portfolio of investments. "That's low, even for you, big brother."

Sonny had the grace to look away. "Never mind that now."

Vero paused outside Nana's room. "Is she conscious?"

Sonny shook his head. "Not since last night. You were the last person she recognized before she drifted into the coma. Ready?"

Vero nodded, and they entered the crowded room. Her parents and Sonny's wife Yuki were seated around the bed, their kids huddled together by the window. Still wearing his mechanic's uniform, Dave leaned awkwardly against a side wall. Her niece Carrie was sobbing softly into her sleeve. Nana Verna had been special to the entire Simon clan, and now she was leaving them. Vero tossed her coat and purse onto the pile in the corner.

"Veronica." Her mother vacated her chair so Vero could sit. "I'm going for coffee. Anyone want something? Dave? Sonny?"

The kids requested hot chocolate. Dave shook his head but didn't speak. Her mother whispered to him as she made her way out of the room. Vero took her grandmother's hand to caress the thin layer of freckled skin that revealed all the ropey veins beneath the surface. How frail she had become, the woman whose strength, courage, and determination had kept the family legacy alive and functioning in Saugatuck long after her husband was gone. Vero never understood why Nana chose to keep the Simon name when she wed. What was so important about passing it on to her son? No way to ask her grandmother now.

Yuki cleared her throat. Waving her hands, she motioned the family closer. "Let's pray for Nana, all right?" Dave rolled his eyes, but Sonny and the children scurried to surround their grandmother's still form. They held hands and bowed their heads. Vero joined them, Cal Castro and his problems relegated to one small corner of her grief-stricken heart.

Cal

The early morning drizzle had transitioned to a sleeting, slushy mess as Cal pulled in next to his father's Lexus. He sat with his hands on the wheel, wondering how he had gotten so far off track. He'd been a high school soccer star with a full ride to Michigan State and the lead singer and guitarist with the Soggy Tucks, a cover band with an album's worth of original songs. Highly sought after around campus and then around the state, the STs were headed for stardom. Although Cal struggled to balance sports with his musical ambitions, he managed until his junior year, when his father showed up outside the apartment Cal shared with his bandmates to have a 'serious conversation' about Cal's future. The talk turned into an invitation to come home early for Thanksgiving break.

The visit turned into an intervention, with the extended *familia* gathered to impress upon him his obligation to the Castro name and the business his father had worked so hard to establish. He refused. Then his grandfather took him for a walk along the lake, pointing out properties they had represented and the importance of providing a legacy for future Castros. With no one on his side and the not-so-veiled threat to cut off funding for the next semester, Cal caved to their demands. He changed his major to business, stashed his guitar in a closet, and signed up for economics and marketing courses. The band moved on, the other members dropping out of school to go on the road, leaving Cal and his soulful vocals behind. After graduation, he returned to Saugatuck, built a client base, played occasional gigs around town. He played the field, dated the evil twins, fended off Cerise's attempt to guilt him into marriage, and stumbled into Gisele's proposal. Easy escorts to work functions, sex, no commitment. Gigi seemed a safe bet, all fun and no expectations, until she turned into a piranha. Shaking off the melancholy rehash of questionable choices, Cal put on a confident face and entered the office.

Associate realtor Lisa Protus, with her big hair, collagen lips, and perpetual smile, raised a finger in greeting, then returned to scheduling showings. Cal waved and kept walking, intent on speaking to his father, but the senior Castro's door was closed, a sign something serious was going on inside. In his office, Cal settled behind the desk, turned on the computer, and thought about Veronica Simon's promise to tell the police about his Friday visit to the jewelry store. It felt wrong to insist when she was in such a fragile state, but Cal had no choice. His life, the family business, the Castro reputation was on the line. He wanted to whine about the unfairness of it all, but self-pity never solved anything. Pulling Barkley's letter from his pocket, he smoothed it over the desktop and considered the best way to approach the man.

Lisa pushed through the half-open door, a sheaf of pink slips in one hand and a mug of coffee in the other. "This a bad time, boss?" He motioned her forward, and she stepped all the way in. "We have a full complement of prospects for the Davidson property. No open house but tons of private showings. A reporter called wanting a statement from Gisele Townsend's fiancé, and an Elgin Barkley called from the Northern Michigan Insurance Company. Oh, and that developer who's tearing down the Scottish Apartments? He wants a sit-down with you and your father. I already informed Antonio."

"Efficient, as always, Lisa." Cal laid the memos on top of the Barkley letter, ignoring the smirk that flitted across Lisa's face. Once, he might have considered responding to her flirty invitations, but the office didn't need the drama, and despite his earlier indiscretions, Cal was working hard to repair his playboy reputation. "I'll follow up with these. When my father's free, come get me."

She frowned, bit her lip, then pivoted and marched out. Voices drifted from the main office. The FedEx guy delivering documents. An associate realtor chatting with a potential client. Water dripped a steady beat from the eaves outside his office window. Cal hurried through the phone calls, ignoring the reporter's attempt to coax a salacious comment on his girlfriend's disappearance and fending off the more tactful expressions of support tinged with skepticism. He didn't have a reputation for violence, but he'd had his share of heated arguments when zoning laws or buyer intransigence didn't align with the client's wishes. His father referred to Cal as the Castro enforcer, whatever the hell that was supposed to mean. Unbidden, Veronica Simon's green eyes flashed in his memory, her dark hair cascading in waves down her back, her delicate, long-fingered hand resting in his. For those few moments in the shop when she'd learned her grandmother was dying, she had needed him. From the fire of Friday's encounter to the wary agreement to support his alibi to the hesitant surrender of today, the woman presented an intriguing blend of confidence and vulnerability. He found the mix curious and intoxicating. Damn it! He couldn't be interested in her when Gisele was missing and probably dead. *But,* his spiteful inner voice crooned, *you don't want Gisele. You never did.* Admitting the truth, even to himself, was a punch in the gut.

A ping from his cell phone reminded Cal he had to call the Barkley fellow to find out what he wanted. He scrolled to voicemail, then pressed the number. An automated message informed him he had reached the Northern Michigan Insurance Company Hotline and to enter the extension of the person he was calling. Cal checked the message once more and punched in the number 101. He was about to hang up when a female voice answered, out of breath and curiously eager.

"Elgin Barkley. To whom am I speaking?'

"Mr. Barkley?" Cal hesitated. He wasn't entirely sure how to address this person.

"It's Ms., actually. A joke my parents played on the universe that I have to sort out every other day." Barkley sighed. She must have checked caller ID because her voice assumed a firm, authoritative tone. "Calderón Castro? Thank you for returning my call. I apologize for the somewhat unconventional contact. I prefer the personal touch regarding matters as delicate as this one."

Cal noted the slight hesitancy before the word delicate. "The letter did catch me off guard, I admit, since I have no idea what it refers to."

Elgin rustled papers, cleared her throat, and lowered her voice. "It seems, Mr. Castro, there is a problem with the application you submitted for a life insurance policy on a Miss Gisele Townsend."

"I'm sorry. What did you say?" Cal clutched the phone tighter. "I made no such request."

"Are you suggesting you didn't apply for the policy on Miss Townsend?"

"That's exactly what I'm saying. I did not."

Barkley's tone grew testy. "Well, we have the documents, Mr. Castro, and my supervisor is anxious that I find out the progress of the missing person investigation before I forward them for processing."

"I don't understand. I've never filled out any papers for any insurance, especially not for Gisele, and certainly not with your company. How did this happen?"

Barkley cleared her throat again. "Mr. Castro, perhaps you can send me a copy of your signature? That way, I can verify whether you did or did not sign this application."

"I'm not sending a complete stranger anything, especially one accusing me of something I didn't do," Cal said. "I want to see the application I'm supposed to have submitted. Before that, I need to see some credentials proving you are who you say you are."

"I understand that you might have reservations." Barkley paused. "I'm based in Holland this week. I could drive over to discuss this and bring the papers with me, but I have to be careful. We both do. Does tomorrow work?"

Cal bristled at the sudden shift in tone, the suggestion that he had something to hide. This didn't sound good. Barkley had started out confident. Now, the woman sounded afraid. What the hell was going on? "No, tomorrow's not a good day. Can we meet later in the week?"

"I'll check my schedule and get back to you. Is the information on the application still correct?" She recited the address of an apartment he had lived in after graduating college.

"Hold up. I haven't lived there for eight years. If you're serious about this, come to the real estate office once we agree on a time." He provided directions and a suggestion that she avoid the ongoing demolition on Francis Street. After Barkley hung up, Cal sent a text to Glenn. This time, he wanted the lawyer with him. Then he dropped his head in his hands and wondered what was going on. Had the person behind Gisele's disappearance taken out a million-dollar policy on the missing woman, pretending to be him? Who hated Cal enough to embroil him in what felt like a conspiracy? Rubbing his temples, he shrugged off the imaginary noose tightening around his neck and called Detective Norsuch. He wasn't going to hide anything, not even this latest wrinkle.

The detective spoke more cordially than he had during their two previous interviews and thanked Cal for the new information. He and Harry wanted to be there when the Barkley woman showed up. Cal didn't object to that either. If he could convince the two bird dogs of his innocence, he would breathe a whole lot easier. He shoved aside his worries to concentrate on the email mountain in his inbox.

A rumble of voices and the tap of shoes down the hall roused Cal from the packet of closing documents he'd been reviewing. Someone rapped on the door, then swung it open. Antonio Castro entered, tugging his cuffs from beneath the sleeves of his dark gray suit. He waited for Cal to look up.

"Your mother informs me the Simon woman will tell the truth?"

"Yes, *Papá*, she promised."

"That's good, *mijo*. The Simons have an excellent reputation in this town. The police will believe her, and you will be cleared of these ridiculous suspicions. But enough of that. Are you free now?"

"*Por favor*. I'm swamped." Cal swept his hand over the papers on the desk.

"All of that can wait, Calderón. I need you in the conference room."

"I have to prepare for the Snyder closing."

Antonio flicked his fingers at the desk. "Leave it. This meeting is much more important. With the Townsend woman missing, Eric Bergeron wishes to finalize a contract with us to handle his purchase of the properties at Goshorn."

Cal flinched. That was the deal he and Gisele fought about the day she disappeared. With her out of the picture, the contract and the hefty commissions would come his way. More grist for the storm of suspicions swirling around him. "That's not a good idea. Taking over that deal will fuel the belief that I had something to do with Gisele vanishing."

"Bergeron believes not. Neither do I. Now, set all that aside." Once more, his father dismissed the folders on Cal's desk with a wave of his hand. "The man and his lawyers have come all the way from Chicago to meet on a Sunday. They are waiting for us now."

Vero

The overcast day turned into a gloomier night. Restless and unsettled, Vero dragged the heavy armchair closer to Nana's bed and placed her phone in silent mode. Her father sent her mother home, then paced the room, unwilling to leave Nana's side. Nurses slipped in and out, checking the monitors and listening to her grandmother's heart. Vero imagined she could hear the old clock in the jewelry store ticking off the final minutes of Nana's life.

"Veronica." Her name popped like a shot in the quiet space. "Go home, sweetheart. I can stay with her until the end."

"No, Daddy." Vero stood and moved to his side. "You don't have to go through this alone."

George Simon wrapped his arms around her. "You always were my mother's favorite. You know that, don't you?"

Vero smiled down at her grandmother. "I do. We share something special, Dad, a connection that's hard to explain. All those days at the lake, paging through old photos or playing pick-up sticks while you and mom went to Sonny and Dave's baseball games. Those afternoons I sat in the shop while she taught me to make beautiful things. Nana's a fighter. I'm not sure she's ready to leave us yet."

"All the more reason for you to go home and rest. Besides, don't you have to move out of your apartment soon?"

"Yeah, I do. Which reminds me. I need to call the realtor and see if he's found a place for me."

"Go do that now, Vero, then go home. Your mother's on her way with clean clothes and a thermos of her famous chicken soup. I promise to let you know if anything changes."

In the corridor, Vero paused to consider all the plates she was juggling, unable to decide which would fall first. She unsilenced her phone, signed out at the front desk and scuffed to her car through a fall of leaves. Halloween was days away. She and Ellie usually hosted a costume party for friends and colleagues. Their themed events were legendary, but she couldn't muster enough interest this year to consider celebrating. Besides, they'd be moving out for good on the thirty-first. She shivered at the thought. Turning up the heat in the car, she dialed Lincoln Storey. He answered on the first ring, startling her into a yelp.

"Hey, Veronica?" he paused. "Glad you called me back."

"Sorry about screaming in your ear. I didn't expect you to pick up so quickly. The thing is, Link, my grandmother is in Hospice, I have to move out of my apartment next week, and I really, really, really need to find a place to live, so I hope you have good news for me. I could use it."

"Slow down, Veronica. I'm sorry to hear about your grandmother. How are you doing?"

"It's difficult. She and I were, are, very close." Vero swallowed the sadness and self-pity begging for release. She wiped her eyes, inhaled sharply, and plunged on. "So, what do you have for me?"

Over the shuffling of paper, Vero heard a dog barking, a big one from the deep howls emanating through the phone. "Kong, enough," Link ordered. The dog whimpered once and retreated. Vero detected the click of nails over a wood floor. Kong? She snorted, coughed once, and asked what kind of dog Kong was. Storey didn't seem to hear her question. "I have a few listings to share," he continued. "I can send the links, but I'd prefer to discuss them in person. Do you feel up to a breakfast meeting?"

"Is there any rush to sign a lease?"

"Well, my advice is not to wait too long. I told you there wasn't much available, and I wasn't wrong. The listings I did find are due to come on the market at the end of the week."

"You're sharing advanced knowledge with me? Is that ethical?" Vero coughed again. The last thing she wanted was to sound confrontational or, holy hells, flirty.

Link laughed, a warm, vibrant sound that crawled through the phone to wrap around her. "Absolutely, Miss Simon. Pre-listings are ethical and smart. Lincoln Storey is always ahead of the game."

"How about Wednesday? If Nana Verna dies tonight—" Vero repressed the urge to scream and blinked away tears.

"Wednesday's fine unless you need to change it for any reason, but don't put off our meeting beyond Friday, or we'll have to start all over. I do have other clients, and several are chomping at the bit for these places."

From sexy to vaguely threatening in a heartbeat. Dismayed but desperate, Vero agreed to meet Link at The Bagel Place at 7:30 Wednesday morning and ended the call. On the drive home, she silenced the classic rock ballads on the radio. In the sudden stillness, memories of her and Nana competed with Lincoln Storey's mercurial comments and Calderón Castro's urgent request. Cal. She had promised to provide him with an alibi. Tomorrow. All right, she would go to the police first thing and get that out of the way. She pulled into the lot in front of the Scottish Apartments, dodging the barrels and the orange netting around the soon-to-be-demolished building. Trudging up the stairs to the second floor took every bit of willpower she had left. If only she didn't have to face everything alone.

The silent rooms chastised her as she slipped off her boots and coat and wandered into the kitchen. Ellie had gone to Ray's, the note on the refrigerator declared. Of course, she had. Vero looked around, noting the empty spaces where pictures had hung and books had occupied shelves. The apartment that had seemed warm and cozy when she first moved in now appeared shabby and cold. A fresh round of tears threatened. Vero grabbed the blanket her mother had crocheted for her eighteenth birthday and huddled on the sofa. A detail from the day washed over her, the warmth of Cal Castro's hand at her waist, supportive without threatening. She should call him, let him know her plan for tomorrow. She pressed his number and listened to it ring. But when he picked up, she couldn't say a word and ended the connection. The last thing she needed was pity from that arrogant man.

Cal

Thirsty after their walk, Amigo and Choco lapped at their water bowls, accepted the proffered biscuits, and settled down next to the couch. Cal flicked on the TV. The evening news featured the usual highway mayhem, political shenanigans, and local sports reporting. He picked up the remote to change the channel when the studio announced breaking news, then cut away to a reporter broadcasting live from a secluded section of Michigan's dunes. Stunned by the crawler announcing a discovery in the disappearance of Gisele Townsend, Cal stared at the screen as the camera panned to a car matching the description of the one seen outside the real estate office the night Gisele disappeared. The vehicle sat partially submerged in the lake. The news banner continued to crawl across the bottom of the screen as a tow truck snagged the back bumper and extracted the car while the female reporter rehashed the details of the alleged crime. The woman sidled closer to peer through the side window, then stood back when a uniformed officer ordered her to move. She concluded the segment with speculation that the darker patches on the back seat might be bloodstains. "Although no body was recovered," the nasal voice intoned, "there is evidence of foul play. Stay tuned for an update at eleven."

Unsettled by the ominous timbre of the report, Cal stabbed at the off button and tossed the remote onto the couch. His mother would suggest the discovery was nothing more than a random coincidence, but he knew that assessment wouldn't last. Choco looked up, barked once, then snuggled deeper into her bed. Alert to the growing tension, Amigo clicked his way to his master's side. Cal scratched the dog's ears, then opened the refrigerator, stared at the contents, and closed it again. When his phone pinged, he read the curt text from Dick Norsuch. Now that the car had been found, the detective had new questions. What more could Cal say? He certainly couldn't tell them the truth, that despite his concern over his missing fiancée and the anxiety of being a suspect, he was relieved, not about Gisele's disappearance and possible murder, but that he no longer had to deal with her constant threats. What happened to him didn't matter. He had to protect the family.

He grabbed an energy drink, popped the cap, and downed it in three long swallows. Amigo returned to his treat. His phone rang, stopped, rang two more times, then went silent. He checked caller ID. Vero. She had phoned and hung up before he could answer, and she didn't leave a message. Was she planning to renege on her promise? Only one way to find out. Cal changed into jeans and a long-sleeved tee and grabbed a fleece pullover. He crouched to give the dogs a final pat and instructions to guard the house. Setting the alarm, he hurried into the garage. If the Simon woman wanted to play games, so be it.

Night had settled in over the downtown. The topsy-turvy clash of warm and cold fronts caused fog to roll in, wreathing the shoreline in swirling mist. Cal texted an order to the Corner Café from the parking lot, humming a few lines from a ballad he'd penned years ago. *"No one left to run to/No one left to love..."* When the Café notified him that the order was ready, he dodged the last of the leaves hurtling down the street, dashed inside for the food, and headed toward the Scottish Apartments.

Pulling into the lot, he shook his head at the caution barrels and fencing already in place. Bergeron wasn't wasting time negotiating with tenants. The developer had gone full bore into demolition mode. Cal checked his phone for new messages, gathered the take-out bags, and exited the car. At the entry door, he debated whether to call first. No, that left her free to ignore him. He tapped his leg, wondering how to get inside, when an elderly couple led by an Aussiedoodle clomped down the hall. As they maneuvered through the door, Cal grabbed for the handle, allowed them to pass, and slipped in. He checked the mailboxes, then took the stairs two at a time. A stack of boxes outside each apartment testified to the frantic departure of people who thought they had a secure lease. Cal would never treat clients so poorly, and he never allowed his buyers to sign without understanding what their contract really said. He always urged everyone to read the fine print, no matter how long it took, even though, or perhaps because, it irritated his father. *We all have our petty paybacks.* Approaching Apartment 2-C, he tucked the car keys in his pocket and rang the bell.

A tenant banged down from the fourth floor, suitcase thumping behind her. She gave Cal a brief nod, looked away, looked back, a speculative gleam in her eye.

"Looking for Vero Simon?" When Cal nodded, the middle-aged woman wearing leggings and a faux fur zebra-striped coat paused on the landing, perusing him with intent. "If you're looking to exercise those muscles, I could find something for you to do."

Cal stepped back, his discomfort causing the woman to chortle. She continued down the stairs, but her voice floated back to him. "I could come up with lots of things for a hottie like you to do...for me."

On the other side of the door, a chain rattled. A bolt clicked free, and the door opened. Vero Simon, barefoot and braless under a white tee, ran her hands down the sides of tight workout shorts. Her eyes were red, her dark hair piled on her head in a messy bun. "Oh." One hand flew to her mouth. She stepped to the side, hiding her body behind the door. "What are you doing here?"

"You called me." Cal held up the food. "And you must be hungry, right?"

"No, I mean, yes. I'm sorry for hanging up. I didn't want to bother you. What's in the bags?"

Juggling the carry-out and drinks, Cal slipped past her toward the kitchen. "The Corner Café's to-die-for Reubens, curly fries, and chocolate lava cakes for dessert. How's your grandmother?"

Tears welled in Vero's eyes. She brushed them away. Her mouth quivered. "She's dying, and I can't do anything to stop it."

Cal considered giving her a hug. Instead, shrugging out of his jacket, he moved toward the cabinets that flanked the window over the sink. "Plates?"

Vero pointed to the one on the left, arms crossed over her chest to hide the nipples peeking through the thin cotton. Cal looked away, unable to stop his mind from a brief fantasy of touching, tasting, and teasing the woman until she begged for more. *Stop it, you dumb bastard*, he ordered.

This woman had no reason to like him. Yet. She might even suspect him of foul play. He needed to play this like a gentleman, assure her he was harmless and sincere, convince her to carry out her promise. Despite the silent admonition to behave, a part of him, growing harder by the minute, desired to do a whole lot more. *Basta, Calderón. Enough.* He needed this woman at his side, not on her back under him.

Vero retreated a step, then another. "I'll be right back. Drinks are in the fridge." She scampered down the hall. He heard her rummaging through boxes, muttering under her breath, and couldn't stop the smile hovering at the corners of his mouth. By the time she returned, wearing a sweatshirt bearing a graphic of the Great Lakes and checkered pajama pants, he had poured her a soda and himself a beer. Veronica Simon raised one eyebrow but said nothing as she claimed a chair across from him, picked up half of a Reuben, and took a bite. Her eyes closed. A moan of delight squeaked out around the mouthful of rye and corned beef.

"That good, huh?" Cal helped himself to the other half of the sandwich, his juvenile brain conjuring scenarios in which he might coax Vero into making that sound in a different setting. He swallowed wrong, choked, and covered the bulge in his jeans with a napkin. What the hell was wrong with him?

Wiping sauce off her chin, Vero sipped her drink and stared into his eyes. "I apologize again. I did call, three times, but I chickened out. I wanted to express my appreciation for your help today. You didn't have to be so nice."

"Why would you think that?" He polished off his sandwich and reached for the second Reuben. Taking a handful of fries, he pushed the rest toward her.

"Your, um, reputation precedes you, Mr. Castro."

"You don't really know me, Miss Simon."

Two spots of color bloomed on her cheeks. How had he missed the allure of this woman? She caught her bottom lip between her teeth, released a breath, and nodded. "You're right. I don't. I also wanted to let you know that I intend to go to the police station at eight tomorrow morning. Is that all right?"

Cal considered offering to drive her there, but that might make him seem too eager. Instead, he rubbed his thumb along his lower lip. "There's something you should know. They found a car," he said. "It looks like the one in the video from the night Gisele disappeared."

"Is it?"

"I have no idea. And I'm worried about my driver. Brad's still unconscious. He was attacked the same night. That can't be a coincidence. And they can't blame that on me because I was with people at the party." He didn't mention slipping out to walk the terrace.

"Will he be all right?"

Cal rolled the beer glass between his palms. "I don't know. He's in the hospital, in a medically induced coma, I think. Hell, no one will tell me anything. And he knows about the ring."

Vero sat up. "You said something about that before, didn't you? I mean, he has the ring you bought for your, um, for Gisele? Tell me again why your driver has her ring?"

Cal raised his gaze to hers. "I decided not to give it to her. Instead, I asked Brad to lock it in the glove compartment. For some reason, the cops impounded the car. I don't know when we'll get it back."

"You're telling me that the ring and the receipt that could prove you were with me when your girlfriend disappeared are both missing?" She gathered the sandwich plates, popped a fry in her mouth, and narrowed her eyes.

Exasperation coated Cal's reply. "They are."

"And that's why you need me."

"Yes, preferably before the detectives question me again."

Vero handed him a spoon and one of the lava cakes on a paper plate. "Are you playing me, Castro? Because I really don't need that right now."

Cal accepted the utensils, set them aside, and stood to face her. "If you believe anything about me," he grabbed her shoulders, "believe this. I am not abusive to women, not to any woman, and I'm not using you."

He waited for Vero to resist or respond. Instead, she stepped closer, and his arms slipped around her. She laid her head on his shoulder and sobbed. He patted her back, eager to comfort her. A surge of protectiveness had him tightening his embrace. When she looked up, Cal forgot his promise to himself. He leaned down, his lips inches from hers, when the front door banged open. Ellie Manzo exploded into the apartment like a cannonball.

"Oh, for the love of God." She dropped the boxes she was carrying, fisted her hands on her hips, and glared at Cal. "What the hell is he doing here?"

Vero hurried to rescue the backpack dangling from her roommate's arm. "Mr. Castro brought dinner. We were discussing my visit to the police station tomorrow."

"Didn't look like any discussing was going on. Back off, Castro. Vero's my friend, and you, you're an opportunist. Time to leave." Ellie drew Vero to her side.

"You must be Vero's roommate." Cal held out his hand.

Ellie ignored the peace offering. "I'm her friend and protector, dude, and don't you forget it. Ray's on his way up with more packing boxes. Thought you might need them."

Vero frowned. "I will, as soon as I find somewhere to live."

Cal turned to her. "You don't have a new place lined up yet?"

She shook her head. "No, but I have an agency looking into it."

Ellie wandered out to the hall, her words floating after her. "God, roomie, get it together. Take your grandma's offer. How is Nana Verna doing today?"

Before Vero could respond, Cal rescued his jacket from the sofa and headed for the door. "Meet you at the station tomorrow, okay?" He started to leave when Ellie's boyfriend staggered down the hall and plowed right into him.

"Hey, sorry, man. You helping Vero? Moving's a shit job, but worth having the honeys at our place, right?" Ray winked and used his butt to push through the door into the apartment. "Later, man."

Back in the car, Cal dialed the hospital again. Maybe this time, someone would tell him how Brad was doing. In the meantime, he thought about the way Veronica Simon fit so perfectly in his arms.

Vero

Cal's footsteps echoed down the hall. His coat rasped against the wall as he dodged boxes. Vero heard the distant clunk of the entry door as it slammed shut behind him. Chilled by the cold air flowing up the stairwell, she shivered. The memory of Cal holding her lingered, as did the suspicion that everything he had done was calculated and manipulative. The man had plans to marry someone else, had bought that woman multiple rings. *Don't be fooled by his looks and charm, by his pretense of caring,* she admonished herself. But she had welcomed his embrace. What possessed her to lean into him, to seek his comfort? Shaken by the conflict inside her, she returned to the kitchen to wipe the table where they had shared food and confidences. When the door banged against the wall, she flinched. Ray winked as he strolled toward Eva's bedroom.

"Didn't realize you were friends with a bad boy," he said.

"We're not friends," Vero responded. She shoved the crumbs of their shared meal into the waste basket.

"Well, I'm just saying, good for you, Veronica. Now, if you'll pardon us, we have to say a final goodbye to this love nest." Ray winked and closed the bedroom door. Giggling soon erupted, followed by the thump of a headboard. Vero groaned. That's all she needed tonight. Listening to other people make love while Nana lay dying. Putting the dirty dishes in the dishwasher and wiping the counters took less than ten minutes. What would she do the rest of the evening? She stared at the near-empty cabinets, wondering if a new place would have room for a set of dishes that matched. As if she could afford them. Her personal bank account hovered near the red zone. It definitely didn't allow for frills. Keeping the store open and the business solvent took priority. She dried her hands, then checked the phone for messages. Nothing. Unable to resist the urge to find out where things stood, she punched in her parent's number, relieved when her mother answered.

"I'm here, Veronica. So is Dad. Nana's still with us, at least for a while longer. Are you at home?"

"I am."

"Try to get some sleep tonight, honey. We promise to call if anything changes. Are you opening the shop tomorrow?"

"Yes, but first I have to go—," she paused, considering whether to inform them about her trip to the police, "I have an errand to run. I plan to stay at SIMON's until six. Then I'll relieve you and Dad."

"That's good, honey. David will be here from midnight tonight until seven tomorrow."

After a few more minutes of discussion regarding Nana's care, her mother ended the call. Vero's shoulders bowed under the weight of sorrow and longing, aware that part of her wished she could spend the night in someone's arms. Cal Castro sprang to mind. She quashed that thought before it could grow legs and overtake her common sense.

Ellie's door was closed, and the banging, both kinds, paused. Vero rapped twice, called good night, then brushed her teeth and hair, shoved earbuds in, and slipped into bed. No reason to change clothes now. She could shower in the morning. Besides, the smell of Cal's aftershave lingered on the sweatshirt.

Weak light filtered through the blinds as Vero woke before the alarm. She hurried through her routine and, by seven-thirty, had time to fix a coffee to go. Ellie and Ray had yet to make an appearance. Sometimes, she wondered if they ever worked. Returning to the bathroom, she examined herself in the mirror above the sink. Did the brown wool pencil skirt and jacket over a cream silk blouse make her look professional and trustworthy? Did the minimal makeup she had applied hide the dark shadows under her eyes? Checking the names of the detectives on the note Cal had posted on the refrigerator, she grabbed her keys and, unable to remember the last time she'd filled the Subaru's tank, prayed she didn't need gas. Nervous, she punched in the address on her navigation app. The Allegan State Patrol Office was not part of her regular route.

Traffic on the Blue Star Highway seemed unusually heavy. Of course, how would she know? She encountered only a handful of cars on her daily ten-block walk along Saugatuck's Lake Street. Today she'd have to forego a stop for bagels at the Corner Café. She eased into the right-hand lane to avoid two semis who plowed past her, tires kicking up slush that sprayed the windshield. She resisted sipping from her travel cup, worried about spilling liquid on her blouse. She didn't want Norsuch and Harry to think she was a ditz. When she finally reached the station, only one Visitor slot remained. Next to the empty space, Cal Castro leaned against a sleek, black Cadillac, waiting for her. She smoothed the lapels of her jacket before stepping onto the sidewalk. She hadn't planned to enter with him, but something in the set of the man's shoulders alerted her to his state of mind - anxious and uncertain.

"Miss Simon." The way he said her name initiated a nervous flutter in her chest. "Thank you for coming."

"Mr. Castro." His warm hand enveloped hers briefly. She caught her breath, exhaled, the air pluming as she did so. "Did you think I wouldn't show?"

The hint of a smile creased his lips while he inspected her outfit. "No, Vero, I believe you always keep your promises. You look nice, by the way." He gestured toward the door and waited for her to take the lead. Inside, a man in a rumpled suit waited to greet them.

"Veronica Simon?" The detective offered his hand and nodded in Castro's direction. "Detective Norsuch. Thank you for coming in."

A second detective played with the zipper of his Michigan jacket, then introduced himself as Duane Harry and asked her to follow him. "You stay here, Castro."

"Wait." Cal grabbed Harry's arm. "How's my driver, Brad? Have you found out who attacked him?"

The detective placed a hand on Cal's chest, but Castro didn't back down. Norsuch grabbed his partner and spun him away, then turned to Vero. "Follow Detective Harry, Miss Simon, while I speak with Mr. Castro."

Vero glanced back, curious about the hushed conversation between the detective and Cal, but Harry hurried her along before she could learn anything new. In the interview room, he offered coffee. She held up her travel mug as she settled into a chair, took a sip, and set the brew on the table. Harry laid out the recorder and explained the rules for the statement. When Norsuch joined them, she clasped her hands and reminded herself to breathe.

"I understand your grandmother is in Hospice, Miss Simon. We're sorry to hear that and appreciate you taking the time to give us your statement. We'll make this as brief and painless as possible." Duane Harry set a notebook and pen in front of her and began the interrogation. "Please state your name, address, and occupation."

"Veronica Simon. I live in the Scottish Apartments on Francis Street, unit 2-C. Along with my grandmother Verna Simon, I operate SIMON's Jewelers on Culver Street in Saugatuck, Michigan."

Harry rested his chin on a hand. "And how do you know Calderón Castro?"

"Mr. Castro was a customer in my shop last Friday. He purchased a ring while he was there."

"So, you were alone in the store with Calderón Castro on the evening that Gisele Townsend disappeared?"

"I was." Vero laid her hands flat on the table. "My grandmother has been very ill for the past few months. Five days ago, she was admitted to the hospital. I was anxious to see her before visiting hours ended, so I decided to close the shop ahead of the normal closing time, which I started to do when Mr. Castro arrived. He came into the shop at five-fifty p.m."

Harry frowned. "How can you be so sure of the time?"

"I told you I wanted to close early. It takes time to empty the display windows and lock the jewelry in the safe." Vero's cheeks warmed. "When he barged in, I was upset and angry. I looked at the clock to see if I could use the time as an excuse, which I tried to do. He didn't care."

"Are you saying Mr. Castro intimidated you?" The detective leaned in, an eager look on his face.

"Mr. Castro is a man used to getting what he wants. He was arrogant and bossy, Detective, but not threatening or intimidating. I responded in kind."

Harry chuckled. "The man does bring out the claws, doesn't he?"

Vero shrugged. "I'm not sure what you mean by that, but I had every reason to be upset. I wanted to close my store and get to the hospital. Mr. Castro demanded that I show him rings."

"Why exactly did he do that, Miss Simon?"

Vero folded her hands again. "He said he had purchased four previous rings for his fiancée, and she didn't like any of them. He appeared frustrated and stressed."

"Why did he choose your store that night?" Harry scribbled something in a notepad and looked up.

"Our shop has a reputation for unique, high-quality jewelry crafted by hand. I design and make all our specialty items. By the way, that information is a well-guarded secret, one I hope you will keep."

"We'll do our best," Norsuch said. Harry smirked but kept silent. "Go on, Miss Simon."

"My particular passion is rings. Each is one of a kind and offered as an exclusive item. If you purchase one of my pieces, you are guaranteed to own something no one else has. Mr. Castro heard about these rings and believed one of them would please his girlfriend."

"Why didn't you tell him to leave and return the next day?" Harry asked.

"I did. He refused to go until he saw what our store had to offer."

"You could have called the police, forced him to leave, even threatened to have him arrested."

"I could have, but I chose not to do that." Vero sipped from her mug, then laced her fingers on her lap. "My rings are expensive. The business has been struggling, and we needed a sale."

"So, what happened next?"

Vero sighed, reliving the moment when Cal's insistent demand and the financial difficulties of the shop overruled her desire to order him out. "I showed him our selections. He was interested in one specific band and had me try it on so he could see how it looked on a woman's hand." The memory of Cal Castro sliding the ring on her finger caused her to blush again.

"Did he buy the ring?" Harry returned to his notes.

"He did. He paid by check and asked me to wrap it for him, which I did." Vero stopped, stunned by the realization that the check still rested in the register where she had placed it. She had totally forgotten to take the receipts to the bank.

"Miss Simon?" Norsuch touched her arm. "Are you all right?"

Vero blinked at him, noticed Detective Harry watching her closely and forced herself to smile. "Sorry, I just remembered an errand I forgot to do. Anyway, I printed a receipt for Mr. Castro and placed it in the gift bag with the ring. He left the shop at six-twenty-two."

"Six-twenty-two? Not three or four?"

She held up a hand to forestall Harry's next question. "I know exactly because it was printed on the receipt, and I double-checked the time with the grandfather clock in the corner. I was upset because I knew I might miss talking with my grandmother, and I was angry."

"Angry? About Mr. Castro's demeanor?" Harry raised an eyebrow.

"No. The ring he purchased was a favorite of mine. Sometimes, an artist has trouble letting go of her babies." Vero smiled, unwilling to reveal how much she had hoped someone would buy that ring for her. One more romantic fantasy shattered. She really needed to get a life.

"Huh. I suppose that makes sense." The detective shrugged. "So, you always record the time and date of sales?"

"Yes, we have a video record as well as a written one on the spreadsheet I keep on my tablet," Vero said. "And in the receipt bag, which I then take to the bank. That's what I just remembered. With all that's happening with my grandmother, I forgot to do that. It's still at the store."

"Is that a problem?" Harry hunched his shoulders and leaned toward her.

Vero shrugged. "My grandmother's condition has me a little disoriented. Usually, I make a daily delivery to the bank." Maybe that's why the bank manager left a message on my phone, she realized.

"One more thing before we have you write out, sign, and date your statement. Miss Simon, when Mr. Castro left your shop, did you notice whether he drove himself?"

"I did. He got into the back of a car idling at the curb a little farther down the street from the shop. I'm not very good at identifying makes and models, but I know it was black and looked expensive. And that's all I can tell you about Mr. Castro's whereabouts Friday night. He was with me in my shop for at least those thirty-two minutes. Whether he returned to the real estate office or went somewhere else, I wouldn't know."

Harry swore softly. "It would have taken at least ten minutes to reach the office, fifteen to get to the country club."

Vero stood. "May I go now? I have a business to run."

"We'll need copies of the written receipt and the video." Vero agreed to supply them. After several more questions about her arrival at the hospital, Duane Harry escorted her back to the entry where Cal waited. Harry looked between the two. "So, you didn't know each other before Friday?"

Cal and Vero looked at Harry, then at each other. "We did not," Vero said. Castro nodded.

"Detective Norsuch and I have a few more questions for you, Castro." When he motioned Cal to follow him, Cal mouthed a thank you before heading after the detectives, leaving Vero to wonder what more they had to ask the realtor.

Back on the road, she mulled over the statement, which she had written out and signed. Had she forgotten anything? When the phone rang, she pushed the answer button on the dashboard screen.

"Vero? Link Storey. Are you there?" She assured him she was listening. "I have a few promising prospects for you, but we need to move quickly, like today. Any chance I can stop by the store this morning?"

After she agreed to meet with Storey at ten-thirty, Vero set aside the Castro problem to concentrate on a more immediate concern. Where was she going to live?

Cal

Cal watched Vero Simon exit the building, the wind blowing her skirt against her long, shapely legs. He remained at the window as she drove away, then acknowledged the detective's command to follow him. The station thrummed with the business of policing. Patrol officers dispersed from a meeting room into the corridor. Still thinking about those legs, he followed Harry to the room where they had interviewed him yesterday.

"Coffee?" Norsuch offered while Harry spoke with a pair of uniforms in the hall. Finally, scowling, he joined his partner. The older detective scratched the bristles on his chin and sighed.

"Miss Simon gave a detailed statement about your whereabouts Friday evening from five-fifty to approximately six-thirty p.m." Norsuch toyed with his Styrofoam cup, his nails leaving crescent marks around the rim. "Her account matches what you told us previously."

"I told you the truth, Detective."

"But that doesn't explain where the ring is now."

Cal leaned toward the detective. "You have the car. You must have checked the glove compartment, where I told Brad to stow the thing. Are you telling me it wasn't there?"

"The ring is missing." Norsuch stared into the cloudy coffee.

"And it appears you're in the clear, for now," Duane Harry said.

"Then I can go?"

"Just a few more minor details." Harry cracked his knuckles. "When we spoke yesterday, you suggested Miss Townsend had a colorful history with other men. Care to elaborate?"

Cal met the detective's stare. Did the man believe he'd offer up other suspects to save himself? "Look, Gigi had an extensive dating history long before we started going out. It won't be difficult to find out who she was involved with."

"Not a jealous man, Castro? No old scores to settle?"

"Not a one, Harry, and if that's all you need, I have work to do before we meet with the Barkley woman. When Brad Hanson regains consciousness, he'll tell us where he put the ring. Along with the receipt and Miss Simon's statement, that should provide more proof that I'm telling the truth." Cal pondered the wisdom of bringing up the news report, then decided what the hell. "You found a car in the water. Is that related to Gisele's disappearance?"

Norsuch eyed him. "Not at liberty to say. Why? You know something about it you'd like to share?"

"No." Cal shook his head and turned to go.

"Have you and Miss Simon known each other long?" The older detective's question felt like a sucker punch. Cal hesitated, then returned to the table.

"I'm not sure what that has to do with Gisele Townsend's disappearance, but I met Miss Simon for the first time when I went into her shop. We did attend the same high school, but she was a freshman when I was a senior. Not on my radar that long ago."

"Is the Simon woman on your radar now, Castro?" Harry raised an eyebrow. "She's a fine-looking lady, and you stated that you and Miss Townsend had relationship issues. Plus, you have a reputation as a ladies' man. Maybe Veronica Simon has another reason for providing you with an alibi."

Cal rose, fists clenched. "Do not go there, Harry. Veronica Simon's grandmother is dying, the woman is struggling to make a go of her family's business, and, based on my less-than-stellar behavior in her shop, she has absolutely no reason to involve herself in this mess. Yet she came here willingly to vouch for me. Don't twist this into something it isn't."

"Settle down, Castro." Norsuch waved away Cal's anger. "You seem more upset about Miss Simon than you do about your fiancée."

"Nothing was official with Gisele." Cal ran a hand through his hair. "To be honest, the engagement was more our parents' idea. Gisele liked the idea for all the wrong reasons - money, prestige, glamor, forging a dynasty, a business transaction, she called it."

"I'm curious, then, what are the right reasons?" Harry waited.

Cal palmed his keys and shrugged. "If you have no more questions, I'm out of here."

Norsuch waved at the door. "Go, Castro, but stay in touch."

Hunching his shoulders against the brisk wind, Cal made his way to the exit, unsettled by the feeling that Norsuch and Harry were toying with him. More disturbing was the need to defend Veronica Simon. Her mix of strength and vulnerability appealed to him at a visceral level, and Harry hadn't been wrong. The woman was beautiful in that quiet way that crept up without warning, then knocked your socks off. Had he ever noticed her in high school? Cal doubted it. Veronica Simon didn't realize how attractive she was, didn't flaunt her assets like the Townsend twins. Her kind of beauty bloomed late and grew deeper with age and experience. She reminded Cal, he realized, of his mother.

Dodging patrolmen and visitors to the station, Cal hurried to get out of the cold. The heater, cranked up to 74 degrees, warmed him as he scrolled through the list of missed calls. Most were from clients and other brokers. One was a message from Huntington Bank affirming a closing set for the afternoon. Good thing he'd finished the paperwork after the meeting with Bergeron. The developer's interest in properties on Goshorn Lake promised a lucrative payout. Still, Cal couldn't shake the warning bell clanging in his head. Gisele made no secret of wanting that contract. If the Castro agency accepted the account, how bad would the optics be for the firm and him personally now that she was missing?

When he reached the end of the calls, he noticed that Cerise Townsend had left a message demanding he contact her ASAP. As bitchy as her sister and even more cutthroat, Cerise had transitioned from the shadow twin into the lawyer you most wanted to avoid in any situation. She was blunt, vicious, and took no prisoners. Gritting his teeth, he punched in her number. A man kept any Townsend woman waiting at his own peril.

"About time you returned my call." Cerise's nasal voice grated.

"Good morning to you, too, Cerise. I've been a bit distracted. What's up?" Cal let the question hang. Let her start whatever conversation this was supposed to be.

"I understand you've spoken to the police several times since Gisele disappeared. Have they arrested you yet?"

"Good one, Ceri." Cal checked the rearview mirror and backed out of the parking spot. "I wasn't anywhere near your sister the night she vanished, and I have proof to back up my claim, so I'm going to say this again. I did not harm Gisele. I'm as anxious as you are to find out what happened to her."

Cerise paused, then changed direction. "I understand Eric Bergeron met with you and your father yesterday. That contract belonged to Gisele. You'd better not try to replace her."

"You have that in writing?" He waited for her reply. When she failed to respond, Cal went on. "No formal agreement then. Whatever Gisele thought she had going is moot, and we didn't pursue the business. Bergeron came to us."

"That land is worth millions, Cal." Cerise changed tactics again, her voice lower, slower, suggestive. "There's enough there for us to share. My sister wasn't interested in half the pie, but I am. Think about it. That merger our fathers had in mind can still take place."

Cal found it difficult to speak. Was she really offering to take her sister's place now? "I have to go, Cerise."

"Call me tonight. We can work something out." She hung up, the unspoken suggestion settling like a tumor in his brain. He checked the road for traffic, preparing to head for the office, when a message from his father popped up.

Brad has regained consciousness. He's asking to see you.

Vero

Traffic had died down after the morning rush. Sipping the tepid coffee, Vero mulled over the interview with the detectives, unconvinced by their good-guys act that they believed her version of Friday night's encounter with Cal Castro at the shop. But why wouldn't they? She had no reason to defend the man, but neither did she have a reason to lie about his whereabouts. Gah! She didn't need Agatha's warning to realize Castro was trouble the moment he had barged into the shop. And then he spoiled things by bringing dinner and holding her while she suffered an emotional meltdown. Her thoughts ping-ponged wildly between suspicion and interest. The man was practically engaged. *For crying out loud*, Ellie would say, *take a chill pill, Vero*. Good advice. She dismissed Cal Castro from her mind, checked the gas gauge, and groaned. One more stop to make before she could start the workday.

The GasWay Fillerup on the corner of the Blue Star Highway and Allegan Street was packed. All the pumps were busy. She queued up behind a white Suburban and read all the bumper stickers twice before the driver returned from inside the mart, donut in one hand and a Big Gulper in the other. The woman eyed Vero before climbing in and proceeding to eat her breakfast pastry. Vero rested her head on the steering wheel and sighed. After an agonizing ten minutes, the driver moved on. Vero edged forward, liberated her credit card from her purse, and tugged her collar up against the wind. She stared into the woods that framed the back of the property, the memory of Cal Castro's embrace warming her cheeks until movement two stalls down surprised her. Although her knowledge of cars was limited, she identified the forest green military-style vehicle with tinted windows idling at the pump as a Hummer. Patrons continued to stream in and out of the facility, but the vehicle remained stationary, and no one exited to get gas. Shivering from the cold and unease, Vero requested a receipt, tore off the paper copy, and scurried back into the driver's seat. Snow began to fall in lazy flakes, decorating the windshield with tiny stars. She set the wipers to intermittent and kept to the speed limit. When she made the turn onto Allegan, the Hummer pulled up behind her.

Vero stepped on the gas, hoping to distance herself from the oversized vehicle, but the driver increased speed, too. She punched on her phone, then scrolled to contacts, intending to call her brother Dave when the cell rang. Flustered and a little out of breath, she answered with a curt, "What?"

"Miss Simon? Jeff Gordon from Huntington. I've been trying to reach you."

"Oh, Jeff, sorry. I apologize for not returning your call." Vero checked the mirror. The Hummer was still behind her. "My grandmother's in Hospice care. I've been distracted."

"Well, I'm sorry to hear that. Verna Simon has been a good customer for many years. Which is why I need to speak with you. Is there any way you can stop by today?"

"Is this about the loan or the fact that I forgot to make Friday's deposit?"

"Actually," Gordon rattled what sounded like a clutch of pens, "um, both, but not over the phone, please."

Vero checked the side mirror. The Hummer had inched closer, its front bumper shadowing the trunk of her car. She held up her phone as if to say, "I'm calling the police." The vehicle did not back off. She waved the phone again. "I'm on my way to the shop now, Jeff, but someone is tailgating me. Can you call the police and tell them I'm being road-raged?"

"Really? Where are you?" He waited while she described her location, put her on hold, and returned a minute later. "Police are on their way, but, Veronica, the meeting?"

"Wait." She held her breath as the Hummer pulled into a driveway, reversed, and sped back toward the Blue Star. "Whoever it was has changed direction. I'm sorry. I'll call and cancel the request. Can I get back to you after I check the calendar? Of course, if Nana passes..."

Her voice trailed off. Gordon's tone softened. "Certainly. Call me as soon as you're in a safe place. But, Veronica, this is very important. Please don't put it off."

Shaken by the tailgater, Vero punched in 9-1-1 and apologized for her unhinged response to a driver in a hurry. Gisele Townsend's disappearance must have rattled her more than she realized. She checked the traffic one final time, then reduced her speed to merge onto Culver. When she reached the shop, she buried her head in her gloved hands and screamed. Was someone really following her or had her imagination taken over her usually rational mind? Did she turn an impatient driver into someone with a more sinister motive? She wanted to feel safe in her own town, and cared for and protected, the way she had last night in Cal's arms. *Foolish girl. You have no one to rely on but yourself. It's up to you to sort things out, and that includes the bank loan.* She supposed that, if pressed, her parents might supply the funds needed to meet the payment deadline, but they didn't share her commitment to the shop or the house on the lake. To them, the store had become a millstone dragging at their forward progress. For Vero, the shop was more than a burden or an outdated reminder of the family's past. SIMON's was her artistic and financial future, and the cabin at the lake, which had grown into a grand home over the past hundred years, was her safety net. The property represented stability, comfort, security. Each place held precious memories of time spent with Nana Verna. Unfortunately, Sonny and Dave, and apparently her parents, too, now viewed the shop as a liability, the house on Goshorn a monetary asset to be liquidated when the time was right.

Inside the shop, the twenty-year old furnace struggled to heat the back office, although the showroom warmed to a toasty seventy-six degrees. Vero adjusted the thermostat down, then opened the register and gasped. The deposit bag was gone. She lifted the money tray, felt around the space. Nothing. Panic loomed. She clutched her chest, and then she remembered. Agatha. Vero dropped to her knees and spun the dial on the safe. When the bank bag flopped out, she rested her forehead on the door and took several calming breaths. Then she reached for her drawing pad, scribbled a note reminding her to deposit the weekend receipts, including Cal's money, today. That had her remembering the promise to make a copy of the sales receipt for the police. She undid the ties on the pouch and plucked the report of the weekend's entries from the band of cash. Agatha had added yesterday's sales to Vero's last statement. Stuffing the paper in her pocket, she waited for the grandfather clock to chime the hour, unlocked the front door, and returned to the register. The back door banged open, ushering in a draft of cold air. Vero reached for the panic button mounted beneath the register.

"Don't press the alarm, Ironica. It's only me." Dave's voice preceded him into the showroom. "Man, why is it so hot in here?"

"Old furnace," Vero muttered. She finished arranging the coins and bills in the slots in the antique National Cash register and raised an eyebrow. "Something Nana and I have been planning to replace for the past two years."

"You shouldn't put any more money into this place. Grandma's not going to be around much longer, so her passing is the perfect excuse to close the business and get a real job."

"Stop, Dave. I like what I do, even if you and Sonny don't give me credit for it, and I'm good at this." She waved a hand around the showroom. "And before you ask again, I'm not going to work in your body shop. That would be a mind killer for sure."

"A lot of high-quality eligible males come into my shop, Vero. You could meet a guy and settle down."

Vero crossed her arms. "Is that all you think I'm good for? Being someone's wife?"

Dave had the grace to look chagrined. "No, but look around." He flung out his hands. "People aren't exactly beating down the doors to get into this place."

Vero ignored the painful dig. "Why are you here?"

Her brother leaned on the counter. "Why were you talking to the police?"

"How do you know I was talking to the police?"

He scratched the day-old scruff on his chin and grinned. "Happened to be passing by and saw your car. Then I followed you."

"Wait." Vero rested her palms on the glass and glared at him. "That was you tailgating me?"

His laughter rang in the empty space. "This is why you shouldn't be running the store by yourself, Veronica. You're clueless about your surroundings. Always have been. You need someone to protect you before something bad happens."

"I can't believe you think so little of me, and I'm not clueless. I just gave a statement so an innocent man won't go to jail."

"What are you talking about?" Dave frowned.

"None of your concern." Vero bent to rearrange the rings in the case, prepared to order him to leave when the front door swung open, filling the room with chilled air. Both Simons turned as Lincoln Storey strolled in. Vero checked the time, then intercepted a strange look between the two men. Storey smirked. Dave shoved his hands in his pockets.

"Mr. Storey," she said, "why are you here?"

"Dave." Link Storey slapped his gloved hands together. "Got my Hummer fixed yet?"

"Link." Dave avoided Vero's frown as he cocked his thumb toward the back of the shop. "As a matter of fact, I just finished up a test drive this morning."

Vero choked off a snarky comment, anger simmering in her gut. Dave used Storey's car to terrorize her? "My brother was just leaving."

"You coming to the rec center tonight, Simon?" Link said.

Dave glanced at his sister and shrugged. "Probably not, dude. My grandmother's not doing well."

Vero had to swallow down yet another response. Nana not doing well? Their grandmother was dying and that's all her brother could manage to say? "Dave."

Her brother threw up his hands in mock surrender. "I'm going, I'm going. Meet you at your office in an hour, Link. We'll discuss that other thing later, Veronica."

A young mother struggled to push through the door with a stroller and a toddler in tow. Vero hurried to assist the woman, her mind on the slam of the back door and the realtor now pursing his lips at her brother's departure.

"Thank you," the woman said. "I need a present for my husband's birthday. Where are your men's watches?"

Vero led her to the display case, offered the toddler a sucker from the bowl under the counter, and blinked at the realtor. "You wanted to see me. Do you have good news?"

Storey slapped the gloves he'd removed against his leg. The customer eyed him, an appraising look on her face, *if I weren't married* echoing, although not a word was spoken. Vero had to admit the man was good-looking, and he knew it. He smiled back at the woman, winked at the little boy, and pulled a sheaf of papers from the inside pocket of his coat. "I thought you might look these over before we meet for lunch tomorrow. If you see one you like, call me ASAP."

"Tomorrow? You mean Wednesday, don't you?" She had forgotten which day they had decided on, or maybe she had imagined discussing a morning meeting. Vero felt herself in emotional overload. Her sorrow and worry over Nana and the weird sense of responsibility toward Cal Castro competed for attention as she scrambled to find a place to live. Dave's stalker prank hadn't helped. "I'll do my best, but right now my life is chaos city."

"Tomorrow. Wednesday, whenever you're ready, I'll be waiting." Link took her hand, drew circles over her knuckles with his thumb. The contact sent goosebumps down her back. He released her to check his watch. "Look at the Omegas," he called to the female shopper. "Your husband will love one of those. Gotta run, Veronica. Text me when you decide on a day."

The door slammed shut behind Storey, startling the boy with the lollipop and waking the baby in the stroller, who began to cry. Bending to rock the infant, the woman raised her eyebrows. "He's one of those guys," she said, including Vero in a moment of female bonding.

Vero laughed. "Apparently. Did you find something you like?"

"Yes, but I can't afford the one he suggested."

Vero joined the woman by the watch display, key to the case in hand. A shadow passed over the front window as the realtor drove away, the momentary gloom sending a second wave of gooseflesh down Vero's back.

Cal

The tease of snow flurries became a full-blown assault as Cal drove to the hospital. Fat, wet flakes pasted themselves onto the windshield, slid down the glass, and collected in the wiper channel. He replayed the session with the detectives, searching for a gesture or a word that might indicate where he stood in their investigation. He thought about stopping by the jewelry store to thank Veronica for her assistance, but Harry's suggestion that she and he had a connection, romantic or otherwise, made him rethink that action. The police would be watching for anything that looked like collusion. Damn it. Even in her absence, Gisele fucked up his life. She'd been nothing but accommodating when they started, a convenient choice for casual dates and sex, someone familiar enough to mix well in social gatherings but not looking for commitment. He sure had that wrong. When she began to drop hints about being exclusive, moving in together, Cal put her off. Too busy working, he'd barely paid attention to her machinations. He'd allowed things to drift, ignored the increase in outings she planned for them, and their nearly non-existent sexual encounters. By the time the occasional dinner with her sister and parents turned into weekly affairs with a dozen dinner guests, he was trapped. Then the *familia* got involved, and his goose was cooked. Ugly image. Trite but true. He'd been maneuvered into a corner much like he'd caved to his father's demand that he abandon music, then join the firm. Anger replaced melancholy.

Cal looked up, only to realize he'd almost driven past the entrance to Allegan General. He hit the brakes, checked the rearview for oncoming traffic, and swerved into the lane directing him to visitor parking. His father had managed to ferret out Brad's room number, so Cal bypassed the volunteer receptionist and angled his way toward the elevators. Outside the chauffeur's hospital room, he paused to gather his thoughts before going in.

Brad Hanson lay motionless beneath a layer of blankets, the usual monitoring paraphernalia arrayed around the bed. A screen mounted on a pedestal whirred softly as it recorded the patient's oxygen, pulse, and blood pressure level. An arrangement of flowers sat on the tray table at the foot of the bed. Someone had taped a handful of get-well cards to the wall below the mounted TV screen.

"Boss?" Brad's deep baritone brought Cal's gaze back to the bed. Hanson was more than an employee. He was a friend. The two shared a bond forged over the past four years of long days and longer nights driving around Allegan and surrounding counties at the bidding of Antonio Castro. The intrusion of Gisele Townsend into their closed circle had irritated both men.

"Hey, don't sit up." Cal offered Brad a fist bump. "You need to take it easy. You're not out of the woods yet."

"What the hell happened?" Brad touched his bandaged head. "Did somebody hit me? Is that why I'm in the hospital?"

"You were attacked, buddy, by an unknown assailant. Took quite a blow to the head. We weren't sure you were going to wake up."

"Well, that sucks. Who did it?"

"Don't know, Brad, but when you feel better, maybe you can tell me what you remember."

"I can tell you now, but it's not much," he muttered, glancing at Cal. A strange look flitted over his face. "Everything's really fuzzy."

Cal frowned. It wasn't like Brad to mumble. Had he suffered brain damage or was something more going on? "Tell me what you do recall."

Brad scratched an unshaven cheek. "Um, I ran some errands, didn't take long. I was back at the Club having something to eat. The other drivers had gone to play pool. Gisele came into the kitchen through the locker room." Brad closed his eyes and swallowed hard.

"Gigi?"

Another awkward silence. "Yeah. She said she wasn't feeling well, that you were being mean to her, and she asked me to drive her home. We went out to the car, but she forgot her purse, so she went back inside to get it."

"It couldn't have been Gisele, Brad. She never showed. She wasn't at the Club."

"She was there, boss, and she was pissed, like always."

Cal laid a hand on the driver's arm. "Take it easy, man. No need to get upset."

"It was dark in the hall, and it was raining outside, but I know I spoke to Gisele and saw her go inside. I don't know what happened after that, but it was her."

"Calm down, Brad. You must be mistaken. She wasn't there, bro."

"Bullshit, Cal. Gisele was at the Country Club. I saw her. I saw her!"

Brad's insistence reawakened Cal's own skepticism about Gisele's disappearance. He rested his elbows on his knees and steepled his fingers. "Whatever, Brad, the fact is she's missing now. According to the police and her secretary, she disappeared from her office the same night you were attacked."

"The police think Gisele's missing? Don't you believe it, Cal, not for a minute. She was at the Club, at least for a little while, and, if she's really gone, well, I'd like to say I care, but," Brad shifted his weight, loosening several of the heart leads on his chest. The monitor beeped. "Uh, oh."

"I'll fix it." Cal straightened the lines, but the machine continued to blare. Soon a nurse hustled in. She reattached the leads, reset the machine, and cautioned Hanson to lie still. Cal waited until she left before speaking again.

"Look, the police think I had something to do with her disappearance and your attack."

"That's bullshit, too." Brad closed his eyes. He kept them closed so long, Cal thought the man had fallen asleep. "I keep trying to remember, but it's all a blur. Man, the alcove where we eat is sort of dark, and outside was even darker with the rain, but I swear the Townsend bitch was there, in the doorway, ordering me to take her home. She had that red scarf, the one her sister gave her, wrapped around her neck and face, and she was wearing that dark raincoat. I don't remember much after we went outside, and she headed back in. I'm sorry, boss."

"Don't worry, Brad. The cops will sort it out. I do have one more question, a very important one. Do you remember me giving you the bag from the jewelry store?" The driver nodded. "Good, and that I asked you to put it in a safe place?"

Hanson snorted, but he didn't meet Cal's eyes. "That I do remember, and I did."

"Where is it?"

The driver pointed toward the locker next to the bathroom. "In my jacket pocket. I never got around to locking it in the glove box."

Cal opened the cabinet door and pulled out the bag holding Brad's clothing from the night of the attack. He unfolded the driver's jacket, reaching into one pocket, then the other, but the gift bag holding the ring was gone.

Vero

Serious snow had moved in overnight, coating the rooftops and medians, turning the streets into another slushy mess. Vero liberated her winter boots from the packing box holding her cold-weather gear and tugged them on over a pair of fleece-lined tights and an over-sized cable-knit sweater. She twisted her hair into a low bun, pulled on a knit cap and the warm navy pea coat Nana had gifted her last Christmas, and started for the store. The early wintry dumping had convinced people to postpone morning chores. The streets were deserted, the layer of new-fallen snow undisturbed as she made her way down the sidewalk and across the side streets. She looked back to examine the trail left by her boot prints, the only marks in the white blanket covering the sidewalk. Her breath plumed in the cold air. A winter girl at heart, Vero welcomed this first taste of the season, no matter that it was too soon to last. By tomorrow, the temperature might climb into the forties, leaving puddles everywhere and a wish in her heart for another round. Snowfall reminded her of holidays at the cabin, Nana's sage-stuffed turkey and her mother's beef tenderloin gracing the Thanksgiving and Christmas tables respectively. Soon there would be no more celebrations with her beloved grandmother at the lake that had served as a second home her whole life. At least she had the memories. A replay of last night's vigil at her grandmother's bedside kept her company on the walk to the shop.

She had passed the hours in silent prayer and yearning. Nana did not wake, nor did she fall deeper asleep. Vero had the feeling her grandmother was waiting for something. Dave showed up around six, muttering about his day and the prank he played on her, while Sonny bustled in and out, consulted Nana's medical chart and spoke with the nurses. Vero remained vigilant to her grandmother's slightest movement. She refused Dave's attempt to discuss closing the shop or selling the cabin. When her parents arrived at eight to take over the watch, Vero was relieved to escape the tense atmosphere. At the apartment, she packed a few more boxes, wrote checks to cover her share of the final utility bills, and chugged down three pain pills before crawling into bed. Once again, she woke before the alarm went off, anxiety prodding her to do more than mope.

Nine pedestrian-free blocks later, she turned onto Culver. A glance at the lake revealed a shoreline decorated with froth. Wind pummeled the collar of her coat. Beyond the corner restaurant, a man stood motionless, staring into the window of the music shop, his shoulders squared beneath a black ski jacket, his muscular build emphasized by the cut of his dress slacks. She took two more steps before she realized that the man waiting on the sidewalk was Cal Castro. What was he doing here again? She skidded to a stop, arms flailing, as he turned her direction. Now that he had spotted her, she couldn't very well run away, so she trudged on, hands buried in pockets, eyes narrowed. When Cal saw her, he raised a hand, a tentative smile lifting the corners of his lips.

"Miss Simon." He took her elbow just as her boots slipped on a slick of ice. "You look like a snow angel."

"What are you doing here?" She thought about pulling free but decided against it. She rather liked his hand where it was, after all.

"I probably shouldn't be." He scanned up and down the block, tugged her toward the shop. "The thing is, after my interrogation yesterday, I visited my driver in the hospital."

"Oh, I'm sorry. I forgot about him, didn't I?" Vero frowned. "Is he all right?"

"He's getting better." Cal released her so she could unlock the door.

Vero gestured toward the narrow strip of snow-covered grass that led to the back of the property. "Have to enter from the alley. Because of the alarm. Did you need something?"

Cal ran his fingers through his snow-crusted hair. "I wanted to thank you again for your statement yesterday. You literally saved my life."

"Are you sure?"

He cocked his head. "What do you mean?"

"Those detectives kept trying to trip me up. They asked how long we knew each other, whether we had dated." Vero settled her gloved hands on her hips, aware of heat rising in her cheeks.

"Would that be so bad if we had?" Cal said.

Vero couldn't think of an answer to that. She skirted around him and darted between the jewelry store and the scented candle shop to the right, wrestling the building key from her purse as she kicked at the snow. Castro caught up and followed behind, one hand resting at her waist to prevent her from falling. Vero thought about telling him to let her go, hesitated. Why was the man so irritatingly attractive to her? She must be crazy to even consider getting involved with a possible criminal. Still, she had vouched for him with Norsuch and Harry, an action that bonded them in a weird way. "Mr. Castro." She stopped and turned, ending up snug against his chest, her boots sliding over the icy crust. Cal's dress shoes skidded. His arms encircled her to keep them both from falling, and she gripped him back. Layers of cold weather gear separated their bodies, nothing but breath the space between their lips. Vero burst out laughing. Cal tightened his grip.

"Would it be so bad?" he asked again.

"You're as good as engaged." Vero nudged him away. "I have to go to work."

"Wait." Cal stretched an ungloved hand toward her. "There's something else you need to know. The ring is still missing."

"But," she frowned, "you told me you gave it to your driver."

"I did, and he had it in his coat pocket when he was attacked."

"Oh, no, his attacker stole it?" When he nodded, Vero inserted the key in the lock, disengaged the alarm, and motioned Cal to follow her in. "So, no ring, and no receipt."

"I'm sorry." He reached toward her. She looked away, trying to mask the impact of this new loss. Instead of touching her, he stuck his hands in his pockets.

Hanging her coat beside the door, Vero shoved her hat and gloves into the pockets and kicked the door closed. She fisted her hands, fighting the tears and frustration. Her best creation, the ring she had wanted for her own, gone. The furnace kicked in, the fan's whoosh drawing out the moment. When she turned to face him, her eyes sparked. "No sense crying about it now. Nana has a saying. 'When something's hidden, you retrace its path until you find it again.' Are you game?"

Cal did reach for her then. Grabbing her shoulders, he leaned closer, the smell of mint and pine drifting over her. She found herself unable to focus on anything but his lips. "Verónica Simon," he said, "you just made my day."

Vero

Good God, Cal Castro was going to kiss her, and she wanted him to. Vero closed her eyes, swayed forward. Cal folded his arms around her, pulled her close, his lips grazing her cheek, and released her.

"You're leaving?" She intended it as a statement, but somehow the words had morphed into a question. He waited for her to look at him.

"I have a meeting. And the less we're seen together, the better, for now. I'll explain later. Will you be going to Hospice after work?" When she nodded, he opened the door, slipped out, and retraced the path along the side of the building, a promise trailing after him. "I'll call you."

Vero stood in the doorway until he trudged out of sight, then moved to the front of the shop. Cal emerged from between the buildings, crossing the slush-covered street in that awkward penguin stride of people who don't wear boots. Huge flakes were coming down, swirling and spinning in the wind off the lake, as Cal pulled up his collar and walked toward his car. Releasing her grip on the display window, Vero shivered. Cal Castro was mercurial, driven, unsettling, and hot as hell. The hard lines of his body fit perfectly against her own, and if she wasn't delusional, he'd been as turned on as she was. She smacked a palm against the wall, hoping the sting would set her straight. *Don't be a fool. And don't be fooled.* Now was not the time to indulge in teenage fantasies. *Get a grip, Veronica.* Ugh. She never referred to herself with her full name, which just showed how unnerving the man could be.

Last night, sitting with Nana, she had completely dismissed Cal Castro from her mind, along with any other male companion, like Link Storey, who made his interest evident. Then her grandmother opened her eyes, half-rose from the bed, and whispered Grandpa's name, her yearning evident in the way her frail body leaned toward the spectral memory. Although Vero could not see Stanislas Holder, his presence was very real to Nana. Vero knew what her grandparents had meant to each other. Even when they fought, and their disagreements were legendary, they took care never to shout words they couldn't take back. That was the kind of love she wanted for herself, one that would last, not a casual hookup with a man who had a playboy reputation and a missing fiancée. And Cal didn't seem very broken up about Gisele's disappearance, not like a man losing the love of his life. Maybe there was more to this whole situation than she first thought. He was hiding something, but then, wasn't everyone? Nana said that secrets held too tightly festered like untreated wounds, but Vero was certain her grandmother had a few of her own. Her insistence that Vero move to the house on Goshorn and find something there, for instance. And her decision to keep the Simon name. Why hadn't Verna taken her husband's surname when she married? That was certainly a bold move in Nana's era. Then there was the campaign by Vero's parents and brothers to convince her to sell the shop and the land. What made them so anxious to be rid of both places? Well, Vero meant what she'd told Cal. Retrace your movements until you find what's missing. If it worked for lost items, it should work for lost information. And that's precisely what she planned to do, as soon as she found a place to live.

To Vero's surprise, despite the weather, customers flowed into the shop in a steady stream for most of the morning. She checked with her parents to confirm Nana's continued, inexplicable survival and reiterated her promise to take the seven to one shift as she had last night. Right before the grandfather clock struck noon, Lincoln Storey sent a text reminding her of their meeting tomorrow, a good thing because she had forgotten to ask Agatha to cover for her. Time was slipping by too fast, leaving her exhausted from the weight of all the problems she faced, the most immediate, after Nana, her living situation. If she didn't find a place soon, she'd be homeless. She sent a text to her roommate, who replied in Ellie shorthand that no one except Ray and Ellie's mother could interpret: `c u b4 clothes fangs 4 munchies`. Vero couldn't puzzle it out.

The sky grew darker. Streetlights stuttered on, their glow diffused by the falling snow. The number of patrons visiting the shop dwindled as the storm continued to lay down coats of white menace. When a late-model Lexus skidded against the light pole across the street, Vero decided to close and head to the Hospice Center before she got snowed in. She triple-checked that all the doors were locked and set the alarm, then switched off the lights. Grabbing Nana's walking stick, she tugged on her boots and used the cane to steady herself as she slogged through the side yard and onto the sidewalk. Throughout the day, most of Saugatuck's shopkeepers had attempted to clean the walkways, but others, like her, had had no opportunity to do so. Ice had formed beneath the most recent coating of snow, making each step treacherous. The wind slapped frozen flakes against her eyelids. Wrapping her scarf across her nose and mouth, Vero trudged on.

She had only gone three blocks when she noticed a car drifting down the street behind her. The driver matched her pace, neither slowing down nor speeding up. She glanced over her shoulder, squinting into the headlights in an attempt to identify the person behind the wheel. Maybe Dave, knowing she was carless, had decided to come rescue her. But her brother would have driven the truck with the snowplow, unless he was pulling another prank. Stupid of him, scaring her like that this morning, and so typical. How many tricks had he played on her over the years? Well, she wouldn't let his immature behavior ruin her day. Vero turned her back on the trailing car, lost her balance, and slipping, butt-planted in a mound of snow. That would teach her to pay more attention to where she stepped. Rolling onto her knees, she pushed up and pressed on, grateful for the metal pole Nana had sworn was good for everything from hiking to snake wrangling. As if Nana ever hunted snakes.

The intersection of Griffith and Hoffman loomed. Vero paused to allow a Prius to glide through the stop sign and swerve to the left, throwing up a fantail of snow and ice. Double-checking for more cars, she scurried across the street, anticipating three more intersections before she reached the apartment building. Glancing back, she realized the car that had been behind her was still there, and it had moved closer. *You really think it's following you?* her inner voice sneered. Her gut said yes. The question was why? She considered stopping to call Dave. But if it wasn't him? That thought provoked another, creepier one. What if the person responsible for Gisele Townsend's disappearance was prowling for another victim?

The heavy snowfall dimmed the effect of the streetlights, casting the town into shadow. Vero knew the way to her apartment, but the gloom and the reduced visibility were disorienting. She squinted into the curtain of snow, seeking the end of the block. An oncoming car crept past, tires slipping sideways every time the driver tried to increase speed. A city plow rumbled by, piling chunks of snow and ice onto the curb and spraying her boots with salt. She planted the hiking stick in each drift and pulled herself forward, glancing from the invisible sidewalk to the car tracking her. She had reached the final block before the Scottish when the headlights wavered, then leveled straight at her. Hurling the stick to her right, Vero dove after it. She tumbled head over heels, pulled herself up, and staggered onto the deck of the Garden Spot Restaurant. The car's bumper brushed the back of her coat, swerved, and slalomed around the corner, its taillights a faint red glow that faded before it reached the end of Stimson.

"What the hell!" A man crunched his way from the restaurant toward her. "You all right, Miss?"

"I think so." Head bowed, hands buried in her pockets, Vero fought the tremors racing through her.

"Saw the whole thing from the window. That car almost ran you over." The man offered a hand, which she accepted. "I'm going to call the police."

"No need. I'm all right, and he or she will be long gone before the cops get here. But thank you for coming to my rescue. I just live one more block down."

"The Scottish Apartments? The ones that out-of-town con man's tearing down?" Her rescuer blinked into the night. "You're shaking, and no wonder. The least I can do is help you across the street. Fool drivers got no reason to be out in this weather anyway. Hope you got no place to go tonight."

Vero bent to retrieve the walking stick, grateful for the man's hand on her elbow. She thanked him again, urging him to return to the warmth of the restaurant. He reluctantly crossed the patio and went back inside. She hurried on.

Orange caution netting greeted her when she reached the apartments. Ignoring the ache in her back from her desperate lunge, she used her pass card to enter the building, grateful for the whoosh of warm air that greeted her. The close call with the out-of-control driver had left her more than shaken. She grabbed the handrail and crabbed her way to the second floor, unable to shake the sensation of being followed. Checking over her shoulder, she unlocked the door and hurried in.

Empty now of most of the furniture and all Ellie's photographs, the living room leered at her. Shadows crowded the corners where lamps used to stand. Boxes filled with her belongings, labeled and taped shut, awaited transport to an as-of-yet-undisclosed location. Still in her coat, she poured Cabernet into a juice glass and chugged it down. Who could she call? Who would believe her if she claimed a car had tried to run her over on her way home from the shop? The clock on the stove reminded her that she was due at Hospice in twenty minutes. She ticked off the names of the few people she could trust and, without considering the consequences, punched in the one person she knew wouldn't dismiss her story. Cal Castro answered on the first ring.

"I apologize for calling," Vero began. Cal cut her off.

"I was about to call you. What's wrong?"

Swallowing back a sob, she squared her shoulders. "Someone tried to run me down on my walk home."

Cal didn't argue or try to talk her down from the accusation. "Are you hurt?"

"No, but," she paused to gather her thoughts, "I need to get to the Hospice Center. My Nana-"

"Where are you?"

"My apartment."

"Stay there until I text you. My company has a plowing service. I'll call them as soon as we hang up. And Vero? Don't come down until you see a Merle's Trucking sign on the side of a white F150."

"What's," she cursed her lack of knowledge when it came to vehicles, "an F150?"

"A very big truck with a snowplow on the front. It can get you to your grandmother safely. Vero? You still there?"

"I'm here." She emptied the last of the wine into the glass and took a sip. "Thank you."

"Did you call the police?"

"Would they believe me?"

111

"Maybe not," Cal said, "but I do."

Vero ended the call. Now she had to pee and change into warmer clothes, dry boots, a thicker sweater, and pants. Twelve minutes later she stood by the first-floor entry, staring at the few car lights that drifted through the storm like wintry fireflies. The tremors had stopped, replaced by anger and a swell of despair that pushed her into deeper musings. As much as she loved her parents, moving back in with them screamed failure. So did the debts piling up like the snow outside. When she met with Storey, she had to impress upon him how much she needed a place of her own. Except now, someone out there, hidden by the freakishly early winter storm and tinted windows, had tried to run her over. Had it been intentional? How could it not be? The car had followed her from the moment she left the shop. The specter of a serial kidnapper invaded her thoughts. Was the person who took Gisele out cruising for another victim...or was he, if it was a man, after her specifically? Was it a coincidence that both she and Gigi were connected to Calderón Castro? Thinking about the possibilities made her head throb. When lights swept across the ice-crusted glass, Vero left the building.

A large truck bearing a snowplow on the front bumper and tires as big as millstones rumbled to a stop in front of her. Letters on the door, partially obscured by a coating of gray slush, proclaimed *Mer...ucking*. She slogged forward, holding the hood of her coat closed against the fierce tug of wind, and reached for the handle. The door swung open. A gloved hand reached out to lift her up. She hung on and struggled forward, falling across the seat and straight into the lap of Calderón Castro.

Cal

The fur-lined hood of her coat shaded Veronica Simon's face as she flopped forward, her head landing in Cal's lap. Heat ignited low in his belly. The hood slipped back, hair spilling free of a tieback to fan over his thighs. Her breath escaped in a rush, sending a shiver of arousal straight to his groin as she struggled to right herself. Her gloved hands pressed against his thigh. He drew a deep breath, ordered his body to stand down, and helped her up. Face flushed, eyes lowered, she reached over to tug the door closed.

"Thank you, sir, sorry for my clumsy—" She brushed snow from her eyes as she turned toward him. "Oh, it's you."

Cal rested his hands on the wheel, willing his nascent erection to calm down. What was it about this woman that irritated and excited him in equal measure every time they were together? Ignoring the sudden urge to haul her into his arms and kiss her, he waited until she buckled the seatbelt, then shifted into reverse. The truck beeped in warning as he backed out, swung onto Holland, and slowed to check for cars at the intersection. "You're disappointed."

"No, surprised. I wasn't expecting to see you." Blushing, she sucked in her bottom lip. "You didn't have to do this."

"I promised to send a truck, Miss Simon."

"I don't mean to sound ungrateful." The color in her cheeks deepened. Melting snow dripped onto the floor mat beneath her boots, punctuating the whir of the fan blasting warm air into the cab. "Don't you have enough to worry about?"

"I do, and your well-being is one of them." He inhaled sharply as the scent of her perfume drifted around the cab. "Besides, I kind of like driving this thing."

Vero made a small sound that resembled a snort, straightened her shoulders, and touched his arm. "I am glad you came, but you said we shouldn't be seen together."

"Yeah, well, maybe we shouldn't, but have you noticed there's a blizzard raging?" Cal slowed for an older model Volkswagen creeping through the intersection at Francis and Griffith, slid around a curve, and chugged on into the wall of falling snow obscuring the roadway. "Don't think anyone will be able to identify us tonight."

"Probably not, although someone seemed to know it was me trudging through the snowdrifts. Or maybe I'm being paranoid." She wrapped her gloved hands around the ends of her scarf and sighed.

Cal remained quiet until they reached the block where SIMON's was located. "Why didn't you tell me you planned to walk home?"

"It didn't come up." Vero abandoned her grip on the scarf to tug the seat belt tighter and stared down the road. "We're not exactly best friends or anything. Your interest is purely self-serving."

Cal frowned at her prickly demeanor. Is that how she saw him, selfish and arrogant and only out for himself? Was that the person he'd become after years of working to please everyone around him, his father, Gisele, the family? Or was Veronica deflecting her own uncertainty onto him? Maybe she was the one afraid to let him see who she really was. What secrets was she hiding behind those wide and startling green eyes? When she sighed again, he glanced over, only to find her staring at him.

"I'm sorry, Cal. That was uncalled for," she said. "I'm not usually so—"

"Judgmental?"

She hung her head. "Is that what I sound like? God, I'm turning into a shrew."

Cal caught her wiping her eyes, which begged the question…Did she resent his presence, his help? Or had the recent close call with a car frightened her that much? Might as well find out. "Since I am here, why don't you tell me exactly what happened after you left the store?"

Vero propped her chin on a fist and leaned against the side window. "Maybe you won't believe me. The old man who dragged me out of the way thought it was simply a careless driver who doesn't know how to navigate in the snow, but—"

"Try me."

"I don't know if I should..."

"C'mon, Vero, you're not a coward. Anyone who walks ten blocks in a blizzard has grit. What's going on?"

"What if...what if the car that tried to run me over is somehow connected to your girl—," Vero peeked at Cal, looked away, "to Gisele's disappearance? What if they didn't intend to hit me, just scare me? My brother Dave did something similar earlier today. He tailgated me in Link Storey's Hummer on my way back from the police station. Had me so rattled I asked the bank to contact the police."

"Your brother made you think you were being stalked?"

"Yeah, but he's the king of pranks gone wild. I don't think he'll ever outgrow them. Only this time I'm pretty sure it wasn't him, so that leads me to wonder why anyone would try to frighten me like that. What if they had hit me? I could be dead and buried in a snowdrift for days before anyone knew I was missing."

The thought of Vero harmed by an idiot driver made Cal shiver. He was considering how best to continue the conversation when she spoke again. "I'm probably spinning this way out of proportion. Maybe it was nothing more than a bad driver losing control in the middle of a snowstorm."

"That's a huge maybe. Here's another one. Maybe there's a serial stalker out there, and he's got his sights on you."

"But, why?" Vero burrowed deeper into the seat.

"I don't know, Vero, and what I don't know bothers me." Cal hunched forward, used his hand to wipe condensation from the glass. "Damn. Can you find a button for the defogger?"

Vero peered at the dashboard, finger hovering over the panel until she found the one she wanted. Air blasted upward from the grates and the glass began to clear. Cal relaxed, gripped the wheel harder, and calculated the remaining distance to the Hospice Center. Minutes passed before he spoke again. "You really don't trust me?"

Vero bit the tip of a gloved finger. "I don't know. Should I?"

"You could try." Cal turned onto the road to the Hospice Center and increased their speed. "Have you found a place to live?"

"Not yet." Vero removed a glove and took out her phone. "But I'm meeting Lincoln Storey soon. He sent over a few possibilities."

"About that. Why did you call Storey instead of me?"

"Why are you angry? You have enough problems of your own to deal with. Besides, I didn't have any other options."

"Bullshit, Veronica. My firm has way more contacts than that son of a bitch."

"Whoa, Castro, what's that all about? What do you have against Storey?"

"Forget it. Forget I said anything." He refused to look her way, refused to let her see how much rejecting his assistance hurt. "Just be careful with that guy."

Cal flicked on the turn signal and coasted over the slick surface of the Hospice lot. The area had been cleared earlier, but the storm continued to coat the surface as the temperature dropped, turning the exposed slush into sheets of black ice. "If you need a ride home, call an Uber."

"Cal." She touched his arm. He drew back. "I'm sorry. I don't mean to be rude. I just don't know what to do. Because I like you, and I shouldn't."

"It's fine, Simon. Believe what you want." He folded his arms and stared over her head. Vero shoved a shoulder against the stubborn door and jumped down.

"Thank you, for believing me. For what it's worth, I believe you, too." She stared up at him, her eyes bright with tears. He noted the shadows beneath, the worry that creased her forehead. He shouldn't have said that about a stalker, shouldn't have warned her off Storey, but things didn't add up. First, Gisele disappeared. Then Brad was attacked. Now Vero had come close to being injured or killed. The only common link was him. Link. Hah! He didn't even want to consider how that narcissistic asshole got involved with Veronica, and he wasn't about to reveal their history of juvenile rivalries to the woman who gave him his first honest arousal in months.

"Truce," he said. "Call me if you need a ride home." She inclined her head and slammed the door, trudged her way to the Center's entrance. He watched until her figure faded into the interior. He wondered if his intrinsic distrust of Storey would do more harm to Vero's fragile control, but he remained unwilling to reveal more of his stormy teenage years. Truth was he wanted Veronica Simon to like him. Scrubbing at the windshield one more time, he crunched the truck over the snow and headed back to the office. He'd stay there tonight while he searched through apartment listings to send her tomorrow. He didn't want Link Storey anywhere near Vero.

.

Vero

The muted strains of a Vivaldi concerto accompanied Vero as she made her way toward her grandmother's room. Her boots squelched loudly over the clean floor tiles. She stopped to remove them and continued down the hall, feet chilling through her socks. When she reached Nana Verna's room, she paused to clear her mind of the day's concerns. She shelved the conversation with Cal, the difficulty of finding a place to live, the continuing mystery of Gisele Townsend's disappearance, and the fact that the store was slipping through her fingers. Tonight, only Nana mattered.

Her grandmother lay on her back, hands clasped over her chest, eyes skittering beneath the thin lids. Somehow, she had grown smaller, her now-child-size body swaddled in blankets, her head swathed tonight in a pink turban. Two vases graced the window ledge, the dozen roses Vero had sent accompanied by a bouquet of fall flowers from Sonny. If Nana woke up, the first thing she'd see would be a reminder of the plants she'd nurtured in the beds around the lake house. Vero draped her coat over the chair back, opened the volume of Emily Dickinson poems she'd been reading aloud last night, and leafed through the contents. A rustle beneath the mound of coverings brought her closer to the bed. Nana lifted a hand and murmured, "Vero."

"Nana? Oh, my God, Nana!" Vero leaned closer. It didn't matter why her grandmother had awakened, just that she had. She grasped Nana's outstretched hand and brought it to her cheek.

"You must," Nana murmured.

"What, Nana? What must I do?"

Her grandmother's eyes, their bright sparkle dimmed by cataracts and the encroachment of death, struggled to focus on Veronica. "Listen to me, child. The lake house. Yours. You must."

"But why? I don't understand. Please."

Her grandmother's hand slipped free, and she gasped twice, the brief moment of clarity gone. Each breath grew softer, her chest barely rising. Alarmed, Vero pressed the call button. By the time the nurse arrived, Verna Simon was gone.

Vero huddled in the last pew in the candle-lit chapel that overlooked Lake Kalamazoo. Down the hall, the staff conferred with the gentlemen from Dykstra Funeral Home, come to fetch the body. Her parents waited in the lobby, determined to accompany the hearse transferring Nana Verna to the funeral parlor. Paperwork detailing instructions about the burial was already on file. Only the day and time of the celebration of life remained to be decided. Despite being prepared for Nana's passing, Vero shivered with grief, her mind struggling to cope with the loss of the woman who had loved her unconditionally all her life. Who would fill that role now? And how could Vero ignore the plea in her grandmother's final words?

An assistant from Dykstra's popped his head in through the chapel door and motioned to her. Vero followed him to the hearse, grateful for permission to ride with them. After she saw Nana settled there, her parents could drive her home. She wouldn't have to rely on Cal again, though a small part of her kept returning to that moment in the apartment when he had wrapped his arms around her, his body warm and solid and utterly capable of shielding her from all her problems. She tried, unsuccessfully, to dismiss the memory of faceplanting into his lap in the cab of the snowplow. She was positive he'd had an erection. Well, that had to be exhaustion, shock, and sadness coloring her thoughts. *God, Veronica, who thinks about sex when a loved one has just died?* Yet she also recalled her flirty, playful grandma urging her to hang out with her brothers' friends when they showed up uninvited at the lake. "They may not know it now, my girl, but they'll be coming to see you in a few years. You're smart and beautiful and fun, my Vero, and life is to be lived, not squandered." Slumping against the seatback, she fought against a fresh round of tears. She wanted to be strong for her father now. Her grieving could wait.

The road back to town had been plowed, although a thin layer of crusted snow crunched beneath the tires as the hearse approached the funeral home. Vero thanked the driver for his kindness and tightened her scarf against the chill. Her mother and father, wrapped in each other's embrace, waited beneath the covered entry. To the left of the main door, three rectangular glass panels cast light onto the mounds of snow-covered flower beds. When the hearse coasted to a stop, she scrambled out and into her father's arms. The car bearing Nana's remains continued around the building. She held her father's hand as the front door hissed open and Samantha Izor, one of Dykstra's funeral directors, escorted them through the hushed foyer into a comfortable inner room. A gas fireplace lent an air of peace and warmth to the space.

"I'm so sorry for your loss. In this difficult time, it's good to know that your mother," Samantha nodded first to Vero's father, then to her, "your grandmother left all her affairs in order. She specifically requested no additional money be spent beyond what she had already paid, which was substantial. In fact, you may receive a refund, depending upon when and how you decide to hold the celebration of life."

Vero's father accepted the three pages of detailed instructions and glanced through them while Izor retrieved a second folder labeled *Celebration of Life*.

"I understand Ms. Simon wished for a limited viewing followed by the opportunity to share fellowship. Perhaps I can offer these suggestions." She handed over a brochure of food and beverage choices as well as one listing available dates over the coming two weeks. Then she picked up a large manila envelope and turned to Vero. "Your grandmother was the most meticulous and organized woman I've ever had the pleasure of meeting. She insisted I keep this for you, Veronica, and give it to you on the day she passed. You may open it now or later. The choice is yours. Now, Mr. and Mrs. Simon, do you see a day and time that might work for your family?"

Vero tuned them out. She examined the writing on the front of the envelope. Satisfied that Nana had indeed written her name on the cover, Vero held it close. How many more ways would her grandmother speak to her? Perhaps this held information that would explain those final cryptic words. The determined note in her father's voice brought her back to the conversation.

"All the people my mother cared about live in Michigan, most of them here in Saugatuck. If it's possible, I'd like to hold the celebration soon, perhaps this Saturday."

Samantha nodded as she entered the information in her laptop. Vero's mother handed back the menu. "I've circled what we'd like to serve," she said. "Do you have easels for photograph displays?"

"We do." The woman slid a thin, rectangular cardboard box next to her mother. "You may use these posters to mount pictures. We will contact the florist and the minister, unless you have a preference in addition to those Ms. Simon selected."

Vero's dad stood up, indicating the discussion for today had ended. Intimidated by the sedate silence of the building, they made their way back through the long corridor and out the front entrance, where another assistant had parked their car. "Vero? Veronica?" Her mother reached over to tap Vero's cheek. "Do you want to go home?"

"I don't have one," Vero said. "Drop me off at the store. Please."

"Oh, honey—" Her mother's words halted abruptly when her father shook his head.

"Not now, Angela." He handed them both in and drove slowly toward SIMON's. Rather than flounder through the snow piled along the curb, her father stopped the car in the middle of the street. He waited for Vero to slip around the building, enter through the back, and wave to them from the front display window before continuing home. Vero watched until she could no longer see the taillights before stepping away. She reset the alarms, climbed the narrow staircase to the workroom on the second floor, and, setting the envelope aside unopened, sat at her drawing board. Tonight, she would design a necklace to honor Nana Verna. But first, she called Agatha Wiggins to tell her the sad news.

The last sound Vero remembered was the chime of the grandfather clock striking two. She woke to the aroma of fresh-brewed coffee and the faint, sweet smell of pastries. Stretching to ease the kinks in her neck and back, she eyed the drawing board and the sketch lying there, then gathered her purse and the envelope and went downstairs.

Agatha Wiggins had set breakfast on the small table in the back office. When Vero approached, she held out her arms. "Oh, my dear girl, how are you doing?"

"I'm so, so sad. I feel like my heart is bleeding."

The old woman tightened her embrace, the hug a precursor to a sob. "Your grandma was my best friend my whole life. I don't know what I'll do without her."

"Me neither. Thank you for opening the shop today, but you can go home now."

"So should you, Veronica. There is no need to keep SIMON's open after such a loss. No one will blame you for closing. Besides, I doubt many people will be out shopping today, at least not until this snow melts. Go home, dear girl."

"I can't. I have inventory, and I'm working on a special design, and I don't want to be alone in my empty apartment. I need something to do, so I'll catch up on the cleaning and spend some time upstairs. Besides, you heard about The Scottish, right? I don't really have a home anymore."

Agatha patted the manila envelope Vero clutched in her hands. "Are you sure about that?"

Vero frowned. "Do you know what Nana put in here?"

"Let's just say I have a pretty good idea." Agatha shrugged into her quilted down coat and slid her feet into snow boots. "Call me when you know the details regarding the funeral."

"I already do." Vero stepped to the counter, wrote on a sticky note and passed it over. "It's set for Saturday. I will close the store so you can be with us."

Agatha noticed Vero's hesitance. "You know, you could ask my granddaughter to mind the shop that day. Shea has always loved working here."

Vero shrugged. "I don't know if that's a good idea. She's been a bit preoccupied over her boyfriend situation lately."

"Well, I'm sure you'll do what you think is best, but you really should consider taking Shea on. She's a real hard worker, despite her eccentric hair and all those piercings. I'll see you Saturday, dear girl, unless you need me beforehand." With that, Wiggins swirled a scarf around her neck, buttoned her down coat, and let herself out.

Alone and sluggish from sleeping at the drawing board, Vero debated locking the front door, then opted against it. Retreating to the back room, she tapped the envelope but decided whatever was inside could wait. She booted up the laptop and switched on the TV. Perhaps a backdrop of local news would temper the emptiness inside her. She had finished printing out a *Closed for a Funeral* poster when the announcement of **Breaking News** caught her attention. A female reporter swathed in snow hat, mittens, and a ski suit addressed the camera.

"Early this morning, a cross-country skier reported finding a body in the snow along the shore of Lake Goshorn. Local police responded to an emergency call at seven-thirty a.m. When they reached the scene, they found the body of a female on the northern shore of the lake. Investigators at the site would neither confirm nor deny the identity of the victim, although one source did indicate that it appeared the woman had suffered a serious head wound. Channel 3 is at the location and will keep you updated as more information becomes available. This is Kirsten Mong with news at noon reporting for WWMT TV."

Vero stared at the screen long after the broadcast ended, torn between relief and terror. Was the deceased the missing Gisele Townsend? Or was the corpse unrelated to Gisele's disappearance? A third possibility occurred to Vero, one sparked by Cal's comment earlier. Perhaps there was a serial killer at work in Saugatuck. She re-entered the showroom to secure the front door. If any customers appeared, she could admit them and re-lock after they were inside. *Just a precaution.* Bolstered by the thought, she stood behind the window display, inspecting the sidewalk in front of the store as well as the area across the street. No stranger stood silently watching today, but that didn't reassure her. She had never feared being alone before, but the events of the past week had eroded her confidence. If only Nana were still alive. Her grandmother's strength and courage had supported Vero for so many years. Now she felt adrift and more alone than ever. When the phone rang, she jumped, then checked the number. Lincoln Storey. Perhaps, finally, a bit of good news.

Cal

"Where's Lisa?" Antonio Castro's worried tone caused Cal to set down the mail he'd retrieved from the receptionist's desk to shuffle through the woman's index cards, one for each day of the month. Lisa Protus had an old-fashioned approach to her role as chief organizer for the Castro empire. If she wasn't in the office, she might be at a showing that neither Cal nor his father knew about, so she left detailed information about her movements in case they needed to contact her. The cards for the past three days were blank. He ran a thumb down the calendar propped next to her computer. It, too, listed nothing beyond Sunday afternoon, a showing at four but no details as to the location.

"That's odd." Cal confronted his father with a post-it note he found slipped under the keyboard. "This says she's taking a few days' vacation. Did she mention anything to you about going away?"

His father shook his head. "Lisa's behavior has been erratic the last few weeks. She's barely been in the office since Gisele disappeared. I suspect she's upset about the increased scrutiny of our business."

Cal settled into Lisa's chair to sort through the mail. He opened the envelopes, skimmed through the flyers, bank statements, and bills, many of them a week old. "It looks like she hasn't been keeping up with the correspondence either."

Antonio leaned against the desk, arms crossed, frowning. "That's not like her. I wonder if something else is wrong. Remember she had that cancer scare last spring?"

Cal rested his elbows on the desk, worry creasing his forehead. "Now that you mention it, she has seemed distant, preoccupied, but I hate to bother her if she really is taking a break."

His father tapped the card box. "Why don't you see if you can contact her?"

Cal dialed Lisa's number, switched the call to speaker. The cell rang ten times, then kicked over to voice mail. The automated greeting echoed through the salesroom. He left a message for her to call the office and hung up.

"Calderón." Antonio's voice faltered as he sank into a chair. "Have you listened to the news this morning?"

Cal abandoned the mail. "No. Has there been a new development?"

"I don't know. When you were with those policemen at the station, they didn't offer any additional details about Gisele's disappearance, right? Because this recent discovery looks bad."

Startled by the concern in his father's eyes, Cal scooted closer. "What discovery?"

"A body was found at Goshorn Lake. A woman's body."

Cal inhaled sharply. Could it be Gisele? Wouldn't the police have contacted him? After Veronica's statement, Cal had to believe he was no longer a suspect. This discovery could place him back on their radar. They'd start hounding him again, especially Duane Harry, and that suspicion would drive them to ignore other possible suspects. He needed to prove his innocence and remove this cloud hovering over the Castro name. Maybe Brad remembered more about the night he was attacked, and Veronica had promised him a copy of the receipt. He gathered the company correspondence, stuck Lisa's note on the top envelope, and headed toward his office.

"Cal?" His father grabbed his arm. "Are you all right?"

Before he could answer, his cell rang. The unknown number glared at him, but he answered anyway.

"Mr. Castro? Elgin Barkley. Is today still a good time to stop by your office?"

Cal rubbed his forehead. He'd almost forgotten about the insurance scam. He checked his watch. "I'm due at a closing in ten minutes. Can you be here around noon?" Barkley agreed, and Cal hung up, feeling only a little guilty about the lie. He needed to check with Glenn Canard about attending their meeting. His father walked with him past the conference room where they met with the developer. Since the initial consultation, Bergeron, eager to begin his land grab at Goshorn Lake, had taken to leaving voicemails at least twice a day.

"That man, Bergeron," Antonio waved toward the round table where they had faced off, "do you sense he's hiding something?"

"I don't know, *Papá*," Cal said. "He offers a lucrative contract if we succeed in garnering the properties, but I don't trust him."

"We have that in common, *mijo*." His father patted his arm and turned toward his own office. Cal was about to sit down when he heard the front door bang open. Five seconds later Cerise Townsend stomped into his office, eyes narrowed, fury trailing her like fog.

"Castro, if that's my sister out at Goshorn, I promise you'll rot in hell."

"Miss Townsend?" Detective Norsuch followed Gisele's sister into the room, Duane Harry close behind. "I told you we would speak with you later today. Right now, we need to talk to Mr. Castro. In private."

The woman rounded on him. "I've hired my own investigator, Detective, and he's working a lot harder than you and your partner to solve my sister's disappearance."

"In that case," Norsuch took her elbow, preparing to escort her out of the building, "there's no need for you to be here, and no reason to confront Mr. Castro."

Cerise fussed with the collar of her coat, briefcase under one arm, purse on the other, then pointed a gloved hand at Castro. Cal's father squeezed in behind the detectives.

"What's going on?" Antonio demanded.

Shaking off the detective's grip, Cerise glared at each man in turn. "Get out of my way. If you did this, Cal, I will watch you burn."

Norsuch followed her out and waited for her to leave before returning to the office. "Sorry to barge in on you, Castro. Seems our missing person's case just got more complicated."

"Detectives." Antonio stepped beside Cal. "Is there a specific reason for this visit or are you simply here to harass my son?"

Norsuch set the nameplate he'd snatched from the receptionist's desk on top of the scattered mail. "Lisa Protus works for you, does she not? When's the last time you saw her?"

"Sunday, around two, I think. She hasn't been in since then. This morning, I found this on her desk." Cal lifted the note he'd found on the keyboard and handed it over. "We were surprised. She hadn't discussed taking time off with me or my father."

Harry snapped a photo of the note, then slipped it into an evidence bag. "Curious that yet another woman associated with you has gone missing."

"Lisa's missing?"

"Actually, I misspoke." Duane Harry folded his arms. "The body discovered at Goshorn Lake this morning is not your missing fiancée, Miss Townsend."

Norsuch never took his eyes off Cal. His partner continued. "The woman by the lake has been identified as Lisa Protus. She didn't die a natural death, and it wasn't suicide."

Antonio Castro braced himself against a chairback, then sat down, one hand fisted against his chest.

"*Papá*?" Cal crouched beside his father. "What's wrong?"

Antonio shook his head. "Nothing makes sense, *mijo*. Gisele disappearing. Lisa dead. The woman worked for us for ten years, never a complaint, always punctual and enthusiastic about her job, the firm. How? Who?"

In the reception area, the phone rang. When no one answered, the caller spoke to voicemail. All four men listened as an anxious voice recited all the reasons why she had to see a certain listing today and not tomorrow, followed by a demand to call her immediately. Cal left to fetch water for his father. When he returned, he invited the detectives to sit. Both declined.

"How long was Miss Protus in the office Sunday?" Harry asked.

Cal exchanged a glance with his father, then shook his head. "I honestly don't know. I was in and out all day. You're welcome to check the call logs. Lisa was meticulous about recording all communications. If she was here, she would have noted each one along with the time. *Papá*?"

"She was here in the late morning. I do not recall when she left, but that's not unusual. Most of us spend more time away from the office than we do here. There's a rotation schedule on her desk. You can check with the other realtors to see if they know anything."

Cal took the empty glass from his father and set it on the desk. "We had a meeting with Eric Bergeron, the developer interested in obtaining Goshorn Lake properties, Detective. Lisa was here then, which is the last time I recall seeing her."

"My son is correct." Antonio Castro stood to straighten his tie, pull down the sleeves of his suit. "That's the last I recall her being in the office. It was a slow day. The gloomy weather kept many people indoors. I left after the meeting to be with my wife. She wasn't feeling well, and I can work from home as easily as I can here."

"This Eric Bergeron. Who is he again?" Norsuch tapped his lower lip with his pen.

"A big-time investor out of Chicago looking to purchase lakefront properties and turn them into resorts for city dwellers," Cal offered. "He's tearing down The Scottish Apartments. And he's interested in properties out at Goshorn, wants our firm to acquire them for him."

"This the deal you and Gisele argued about?"

"Yes."

"Do you have any objection to us looking through Protus's desk? Her files?"

"No. We have nothing to hide." Cal ran a hand through his hair. "It feels like we're being set up, like someone is deliberately trying to damage our firm."

"That's one way to look at it," Norsuch said, directing his stare at Cal. "Of course, you might have a larger game at play here."

"What would that be, Detective? Because at this point, I see nothing to gain and everything to lose."

Harry pulled out his notebook and flipped to a page. "Perhaps this insurance investigator, Elgin Barkley, can shed some light on that? He's in town to see you."

"Barkley is a woman, and we're supposed to meet here at noon. What do you know about her?" Cal said.

"He's a she? Right. Well, apparently Barkley heard about the Townsend woman's disappearance and, as a concerned citizen, contacted the station via email. Seems million-dollar policies don't roll across insurance desks every day."

"She must have gone to you after she tried to scare me into admitting something else I didn't do. I want it on record that I never took out any such policy on Gisele. Ever. End of story."

"Curious, then, isn't it," Harry said, "that Barkley contends it's your signature on the application?"

"We'll see about that." Cal helped his father to the door. "Right now, my priority is my father's health. I'm taking him home. Then I have a closing to attend, and I'm already late. You're welcome to return when Barkley shows up at noon."

"We'll do that," Norsuch said.

The detectives headed out the door, a scatter of snowflakes drifting in as they exited. Weak sunlight pawed at the windows, unable to dispel the gloom settling over the interior despite the glare of the overhead lights. Cal noted an ashy tinge to his father's normally olive skin. Perhaps Antonio should see a doctor or even go to the hospital. One more worry to add to the growing pile.

"*Papá*, no arguments. I'm taking you home."

"No, *hijo*, I'm all right. It's the shock. Lisa has been a good employee. I can't believe anyone would harm her."

Cal ignored his father's protests. He slipped into his coat, the one that retained a hint of Vero Simon's floral scent. Checking his cell, he found a text from their lawyer asking to join the noon meeting via phone. He sent a quick reply, then messaged the bank that he'd been unavoidably detained but would be there in half an hour. Finally, he sent a group text to the other Castro realtors, informing them that the office would be closed until eleven-thirty. As he sent it off, an incoming message pinged from the Bergeron corporation, requesting a second meeting later that afternoon. *Ready to move on the property*. Cal thumbed in a time, set the reminder, then helped his father into his own coat. He locked the doors but left the lights on, unwilling to shutter the business completely. He'd be back soon enough to deal with Barkley and the detectives and the developer.

The cold bit at his ears. He watched sorrow settle over his father's features, a sadness he shared. Lisa was dead. Gisele was still missing. Cerise remained convinced he had harmed her twin. A mystery man tried to run over his alibi, and someone had forged his signature on an insurance policy. Cal needed a strong drink and a keen mind to help him sort through the chaos his life had become. He ticked through the names of colleagues and extended family, his lawyer, even the two annoying detectives, surprised by the fact that the only person he really wanted to talk to was Vero Simon.

Vero

Vero finished the inventory of the watches and sagged against the counter. Sadness dragged like a too-heavy coat. Only one hour gone, six more until she could close the shop. Perhaps the walk home would clear her mind and lift her spirits. But what if the mysterious stalker returned? She checked her phone for updates from her parents. The screen remained empty. She liberated a tray of loose gemstones, part of Nana's secret stash, from the second safe in the upstairs workroom. Her grandmother never explained where the stones came from. Even though Nana claimed to fly to New York and Amsterdam once a year for trade fairs, the ones she offered Vero never showed up after those trips. And it was from the mystery hoard that Vero had selected the diamonds for the ring Cal bought. She should have listened to her gut and hidden it before he ever came into the shop. She'd done exactly that the week before when a woman with a Brooklyn accent and an inflated ego had insisted on trying on every ring in the shop. *Always trust your gut*, Nana used to say. Agatha Wiggins echoed the sentiment, but then both were into tarot cards and palm readings, too. Smiling at the memory of the two old ladies sharing their experiences of the occult while they sipped wine coolers on the dock at the lake, Vero scrubbed away the tears. Her phone chirped. A new text scrolled across the screen.

sorry to learn of your grandmother's passing missed
you this morning something's come up any chance you can
meet this afternoon? say 3 at Oliver's? link

Oh, shit, she'd forgotten their early meeting. Anxiety filled her, followed by the tiniest hope. Maybe Storey had located an apartment close to the shop. And meeting him would take her mind off Nana's passing, if only for a few moments. Cal's warning sounded, but he didn't have the right to tell her who she could and couldn't see. *Now who's being bitchy,* her inner voice crowed. *He offered to help you, too. You turned him down!*

Ignoring the internal war of wills, she texted an affirmative reply, then contacted Shea about coming in to work for three hours. The woman's prompt acquiescence boosted Vero's confidence. If Storey had located a place for her, she wouldn't have to move to the lake. The creak of the door brought her back to the present. She greeted the customers and spent the next half hour discussing charm bracelets and whether gold or silver hoops were the better choice for a fifteen-year-old. When the shoppers left, Vero grabbed a quick bite from her stash of energy bars. She turned on the TV, hoping for more information about the identity of the body discovered at Goshorn. What a weird coincidence that a corpse would turn up near the Simon family cabin.

The local newscaster droned through the usual segments on national politics, continuing COVID immunization efforts, and weather. The freak blizzard had moved on, roads were returning to normal, and temperatures were predicted to climb into the forties for a few days before another upper-level disturbance threatened. Vero kept one eye on the sales floor and the other on the TV. When the station transitioned to an on-site location, she focused her attention on the interview between a reporter and a representative of the State Highway Patrol. A reference to Castro Realtors intensified her interest. The policeman stepped off camera, and the reporter faced the viewing audience.

"Authorities have confirmed the identity of the dead woman as that of Lisa Protus, forty-three, of Saugatuck, a long-time employee of Castro Realty, the same firm connected to the disappearance of Gisele Townsend five days ago. Officials would neither confirm nor deny any ties between the women except for their work in real estate."

Vero clicked the remote. The sound and picture dissolved, leaving her alone in the silent room. The drip of snow melting from the eaves matched the suspicion growing inside her. Another woman connected to Cal Castro had come to grief. Was it a coincidence that a stranger had attempted to hit Vero during the snowstorm? Harm her or warn her? Cal was worried about her safety. Did the accidental pursuit intend to frighten her into staying away from him? A contrary idea wormed its way forward. Was someone out to destroy the Castro family itself? That, she conceded, was a major leap of conclusions. Best to set it aside for now, print out a new receipt for the man, and wash her hands of the whole mess. It wasn't as if she had no other worries. Depositing the energy bar wrapper and the empty yogurt container in the trash, Vero washed her hands, took several more gulps of water, and returned to the sales floor as two new patrons entered the shop.

At two-forty, Shea arrived with a flourish, wearing her latest thrift store find. "Like my coat?" she crowed.

"Magenta is definitely your color." Vero shrugged into her navy peacoat. "I don't plan on being gone more than an hour. Mr. Storey may have found a place for me to live. At least, I hope that's why he wants to meet this afternoon. I really need one thing to go right today."

"You're meeting realtor and ex-jock Link Storey? One of Saugatuck's three most eligible bachelors, along with your brother Dave and that hunky Cal Castro?" Shea twirled a lock of purple hair around one ringed finger. "I've heard some stories about that man would curl your hair. Well, yours is already curly, but you know what I mean."

Vero worried her lower lip. "Which one?"

Her associate arched her eyebrows and giggled. "All of them, actually. They are sexy to the max, Vero. But Dave is, like, your brother, so off limits, right? I'd do Castro in a sec, if he asked. Storey's a different animal...keeps his life very, very private, which hints at dark and dangerous, in bed, if you know what I mean."

"Stop with the nods and winks, Shea." Vero couldn't resist smiling back. "I don't plan to sleep with either of them."

"Fine, girlfriend. But you might be denying yourself some fabulous sexual pleasure." Shea disappeared into the back, returned without her coat. Vero handed her a list of items to polish and reshelve.

"Seriously, if you know anything about these men, please tell me. Should I be concerned about working with Storey?"

"About men, I know everything, including that wolf of a boyfriend I just dumped." Shea leaned on the glass case, her frown causing the spider tattoo on her forehead to jiggle. "As for the Storey man, where are you meeting him?"

"Morrow's Café. I hope he'll have some good prospects for me."

"Well, enjoy the time away from SIMON's, but keep your guard up until the guy shows his true hand. You know, beat him at his own game."

"I'm not good at playing relationship games, Shea."

Shea set the to-do list on the counter and hugged Vero. "Sweetness, I'm so sorry about your grandma, and I know you're worried about things here, but I'll take good care of the shop for you."

"I know you will." Vero weighed Nana Verna's envelope, then tucked it into her purse, slipped out the front, and headed down the block. She hugged the inside of the walkway, suspicious of every car that passed, but she spotted no dark SUVs, no erratic drivers. Five minutes later she reached the café. Sidestepping a gaggle of young mothers with toddlers in tow, she caught the door before it banged shut and dragged her boots over the doormat to knock off any lingering snow.

The aroma of coffee and savory pastries enticed her as she stepped up to the counter. She ordered a cappuccino, then glanced around. A mix of young and old patrons filled half the tables, most hunkered in front of a laptop. A man in a camel-colored topcoat sat alone in the corner, head bowed over his phone. When he looked up, Vero recognized the all-American features of Lincoln Storey. He wore his hair close-shaven on the sides with a carefully styled mop of curls on top. His light-colored eyes and wide grin projected an innocent, boyish quality, but intelligence and cunning lurked behind the façade. It would be as easy to be taken in by this man as it was to gravitate toward Cal Castro. What, she thought, were the odds of meeting two such dominating personalities in the same week?

When the barista called her name, Vero picked up her drink and approached Storey's table. He stood, offered a smile and a hand, held hers a fraction too long.

"Again, I'm so sorry to hear of your grandmother's passing," he said.

"Thank you. It's not unexpected, but she and I were close." Vero accepted the invitation to sit and slipped off her coat. Her bracelet snagged in the cuff. As she bent to untangle the charms, her sweater pulled tight, highlighting the swell of her breasts. Storey noticed.

"Maybe now is not the time to say this, Veronica," he tapped his cell against the table, "but you've changed a lot since high school. I should have paid more attention back then."

"We've all changed, Mr. Storey." Vero tugged the sweater into place and settled onto the hard wooden chair. "Some of us for the better, others for the worse. Please tell me you have good news."

"I told you, Vero, there's no need to be so formal. Call me Link. I'm afraid my news isn't that great." He spread three papers in front of her, one for a tiny bungalow, another for a condo along the waterfront. The third, nothing but an architectural sketch promising details of an apartment in Holland, wasn't available until the end of next month. Vero took another sip, disappointment coating her tongue. She shuffled the sheets, read through the specifics, and shook her head.

"Seriously, Link? Holland is simply too far away. I can't afford to buy a house, and the condo is also out of my price range. "

Link placed a hand over hers. "Not if you split the expense."

She met his gaze. "My current roommate is the only person I trust to share an apartment with and she's moving in with her boyfriend. I don't want to live with anyone else for a while. Is this really the best you could do?"

He studied her while she spoke, then shook his head. "I'm sorry, Veronica. Right now, Saugatuck's market doesn't offer much for singles or young entrepreneurs trying to make a go in business. What apartments are available are snapped up by students at the college in Holland. Could you move in with your family until a place comes on the market, or rehab the second floor above the shop? Your credit is solid, although the shop itself has problems."

"How do you know that?"

"I checked you out, of course. It's my job." He ran a finger around the rim of his cup, looked away, looked back. "I know your brother from back in high school and from his business. We run into each other at the gym, go out after our workouts. Dave talks about how close you were to your grandmother and how hard it is to run the place without her. And it's no secret all our small businesses are struggling. But this out-of-town developer is holding out a lifeline to us. That land your family owns at Goshorn, your brother thinks—"

"It doesn't matter what my brother thinks. The Simon land is not for sale, end of discussion." Was every realtor in town frothing at the mouth for a share of that sale? Was her family so willing to dispose of their heritage for money? She squeezed the carry cup before she said something she'd regret. "I appreciate your efforts, and I'm sorry I wasted your time. Was this all you had to tell me?"

"Actually," Link stared at her with an intensity that caused a shiver to race down both arms, "I like you, Vero, and I know the timing isn't great, but I was hoping that you might have dinner with me sometime soon."

Vero tossed the papers back at him, gathered her things, and stood up. "That's not going to happen, Mr. Storey. I'm not looking for a hookup, and before you say anything else, I want you to know I'm not interested in dating anyone right now."

Link stood, too, a sly grin stretching the corners of his well-formed mouth. "I can be very persuasive, Veronica, and I know people at the bank. You might find it advantageous to have me in your corner."

No smart retort came to mind as she struggled into her coat, yanked the door open, and shut her eyes against the glare from the piles of snow lining the street. Storey's words blinked like a neon sign in her mind. Was his offer a solution or a threat?

Cal

The associates of Castro Realty crowded into the conference room. A few stared blankly at the impressionist painting on the wall. Others clustered in small groups, whispering as they cast furtive glances at Cal and his father. When the last of the realtors arrived, Antonio called for order.

"My son and I want to thank you for coming in on such short notice. We are saddened and appalled at the news about Lisa, but Castro Realty has a solid reputation, and this tragedy will not keep us from continuing the important work we have always done for the citizens of Allegan County." Antonio met their uncertain glances with resolve. "My son would like to say a few words as well. Then, we will discuss what can be done to assist the investigation, and how we can help Lisa's family at this sad time. Cal?"

Cal took his father's place at the head of the table, making eye contact with each person before speaking. He murmured his sympathy to those who had been particularly close to the dead woman. "Coming as this news does on the heels of Gisele's disappearance, I know you have questions, perhaps even suspicions, about what is going on. First, I want to state, in clear and unequivocal terms," he leaned on the table, "I had nothing to do with either of these events. Although my relationship with Miss Townsend could be stormy, I never harmed her or any other woman. As for Lisa Protus, other than our contact here, she and I did not interact outside of work. Please believe me, no one will be happier than me to see Gisele returned to us and the person who harmed Lisa arrested."

No one spoke. Cal noted a few eyerolls whenever he mentioned Gisele, but for the most part, they appeared to believe him. He hoped they did. Sean Perry rose to refill his coffee mug, then turned toward Cal and his father.

"How can we help?" Perry said.

Antonio rapped his knuckles on the table. "That is the best question of the many you may have. If anyone has any information, no matter how small a detail, about Lisa's movements the last few days, you must share it with the police. The detectives working on both cases will join us later today. If you can stay to speak with them, please do. If you have showings scheduled but wish to share something relevant, write down your name and number. Cal will pass your info along. Now, Lisa wasn't married."

"She was once," Silvia Atkins blurted out. "And divorced. But she had a new boyfriend."

"More than one," Rosa Aquino murmured. When everyone turned to stare at her, she sat up straighter. "I mean, Lisa liked men. Lots of men."

Cal rubbed his chin to hide his discomfort. Despite his obvious non-interest in her, Lisa had let him know she was available should he change his mind. His father touched his arm, then pointed to his watch. "Barkley," Antonio mouthed before addressing the group. "Please, save these observations for the police. Right now, let's discuss what we can do to help Miss Protus's parents. I understand they're coming up from Detroit later today. I have contacted Best Western out on the Blue Star Highway and reserved rooms for them. As soon as the coroner releases the body, I will share the arrangements with you."

"Should we, you know, release some kind of statement and, I don't know, start a Go-Fund-Me account or something?" Perry wiped a bit of foam from his mustache.

"What about a memorial scholarship?" another voice suggested.

Silvia snorted. "Lisa wasn't really interested in higher education. Said she didn't need a degree to sell houses. Maybe we should plant a tree in the park or a new flower bed out front in her honor."

"All good suggestions," Antonio said. "We will send around an email and let you all vote on the one you prefer." The buzzer on the reception desk in the outer room, the one Lisa usually monitored, signaled the arrival of a visitor. Antonio nodded at Cal, who excused himself to greet the insurance investigator. Elgin Barkley, short, plump, her cheeks reddened from the cold, pushed her glasses onto her head, stuck out a hand. Her brown eyes narrowed.

"You're even more impressive in person than in your picture, Mr. Castro."

"My picture?"

"Is there somewhere we can talk?" Ms. Barkley looked around as she juggled scarf, purse, and briefcase. "Somewhere more private?"

"This way." Cal led her past the crowded conference room and into his office. His father glanced up as they passed, then returned to the discussion about a memorial. Cal relieved his visitor of her coat, hung it on the rack in the corner, and motioned to the chair opposite his own. Barkley settled with a sigh, heaved her case onto the desk, and snapped it open.

"That's quite a group in there." She cocked her head toward the room down the hall. "A business meeting?"

"One of our employees was found murdered this morning, Ms. Barkley. We're trying to decide how to move forward."

Barkley didn't act surprised. Instead, she murmured something under her breath. "That's not good news for you, is it, Mr. Castro?"

Ignoring the undercurrent of glee in her voice, Cal folded his hands and waited for the woman to begin the interrogation. He dreaded it. Norsuch and Harry had been relentless in their interviews, seeking to trip him in some imagined falsehood. They had planned to be here, too, but a text from Norsuch indicated they were out at Goshorn and wouldn't be back in time. Now, this woman, who had yet to prove her identity, was sizing him up behind the tortoiseshell frames. He sent a quick reminder to Canard to join the meeting via Facetime and opened the app, ready to connect with Glenn as soon as he rang. "Before we begin," Cal said, "may I see your credentials?"

"Of course." Barkley rooted through her purse, pulled out a driver's license and an ID badge with her photo and the name and address of the company for whom she worked. She left them lying on the desk as she extracted a thick folder from the briefcase, shifted the case to the floor, and scooted the chair forward. All the rustling made Cal slightly nauseous.

"Would you like something to drink?"

"Water would be fine, although a cup of chamomile tea would be even better. I can't seem to get warm." Her fingers shook as she spread out the papers in the file.

"I'll be right back." Cal hustled from the room into the kitchenette at the rear of the building. He filled a mug with water, rooted through the tea caddy before deciding to bring the whole thing with him, and set the microwave for two minutes. Bearing the tea selections and the now-heated mug, he returned to his office, only to find Miss Barkley examining the award plaques lining the wall next to the bay window. He shifted his work files to an adjoining cabinet, set down the drink supplies, and resumed his seat behind the desk. Glenn had responded with a request to dial him in. Cal did so, set the phone on the desk, and gestured toward the teas. "Help yourself."

Barkley returned to her chair and, selecting from the caddy, dunked a teabag repeatedly in the hot water as she glanced at him. "In a moment, I'm going to ask you to look over the paperwork we received concerning an insurance policy in the amount of one million five-hundred thousand dollars for a Gisele Townsend, birthday July 16, 1992, a resident of Saugatuck Michigan in the county of Allegan at 190 Crofter's Lane. Said policy was for the life of the insured as well as for injury or illness affecting the performance of her job with a specific codicil covering existing and future personal belongings, specifically jewelry in the amount of one hundred thousand dollars. Do you deny any knowledge of this request?"

Stunned by the specificity of the application, especially the mention of jewelry, Cal wondered if he was having an out-of-body experience. He lifted the phone so the lawyer could see the documents. "I do. I never requested such a policy and have no knowledge of any of the things you mentioned. Plus, as I told you, that is not my current address, and Gisele did not live with me. She has her own place. And Gigi Townsend was, no, is, a successful businesswoman. She insisted that she would always keep her finances separate from any partner."

"I understand," Barkley interrupted, "you and she planned to marry."

"We discussed it. Our families favor the merger."

Barkley twisted the gold band on her left ring finger. "A good marriage is more than a business merger, Mr. Castro. Which of you was more in favor of the arrangement?"

Cal leaned back. "Gisele."

"You were having second thoughts?"

"How is that any of your business?"

"Your relationship, or lack thereof, has a direct bearing on the motive for taking out such a large policy."

Cal suppressed the rage demanding to be expressed. "Gisele is high maintenance. I grew concerned about what that might mean if we were married."

"Given your hesitancy, I can see where an insurance policy," the woman waved her hand over the documents, "might not be a priority for you. However, I've been doing this long enough to know human beings don't always use common sense. Greed is a powerful motivator, don't you agree?"

"Miss Barkley, I'm very good at my job. I have a healthy portfolio and no need or desire for more money."

"Had you gone as far as drawing up a pre-nup?" She cocked her head, a bird deciding whether to snatch a crumb or wait for more to fall.

"If we got officially engaged, yes, we intended to have her sister, Cerise, draw one up for us."

"Cerise? Miss Townsend's sister? She's a lawyer?"

"Yes, and she and Gisele are twins."

Barkley sat up straighter at that remark. She appeared to retreat into herself, humming a little as she tapped her index finger on the arm of the chair. Abruptly, she picked up the initial policy paperwork and handed it over. "Look over this application and tell me if anything seems familiar or strange to you?"

Cal laid the papers out and read through them. Each line of information had been printed in small, precise letters. The entire form had been scanned and sent via email. The date stamped at the bottom read 08/21/2022. The time: 1:00 a.m. He slipped the papers back into the folder and handed it back. "I couldn't have done this."

"Why is that, Mr. Castro?"

"On that date, I was playing a gig at The River City Saloon in Grand Rapids. It was a hot night, the bar was crowded, and the owner asked me to play an extra set. You can check. I just ask that you don't mention it to my family."

"And why shouldn't I mention that to your relatives?"

"When I agreed to join the firm, I promised to shelve my musical ambitions."

"Did Miss Townsend know about your extracurricular activities?"

"No, Miss Barkley, no one in Saugatuck does, and I'd like to keep it that way."

Vero

Vero cradled the receipt bag, squared her shoulders, and pushed through the doors of Huntington Bank. When she entered, Jeff Gordon stood to greet her. He waved her over to his corner cubicle, then picked up the phone. Vero watched an older woman in another office answer, nod, then hustle to join them. "Miss Simon. I'm so sorry to hear of your grandmother's passing."

"Thank you, Jeff." She set the deposit bag down and rested her hand on it, aware of Cal's receipt nestled among the cash. "Sorry for the delay in bringing this by. I've been a little preoccupied."

"Understandable. Mary will make the deposit for you." Gordon started to hand the bag to the teller. Vero refused to let go.

"I need copies of the receipts, all of them. It's important," she drew a quick breath, "to check them against the entries in my ledger book. I'm afraid I've been neglecting that, too."

Mary liberated the bag from Vero's grasp. "Of course, Miss Simon. I'll be right back."

The muted rumble of traffic from outside filled the silence until Gordon nudged her folded hands, drawing her back to the moment. "I know this is bad timing, and I'm sorry for that. Your grandparents were trusted clients of Huntington for fifty years. However, when you and your grandmother co-signed the refinancing loan for SIMON's, you agreed to settle the debt by a specific date. That balloon payment is due at the end of November. If you can't pay then, you may be able to re-negotiate, but the interest rate will increase, per the terms of the contract."

"I can't afford an increase, Gordon. Is there anything I can do to avoid it?"

"You have no real choice, Veronica. You pay the amount due in full or take out a new loan and meet the increase in monthly payments."

"And if I don't?"

"The bank will have no choice but to foreclose on the shop. To save SIMON's, you may have to file for bankruptcy. Of course, you can always sell the business. That would solve your problem."

Vero glanced at the bottom figure on the balance sheet Gordon handed her. Cal Castro's purchase money would defray a third of the sum, but that left thirty thousand dollars owed. Folding the sheet, she crammed it into her purse. "I have five weeks to figure this out. Don't start any actions until I contact you."

"Look, Veronica, if there were any other solution—"

She shook off his apology. "I can't stay and argue with you, Jeff. I have a business to run and a funeral to help plan. Thanks for your time."

"At least let me—" He paused as Mary approached, copies of the store receipts and a deposit form in hand. Vero snatched them from the teller and turned away, heading for the exit before the rage and frustration erupted into a fierce yell or, worse, a torrent of tears. She was not a weepy woman, but the events of the past few days had eroded her self-control. Grateful that no over-sized pursuit vehicle awaited her in the parking lot, she scrambled across the slick mounds of snow and hurried toward Culver Street, the voice inside her head whispering of failure at each step.

Shea was dusting the Lladró figurines on the corner shelf when Vero emerged from the back room, rubbing her cold hands to ease their tingling. A trio of elderly women wandered from one case to the next, exclaiming in soft voices about the quality of the gems on display. She greeted them, offered to show any piece that caught their eye, then joined Shea by the statuary. "No problems while I was away?"

"Yoo-hoo, young lady," one of the women called.

Shea waved the duster in the air and called, "I'm coming," before whispering, "Only the usual. Everyone wants a bargain."

"Can't blame them. I could use one myself."

Shea started toward the shoppers, hesitated. "There was one weird thing. Some dude in a trench coat came in asking for you. Really, a trench coat in Saugatuck? He asked about your special rings, but I told him we were all sold out."

"What did he look like?" Vero said.

"Tell you later." Shea frowned and rolled her lips, duster in hand, before skipping over to the ladies. Vero returned to the office. She checked that the back door was secure, then extracted the receipts and the deposit slip from the bag and booted up the accounts file. She spent the next half hour entering the sales data she had neglected since Friday. When she was done, she sat and stared at the calendar on the wall, calculating the inventory available for her designs. She'd been neglecting those as well, and now that Cal had purchased and lost her favorite piece, she needed to create a new line, something beautiful and meaningful, items that would honor her bond with Nana Verna. Thinking of her grandmother reminded her of the envelope she'd received at the funeral home. She dragged it from her purse, slit the seal, and dumped the contents over her workspace. A smaller envelope, the size of a birthday card, landed with a thump. She opened that, too, and read the inscription inside.

Dear Veronica,
You have always cared about the Simon legacy. Now it's in your hands. This key will open two doors, one to the past, the other to your future. Guard it well and keep my memory close to your heart.
I love you, granddaughter, more than you know.
Nana Verna

Vero held the key up to the light, twisting it in her fingers. She had no clue what it might open. Another of Nana's games, she supposed. Well, finding the lock would have to wait. She tucked the key into a zippered pocket in her wallet, stuffed the note in her purse, and discarded the larger envelope. With her grandmother gone, the shop belonged to her, and she was determined not to lose it. Her thoughts turned to Lincoln Storey and his demeanor at the Corner Café. He had caught her off-guard with the blatant attempt to hook up, but at least he had been honest about her chances of finding living space near the shop. She felt boxed in by circumstance. Moving into the lake cabin offered one advantage. She could apply the money she'd spend on rent toward the loan. It wasn't enough, but it was something.

She sighed, fingering the slip of paper proving that Cal had been with her Friday when Gisele Townsend vanished. He'd be relieved to know she had proof of his alibi. She moved to the copier, placed the receipt facedown, and closed the cover of the machine. The scanner marched back and forth, much like her thoughts, storing away information to be printed out and distributed for another to examine. She rescued her phone from the pocket of her coat and sent a text. `I have your receipt want to meet?`

Out in the showroom, delighted voices rose as Shea rang up the purchases of the women and wished them a good day. Another customer entered, an out-of-towner by the cadence of his speech. Vero intended to join the salesclerk in the showroom, but something in the stranger's tone made her hesitate. She recalled Shea's statement about a man asking for her earlier. The young woman seemed unsettled, an unusual response for her. Shea came from a family of sturdy outdoor people who laughed at blizzards, lived year-round in their home on Goshorn, and excelled at every winter sport possible. Nothing rattled them. Gliding along the wall to eavesdrop on the conversation, Vero realized she'd left her phone on the desk. If it pinged now, the stranger would know she was here. Shea must have realized the same thing. The young clerk's voice rose.

"The owner's not back yet, sir, and, as I told you, we are out of the special stock."

"Is that so?" A humph of disbelief accompanied the words, followed by a thump on the glass case holding the engagement rings. "What are those then?"

Vero decided not to leave Shea alone any longer. Rustling papers, she snatched her phone and backed into the showroom, carrying an unopened box of watchbands under her arm. "Miss Wiggins, can you set these out for me? Oh, you have a customer."

The man, of medium height and in his late thirties, straightened. He removed his stocking cap, revealing a full head of red curls. His eyes narrowed as he stared at Vero. "I see the resemblance," he said. "You are Verna Simon's granddaughter, aren't you? And I'm betting you know where she hid them."

Vero dumped the watchbands into Shea's outstretched hands and nudged her away from the register. "I'm sorry, but you're being very rude. I have no idea who you are and what you're referring to, so unless you can explain yourself, I'm calling the police." She lifted her phone, thumb resting on the emergency call button.

The man reached into the inside pocket of his coat, pulled out a business card, and slapped it onto the glass. "Frank Holder. Yes, Ms. Simon, Holder. Recognize the family name? I'm a private investigator, here in Saugatuck on another matter but glad to follow up on a personal one as well. I can show you my license if you wish. No? Fine. Here's the deal. My great-grandfather and yours were cousins and eventually business partners, although I doubt anyone told you about either connection."

A relative who was a PI? Vero closed her eyes, hoping when she opened them, this whole bizarre conversation would dissipate like morning fog and this intense man with it. No luck. Frank Holder continued to stare at her from across the counter. She cleared her throat. "Are you here to discuss our shared genealogy, Mr. Simon? Because right now, I could care less."

"Family ties aside, what you need to know is our great-grandfathers planned to establish a jewelry business together. But before they could form a legal agreement, they had a falling out. Mine died, and yours vanished, along with a collection of gems worth well over a million dollars, even in 1922."

The man's voice continued to rise. His face flushed as he leaned toward her. Vero backed away. "Mr. Holder, if that's really who you are, that's a fantastical story, but it has nothing to do with me."

"Oh, but it does. It's taken me a while to verify our lineage, but now that I have, I want what's rightfully mine, what should have belonged to me and mine all these years."

Shea hustled over, feather duster in one hand, cell phone in the other. "You want me to call the cops, boss?"

"Not yet." Vero flicked the man's card with her thumb, wondering if he was who he said he was. Had Nana Verna known about him? Had her grandmother kept this part of the family history hidden on purpose? Were the man's claims legitimate? "If we're related, and if any of what you told me is true, this is a matter for the family to discuss, and right now, we're planning our grandmother's funeral. So, whatever you think we know or don't know—"

"Fuck." Frank Holder slumped at the news of Nana's death, all the righteous fire inflaming his tirade quenched. He bowed over the counter and buried his head in his hands. "Verna Simon's gone? That's not good. I can't return empty-handed."

"Return where?" Vero asked. Shea echoed her. The women moved closer together, finding strength in solidarity. Built like an ironworker, the man was physically intimidating, but, deflated as he was by the news of Nana's passing, he appeared more sad than threatening. He waved away the question, rubbed a hand over his face, and braced himself against the edge of the case. Vero had too many questions percolating to stand still. She paced the counter, picking up and replacing brochures advertising class rings and custom necklaces. "Frank Holder. Is that really your name?"

The man pulled out his wallet, extracted his license, and slapped it on the glass. Shea slid it across the counter, held it close, and snorted. "Dude's telling the truth, Vero. He's thirty-eight, doesn't need glasses to drive, and he's from Chi-ca-go."

"Satisfied?" Holder snatched the license from the clerk and stuffed it back in its slot. He looked around the shop. "This is a nice place. Rumor has it you're in some financial difficulty, though. You help me locate the gems, and I'll be in a position to help you."

"Help me? I don't even know you, and I sure as hell don't know anything about a secret stash of gemstones. Now," Vero nodded at the mother ushering her teenage son in through the door, "I have customers to attend to."

"Hey," Frank grabbed her wrist, "I'm not kidding about wanting my share. Tell me, who owns this shop now that your grandmother is gone?"

Vero worried her lower lip. Should she tell him? Did it matter? It was no secret within the family that Nana wanted Vero to have the business. Had her grandmother mentioned it to many people in town? If so, did this man need to know that? Mulling her choices, she sent Shea to assist the clients, then stared at him until he released his grip. "Who owns SIMON's now? I do."

Frank dropped his voice. "And if something happens to you?"

Vero's mouth dropped open. "I have no idea."

"Your brothers? Sonny, the doctor with med school loans to pay off, and Dave, who has his own hidden addictions to deal with? Yeah, they're both salivating for the inheritance."

"How do you know all that about my brothers? And," she sputtered, inhaled, struggled on, "they're not that callous."

"No? They haven't suggested you sell?"

Shea approached with the mother and son in tow. She elbowed Frank Holder aside, picked up a class ring brochure, and suggested they sit on the loveseat by the free-standing fireplace and look through the choices. Holder took the hint. He pushed the business card toward Vero.

"I'm staying at The Hotel Saugatuck. Call me tonight after work and we can discuss this further." He replaced the stocking cap, rapped the counter with his knuckles, and left. Noting that Shea had things under control, Vero escaped to the back room. Her brothers had been pushing to sell the lake property and the shop. Did they need money that much? And what was that comment about Dave's addiction and a secret cache of stolen gems? Was Frank Holder accusing her grandmother of being a thief? No, Nana wasn't born until 1942. If there were hidden gems, she would have inherited them, but could the tale of the shop's origin include thievery? Was this man behind the attempt to run her over? Then there was the name. Holder. Nana married a Holder. Did that suggest incest? Yuck. Not to mention that sly reference to being on a case. Really? Was he investigating Gisele's disappearance or Lisa Protus's murder, or both? She flopped into the desk chair, massaging the headache gnawing at her temples. She would have to meet with this man, if only to tease out more details. Meanwhile, she would look him up on the web. First, though, she needed to check her phone. It had pinged several times during the conversation with the investigator. She touched the screen and there it was, Cal's response. `Meet? Yes. But we have a new problem.`

Cal

Wind whipped the flags lining the waterfront, its low keening counterpoint to the turmoil in Cal's gut. With Glenn's approval, he had agreed to contact Barkley if any new information crossed his desk. The insurance investigator acted like she believed him, especially after she compared his signature to the one on all the documents. Not one matched the neat printing and precise *Calderón Castro* on the application filed two months earlier. But her eyes remained accusatory, even as she shook his hand, asked him to stay in touch, and departed. Her mistrust left Cal off-balance and wondering if she would keep his confidence regarding the music gig. He fervently hoped she wouldn't reveal his secret. He'd managed to hide that part of his life from everyone for a year now. Music kept him sane, balanced, alive in a way selling real estate never did. What, he mused, would Miss Veronica Simon think about his clandestine evenings in dimly lit out-of-the-way down-home bars around the Upper Peninsula?

Thinking of Vero must have rung some psychic bell, for his phone pinged. He started to open her message when he noticed three calls from the same unidentified number, the last with a voice mail component. He delayed reading Vero's text to punch in the audio. A voice that sounded familiar but which he couldn't place greeted him with a verbal sneer: *Castro. You want your girl back, get a half million dollars in small bills and wait for the next call. Of course, no police or she's a dead woman.* A dial tone replaced the disembodied voice, leaving Cal to wonder where in Saugatuck or the surrounding towns one could find an old-fashioned rotary phone. The only places that came to mind were cabins like the one the Simons owned out on Goshorn Lake. He should contact Norsuch and Harry, but the threat to Gisele sounded real. Maybe he should wait until the follow-up call before reporting the ransom demand. One more damning decision laid on him. No matter what he decided, it spelled disaster. He rubbed his eyes and groaned.

Antonio Castro knocked, then stepped in. "Are you all right, *mijo*? Your mother still isn't feeling well, so I'm going home. We have the plans for the memorial for Miss Protus ready to go, but you do not have to worry about anything. Take care of your closings. Oh, if Bergeron calls, you decide what to do about his offer."

"Why me, *Papi*?"

His father, who always stood ramrod straight, slumped against the jamb. "This business with Gisele and now Lisa. It is too much, Calderón. I want to enjoy my life, not look over my shoulder for the next catastrophe. I thought perhaps a marriage between our family and the Townsends would be an advantage. Now, it brings nothing but trauma. I know you do not love the woman, but do you care for her enough to mourn?"

Cal shook his head. "I will only say this to you, and maybe to one other person." Cal stabbed the desk with a letter opener. "I truly hope nothing bad has happened to Gisele, but I don't care enough to marry her."

"You always were so honest, my son, but sometimes the truth hurts more than a lie."

Cal didn't look away from his father's earnest gaze. When Antonio finally left, the weight of the secrets he carried gave him heartburn. He reached for a file, knocking his phone to the floor, which caused the screen to light up. Reminded that he hadn't yet read Vero's message, he retrieved the phone and skipped to her text. I have your receipt want to meet?

He pictured her green eyes flashing as her elegant fingers sped over the keys, the fire and sometimes fury that lit her like a flame. Did he want to meet her? Hell, yes. Unbidden, the thought of other things he might do with Veronica Simon pushed aside the dread circling like a vulture. But how could he even think about the woman that way? She was grieving her grandmother's death, an emotion that overrode all other concerns, including any attraction she might feel toward him. He wished he knew who had tried to run her over. The idea of Vero coming to harm felt like a physical blow. Despite her reservations, she agreed to come to his rescue again. Did he have the right to involve her further? Maybe not, but he didn't even fight the urge to respond. `Meet? Yes. But we have a new problem.`

He sent the message before he could rethink the decision. Then he sent a voice mail to the detectives with a brief explanation of the ransom call. Finally, he settled in to finish the afternoon's work. If he needed half a million dollars to free Gisele and lift the stone from his neck, he'd better make sure all the deals went through, including the contract with Eric Bergeron regarding the purchase of properties on Goshorn Lake.

Vero

The change in weather and the looming Halloween celebrations prompted more than the usual number of patrons to wander in and out of the shops along Water Street. Despite the chill wind, the tourist crowd had even wandered to the waterfront off Culver to stroll the beach. Morrow's café drew them in with the enticing aromas that floated streetside, then sent them strolling to the Music Store and SIMON's just beyond. Vero had no time to parse out Cal's latest cryptic message. Besides, she had a new problem of her own to puzzle through. This previously unknown cousin, Frank Holder, might be a legitimate family connection or he might be a con man, though what he'd want with a struggling business, she couldn't fathom.

After reorganizing the supply closet, Shea left, promising to work Saturday so Vero could attend Nana Verna's celebration of life. The official notice of the event had gone up earlier on the funeral home website. Vero read through several of the comments left by her grandmother's friends before grief forced her to stop. Wallowing in sorrow did not suit her. Nana would not approve, either. What she really needed was an afternoon in her workshop, a chance to lose herself in her art.

As a young girl, Vero had reveled in the gifts from her grandmother that allowed her to craft bead and thread bracelets, to draw and then glue together kitschy necklaces and makeshift rings. When she outgrew the basic kits, her grandmother arranged for her to attend jewelry-making classes at a local art collective. Then she began to teach Vero herself. She had cleared a special place in the upstairs workroom where a second, secret safe harbored a glittering assortment of gemstones and two free-standing cabinets housed gold and silver wire plus all the tools necessary to bend, fuse, and polish until the hand-crafted pieces were ready for display. The memories of those afterschool hours spent in the shop, along with the long, lazy summer vacations spent at the lake, consoled her. Even at Goshorn, Nana had a room devoted to her jewelry art, and Vero's work had a shelf there, too. Rainy summer days when she couldn't swim or paddleboard, she spent with Nana in the 'dungeon,' the locked, basement storage room they had transformed into their private space. Her parents were only admitted for brief periods. Her brothers had no interest and rarely did more than peek inside. While the sky thundered and lightning crackled across the lake, she and Nana would listen to old blues records and work on creating something beautiful.

Vero recalled the first piece she had designed, a silver band with a simple amethyst shaped like a pear. She had crafted two slender silver wings to hold the stone, giving the illusion of flight. Nana had held the ring to the light, her eyes sparkling with approval, and announced, "Today a new jeweler joins a long line of master craftsmen. Congratulations, Veronica." The hug that followed warmed her to her toes, but the news, a week later, that the ring had sold for five hundred dollars made her grandmother's words true in a different way. Her portion of the sale became the basis of her college savings account and fueled her determination to see Simon's succeed for another century.

Now, perhaps, a lost cousin, Frank Holder, endangered the hope that she might carry on the family tradition. More probably, her failure to pay off the loan due soon would doom it irrevocably. And what about the man she'd spotted watching the shop last week, or the mystery driver who tried to run her over? Vero groaned. OMG, was Frank behind both those incidents? She should have asked if he had followed her the night of the snowstorm. Disturbed by the thought that her attacker may have been in the shop only a few hours ago, she considered her next steps. First, she would meet Cal and give him the copy of the receipt. Once she did that, she could check him off her to-do list. She gnawed her thumbnail. She wasn't certain she never wanted to see Cal Castro again. Of all the people in her life, he was the only one who believed in her. Twice now he had supported her when no one else would or could. Plus, his text indicated a new difficulty had cropped up. Curiosity, that little imp, dogged her as she responded to customers' questions, rang up sales, and tidied counters marred by fingerprints. Shortly before five-thirty, what she hoped was the last of the day's patrons wandered in. While the gentleman considered a display of pearl earrings, Vero inspected the front window. The spider didn't make an appearance, but she noticed the leading strand of a new web. Tomorrow she would have to spray the crack with bug killer. Ugh! The thought of smelling insecticide all day changed her mind. She would douse the area tonight.

The grandfather clock struck six. Vero locked the front door, then hurried to place all the expensive items in the safe. She extracted the deposit bag, included the day's receipt log, and stuffed it into her purse. Unearthing the can of bug spray from its hiding place in the supply closet, she sprayed the spider's lair. Only a small part of her felt guilty. "You don't belong inside my store, Mr. Spider," she murmured, holding her breath as a cloud of toxicity rose around her. She turned to go, then glanced across the street.

The watcher had returned. He wore a heavy coat with the collar pulled up around his ears. A balaclava obscured his face. The fickle October weather had warmed enough that the mask was overkill. Vero wished she had binoculars. The man might be Frank Holder, but she doubted it. This person appeared shorter, thinner, even in the bulky coat. The last of the light gleamed faintly off the water beyond. The stranger's presence rekindled the apprehension she'd felt the night the car almost hit her, along with a flush of anger. Vero looked at the can and decided to carry it with her. Didn't they, whoever they were, say an ounce of prevention was better than a pound of cure? Well, a can of whoop-ass bug spray might be better. She stuffed it in her purse and pulled out her phone. Cal answered on the first ring.

"Vero? Everything all right?"

"So far. When did you want to meet? And where?"

Cal didn't speak immediately. When he did, she realized he wasn't alone. "I'll let you know after I finish with the detectives."

The police were talking to him again? Her worry index shot up. "Of course. I'm leaving the shop now."

"Meet you at the apartment." He hung up before she could reply. Vero checked the street. The stalker remained in place. So, if he thought she was still inside, he wouldn't go anywhere. Instead of turning off the lights, Vero left them on. In the back, she set the alarm, slipped out the back, and followed the alley down to the café. She eased around the Arts Center and turned left on Mason. She paused to dial for an Uber, then kept walking. When she reached the next intersection, she huddled behind a screen of leafless honeysuckle and wrestled the bug spray out of her purse. A new text pinged. She noted Ellie's ID in the window. They hadn't spoken to each other for two days, so it surprised her to see her ex-roommate's name. More alarming was the message. `someone broke into the apartment Ray's hurt`

Cal

Cal spotted Veronica standing under the eaves of the old Victorian on Hoffman Street, dark hair spilling from beneath a red ski cap, the over-size purse she lugged everywhere pulling at her left shoulder. She looked lost and sad and angry, and all he wanted to do was scoop her up and carry her away, preferably to a secluded spot where he could explore other ways to erase the sadness. *Calm down, Calderón*, Cal murmured as he approached. Despite her obvious need for comfort, he didn't want to frighten her off. The old Cal would have followed the impulse to leap from the car and wrap her in his arms, to ignore her needs for his own desires. This time, with this woman, he wanted to do things differently. He slowed to take her in, the wind-whipped curls, the expressive eyes, the way she clutched the collar of her coat like she had something to hide or protect. Unexpectedly, a melody surfaced, along with a lyric: *brave beautiful ember, glow for me*. He repeated it until he knew the words would be there later when he had a moment to write them down. He coasted to the curb and rolled down the window.

"Vero?"

She raised tearful eyes. Her hand was shaking where it clutched the strap of her purse. Cal threw the car into park and hopped out. He reached her before she turned away. He swore softly and lifted her chin. "What's wrong, baby?"

She blinked twice, like an owl waking from a dream. He didn't think she heard his last word, the one that slipped out, the one he didn't want to take back no matter how foolish it sounded. She relaxed against his chest, took a deep breath, then pushed him far enough to create some space, but she didn't step completely away. "I don't...Ellie...someone broke into the apartment and her boyfriend got hurt. I need to go there."

"I'll take you."

She opened her bag and rummaged through the contents, mumbling about where did she put the damn thing. If she didn't look so wounded, he might have chuckled at her dismay.

"Here." With a triumphant cry, she yanked the copy of the ring receipt out and, hand trembling, stuffed it between the zipper of his coat and the pullover he was wearing. Veronica Simon had kept her promise. Cal tugged the paper free and shoved it into an inside pocket.

"Let's go."

"How did you know where to find me?"

He retied the scarf around her neck, unable to explain the impulse that led him to check the shop before going to her apartment. "Instinct."

"Wait." She stopped midstride. "I forgot to cancel the Uber."

Once she completed the call, Cal led her to the car, loaded her in, and drove as fast as the traffic allowed to The Scottish. Two police cruisers and an ambulance with lights flashing blocked the remaining parking spots in the cordoned-off construction site. Cal angled the company Escalade between a Prius and a dumpster, then grabbed Vero's hand as they raced for the entry. A cop stationed there stopped them. After Vero explained who she was and vouched for Cal, the female officer escorted them into the building. The EMTs were bringing Ray down, Ellie close behind. While she and Vero hugged, Cal asked one of the techs what happened.

"Knife wound," the guy responded. "Step aside, sir, so we can get him to the hospital."

Ellie scurried after the gurney. "Vero, call me," she shouted as she passed them. Cal followed Vero up the stairs to the apartment. Inside, another uniformed officer was taking photographs while a third appeared to catalogue the scene, talking into her voice recorder as she wandered from one overturned box to the next. The place was a mess. Clothes strewn everywhere, kitchen utensils and cutlery piled on the floor, shards of broken plates scattered over the stove and countertops. A shell-shocked

Vero stood in the center of the chaos, tears streaming down her face, one fist clenched in rage. "What the fuck!" she screamed.

The female officer swallowed a grin. "My sentiments exactly, Miss Simon. Sir? Are you family?"

"No, just a friend. Can I stay?"

The officer looked at Vero, then at her partner, who eyed Cal like he was responsible for the attack. "Miss?"

Vero turned toward Cal, their hands still linked. She gripped his tighter. "Please let him stay."

Cal released her hand to move behind her, offering his body as a bulwark against the chaos. He remained silent, rubbing her back in slow circles to let her know he was there while the policewoman proceeded to ask the standard questions. Where had Vero been? When did she usually return home from work? Did she have anything of value in the packing boxes? Would she be willing to look through them now to see if anything was missing?

"I don't even know where to begin. What happened to Ray? How badly is he hurt?"

"Your roommate's fiancé tried to stop the intruders. One of them had a knife and used it on him."

"Intruders?" Vero held a hand to her cheek. Cal felt the same disconnect. He snaked an arm around her.

"Are you telling us there was more than one person involved in this burglary? Robbery?"

"Robbery, Mr. Castro, since a weapon was carried in and used by one of the perpetrators. Yes, I know who you are. The question is why are you here?"

Vero glared at the policewoman. "Mr. Castro was kind enough to offer me a ride when he saw me on the street. I-I had just gotten Ellie's text, and I was distraught. But I'm okay now, and I'm furious. Do you have any idea who the men were who did this?"

The female cop shook her head. "Not yet, but it wasn't two men."

Vero cocked her head. "What?"

The woman stuck her thumbs in her belt. "Two suspects, one male and one female."

"How do you know that?" Cal said.

"The roommate, Ellie Manzo, managed to snatch the hat off the female. Guess she had a lot of hair. However, both the perps wore masks, so all we have is a general description. Both tall, fair-haired, foul-mouthed idiots looking for something to steal." The male cop continued to prowl and poke through the debris. "You're one of those creative types, aren't you, Miss Simon? You and your roomie? You like the arts and that kind of stuff. Do you have any drugs on the premises?"

Vero's eyes grew wider. Her cheeks reddened. "Neither Ellie nor I do drugs. We never have."

"What about jewelry, ma'am? After all, you own a jewelry store, don't you?"

The mention of the shop created an uneasy buzz in Cal's gut. Vero glanced at him, then returned her focus to the officers. "I never keep merchandise here. Now, you asked me to look around. I will, but it will take a long time to sort out this mess."

Cal stayed where he was, watching Vero square her shoulders and march into the jumble of belongings. She picked up articles of clothing and folded them into piles as she moved from one box to the next. He didn't think the police noticed the way her shoulders slumped at the shattered picture frames, the books torn and tossed into the corner. Twenty minutes later, she rejoined him in the kitchen. "I can't stay here," she said.

He leaned to whisper in her ear, "You don't have to. You're coming home with me. You need food and a glass of wine. Or two. We'll figure it out from there."

The female cop raised an eyebrow. "Before you leave, give me a contact number to reach you, Miss Simon. Tomorrow you can come back and do a more thorough appraisal. For insurance purposes, of course."

"Will you be here for that?"

"Not necessary, but I can be." They exchanged information. "Why don't you gather a few things to take with you," she zeroed in on Cal, "wherever you'll be staying?"

Cal tiptoed around the broken crockery to lean on the counter. The cop followed him. "Home invasions are a lot like rapes, Mr. Castro. The sense of violation is real and can be lasting. It takes time to process and then deal with the desecration of your private space. If you're only here to take advantage—"

He cut her off mid-sentence. "Miss Simon is a friend, one I plan to help in whatever way she needs me."

"So long as you don't hurt her more. Word around the station is that you lose girlfriends like some people lose change."

Cal started to reply when he heard Vero clear her throat. He raised his head to that intense Simon gaze and the knowledge that the policewoman had just erased all the good credit he'd been building.

Cal

Ignoring the raised eyebrows and pursed lips of the male cop, Cal grabbed Vero's bag and, with a firm grip on her elbow, guided her down the stairs and out the door of The Scottish. She clambered into the Escalade, shoving her oversized purse into the space at her feet, and clutched her ungloved hands to the collar of her down coat.

"What a shit day," she said. "I ought to go back to the shop and get my car."

Cal reached toward her, hesitated, then resettled himself in the driver's seat to concentrate on backing out of the crowded lot. The ambulance had departed, but the police cars and the vehicles that belonged to the remaining tenants clogged the exit. "The car can wait. You need a drink."

"More than one." She worried her lower lip. "And I'm starving. How can I be hungry when so much has gone wrong?"

"It's called being human, Veronica. You're allowed to be one, you know." He checked for cars and pulled onto Francis Street.

She smiled at the tease in his words. "Right. No superheroes here."

"When's the last time you ate anything substantial?"

"I don't remember." She rested her head on the seatback and closed her eyes. "Any ideas about where we can go that won't send the rumor mill into overdrive?"

"Actually," Cal said, "I do, and there are some friends of mine I'd like you to meet."

Vero's eyes popped open. "You have friends?"

Cal smirked at the skepticism in her words. "Actually, more than one, but these friends are very special, and they're going to love you."

"Is it anyone I'm likely to know? Maybe another guy from high school who didn't acknowledge my existence when I was fourteen? If so, better tell me now."

"I think I'll keep it a surprise." Cal winked at her. Vero frowned. She didn't like being kept in the dark. "But I think you'll like them."

"That will be a nice change of pace, especially after today." She burrowed deeper into the coat and stared out the window. Cal tapped the wheel, then cleared his throat.

"Care to share?" That shouldn't be too intrusive a question, and he needed to know what had happened.

She glanced at him, turned back to the window, and shuddered. "Well, first, some man came to the shop claiming to be a long-lost cousin and ranting about a stolen inheritance and how I owed him. Then he warned me I was in danger. After he left, I spotted someone watching the store from across the street. I'm certain he's been there before. Across the street, I mean, just staring at SIMON's. In fact, he was there Friday right before you came in."

"You saw this person when you left today? Did he follow you?" Cal checked the rear and side mirrors, then decided on a less direct route to his destination.

"Yes, but I don't think he followed me." Vero worried the ends of her scarf. "I thought about confronting him, but then I decided to leave the lights on in the showroom, so he'll think I'm still there, and I sneaked out the back. If my car's there, I am, too, right?"

He glanced over, warmed by the grin that had replaced the frown. Neither looked away until she pulled out her phone to stare at the screen. Cal rested a hand over hers. "There's something else, isn't there?"

"Didn't figure you for the intuitive type, Castro."

"*Ay, madre,* you wound me." He placed a hand over his heart, then grew serious. "I'm not that guy everyone thinks I am, and it hurts that you see me that way. You don't even know me."

She straightened her shoulders and sighed. "You're right, and I'm sorry. I'm feeling guilty about Ray. He got hurt because of me."

"Call Ellie. Find out how he's doing."

She hummed as she waited for her roommate to answer, a melody Cal recognized from an old Boz Scaggs album he loved. What were the odds this woman knew it? "Ellie?" Her voice climbed an octave. "How's Ray?"

Cal checked the mirrors, watching each car that followed behind them until it turned away. He doubled back to Culver to see if Vero's stalker was still there, while she nodded at her friend's detailed recital of the events at the apartment. Satisfied that whoever had been watching Vero was gone, he eased down the alley and halted next to her car. It and the building remained secure. Vero ended the call.

"Ellie apologized to me! Stupid, silly girl. Best roommate ever." Vero swallowed hard. "She claims she and Ray were, um, saying good-bye to the place when two people wearing masks forced their way in through the door, which she forgot to lock. They threatened to gag her if she didn't stop yelling. Ray went ballistic and charged the male intruder, who pulled a knife. They fought while the other one raced around tearing open all the boxes. Ellie jumped on his back. That's when she grabbed the cap and found out it was a woman. Then Ray got stabbed, and she screamed, and the woman waved a gun. She made Ellie stand by her while the man finished looking for whatever they thought they'd find, and Ray lay bleeding on the floor."

The bleak look on Vero's face almost had him leaning over to give her a hug. Instead, he lifted his chin in the direction of her car. "Leave it here for tonight. If anyone is watching the shop, they'll assume you're still inside."

"All right." Her quick agreement convinced him that she needed a safe space to process what had happened at the apartment. Keeping an eye on traffic, he outlined their next move. "Here's the plan for tonight, if you agree. You're coming with me. You'll meet my friends. Eat some comfort food. Listen to great music, and then you are going to get a good night's sleep before you tackle the mess in the apartment. Maybe by tomorrow the police will have caught the robbers."

"Maybe." She closed her eyes, leaned back, then sat up as though she'd just remembered something. "OMG, I'm so inconsiderate. I totally forgot about your bad day. You haven't told me about the new problem."

He rubbed a thumb across his lower lip. "I received a ransom request. I shared the information with Norsuch, even though the caller said not to. I don't want the police to think I have anything to hide."

"Just a ransom request? You have a talent for understatement, Castro." Vero patted his shoulder. Her hand slipped to his thigh, sending a jolt of electricity straight to his loins. He swallowed hard, glanced over. Vero's lips parted, reminding him of what lips can do to certain aroused body parts. He almost groaned aloud. *Please, God, don't let her see I have a hard-on.*

"How much of a request?" she said.

"Half a million, in small bills. Sounds like a movie script, right?"

"It must be hard," she said. He coughed to cover his distress. "To raise that kind of money."

"Yeah, it is," he managed to squeak out. Her hand remained on his leg, the connection grounding them as he pulled into his driveway, pushed the remote, and glided into the garage.

"Cal, where are we?"

"My place, Miss Simon. It's warm, secure, and fully stocked with good food, and no one knows you're here. Are you coming?" When she let out the breath she'd been holding, Cal knew he'd won the first battle.

"I'm too tired to fight you." She shifted to open the door. He helped her out, hefting her purse despite her objections, then ushered her into the foyer and disarmed the security system. A chorus of barks greeted them as they entered, followed by the scrabble of paws across the wood floor as the two dark-coated Labrador retrievers barreled toward them. Cal knelt to nuzzle the first, while the second wriggled its hindquarters and sniffed Vero. Cal rubbed his hands down the larger dog's back and smiled up at her.

"Meet my best friends, Vero. This is Amigo, and this," he pulled the second dog into a headlock and scratched her ears, "is his sister, Choco. Hey, guys, I want you to meet a special friend of mine. Her name is Verónica. She's coming to stay for a while, so treat her right."

Vero arched an eyebrow and mouthed, "A while?" Cal shrugged, waiting for her to decide her next move. One eye roll and two big sighs and Vero crouched to offer an ungloved hand to Amigo, who sniffed, licked her knuckles, then circled both humans, rear wagging madly. Choco shoved her way forward to repeat her brother's inspection before nudging Vero for a pet. Amigo whined and lowered himself onto the toes of Vero's boots.

She buried her face in the dog's neck, hands stroking down his back. When she raised her face, tears glistened.

"Your best friends?"

"Yep. Now they're yours, too." Rising, Cal slipped around Vero and headed into the kitchen. Slinging his coat over the back of a bar stool, he washed his hands before dragging ingredients from the refrigerator, trying hard to ignore the fantasies screaming at him about the woman on her knees at his feet. How would her lips feel wrapped around his cock? How would she taste? An urge to explore the fantasy thrummed through him as he watched her murmur endearments to Amigo. When she looked up, her eyes were shy with unshed tears. She smiled and offered him her hand. "They're wonderful, Cal. Thank you."

He squeezed her fingers and, shaken, turned away. No woman had looked at him with such warm approval in a very long time.

Vero pushed to her feet to wander into the great room. Amigo and Choco trailed behind, nudging her legs with every step. She tossed her coat over the back of a recliner, dropped onto the couch, and patted the cushion beside her. The dogs hopped up on either side to curl into compact balls of contentment. "What are you going to do about the money?"

Startled by her abrupt return to their previous conversation, Cal set out bacon, a block of parmesan cheese, and a packet of sun-dried tomatoes. He poured two glasses of wine, passed one to her, and returned to prepping dinner. "I don't know. Norsuch thinks we should set up a meet. Harry thinks it's another Cal Castro ploy. Hope you like the cabernet."

Amigo hopped down when Vero stopped petting him. The female remained on the couch. Vero joined Cal, tasted the wine, then twirled the glass between her palms. "This is delicious. Evidently, your good taste in dogs extends to drinks."

"I have a very discerning palate, Miss Simon, and taste is one of the senses overlooked by most people." He picked up the bottle to examine the label. "Sensual Nun. A full-bodied, complex, layered red wine, a mystery that deepens with every sip only to reveal itself after you peel back the layers. Sounds a lot like you, Vero."

She opened her mouth to reply, closed it, took a bigger sip, a blush creeping over her cheeks. Cal gnawed his lower lip. *Too much, too soon, Castro. Change the subject.* He returned to slicing mushrooms. "I hope you like my version of carbonara."

"Any pasta is my favorite." She choked on the third swallow, covered her mouth until she recovered. "Why is that one detective so suspicious of you?"

"Duane Harry? Besides the fact that, statistically, most crimes against women are committed by those closest to them, he's still carrying a grudge from the last ballgame we played against each other. Go figure."

"Last game? Wasn't that, like, twelve years ago?" Cal nodded, watching as she swirled the wine, apparently intrigued by this glimpse into his past life. Her brother Dave probably knew all this, but she wouldn't. "What sport did you play?"

"You name it, I played it. Soccer and baseball were my favorites. More wine?"

"Stop deflecting, Castro." She eyed him over the rim of her glass. He continued chopping mushrooms and onions. "Did you have some kind of rivalry?"

"Harry played for Holland. Final game our senior year, bottom of the ninth, winning runs on second and third, two outs. He hits a smoking line drive that would have sent at least one runner home, maybe both. I catch it, which ends the game. Saugatuck clinches the league title. Harry missed out on being MVP, which chapped his ass big time."

"Hardly seems worth harboring bad feelings for over a decade."

Cal added the chopped ingredients to olive oil heating in a skillet, then dropped the pasta into boiling water. "Cost him a scholarship offer and his prom date."

"So, it was really about a girl." Vero took another long swallow. "I guess your reputation is well-earned, then."

All the validity he'd won for the dogs evaporated. Cal wanted it back, that soft glow of approval and admiration he'd glimpsed when she'd knelt before him. His stomach tightened. "Verónica." He faced her. "I haven't always been a good guy, but I've never been the son of a bitch people claim I am. Do you really believe, in your heart, I'm guilty of harming Gisele?"

Her green-eyed gaze unnerved him. On the stove, the sauce burped. If he didn't attend to it, the mixture would burn. He started to turn away when she reached out, her touch lighting a fire on the skin below his rolled-up sleeves. "No," she said. "I don't."

"But?"

She edged around the island to stand beside him, one stockinged foot pressed against his bare one, their calves and thighs touching. "I think there's a lot hidden beneath your surface, Cal Castro." She took the spoon from his hand, dipped it into the sauce, and lifted it to her lips. "Maybe more than I know."

Unable to resist, Cal slipped his free arm around her. "I'll tell you my secrets if you tell me yours, Verónica Simon."

"I—," she said. He bent forward to lick a bit of sauce from beside her mouth. She shivered but didn't pull away. He leaned closer to kiss her, a sweet, slow, steady press of his mouth to seal the moment, sending an invitation and a promise he hadn't expected to extend. The pasta water foamed, threatening to spill over. Releasing Vero, he lowered the flame, stirred the noodles. She stood still, fingers to lips, an expression somewhere between awe and fright in her green eyes.

"Will you set the table?" He lifted his chin toward the cabinet where the dishes nestled. Wordless, she set about the task, Amigo clicking behind her. Choco settled into her doggie bed, watching every move with intent. Cal drained the pasta, added the sauce, and plated the meal. He poured more wine before he sat. Vero toyed with her fork, a grin tugging the corners of her mouth. When she looked up, the grin became a full-blown smile.

"You're a man of many talents. Maybe I do want to know more about them."

"It would be my pleasure, Miss Simon. Amigo, settle." The male lab circled the room, then dropped to the floor, draping his head and paws across Vero's feet, and sneezed. They laughed, then turned their attention to the food, eating between bursts of conversation, avoiding weighty topics until the meal was done. Cal stashed the last dirty plate in the dishwasher, dried his hands, and refilled the dogs' food and water dishes. Amigo sniffed at the additions but refused to eat. "Sorry, buddy. We're all out of rawhide chewies. Guess it's time to visit the pet store."

"I'm so sorry, Cal." Vero said. "My drama is keeping you from your life."

"What life?" Cal gestured at the big-screen TV above the gas fireplace. "Most nights I take the dogs for a run, eat takeout, and fall asleep watching reruns of the Bundesliga."

"Really?"

"Really." He retreated behind the counter to avoid joining her on the couch and repeating that kiss. "I think I said something about music and then off to bed."

She blushed again, a deeper red that highlighted the olive of her complexion, and, to cover her reaction, blurted out, "Where are the bedrooms?"

Cal crossed his arms, dimples flashing. "Thought you'd never ask. There are two, in case you were wondering."

"Wait, I didn't mean." She grasped the neck of her sweater and pulled it tight. "I need to use the bathroom."

"There are two of those, too." He moved closer. "One in the guest bedroom, and one in the master, a much larger one. We can switch rooms, if you like."

"Thank you, but I can't stay here." Vero waved her hands around. "I'll just use the restroom, and then you can take me to a hotel, or something."

"You're welcome, Verónica," again he pronounced it with the Spanish emphasis on the *o*, unable to resist the pleasure it gave him to watch her reaction when he did so. "But you're not going anywhere. Remember what I said before? I have an excellent security system, a spare bedroom, and no one knows you're here. My condo is the safest place for you tonight."

"I'm not sure that's true," she said over her shoulder as she headed toward the guest bedroom. Cal watched her walk away, wondering what argument he could make to convince her to kiss him again.

Vero

The guest bedroom was decorated in soft blues and grays, with a queen-size bed bearing a striped navy comforter and a mound of pillows. The ensuite bath continued the color scheme but included nautical touches like a seashell shower curtain and a print of a Michigan lighthouse. It was charming, intimate, and equipped with a shelf of toiletries for any guests who might stay the night. Vero lingered at the sink, washing her hands and staring at herself in the mirror. She should leave, right? It wasn't wise to stay. She pulled down the neck of her sweater, touched the top of the scar that divided her chest from just below the neck to her belly button. She'd never had a serious sexual relationship because she couldn't bear for a lover to see her naked. *Stop, Vero. You're imagining an interest that isn't there.* But the way Cal looked at her, the way he spoke her name...gah, she was making herself crazy. The kiss was fabulous, but it was just a pity kiss. Best to get out of here before things went any farther. She sighed, wrestled her meds from her bag, and popped the required dose. Then she returned to the great room. Amigo and Choco raised their heads to watch her approach. Cal waited, hands in pockets, face set in a determined frown.

"Vero Simon, you are staying here tonight. No discussion."

"I can't. What if my presence puts you in danger? What if the police find out? What will people think?" She blundered on, caught between concern and desire. The truth was, despite her insecurities, she wanted Cal to kiss her again, ached to explore the invitation his lips had extended.

"No people here, Vero. No one to answer to or convince."

"I don't want to be any trouble." Her words sounded small, fearful.

He moved closer, ran his hands through his hair. "You're not trouble, Verónica. You're salvation. Can you just accept that I want you here? Besides, I owe you, big-time."

"No, I can't, really. It's too much. All I did was copy your receipt."

"You did more than that." He leaned closer. "You believed in me. You still do. I can see in your eyes that you trust me."

Vero didn't move. All the light touches he'd given her, the way he had her back at the apartment, his insistence that she stay safe, even their conversations had erased her initial suspicions of the man. And her body woke to his, her blood stirring at his approach. Despite all the cautionary notes from her inner voice, she wanted him to touch her again, to kiss her, to wrap her in his arms and assure her that nothing and no one would harm her. At least not for tonight. He closed the distance between them, gathered her in, careful not to move too fast. "Vero, do you want me? Because I sure as hell want you." He waited one breath, two. Her acquiescence slipped out along with a sigh. Then his lips settled on hers, settled in, kissed and teased away all misgivings and left her breathless. His hands rested on her hips. She pressed against him, her action a wordless command to begin a dance they both craved. One hand slipped beneath her top, teased along her spine, palmed her breast through her bra. He tugged the sweater up. She broke the kiss, clutched her arms tight to her sides to prevent him from exposing her.

"*Querida*, what's wrong? *¿No tienes ganas?* Don't you want to?" She struggled against him, but he held her tight. "Has someone hurt you? Do you not trust me?"

"No. Yes, I trust you." She took one deep breath, another, ragged and uncertain. This was the moment to retreat behind the walls she had erected or take a chance, tell the truth, her truth, find out what Calderón Castro was really made of. He started to remove his hands. Then, grabbing his wrists, she pulled him close and replaced his hands on her hips. She tugged the sweater up and over her head, tossed it aside. Her nipples strained against the lace cups of her bra, drawing Cal's eyes to her chest and the scars that marked it. One long vertical line ran from right below her breastbone to her navel. Two faint lines marked the skin beneath her rib cage on both sides. She watched him as he traced a finger down the middle of her chest. When he reached the bottom, he ran his whole hand upward, his touch a benediction. He brought his lips to the top of the scar, pressed a kiss there, trailed kisses down, his hand brushing one nipple, then the other, sending signals to her core.

"You're so beautiful, Vero. Tell me."

She did, every detail of her infant journey through numerous heart surgeries to repair faulty valves, to restore proper blood flow, to keep Veronica Simon alive until a heart could be found to replace the one she'd been born with. When she finished, she was trembling. "I didn't want you to see them, see me."

"Do you really believe these would scare me away? Oh, Vero, this only makes me want you more. My brave, lovely Verónica."

This time when he kissed her, she kissed him back with no reservations. Unbuttoning his shirt, she eased it off to splay her hands across his chest, exploring the muscled ribs, the firm abdomen. Eased one hand lower to cup him through the jeans. She stood on tiptoe, eager to line up their bodies, to feel him even through the layers of clothing. Her desire made up for her lack of experience. She knew he'd show her what to do and she relished being in his capable hands.

"I do want you, Cal, so very much I can't breathe. Show me how to please you." Her words, at once innocent and sensual, made him harder. He had to get her naked and soon, or he'd explode like a teenager at his first fuck.

"*Ah, querida,* how much I want you." He scooped her up, wrapped her legs around his waist, braced her against the wall to grind against her when his phone chimed. Hers did, too. He groaned, resting his forehead against hers. "Don't answer."

"I have to." She disengaged from his embrace to rescue her cell from the bottom of her purse.

"It's a text from Ellie. Ray's going into surgery." She raised her eyebrows at the look on Cal's face. "What does yours say?"

"Instructions, about where to leave the money, and a photo of Gisele." He held up the phone. A video of Gisele Townsend bound and tied to a tree, her mouth open in a scream they couldn't hear, scrolled across the screen.

Vero

The detectives left at midnight, promising to have a plan in place by morning. Curious about Vero's presence at the realtor's condo, Harry interrogated them separately, then accepted Castro's explanation that, with her apartment a crime scene and her parents hosting relatives arriving for Verna Simon's funeral, she had no place else to go. She kept her distance from Cal, avoided eye contact, her unease real and transparent. Norsuch took her aside right before he and his partner left.

"Are you certain you want to remain here, Miss Simon?"

Vero managed a smile. "Mr. Castro has been nothing but kind to me since all this," she waved a hand at the events of the past few days. "I trust him."

"Do you?" Harry joined them.

"He didn't send that video to himself, Detective, and he didn't call with a ransom demand. I've been followed, almost run over, harassed by a stranger, and driven from my home by intruders. I don't see either of you offering me a place to stay."

Norsuch wiped a meaty hand down his face. "We can put you in a secure location," he said.

"This is secure. You've tapped our phones, stationed a patrol car on the street, and made it clear we'll be followed if we try to leave." She clapped a hand over the yawn that interrupted her tirade. "I'm exhausted."

Both men looked at Cal, standing with his hands in the pockets of his jeans, Amigo beside him. "Behave yourself, Castro," Harry said.

Cal removed a hand to give Harry a mock salute, then looked at Vero. "I'll protect Miss Simon with my life. You can bet on that."

As soon as they left, Vero excused herself and fled to the guest room. She leaned against the closed door, breathed deeply, and debated the wisdom of continuing what she and Cal had begun before the phone calls. Another yawn, and she sighed. She was too tired to do more than a cursory washing up before changing into sleepwear and burying herself under the duvet. Her last conscious thought was of Cal lifting her up to mold their bodies together. It felt so right.

Darkness engulfed the room, layered and mysterious. Vero didn't know what woke her, only that she lay curled beneath the flannel sheets and soft waffle-weave blanket, the blue tones of the comforter unseeable but soothing. She stretched and rolled, trying to convince her mind to return to the oblivion of sleep, but the events of the day played like movie credits. After half an hour of restless movement and one trip to the bathroom, she decided to abandon the effort and get a drink. She crept into the great room, cardigan clutched around her camisole top and short shorts, the only items she'd packed besides clothes for work tomorrow. Today, she corrected herself. She crossed to the sliding doors that opened onto Cal's balcony. Beyond the short expanse of withered grass, the harbor glimmered under a waning moon. She strained to catch the sound of waves lapping against the shoreline. The night sailed on a windless stream of memory and regret. If she'd been smarter, maybe she could have figured a way to meet the looming loan payment. If she had paid more attention to the city government, maybe she would have seen the redevelopment coming and found a place to live before being kicked out of the apartment. And why hadn't she thought to question Nana years ago about the jewels in the secret stash? *Because I'm an idiot.* The realization made her grimace. She rested a palm against the cool glass, the need to decide about the lake house gnawing at her.

"Verónica?" Cal's voice, low, thick with sleep and something more. Concern? Caring? Desire?

"I didn't mean to wake you." She turned to go back to the guest bedroom. He blocked her path.

"I couldn't sleep either." He rubbed his chest, drawing her attention to the tee clinging to his abdomen, the boxers hugging his thighs. She inhaled the maleness of him, the strength radiating off his tall frame.

"I can't stay in my apartment ever again." She moved to pass him, but he captured her hand, laced his fingers through hers. "And before you say it, I can't stay here. I can't be around you."

He lifted his free hand to touch her cheek. "Because people might talk."

"Yes, and because I don't trust—"

"You don't trust me," he traced a finger over her lips and down her neck, "or yourself?"

"Cal."

"Don't say anything, Vero. Here, in the dark, we can be whomever we wish, take whatever we wish." He eased her body next to his. How easy it was to surrender to a need she hadn't acknowledged until he stood there, offering comfort and consolation, abandon and oblivion. "And I want you, baby."

She rose to press against him, buried a hand in his hair, met his lips. When he teased her mouth open, she didn't draw back, the taste of him fanning the need to be consumed by something other than sadness and fear. It was impossible to stop the moan in her throat that matched his growl as he cupped her rear. She raised a leg, curled it around his, her body no longer hers to control but his to command. She wanted him now, on her, in her, with all the complications that came with that desire. When they broke apart, both out of breath, he cupped her face, his eyes sparkling in the spray of moonshine coming through the glass.

"Will you give me one night, Vero? Forget who I am and all the crap swirling around us and let me make love to you, just you, the most beautiful soul I've ever met?"

"Cal, if we do this, and the police, the press, find out—"

"I know. But you're here, in my home, in my arms. I want you in my bed, Vero, please. I may never get another chance to be with you." He breathed in her scent and her uncertainty, rubbed his hands over her back. "We'll use protection, mi amor. I never want to do anything to put you in any kind of danger."

"What if," she hesitated, the words pushing to be free, "what if I want more than one night?"

"Then we'll find a way." He stopped her next words with his mouth and his hands, removed the sweater and the camisole to caress her breasts. When she murmured his name, he bent to suck her nipple, and she gave up the struggle. Cal was right. She was here. She wanted him. Tomorrow crouched a few short hours away. She raised the hem of his tee, tugging until he allowed her to pull it over his head. She hooked her thumbs into the waistband of his boxers, careful to ease them over the evidence of his desire.

"I want to taste you," she said, hesitant. "I want to please you."

"And I you, *bella*. We'll take turns." He held her as she grazed her tongue over the dark hair on his chest, slipped past the vee of his stomach and onto the length of him, a long stroke up his shaft before she licked the tip and sucked him into her mouth before he pulled her up. "Enough, Vero. I said we'd take turns."

He carried her to his bed, laid her down, and eased her to the edge of the mattress. "Give me permission, mi amor." When she whispered yes, he spread her legs and put his mouth on her. She shuddered from the pleasure, spoke his name, an incantation and a plea. He reached into the bedside table, drew out a condom, and handed it to her to open. And when he finally moved in her, nothing else mattered.

Gray fingers of dawn climbed the wall opposite the window. She watched Cal watching her, his fingers idly stroking her hair. He caught her hand, kissed each finger, drew one into his mouth, sending butterflies of desire to her core. "It was good, yes?" The dimples danced when he smiled.

"More than good. I've never," she turned away, but he forced her gaze back to him.

"You can tell me anything. I won't judge you, Verónica."

"I've never had an orgasm during sex."

He dipped his head, suckled a nipple, kissed her mouth, then her nose. "We can do it again, *querida*, make sure it wasn't a one-time thing."

Vero started to protest, but her body refused to listen, and as Cal stroked her toward a climax, she managed one rational thought. As soon as possible, she would move into the lake house.

Cal

A watercolor sky bled into morning as Cal drove Vero to SIMON's. Neither spoke beyond a few murmured pleasantries, their hands entwined on the seat between them, the air tinged with unexpected joy. Too soon, he thought, to break the seal on last night's act of acceptance and forgiveness. Maybe even commitment. No. That was a wishful fantasy, and he had abandoned such thinking when he changed his major from music to business, but if it brought Veronica Simon to his bed again, he'd entertain the thought. At least she didn't hate him. He hardened thinking of her shouting his name as she climaxed. The copy of the receipt for the ring crackled in his jacket pocket as he lifted her hand to press a kiss to her knuckles.

"Want me to help clean up your apartment tonight?"

She bit her lip before offering a shy smile. "You've done so much already. I'll manage."

"Where are you going to go?" He bit out the next question. "Did Storey find you a place to live?"

"No." She squeezed his hand, then withdrew hers to pull out her cell phone. "Nana did."

"I don't understand." He waited for a pedestrian to cross at the light, then made his way down the alley behind the jewelry store. Vero's car waited, a smear of ice coating the windows.

"My grandmother wanted me to move into the lake house. I thought it was too far from town. Last night I realized I have no choice. Besides, the money I save in rent can go toward the loan." She froze. Cal pounced.

"What loan?"

She brushed away his question. "A business thing. I'm on it. Let me get my keys out."

"Vero, let me help."

She gazed into the morning, eyes distant and thoughtful. When she turned to him, he noted the sadness was back. "You've done so much, Cal. Thank you, for everything. Last night was very special to me."

He wanted to embrace her, kiss her until she responded the way she had in his bed, the need to reclaim her urgent, but he saw that she had retreated again. *Paciencia, Calderón*, he reminded himself. "Beyond special, Verónica. You have my number."

He waited until she entered the shop before heading to the police station on the Blue Highway, the receipt a counterweight to the dread he'd lived with since Gigi disappeared. Norsuch and Harry had better have that plan in place. Even if it took all the money he had, he'd give it away gladly. When Gisele returned, he'd tell her they were through, whatever the cost, even if it meant being blackmailed for the rest of his life. After last night, he'd do anything to extricate himself from the Townsends and win Vero Simon for himself. Finally, he knew what he wanted, and he intended to get it.

Cruisers lined half the lot when he arrived. A swat team milled around an armored vehicle. Inside, Cal spoke to the officer at the desk, then leaned against a wall to check his messages. His father had left a voice mail, the transcription typically cryptic but essentially nothing more than a demand that Cal call him as soon as he got the message. He spotted Duane Harry before the detective saw him and prepared himself for the suspicion Harry exuded. When the man simply shook his hand and escorted him to an interrogation room, Cal suspected something else had happened.

Norsuch raised his head from behind a stack of file folders to offer Cal a seat. "Thanks for informing us of the ransom demand. Am I correct in thinking there's been no new contact?"

"Were you able to grab anything from the voice message?"

Norsuch shook his head. "Nothing useful. You have no idea who made the call?"

"Honestly, no. But I'd definitely say it was a male." Cal extracted the receipt from his pocket and slid it across the table. "Here's the proof about my whereabouts last Friday. I'll do what I can to get the money, as long as you guys take the lead on the meeting."

"That's good, Mr. Castro. And you haven't received any more communications?"

Cal shook his head, unlocked his phone, and scrolled to the last voice mail. Harry doublechecked the instructions and returned the phone.

"All right. One of our FBI colleagues is coordinating the contact phase of the recovery of Miss Townsend." Norsuch cleared his throat. "There's been another development. In searching the home of Lisa Protus, our investigation uncovered a quantity of jewelry. Among the items was a ring we believe is the one you claim to have purchased from Simon's. We're going to need you and Miss Simon to confirm that it's the same ring."

Cal sat stunned. How did Lisa end up with the missing ring? What the hell was going on? His mind pinballed around the events of the previous day. Vero's stalker. A home invasion. Two strangers in town. Whoever Elgin Barkley and Frank Holder were, they seemed connected to Gigi's disappearance, but how? "Do you have the ring here?"

Harry hoisted an evidence box onto the table, removed the lid, and lifted out a clear plastic bag. Drawing on gloves, he undid the seal and placed the unwrapped SIMON's jewelry box in front of Cal. Detective Norsuch pointed at the evidence.

"Is this the ring you purchased from Veronica Simon?"

The ruby caught the light, sparkling in the rose-petaled setting. The four tiny diamonds around it provided the perfect counterpoint. He was struck again by the simple beauty of the design. Harry nudged the box closer to Cal. "That young Simon woman is quite an artist, isn't she? My girlfriend ever sees this, she'll want a copy in a heartbeat."

Norsuch snickered. "SIMON's doesn't do copies, Duane. This is a one-of-a-kind piece."

Rocked for the second time in less than an hour, Cal clenched his hands, his mind taking him back to his initial visit to the jewelry store. Vero designed this? What an idiot he was not to have realized it sooner. Despite all they had shared, she had never corrected his mistake. Now, her despair over losing the ring made more sense. She was the one behind the shop's unique offerings.

Vero

In between waiting on customers and paying bills, Vero contacted a moving company. She dreaded a return to the chaos of the apartment, but by tomorrow, she would be moved into the lake house. Saturday, after the funeral, she could fold herself into the memories inside the house and have a good cry. Maybe Nana's spirit would visit her and suggest a way out of the forest of debt in which she found herself. That only left the problem of where to sleep tonight. She thought about asking Cal, which made her blush. She fantasized returning to his condo, relaxing with Amigo and Choco at her feet, helping prepare dinner. She longed to share his bed and his body again, to return to the haven they had created last night. But could she be certain she wasn't just another conquest? As real as their connection felt, did Cal Castro offer anything beyond the moment? Too many questions. Not enough answers. Returning to her childhood home seemed the logical choice. Her parents would welcome her, their I-told-you-so's escaping in sly, sideways glances. She ignored the sick feeling inside and began to dial her mother when a different plan occurred to her. Grabbing her purse, she rescued Frank Holder's card from the detritus and flicked it with a finger. He mentioned staying at The Hotel Saugatuck. The inn was pricey, but perhaps she could claim it as a business expense, and no one would suspect her of staying there. She could meet with the pushy investigator to find out more about their purported familial connection.

Not the optimal solution, but at least a step forward. Now that she had a plan, she dialed the hotel, inquired about availability, and, with trepidation and a glance at her bank balance, booked the only room available, a king suite with a view of Lake Kalamazoo. She choked as she read out her credit card numbers, certain that this expense would finally tip her into freefall, the depth of her financial chasm growing deeper by the day.

Returning to the apartment took all her courage. She triple-checked that the lock was set and dug into the mess. By seven-thirty, she had finished repacking all her belongings. Not that she had that many to begin with. Except for her bedroom suite, most of the furniture had belonged to Ellie. As she scooped up the last of the broken items, she spent precious minutes mourning the loss of the Lladró statue Nana Verna had gifted her when she graduated from college, but she wouldn't miss the vintage Fiesta ware she'd picked up at a yard sale. *It would be fun*, she mused, *to shop for china and glassware with a husband-to-be*. Since no one stood beside her on the threshold of that fantasy, she salvaged what she could from the trashed dishes and sealed the last box.

Marking the ones destined for the lake with a black marker, she dragged two bags of trash to the outdoor dumpsters and set the donations for Vietnam Vets pickup in the lobby. Her footsteps echoed as she perused the apartment one last time. After tomorrow, she'd never see it again. Recalling the attack on Ray, she shouted, "Good riddance," then regretted the remark. The place held good memories, too. She and Ellie bonding as they practiced yoga along with the phone app. She, Ellie, and Ray playing Bananagrams on rainy nights when no one wanted to go out. The night Cal brought her dinner. The first time he held her while she sobbed through the loss of her grandmother. She squeezed her temples to banish Calderón Castro, but her mind revolted. Last night replayed itself, the way he ran his hands and his lips over her body, the feel of him moving inside her, the endearments he murmured in Spanish. Why torture herself? She should just accept it as a one-time thing and let it go. Well, tomorrow she would banish Cal and his lovemaking skills. Tonight, she had some interrogating to do.

Hotel Saugatuck billed itself as the town's most romantic getaway, and from what she could observe, the place lived up to its hype. Tall trees shedding the last of their leaves loomed at the end of a brick walkway that wound around the outside of the building past the decks gracing each room. In the near distance, the lake shimmered under a waning moon. Warm orange light seeped through slatted blinds covering each of the windows. She lugged the same tattered bag she'd packed last night up the steps and into the lobby. The aroma of fresh-baked cookies wafted at her, along with the scent of cinnamon and pumpkin candles. Her stomach growled, a reminder she had missed lunch again. She didn't recognize the receptionist at the desk but smiled in response to the young woman's greeting.

"I have a reservation," Vero began.

"You must be Veronica Simon, the last of our guests this evening." The woman checked the display screen in front of her, hit several keys, and handed Vero a card. "We have you in Twin Gables. It's on the second floor and has a wonderful lake view. I'm sure you will have a restful night there. Have you eaten dinner yet?"

"No. I think I'll take a walk down to **Grow**."

"Good evening, Miss Simon. Thought I'd see you last night, but tonight works, too." Frank Holder leaned on the counter and tapped his room card on the wooden surface. "I was about to ask for a dinner recommendation. Mind if I join you?"

Startled by his stealthy approach, Vero backed away.

The woman behind the desk looked back and forth between them. "Is everything all right, Miss Simon?"

"Yes. He just surprised me." Vero tucked her room card into a pocket and glared at Holder. "If you're serious about wanting dinner, there's a great place just down the street. We can go together after I drop off my bag."

"Perfect. I'll wait for you here." Holder strolled to an armchair next to the gas fireplace and plopped down. Vero scooted toward the stairs, amazed that her plan was already in play. The upstairs room was as lovely as advertised. The print on the window curtains matched the thick bedspread piled high with fluffy pillows. Soft mint walls reflected a warm glow from the recessed lighting. The bathroom beckoned, a thick robe hanging invitingly over a hook on the door. She placed her bag on the bed, checked her hair and makeup, and slipped the strap of her purse over her shoulder. Then she went down to meet her purported cousin. When her cell chimed in the elevator, she answered without checking caller ID.

"Verónica?" Cal's rich baritone surprised her. "Are you still at the apartment?"

"No, it didn't take long to pack. I didn't realize how reduced in size my life has become."

"Well," he hesitated long enough to make her nervous.

"Cal? Are you all right?"

"Yeah, well, I think so. Did Norsuch or Harry contact you today?"

"Maybe. I haven't had time to check my emails or messages. Why?"

"They found your ring, Vero." The emphasis on the word your made her blink. "Vero? You there?"

"What aren't you telling me?"

"Where they found it, which makes no sense."

Vero stared at her reflection in the mirrored wall of the elevator, dread pooling in her chest. "Where was it, Cal?"

He continued in a hushed voice. "In Lisa Protus's house."

The door opened onto the lobby. She stepped out to lean against the wall. "I don't understand."

"Neither do I. Where are you? Do you," he paused again. She almost heard his nervousness. "Do you want to stay with me tonight?"

"I booked a room at The Hotel Saugatuck. I'm having dinner with that guy who claims we're cousins. Maybe I can find out more about his claim."

"That's not a good idea. You don't know anything about him."

"I know, but I have to do something." Vero walked into the lobby, looked toward the fireplace, then around the space. The woman who welcomed her had disappeared into a back office, and the room appeared empty. The man calling himself Frank Holder was gone.

Cal

Instrumental music played in the background, overridden by Vero's gasp. Cal nodded at the clients inspecting the house but moved out of hearing range. "Vero? Talk to me."

"He's gone. He said he'd wait for me here, but he's gone. I have no idea… wait. Miss? Have you seen that man I was talking to earlier?"

Cal listened to the muffled sounds as the woman inspected the lobby before responding to Veronica. "No," she said. "But he answered his phone while you were in your room. Perhaps some pressing business?"

"Thank you. Cal?"

"Don't leave the hotel, Vero." He checked his watch. The couple had already spent forty minutes exploring the American four-square. They must be interested. "Listen. I'm with clients, but I should be finished by nine. Can we go somewhere, have dinner, talk?"

"I'm tired. I think I'll order a pizza and spend the evening balancing my checkbook."

"Vero, what about the ring?"

"What about the ransom demand?" she asked, deliberately avoiding his question.

"See why we need to talk?" The married couple clomped down the stairs to the lower- level rec room, the woman with a smile, the man wearing that

'I'm ready to negotiate' look. "Stay where you are, Verónica, please? Cancel your pizza order. I'll bring food as soon as I finish here."

He sensed her reluctance, but she finally agreed and hung up. Cal returned to the potential buyers, wishing for the thousandth time he was sitting in a bar strumming his guitar and singing ballads while Verónica Simon sat at a front table, enticing him with those captivating eyes.

It took another hour and a half to write up the contract. Cal did his best to convince the buyers to add inspections, but they were eager to make an offer before another bidder closed them out. By the time he filed the paperwork, contacted the sellers, and locked the deposit check in the safe, it was after ten. He went by the condo to pick up the dogs, stopped by the Pizza Oven for a medium deluxe and a six-pack, and made his way to The Hotel Saugatuck.

The illuminated façade of the hotel, muted and glowing, reinforced its claim to most romantic inn on the North Coast. He had neglected to ask Vero's room number, so, ordering the dogs to stay, he tented the food with his jacket to avoid a doggy disaster and went inside. Five minutes of sweet talk and a promise of free tickets to next summer's Homearama and Cal had the information he sought. When he returned to the car, Choco yawned. Amigo stretched and farted.

"C'mon, buddy. Mind your manners, okay? And, guys, stay close. What the proprietors don't see, they can't object to, right?" Cal waited for the clerk to leave the reception desk, then scooted quickly through the lobby and onto the elevator, the labs at his heels. He checked the corridor before exiting and hurried down the hall to the door marked Twin Gables. One more scan of the area convinced him they were alone. He rapped twice, then scrubbed his chin with his free hand. What if Vero wouldn't let him in? He swore he heard her breathing on the other side of the door. Good. She was being careful. "Vero? It's me."

The door creaked open, and she peeked out, her hair loose and flowing down her back. She was wearing sweatpants and a camisole, the same one he'd removed during their first coupling. His body responded as it had last night, with immediate and unconcealed arousal. She crossed her arms over her chest and licked her lips.

"You came."

"You didn't believe me?"

She stepped back, waving him in, knelt to pet the dogs. Then she straightened and stared him down. "What happened to the ransom plan? I thought you were meeting the caller today?"

He moved past her. "I was. I did, but no one showed. Then I got a new message, rescheduling the drop for tomorrow."

"That's weird. What's all this?"

Cal thrust the pizza box at her. "Dinner." Amigo and Choco crowded his calf. "And friends."

She swept her eyes over the offering, noted the beer. The scowl gave way to a grin when she made eye contact with Choco. She crouched to pet the lab, then Amigo, who nuzzled her hand, then pushed past her into the room. Cal followed, his eyes resting briefly on the taut nipples pushing against the thin top. He closed his eyes against the desire that urged him to forget dinner and move on to dessert. Eyeing the room, he spotted a bistro table near French doors that opened onto a balcony. Through the branches of a heritage maple right outside, the lake wavered like an impressionist painting.

"You didn't have to bring all this. I had an energy bar and some juice." She stood still, wringing her hands, when her stomach growled, loudly. He raised an eyebrow and crossed his arms.

"Sit, Vero. Please. Eat. We have things to discuss."

One more moment of hesitation and she capitulated. Rescuing a sweatshirt from the bed, she tugged it on, giving him another glimpse of her enticing chest before the U of M logo covered it up. He popped the tab on two cans of Saugatuck Brewery's *Paled It* and set one in front of her. The pizza occupied most of the table, the aroma of cheese, sauce, and pepperoni filling the room. Vero helped herself to a slice. Cal watched her eat, noting the slow, careful bites, how she savored each mouthful. She wiped a smear of sauce from the corner of her mouth. That mouth. Cal forgot to chew, his mind spooling back to the previous evening and the various ways he had experienced that mouth on his body.

Vero caught him staring and licked her bottom lip. "What do we have to discuss?"

He refocused his thoughts to answer her question with one of his own. "The detectives didn't contact you about the ring?"

She set her beer down and frowned. "OMG, I still haven't checked my messages. I'll do that right now." Setting her cell on the table, she began to press keys until she reached voice mail. When she turned up the volume, Cal listened as Detective Norsuch explained what they found at the home of the deceased Lisa Protus. Vero looked up. "You saw it."

"It's your ring."

Vero blushed. "Not anymore. It belongs to you and Gise—Miss Townsend."

"No, Vero. I never asked her, not formally, and I never offered her that ring." He covered her hand with his. "Why didn't you tell me you designed it?"

She shrugged. "You had made up your mind about the designer. I didn't think you'd believe me."

"Why?"

She folded her arms and glared at him. "No one ever does. Because of my medical history, they all think I'm incapable of leading a normal life, of running a business. My own brothers have refused for years to credit me for my work. They are convinced someone else makes the jewelry and sends the pieces to us."

"Why don't you tell them the truth?"

"Part of the Simon mystique has always been the mystery behind the jewelry designs. Where the gems come from. Who cuts and polishes each one. Who sets them. It's an art and an obsession, passed down from one generation to the next, and a secret only revealed once you commit to it."

"Did your grandmother swear you to secrecy?"

Vero nodded. "I suppose the detectives know now, and you. Once Nana Verna began to teach me, she cautioned against revealing the artist behind the work. Even my parents don't know the truth. They still view me as the weakest link in the family. Especially now that the future of the shop is up in the air." She picked up her beer, took a long swallow, then wandered away, tapping the can with the rings she wore. Cal teased the drink from her hand. He gripped her shoulders, forcing her to look at him.

"Let me help you, Verónica. *Por favor, querida*."

"Don't lay that infamous Castro charm on me."

One corner of his mouth lifted. "Why not, Miss Simon?"

"Because it's working, damn you." She resisted only long enough for him to tug her closer.

"Good, because, whatever's got you worried, I want to make it right. Later. Tomorrow. Next week. Right now, all I can think about is charming you out of these clothes and into that beautiful bed. How's that sound?"

"Like a plan." She reached beneath his long-sleeved tee to skim her fingers over his chest, tugging gently at his nipples and tracing his abs. "You know we shouldn't be doing this."

He kissed her deeply enough to leave her breathless. "We shouldn't," he said, "but we are."

She allowed him to walk her backward until her knees hit the bed. He pushed her gently until they collapsed in a tangle of limbs and desire. Over by the window, the labs snored softly, paws twitching in doggy dreams.

Vero

The rattle of a suitcase on the sidewalk below woke Vero. She hummed and stretched, bumping up against Cal's naked body. The hard evidence of his morning desire rested between her thighs. Blushing, she inched away, but he snorted and wrapped an arm around her waist. "Unfinished business, Miss Simon," he murmured.

She squirmed, but not for long, warmed by her own flush of arousal rising from a well of need she hadn't acknowledged in years.

"Why in such a hurry, *querida*?' He nuzzled her hair.

"I requested breakfast at seven. For one."

"Guess we'll have to share, then, but first," his hand splayed across her belly, crept lower, pressed the soft swell of her sex, "I want to say a proper good morning."

"How are you so good at this?" She arched under his touch. "No, don't answer that."

He kissed her neck, her shoulder, the soft spot behind her ear. "I won't lie, Vero. I've sown more than a few wild oats, but I swear I'm not playing you."

"I hope not, Castro, because…" She bit her lip to stop herself. What she was feeling was nothing more than a release of years of accumulated sexual frustration. The anxiety and uncertainty of the past week had unsettled her. That's all it was, right? Her inner voice remained silent. Despite misgivings, she wanted this, wanted him. He kissed her mouth, her neck, teased a nipple with his tongue and she surrendered. The knock at the door reminded her of where they were and what she had to do today. Cal groaned, then released her. Eyes closed, he scowled. "You owe me, Simon."

"No, baby, you owe me." She giggled and hopped from the bed, eyes wide, aghast at the word that had slipped from her lips. Baby? Oh. My. God. Maybe Cal didn't hear it? Snatching up her sweatpants and hoodie, she pulled them on to answer the door. A cart sat in the hall, a carafe of coffee and a smaller one of hot water beside a teacup and a platter with a metal cover to keep the food warm. She rolled it through the open door and over to the table. Removing the empty pizza box, they'd finished off the pie in between lovemaking, she set out the breakfast. Cal had gone in to take a shower. She sniffed her armpits and decided he'd better hurry up when a wet arm snaked out from the bathroom, finger crooked in her direction.

"Get in here, woman." When she didn't move, he stepped out, naked and dripping and sexy as hell.

"All right, I'm coming." Vero removed the sweats and followed him, grumbling a little about this being a bad idea.

"You will be," Cal said. Amigo stretched and yawned, then cocked his head, while Choco circled the room. Reaching to liberate a slice of bacon from the breakfast plate, Vero fed it to the male lab, who looked at her with adulation as she slipped into the bathroom.

Twenty minutes later, flushed, legs still quivering, Vero dressed and joined Cal at the bistro table. Scones, a rasher of bacon, three pancakes and an egg later, she sat back with a sigh. Cal leaned over to touch her cheek. "You look content, Verónica. I hope I had something to do with that."

Vero grasped his hand and held it to her face. "You know you did."

"Wish we could call off sick today, forget about ransom demands and long-lost cousins. We could spend the day working off that breakfast."

She blushed again, her body eager to repeat the exertions of the past ten hours, but reason intruded. "Stop, Cal. The dogs need a potty break." She leaned down to fasten their leashes and handed them over. The labs whined and pranced as Cal hurried to the exit stairway, sneaked out the back door, and jogged toward the beach. He returned to a made bed, a cleared table, and a Veronica with her serious face on.

"While we finish the coffee and tea," she said, gesturing at the empty chair, "you can fill me in on the ransom deal."

"What? I don't get a thank you or a kiss for doing my duty as a doggie daddy?"

She smirked but met him halfway, her lips as warm and willing as they had been earlier in the shower. He reached to draw her onto his lap, but she pushed him away. "Tell me."

He winked but relaxed backward, thumb running over his lower lip, forehead creased in thought. "Today Norsuch and Harry are following me to the drop point. The SWAT team will be in place but hidden. If we're lucky, we'll catch whoever is behind this whole thing and rescue Gisele. What?"

Vero shook her head. "It's too dangerous. If what you saw in the video is true, you could get hurt. Besides, if you find Miss Townsend—"

"You're worried for me."

"I am, but—"

"Everything is different now. When we get Gisele back, I'm going to end this farce of an engagement."

"Really? Why would you do that?"

"I'm already working a job I hate. Why would I want to end up married to a woman I despise, especially when I've found one who makes me happy?"

"I make you happy?"

"Do you doubt it, Verónica?' He ran a hand up her arm, pulled her in for a kiss. "Now, what time shall I pick you up after work today?"

Vero sipped the last of her Earl Grey, uncertain of his response to her next words. "I won't be able to see you tonight. I'm moving into my new place."

"No, you're moving in with me."

"No, Cal, I never agreed to that."

"Why not?"

"You said it before. Our being together looks bad."

Cal paced the room, one hand on his hip, the other ruffling his hair. "Damn it, Vero, be reasonable. Wait. Did Storey find you an apartment here in town?"

"No." She gathered her purse and overnight bag. Slinging her coat over one arm, she picked up the room key. "I've decided to honor my grandmother's wishes. I'm moving into the lake house."

Cal

Cal cautioned the dogs to stay, then watched Vero hustle down the hall to the elevator. He bit his lip to forestall calling her back, last night's revelations about her jewelry art and the shop's financial difficulties a solid weight in his chest. Despite all she had been through, the woman insisted on making her own way, but this plan seemed perilous. Vero was beautiful and brave. However, moving to a cabin on a deserted lake where a murdered woman's body had been discovered sounded crazy. Well, it wasn't his decision...yet. He checked the corridor for inn guests. When the way was clear, he leashed the dogs and once more slipped down the stairwell and out the back door. He checked the time, then released Amigo and Choco for a run before meeting with the detectives. Delivering ransom money took precedence over convincing Vero not to live by herself, and he had to admit that their moving in together would raise suspicions about her motive in supplying Cal's alibi. In a small town like Saugatuck, suspicions tended to linger longer than truth.

But what was the truth? He no longer felt anything for Gisele, although he did wish they'd find the woman so he could convince her to let him go, appeal to whatever passed for a conscience in Gigi's icy heart. If she insisted on revealing what she knew about his mother... Cal shook his head. Maybe it was time to talk with Mamá. Perhaps Gisele's blackmail was nothing but one more con game added to the ones she and Cerise had played on him in the past. One way or another, he was determined to close that chapter before moving on to his next big decisions, the most important of which involved his relationship with Veronica Simon. The other revolved around that invitation from a record producer who had cornered him at his last gig. When they reached the car, he waited for the dogs to hop in, then scooted behind the wheel. He had time to drop them at the condo, check emails, and dress in warmer clothes before the meet-up by the water.

The Sergeant Marina occupied land at the south end of Griffith, not far from SIMON's Jewelers, with slips for deep water boats, a clubhouse, and a gated parking area. Popular with long-time residents as well as seasonal boaters, the facility also provided dependable Internet service. Norsuch and Harry had determined that using a boat to cross the lake would attract less attention than a convoy of vehicles. Prior to his arrival, the SWAT team members would hide themselves in the forest edging the stairway up to Mt. Baldhead. Only Cal would climb the two-hundred and eighty-two steps that led to an overview of the town to the east and the sand dunes of Lake Michigan to the west.

Norsuch had promised Cal he'd be under observation at every stage of the ascent. How the task force would manage that and remain unseen worried him. In the video, Gisele appeared bound and in pain, her captor impervious to her suffering. And if the man had murdered Lisa Protus, Cal didn't like the odds of surviving an encounter with him. Which is why he tucked a small tube of bear mace into his boot. Not much use against a gun or knife, but all he needed was a distraction and the speed he had cultivated all those years ago as a striker on his college soccer squad.

Duane Harry accosted Cal as soon as he exited the car. "Where you been all night, Castro? We've been trying to reach you."

"Getting some rest, Harry. Besides, why do you care? I'm here now."

"We had a car stationed at your condo. You never came home."

Cal ignored the detective's tone and headed toward Norsuch, who spoke in curt syllables to two cops in running gear. "Cut me some slack, Harry. I went to see my mom."

Duane Harry frowned but made no further comment, trailing Cal like a bloodhound on the scent of something foul. Cal hoped no one had spotted him at The Saugatuck. For Vero's sake as much as his own. Harry's long-held grudge was a thorn that dug deeper under Cal's skin with every new development. Cal was certain that, given the opportunity, the man would arrest him, facts be damned.

Norsuch greeted him with a nod and handed over a backpack. "Not half a mil but enough real money on top to look believable, and the weight is right," the detective said. He tightened the straps before slipping a phone and ear buds into the pocket of Cal's jacket.

"What's this for?"

"Looks like a music player, works like a walkie-talkie. Allows us to stay in touch with you throughout the encounter. You good?"

"Do I have a choice?"

Harry brushed past him to climb into the Bayliner 160 Bowrider idling next to the dock. "Let's get this show going. Dick and I will tie up by the chain ferry. Castro, once you start up the hill, you're on your own until you reach the stairway up Mt. Baldhead. The team's already in place all along the climb."

"Good to know." Cal hopped in, and Harry piloted the craft across the lake. Once everyone was in position, Cal closed his eyes, imaged the details of the plan, then began his ascent toward the stairway. He'd jogged this road before, but never with so much at stake. Twenty minutes of effort brought him to the base of the hill. The stairs loomed, the gentle first rungs masking the effort it took to climb them all. Locals and tourists alike challenged themselves to master the almost-three hundred steps to the lookout at the top. He checked his phone once more for any last-minutes changes and sent a text to Vero.

`last night was special…call if you need me`

He was about to hit send when he decided to add `Stay safe`. Then he gave himself the same instruction, adjusted the pack, and started to climb. The first few flights didn't tax him, but soon his thigh and calf muscles protested the unusual exertion. Grateful for the benches that provided resting spots, he varied his pace. The message had specified he arrive no later than ten a.m. An older couple, regulars by their clothing and gear, greeted him along the climb, then resumed the downward trek. Each time he paused, he checked the woods, hoping the undercover team was in place as promised. When he reached the halfway point, he spotted a woman on the next uphill bench. Slender, dressed in camouflage joggers, the woman's hair was caught up in a stocking cap, making it difficult to tell its color. As Cal drew closer, he considered his next move. When he resumed the climb, the woman pivoted to look at him. Cal lunged upward, taking the risers two at a time until he reached her.

"Cerise!" He cornered her before she could dart away. "You took Gisele?"

Cerise shoved him away. "Hands off, Calderón. You're the one who lured me here. I know you were behind her disappearance."

"Don't be stupid. I'm bringing ransom money to free Gisele. Why the hell are you here?"

"But, but—" She stopped talking and turned around, revealing a pack strapped around her waist.

"What is that?" He pointed to the thick, black band.

"I don't know. It showed up outside my office door last night. There was a text from you on my phone, demanding I wear it to save my sister."

"I didn't leave any note, Ceri, and I sure as hell didn't ask you to wear that." Cal backed away. He pulled the miniature radio from his pocket, clicked it on. "Norsuch? Harry? I hope you're listening. Cerise Townsend is here, and I'm pretty sure she has a bomb strapped to her waist." He whispered the last part, but something in his tone must have given him away.

"Wait, what? This thing is a bomb?" She reached to unstrap the pack. Cal stopped her.

"Don't touch that, Ceri."

She snatched her hand back, visibly shaken, and held up her cell phone. "You swear you didn't send this?"

He leaned closer to read the message. `put on this fanny pack at the foot of mt baldhead and wear it as you climb come alone and your sister goes free`

Cal checked the time. If he remained with Cerise, he would miss his window with the kidnapper. The transmitter crackled to life. Shouting followed by a command to put your hands up and get on your knees. Heavy breathing, the sounds of a struggle, curses, and a woman's voice shouting, "The perp is down."

"Cal, don't you dare leave. Please." Cerise's plea startled him. Like her sister, Ceri never asked nice for anything, but she was begging now, her body quivering with fear and rage. The device sputtered in his ear.

"Castro?" Harry said. "Stay where you are. We're on our way. Tell the lady to remain very, very calm."

After Cal relayed the instructions, he listened for the sound of booted feet coming down the mountain, the shuffle of others working their way up. Cerise listened, too, arms wrapped tight around her. He should give her his jacket, but if she was wearing a bomb, any movement might trigger it. "Why are you really here, Ceri?"

She shook her head, the consummate lawyer shuffling through facts before selecting one to share. He repeated the question. When she looked up, her eyes blazed with fury. "That message has an attachment, a video of Gisele bound and bloody. I responded with an offer of money but got no reply. I didn't think you or the detectives were doing much to find her, so I had no choice but to follow the instructions. I thought the demand came from you. I'm still not convinced it didn't."

"For Christ's sake, Cerise. I may not want to marry your sister, but I don't want to see her hurt." Cal ran a hand through his hair. "I got a message to bring ransom money two days ago. Then the bastard changed the drop to today. I went to Norsuch and Harry, and they set up a meet. I hope they caught the guy, but what if he won't tell us where he has Gisele?"

Cerise didn't answer. Off to their right, three SWAT team members hustled out of the woods and onto the stairs. One handed his weapon off and approached Cal and Cerise. "Sir, I need you to go on down with Sergeant Miles here. Ma'am, I need you to not move until I know what we're dealing with." The man bent to inspect the fanny pack. Cerise sent another pleading glance toward Cal, but the officer grasped his arm and urged him down the stairway. They were twenty steps closer to the bottom when the transmitter crackled again. "All clear. No incendiary material discovered. We'll bring Miss Townsend down immediately."

Groups of law enforcement and emergency personnel had congregated at the bottom of the steps, Norsuch and Harry among them. The balding detective relieved Cal of his backpack and transmitter but refused to comment on the swarm of SWAT vehicles and personnel. "No comment, Castro. Stay put until we sort this out." Forty minutes passed before the team assigned to the top of the mountain came into view, a middle-aged man with a paunch handcuffed between two of them. Harry strode over.

"This our kidnapper?" he said.

"I never," the man mumbled.

"You never what?" Harry lifted the man's chin to look in his eyes.

"I want a lawyer."

"Oh, my man, a lawyer can't help you out of this mess. Where's Miss Gisele Townsend?"

"I don't know. Some guy online offered me a thousand bucks if I sent two messages and included a video with it."

"You didn't make the video?" Norsuch joined his partner.

"Damn straight I didn't. Check my email feed. I didn't do nothing wrong."

"Well, that's not strictly true. You issued threats to two individuals, demanded a ransom, insinuated you knew where our missing person was, and," Norsuch held up a plastic evidence bag containing a hunting knife and a .38., "you were carrying weapons. If you're a convicted felon, that is enough to send you to jail."

"I have the right to protect myself, man."

"Maybe. Hope you have a permit for the gun. Covich, you and Miles take this man to the station. We'll be there shortly." Norsuch motioned Cal over. One of the EMTs escorted a shaken Cerise to the detectives.

"Miss Townsend. Any reason you didn't notify us when you received this message?"

She stared at the phone clutched in the detective's meaty hand, lifted her shoulders, and smoothed her hair. Cal realized Cerise the lawyer was back in charge. "I was trying to find and free my sister, something you all have failed to do. It's been almost a week and she's still missing."

"Your actions today set us back. I could bring you in on a charge of obstruction."

"Doesn't matter what you do to me." Cerise glanced at Cal. "At least Castro and I aren't standing around with our thumbs in our belts speculating. Go ahead, bring me in. If it helps you find Gisele, it'll be worth it."

Norsuch shrugged. "Detective Harry will escort you to the station. Mr. Castro, I'll drop you at the dock and you can pick up your car. I'll let you know if we find out anything else. Seems someone's playing prankster, and I am not amused."

Cal didn't protest. He had a contract to present to the sellers of the colonial, another closing at one o'clock, and dogs to walk in between appointments. He checked for messages from Vero but found none. After the rush up Mt. Baldhead, the bomb scare, and the arrest of an opportunist trying to pull a con, he felt deflated. Despite their efforts, Gisele Townsend remained unaccounted for and Cal's future along with her.

Vero

Every chime of the bell announcing a customer startled Vero from her thoughts. She couldn't forget last night with Cal or the way her heart fluttered at the sound of his voice on the phone. If she didn't know better, she'd think she was in love with the man. But there was no way, right? She didn't dare imagine a future when her present remained in chaos. And, come on, didn't Nana always say leopards didn't change their spots? Despite their recent and undeniably amazing chemistry, Cal was an arrogant, self-centered, egotist. Wasn't he? Right, a man with devilish good looks and a talent for making her forget her problems. He hadn't recoiled from the scars on her chest. In fact, he'd kissed them, each press of his lips a reminder that the past didn't define her. Gah! She finished printing the details about Nana Verna's Celebration of Life and taped it to the window. She hoped Shea wouldn't be late today. Agatha was right. Despite her unconventional appearance, Shea had a proven ability to sweet talk customers. If she agreed to come on full-time, Vero could get back to designing new items. Her fingers ached to create something beautiful again, jewelry to rival the missing ring.

The bell jangled and Frank Holder, gloves in hand, thundered in. He paused in the doorway, shifted his shoulders, and marched to the register. The other customers looked around, apprehensive in the face of his belligerence. Vero lifted her chin. She would not be intimidated by him today. "Where were you last night, Mr. Holder? I thought you wanted to talk with me."

He tossed a sheaf of papers on the glass and anchored them with a fist. "Something unexpected happened. You need to read this."

"What is it?"

"An inventory of all the gems our great-grandfathers claimed before yours stole them all away."

Vero swept her eyes around the showroom, playing for time until she could control her temper. She wished her grandmother were here to confront the lie in the man's tale. "I'm working, Mr. Holder. Leave them here and I'll look them over tonight. Meanwhile, please step back while I tend to my customers."

He opened his mouth, closed it, then slapped the counter with the gloves. "One way or another, I'll have what's mine."

"Are you issuing another threat?"

He faced her, eyes narrowed. "I'm making a promise, Veronica Simon. We will resolve this between us now, or we'll let the courts decide. Either way, I will have what I'm owed."

Shea chose that moment to sweep into the shop, a red wool cape swirling around her black boots. She had re-dyed her hair, adding orange, red, and brown highlights. She walked right up to Frank and poked him in the chest. "Get lost, ogre-boy, or I'll sic the cops on you. Hey, Vero, like my new locks? I'll change to red and green in December."

Frank Holder refused to back down. "I knew appealing to your decency wouldn't work, that we'd have to take more drastic action."

"Mr. Holder or whatever your real name is, I have no reason to believe your claim is legitimate. If you can prove that we're related, then we'll talk." Vero pressed her thumbs against her temple to stave off the burgeoning headache. "Now, please leave."

"A simple DNA test is all the proof I need. Are you willing to do that?" Vero and Shea exchanged a look, and Vero nodded, erasing some of the tension between them. His tone mellowed with his next words. "The funeral's tomorrow, right? I'll see you there."

"You're not invited."

"It's a celebration of your grandmother's life, isn't it? A time for family and friends to remember her? Well, I'm family, and I'm going to be there. Hands off, weird girl."

Shea released her grip on Holder's coat sleeve and threw up her hands. "No need for name-calling."

Frank Holder backed toward the door, staring at Vero as he did so. "See you tomorrow, cousin."

Vero shook off the angst the man produced to help a man inspecting a display of bracelets, then scooted to the window to watch Holder jog across Culver. Her phone vibrated, reminding her of all the loose ends to tie before tomorrow. "Take care of our customers, Shea. The movers just texted to meet them at the apartment."

"Go, boss. I've got you covered. Except for what to do at the end of the day." Shea smiled at the couple inspecting the ornamental vases.

Vero scribbled a note about how to close the shop, lock up the expensive pieces, and set the alarm. A blast of chill air greeted her as she left the building. The sun had melted the thin layer of frost covering the back window of her Subaru. By the time she arrived at The Scottish, she felt more composed and in control. A DNA test would put to rest the man's claim. And if, by some chance, they were related, well, she would sort that out later.

Five minutes after her arrival, a van bearing a Two Men and a Truck logo pulled up to the entrance to the apartments. She greeted the movers and led the way upstairs. It took less than an hour to load her stuff. Satisfied that she'd left nothing but memories behind, Vero locked the door for the last time, then stared at the key in her palm, reminding her of the other key, the one her grandmother had willed her. Did it matter if she threw this one away? Another month, and The Scottish would be gone, the lot cleared and awaiting new construction. The bittersweet taste of yet another loss accompanied her as she followed the truck out of town.

Leaves cushioned the crunch of tires down the lane to the cabin. Beyond the house, the lake drowsed in the weak October light. As she pulled into the graveled parking area, a memory surfaced. Labor Day weekend. The last time she'd been here with Nana Verna. After closing the shop, they had driven over to prepare for the official season-ending family cookout. The following week Nana had been diagnosed with advanced-stage pancreatic cancer. Two weeks after that, her grandmother had surgery, which only confirmed that the cancer had metastasized. Nana could no longer live alone at the lake. Overwhelmed by the reminder of that final happy weekend, Vero braced her head on the steering wheel and clutched her waist, unable to suppress the keening sound of loss. The movers crunched their way toward her.

"You all right, Ma'am?"

Vero pushed herself upright. "Sorry for the meltdown. It's been a stressful week."

The young men scuffed their boots against the gravel, shrugged, and returned to the van. She didn't blame them for being nervous. It wasn't their job to comfort a sobbing client. She propped the door open with the tree stump carved like a bear and went inside. The interior was freezing. Her first act was to switch on the power. Then she bent to open the flue, added a log to the grate, and used kindling to start a blaze. Once the fire was going, she removed her boots and stomped to the basement to turn on the water and check for mice. Although they had regular service by the local pest control company, the creatures were adept at finding a way in. Upstairs, the movers clomped across the hardwood floor, stacking everything in the hall. She abandoned the critter search to head upstairs. If they didn't get the boxes in the right places, she'd be dragging items from one spot to another for days.

"The ones marked master bedroom belong in there." Vero gestured down the hall to the right. "Be careful. There are two steps down." It took even less time to unload her sparse belongings than it had to empty the apartment. She wrote a check, then crossed her fingers that it wouldn't bounce. As soon as they drove away, she filled the kettle, put it on the burner, and got to work in the bedroom. When the whistle sounded, she returned to the kitchen to pour a cup for tea. She warmed her hands around the mug, then rummaged through the end table in the great room, searching for the journal where the family recorded details of each visit, a tradition stretching back almost a hundred years. The current volume only covered last year. Where were the ones from the past? Where had Nana stashed all those old records? Unable to locate them in the great room, Vero went down to the storage room.

Shelving units bowed under the weight of backpacks, while sand toys, gardening implements, and hiking gear lined the perimeter of the room. A hutch stood against the far wall, its surface cluttered with knickknacks and fishing lures. She yanked on the top drawer. The wood had swollen, making it difficult to open. Vero braced her feet and pulled harder. The drawer popped free and fell, landing on her foot. "Shit! Shit! Shit!" She grabbed her toes and hopped around the room until the initial pain morphed into a steady throb. The contents lay spilled across the cement floor.

Kneeling, Vero gathered the diaries and checked the inside cover for the dates of entries before stacking them in order. When she opened the one labeled 1923, her hand trembled. Easing to her feet, she winced. She remounted the drawer, placed the rest of the diaries back inside, and hobbled upstairs, 1923 clutched to her chest. She took out a fresh tea bag, added hot water to the mug, and, as an afterthought, a splash of whiskey from the bottle under the sink. She carried the drink and the diary to the couch, now warmed by the fire she had started. Unfolding one of the blankets Nana Verna had crocheted, Vero snuggled in to read.

And so it begins, this new life we Simons are crafting for ourselves. The cabin is complete. Violet is pregnant. SIMON's will open in the spring. All is good. I pray the past stays in the past. No ghosts are permitted in this new home.

Cal

While the dogs enjoyed their after-walk treats, Cal showered and dressed for the day's business. Adjusting his tie in the mirror, he examined the face that had gotten him into so much trouble over the years. What did women see in him? Maybe it was the family money that explained the way they came on to him. When he was younger, female attention flattered his ego, but being pursued for shallow reasons grew stale. Maybe that's why he'd fallen into a liaison with Gisele Townsend. She was a safe date, until she wasn't. If... no, when, she came back, he had to break it off with her, but only after making sure his mother's secret would never be revealed. Right now, he didn't know how he'd arrange that. He only knew that it had to be done before he could move forward with his feelings for Veronica Simon.

Gathering his thoughts for the meeting with Bergeron, Cal stood by the window, watching the waters of the lake ripple in the strong north wind. Seeing Cerise on Mt. Baldhead had shocked him into considering whether she had a hand in her sister's disappearance. Despite the text message luring her there, her presence on the stairway felt more calculated than coincidental. He pitied the poor schmuck the cops arrested. From the man's denials as the officers hustled him away, Cal pegged him for one of those online conspiracy buffs who saw dollar signs in claiming responsibility for Gisele's vanishing. That led him to consider Veronica's long-lost cousin as Gisele's possible kidnapper. Thank goodness Vero hadn't accompanied Holder to dinner, or she might have vanished, too. Cal narrowed his eyes at the thought of Vero being in danger. And she was, wasn't she? A stranger watching the jewelry shop. A previously unknown relative showing up to claim a stolen inheritance. What did that even mean? If there was some truth to the man's story, had Verna Simon known about her family's nefarious past? Did she deliberately hide the truth from her granddaughter? Or was Frank Holder another con man looking to score off a family tragedy? Cal had his own possible stalker in Elgin Barkley. The woman questioned every statement he made, determined to prove him guilty of something. Well, he wanted to know the truth, too. Who had taken out life insurance on Gisele? Was it just another scam, or had someone deliberately intended to discredit the Castro family and ruin them for good?

Amigo padded over. Cal reached down to scratch his ears. "You're the best, buddy, you and your sister, and I want to stay with you guys, but a man's got to work. Bob will be here later to take you both for a run." Cal paused at the door, thought about the guitar tucked in the closet, of the song germinating every time he saw Vero Simon, and pursed his lips. He set down the briefcase, took the dogs out for one more potty break, then drove to the office.

One of the new associate realtors, Amy Johansen, had set up a reception desk next to the one Lisa Protus had occupied. No one wanted to claim the deceased woman's space, the violence of her passing too raw to overlook. Cal accepted the pink memos Johansen handed him. Thanking her, he turned to leave when she tapped his wrist.

"There's a woman waiting in your office." Amy shuddered. "She's a little upset."

Cal wondered if Vero had come to see him but dismissed that thought as soon as it occurred. The only person who might commandeer his office was the insurance investigator, Barkley. What fresh conspiracy did she intend to spin today? Well, he was in no rush to see her, and one more cup of coffee would fortify him for the day ahead. In the break room, he popped in a Keurig, then prepared to confront Barkley. His father caught him before he reached the hall.

"Calderón? Do you have a minute?"

Cal glanced at his closed door, then followed Antonio into his office.

"It's a busy day, Papá, and that insurance woman is waiting in my office."

"I only need a moment. Eric Bergeron has signed a contract with The Castro Group. We are to represent him in all deals with landowners on Goshorn Lake."

"That's good news, I guess, but the lake people won't be in favor of more development, and they won't be eager to sell. Besides, half of them won't be back until spring. Convincing them to sell to an unknown entity won't be easy. We should stall, advise him to look for other sites to build his resort."

"You may be right, Cal, but he insists we try it his way first."

"How does this concern me?"

"Bergeron requested that you personally meet with the property owners. He believes you have the power to persuade them to relinquish their land."

Cal's interior radar went off. There was something he wasn't seeing. "Why does he think that?"

His father picked up a paperweight Cal had gifted him years ago, the inscription worn by time. *Greatest Dad Ever.* "He believes you have a special connection to the owners of the largest property."

"Who are they?"

His father rolled his lips. "The Simon family. He claims the business is in trouble, and they need capital. Besides, you and the Simon woman have grown close."

"How does a real estate developer from Chicago know about a local business's financial difficulties? Or my friendship with Veronica?"

Antonio rescued a folder from his inbox and handed it to Cal. "It's more than friendship, *mijo*. They have pictures of you and Miss Simon together."

"We're not together."

"They believe you are. She spent the night at your place two days ago. Last night you were with her at The Hotel Saugatuck." Antonio held up a hand to forestall Cal's next words. "Bergeron said he would send the photos to the police unless you secure the Simon property for him."

"No." Cal tossed the photographs on the desk. "This is blackmail. I want no part of it."

Antonio picked up the folder and handed it back to Cal. "The photos can't hurt us, Calderón, but they can destroy Miss Simon."

Cal stormed from the room, wondering how and where surveillance had caught him with Vero. The pictures did not display any real intimacy, but it was clear from their body language that they were drawn to each other. He strode through the door, slapped the folder down, and glared at the woman sitting primly behind his desk. "I don't have time for this, Barkley. Say what you have to say and leave."

The insurance investigator smoothed her skirt and picked up her attaché case. She set it on top of the folder, opened it, and waved a hand over the contents. "You might be interested to know, Mr. Castro, that with the help of the Post Office, we've been able to trace the origin of the signed documents to this very office."

"That's impossible." Cal peered at the contents inside the case. "I never signed those papers, never even saw them."

"Yes, so you said." She separated two sheets and laid them in front of him. "Your assertion that it's not your signature has been corroborated, and so has my suspicion that someone from Castro Realty did endorse the request by forging your signature. Any idea who that might be?"

Cal shook his head. "I have no idea who hated me that much."

Elgin Barkley returned the papers to the case. "Think carefully, Mr. Castro. Who in this establishment had access to your information? Who oversaw transactions, served as notary when required? Who might have had a reason to feel overlooked or slighted and acted on that hurt?"

Laughter filtered down the hall. Footsteps clicked in the tiled entryway. A phone rang. Amy answered, recited the standard Castro Realty greeting Lisa Protus used to say. "Not Lisa. Not possible. We, I, trusted her with—"

"Everything." Barkley waited for him to look up. "And she used that trust against you. The question is why? What did she have to gain?"

A memory surfaced. The Fourth of July office party at his parents' home, Lisa following him around, waiting for Gisele to detach herself from his side. When Gigi joined another group of guests, Lisa suggested they walk down to the lake.

"You don't seem to be enjoying yourself, Cal."

He wasn't. The pressure to marry Gisele had reached critical mass, and Cal's discontent with his role at the company gnawed at him. He couldn't see a way out, but he had no reason to share any of that with Lisa. "The last few months have been stressful."

She ran her fingers down his chest, tightened her grip on his arm. He pulled away with a little more force than expected. Lisa stumbled. He caught her by the elbow, released her as soon as she was upright, but something flickered in her eyes. "I would be a better match for you, but you never seem to see that."

"Lisa, don't go there." They'd had one night when she had first come to work at Castro Realty, one drunken encounter.

"The age difference doesn't have to matter, but then you Castros are all hung up on image, aren't you?" She brushed off his denial. "Fine, no harm, no foul. I won't hold our night together against you, but I won't forget it either. Here's the thing. I've been waiting a long time for a promotion. I think it's time I got one."

"My father is the one who makes those decisions."

"He listens to you. You could put in a good word for me. After all, he'd be disappointed to find his son is guilty of sexual harassment."

"I wasn't hired until after we hooked up." He glanced back at the house, spotted Gisele staring at them. "Don't do this, Lisa."

"Fine. Forget I even brought it up. Go." She pushed him toward the gathering on the patio. "There's more than one way to bell a cat."

"What the hell does that mean?" he said, but Lisa had turned away to wander farther down the dock. Disgusted by his own past behavior and unsettled by her threat, he hurried back to the group and the untenable situation he found himself in.

"You remembered something." Barkley edged closer.

Cal rested his head in his hands. "When I came home from college, she and I spent a night together. It meant nothing, a drunken hookup with a good-looking older woman, but it must have meant more to her. At a work party at my father's house last July, she threatened to accuse me of sexual harassment, but she had no grounds. I never thought—"

"It's a natural response for a man, to discount a scorned woman."

"She wasn't scorned. She came on to me and I, stupid college boy, felt flattered. That makes me an idiot, not a harasser."

"Well, we have her motive, but she couldn't have physically abducted Miss Townsend. Your fiancée—"

"Not officially."

"I stand corrected. Your girlfriend was bigger and stronger, and Protus's alibi checks out."

"Not to mention someone killed her, and they found the ring at her place."

Barkley raised a hand. "What ring?"

Cal explained the purchase at Vero's shop and its disappearance from Brad's jacket. The investigator sniffed. "I'd like to see this ring."

"Why? It has nothing to do with," Cal gestured toward the life insurance papers, "your case."

Barkley pinched her lips with her thumb and forefinger. "Never mind. What you need to know is that I'm officially clearing you of the fraud charge."

"So, we're good then?" Cal stood as she closed the case, hiked her purse over her shoulder, and almost sprinted toward the door.

"For the moment, Mr. Castro." She gave him a Mona Lisa smile and scampered in the direction of the reception area, her Cuban heels tapping out a solid rhythm. Cal watched her go, unsettled by the calculated glee that crossed her face just before she turned away.

Vero

Vero dozed off, three of the diaries from the basement scattered at her feet. The others had fallen from the couch and spread over the rag rug. Early the next morning, she bolted awake, grateful the fire had burned itself out without throwing any sparks over the screen that guarded the opening. Beyond the French doors, the lake glistened, calm and unruffled as dawn gilded the surface. She checked the time and hurried to shower. Thank goodness she had turned on the hot water heater before she drifted off. It took a while to locate her dress for the Celebration of Life, longer to set up the ironing board and press out the wrinkles, which only left time for a piece of toast and a glass of juice before heading into town. The euphoria of being with Cal two nights ago was overshadowed by the sadness looming ahead. She ignored the distraction of using cell phones when driving and called Shea to make sure the woman was prepared to run the shop. The ache in her chest joined the throbbing behind her eyes.

The funeral home had posted Verna Simon's name on the outdoor sign listing the ceremonies scheduled for the day. Several older couples lingered at the entrance, Vero didn't recognize them, but perhaps they were here for someone else's memorial. She spotted her parents' car, then Sonny's. She had just pushed the door lock on her key fob when Dave roared into the lot, his newest muscle car an affront to the quiet neighborhood. She waved but decided not to wait for him.

An assistant she didn't recognize directed her toward the salon reserved for Verna Simon's celebration. She signed the condolence book, nodded at Agatha Wiggins, and went into the event room. Her parents stood next to a table bearing Nana's urn surrounded by a heart-shaped display of pink roses. Four easels bearing photographs of her grandmother's life flanked them. Tables had been set up around the perimeter. Near the facility's kitchenette, a serving counter held the initial offerings of the food service. The spread was tasteful, appealing, and bountiful. Vero recognized her mother's touch behind the decorations and the food choices. Her stomach growled, but she ignored the urge to help herself. A tiny voice inside wished Cal were standing beside her, his hand warm and supportive on her back. She silenced that thought before it could grow wings.

"Veronica?" Her mother hugged her. "Sonny's here. As soon as Dave arrives, we need to meet with the director. It seems Nana Verna left letters and requested that they be given to us before the celebration."

"More letters?"

Her mother blinked and led her over to her father, who was staring at pictures of his mother as a young girl, a teenager, and a mother. Vero ran her fingers over the photographs, warmed by the images of Nana in happier days when one of the pictures caught her eye. Labeled *Reunion 1946*, the black and white photo showed a gathering of the extended family, young children sitting or kneeling in front, the elders arranged behind the cousins and married couples. "Who are they?" She tapped the stern faces of two men, one white-haired and smiling, the other bald and snarling.

Her father leaned closer, lifted his glasses to peer at the photograph. "I think that's Grandpa Simon and Jacob Holder."

"Holder as in my grandfather?"

"Not exactly. It's complicated."

"Can you uncomplicate it, Dad? Please."

Her father gripped her hand as he tapped the image. "Jacob Holder was Stan Holder's father. Johan Simon, your great-grandfather, and great-grandma Violet took Jacob in when his parents died of the Spanish flu. They treated him like a son. Even had legal papers drawn up to include him in the family."

"But Nana married a Holder. Wasn't that, er, creepy?"

"Well, a distant Holder cousin. The bloodlines were separate, Vero, and, because of the enmity between the factions, my mother fought to keep them that way. That's why she insisted on retaining the Simon name."

"So, Simons and Holders are related but not really. Why don't I know any of this?"

Her father hunched his shoulders. "At some point, Johan and Jacob had a falling out, an actual knock-down, drag-out fight. Jacob left. Johan ended up in the hospital."

"Where did Jacob go?"

"According to family lore, he disappeared after the fight. No one ever saw him again."

Stunned, Vero tried to fit the new information into the story Frank Holder had shared yesterday. She caught her dad's eye, intending to press for more about the family history when Sonny and Dave emerged from the crowd. "Mr. Dykstra," Sonny waved a hand toward the outer hall, "wants to see us before the program begins."

Dave rubbed his hands. "Maybe we can decide what to do with the store and the lake house while we're together."

Vero crossed her arms. "We're not doing anything with them, Dave, because they're not for sale."

Sonny narrowed his eyes, and, taking her arm, propelled her toward the hall, "Not here," he said. She had no choice but to walk with him while Dave herded her parents along. The funeral director intercepted them and led the way to his office. Once inside, her parents took the seats across from him. Her brothers plopped down on either side. Vero declined to sit, Dave's words clinging like barnacles to her raw emotional boat. Dykstra cleared his throat.

"George. Angela. You have my deepest condolences for the loss of Verna. She was a loved and respected member of our town, and she will be missed." He paused, cleared his throat a second time, and picked up five envelopes. "When your mother arranged her funeral, she was quite specific in her requests and generous in making sure all expenses were covered prior to her passing. She also insisted I deliver these to each of you before the Celebration of Life began, with the caveat that you were not to open them until afterward." Mr. Dykstra smiled. "Verna never could resist getting the last word. While I can't hold you to her request, I caution you to heed her wishes. Letters such as these usually carry quite an emotional punch. I hope you will abide by her wishes. Any questions?"

Sonny crossed his legs to toy with the cuff of his dress pants. "How long ago did my grandmother write these letters?"

The director consulted a file. "She brought them to me two months ago."

Vero's mother wiped her eyes with a tissue. "That's about the time she received the cancer diagnosis."

"Nana Verna didn't like loose ends," Vero murmured.

Dave huffed. "Well, she left a few. When do we get a look at the will?"

"I've already looked at it."

"You did?" Sonny said.

Dykstra blushed. "She chose to share that information with me when she and her lawyer came to finalize her plans."

"That seems peculiar."

"Perhaps. Verna was Verna, after all. In any case, your grandmother provided adequately for you and Sonny." George Simon turned to Vero. "But she knew who she wanted to have the properties most dear to her. Your sister gets the shop and the lake house."

Sonny looked at Vero, his face a mix of anger and despair. Their father stepped between them. "Now is not the time or place to discuss the disposition of your grandmother's assets. No. You will not say anything to your sister you might regret later."

"We talked this over, Dad. You and Mom agreed."

"Enough." George reached for Angela's hand. "We're going out there as a family to honor Nana's life."

Vero remained behind, the envelope clutched to her chest. Her brothers' intentions had been clear for some time. They had no interest in the jewelry business and, although they liked the lake house, they enjoyed the idea of a big payout more. Apparently, none of the Simon males had inherited their grandmother's ability to spin straw into gold. That's how Nana Verna always explained it when Vero asked how she managed to wring a profit from such a small family business. Her mother caught Vero's eye and winked. Then she slipped an arm around the boys and guided them into the hall. Tucking her grandmother's letter in her purse, Vero followed, the mystery of the family tree trailing after her.

The room was full. Funeral home assistants scurried in and out, dragging more chairs for those standing along the walls. The minister from the United Church of Christ had arrived, his face somber, Bible in hand.

He spoke with George and Angela, then waited for the group to quiet. An aisle had been created down the center, allowing anyone who wished to speak to make their way to the podium. Vero scanned the crowd, acknowledging the silent greetings of extended family, neighbors, friends, and business acquaintances. She paused when she spotted Frank Holder sitting directly behind the family seats. A woman in a conservative brown suit sat beside him, her sparrow eyes canvassing the room. Before Vero could inquire about the woman's identity, her mother waved her to sit.

Following formal prayers, a homily, and a spate of personal anecdotes about Verna Simon, the minister ended the service. George Simon encouraged the crowd to find refreshments and celebrate the beauty of his mother's life. Tears gave way to pockets of laughter, memories of Nana Verna's life escaping in bursts. Vero wandered the crowd, following Frank and his companion as they circled the room. Each time she thought to approach him, someone grabbed her hand or gathered her into an embrace. By the time she worked her way through the mourners, Holder and the woman were nowhere to be found. Thirsty and defeated, Vero helped herself to a bottled water and eased into a chair in the corner. She leaned her head against the wall, closing her eyes against the sunlight ricocheting off the tinted windows, and allowed a warm reminder of Thursday night to trickle into her mind.

"Veronica." Sonny's demanding tone intruded. Vero blinked. Both her brothers loomed over her. Dave held his envelope like a blade. "Let's go somewhere quiet and talk."

She carried her empty bottle to the trash, determined to be as brave and bold as her grandmother believed her to be. "Sure. Go get mom and dad."

Dave's hand shook. Sonny pushed the envelope down. "Not here, bro, and Mom and Dad don't need to join us. It's up to us to decide."

"You opened your letter, too? Why am I not surprised?" Vero grabbed her coat from the hall and led the way out. They exited through the back of the building. Only a few cars remained. The caterers were loading leftovers to donate to a nearby nursing home. Vero stepped aside but refused to go farther than the bench in front of a planting of dormant rose bushes.

"I guess you didn't have to open your letter to know what it says." Dave's attack was predictable, but she still flinched. "You always were Nana's favorite."

Sonny placed a hand on his brother's arm. "Easy, Dave. The thing is, Veronica, with your health issues, the store is a constant stress, and the financial picture looks bleak. Selling the lake house offers all of us security for the future."

"My health," Vero hugged herself to keep from lashing out physically, "is fine, thanks, and none of your business, and I'm working on the money issues."

"Yeah, well, if you're determined to keep the shop, selling to that developer would provide more than enough capital to stay in business."

Sonny acting like it was in her best interests pissed her off. "What's the matter, big brother? Didn't our grandmother leave you enough to cover your gambling debts?" He took a step back. Vero advanced. "You think I don't know why you've been working so many extra shifts? Saugatuck's a small town with a big appetite for gossip. When it's two a.m. and the only sound is the rattling gasp of a dying patient, the nurses at the Hospice Center talk to relieve the tension. But you wouldn't know that, would you? How many times did you visit Nana Verna these past few weeks?"

"That's cold, Vero," Dave said. She rounded to face him.

"Is it? You're no better, D. What have you been up to that has you acquiring an expensive car and making plans to expand your body shop? Did you make promises to get a loan, ones dependent on convincing your baby sister she was too weak and too stupid to succeed at the one thing she loves?" Tears threatened. She shook them off. Scrabbling in her purse for her letter from Nana, she jerked it free, broke the seal, and unfolded a single, hand-written page. She scanned the contents, then re-read the words her grandmother had sent to her. "Nana believed in me, even if you don't. She left the store and the lake house to me. You both got enough to dig yourself out of debt but not enough to play with."

"Boys?" Angela Simon burst through the back door, skirted the caterers, and headed toward them. "Veronica Grace Simon. You all should be ashamed for arguing at your grandmother's wake."

Sonny intercepted his mother. "We're just having a discussion, Mom. No need to worry. We're working things out, right?" He glared at Vero. She glared back, tightening her grip on the letter, her thumb resting on the final line of her grandmother's note. *Play the hiding game, Vero. Play it soon.*

Cal

The last of the maple leaves scattered across the balcony, the wind piling them into a heap against the outside wall. Cal yawned, stretched, unfolded his long body from the recliner where he'd spent the night. Aside from a brief text to make sure Veronica was safely ensconced at the lake house, he had refrained from calling. God knows he wanted to. More than hearing her voice, he wanted her in his bed, naked and warm and aroused. He admitted his desire was physical, that lust was a factor, but something deeper tugged at him, a sense of rightness every time she was near. Veronica Simon, puzzled, excited, amused, and flushed from sex, moved him. He flung off the comforter and ran a hand down Amigo's back. "You like her, too, don't you, boy?"

The dog pawed at Cal's bare feet, then rolled over, inviting a belly rub. Choco looked at him, stretched, farted, and clicked her way into the kitchen. Cal indulged the male lab in an extended pet, then rose to prepare for the day's appointments. His father's request, aided by Bergeron's not-so-veiled threat of blackmail unless he persuaded Vero to sell her land weighed on him. He understood how much the family legacy meant to her. Her brothers and parents might not care as much as she did, but if the lake house belonged to her, they wouldn't have a say in its disposition. Still, if his father was correct, the Castro family future was tied to a successful acquisition of the land. As if that wasn't enough to bring on a headache, the Barkley woman's interest in the ring confounded him. He recalled how her eyes lit up at the mention of it. He wondered how long before the police would release it to him, although what he'd do with it remained a mystery. Most surprising was the fact that Lisa Protus had it. Did she attack Brad? Not likely. Did the person who stole it give it to her? Probably, but how did they even know that Cal had purchased it or that he'd given it to Brad. Thinking of his driver reminded him that he hadn't checked on the man's progress for days. Moving that to the top of his to-do list, Cal filled the dogs' food and water bowls, wrote a check to the pet sitter, then went to dress.

Empty of visitors at this early hour, the hospital atrium dozed in the gloomy autumnal light. The gift shop already displayed Thanksgiving arrangements amid the falling leaves and chrysanthemum garlands decorating the corners. Cal paused to peer at the flowers and made a mental note to send some to Verónica, then headed to Brad's room.

A nurse exited at his approach, paused in mid-step as if to say something, then shook her head. "Mr. Hanson will be discharged shortly. Have you come to take him home?"

"Sure." Cal scooted around the woman and pushed into the room. Brad dangled his legs over the edge of the bed, a sock in one hand and a harried look on his face. When he realized he was not alone, he flopped back against the pillows. "Hey, buddy," Cal said, "were you planning to escape without telling me?"

Brad struggled to sit up. "I didn't want to cause any more trouble."

"Who's coming to get you?"

Brad avoided Cal's eyes. "I called an Uber."

"Cancel it. I'm taking you home. Here, let me help." Cal took the sock and eased it over the man's foot. He grabbed the other one to do the same, then balanced Brad's weight against his shoulder as the man finished dressing, chattering about the weather and office politics until Brad was ready. "Have you signed your discharge papers?"

Brad waved a hand at documents on the tray table. "Done."

"Sit, Brad. They won't let you walk out, so while we're waiting for a wheelchair, can I ask you something?"

The driver worried the zipper on his jacket. "I don't know who hit me, and I don't know where your ring is, boss. I feel bad about losing it."

Cal waved off the apology. "I need to know one thing, Brad, and it's crucial to figuring out who did this to you. Who besides me knew you had that ring?"

A cart rattled down the corridor. Voices murmured as they passed the open door. Cal crouched in front of his employee and friend, rested a hand on the man's knee.

"I've tried to remember what happened, but everything's foggy." The man looked everywhere but at Cal, rubbing his hands over his thighs.

"All right. Don't work yourself up over this. We'll figure it out." Cal moved to the locker to retrieve Brad's personal items. As he swung the bag, it clunked against the wall, revealing something heavy in the bottom of the bag. Cal reached in and pulled out a cell phone. "Can I look at this?"

"Sure," Brad said, but he didn't look sure. He looked scared.

"What's your passcode?"

Brad rattled off numbers, and Cal entered them. The home screen popped up. He pressed the phone icon to bring up recent calls. The last six days offered a long list from people Cal didn't know. He showed the screen to Brad. "These your friends?"

"Mostly." The driver wrung his hands. "Not all of them."

Cal scrutinized the numbers, noting the ones that had no caller ID associated with them. He took out his phone to enter the unknown numbers, then returned to scrolling the list. He had reached last Friday when he found a call at 8:43 p.m., the night of Brad's attack. He checked twice to reassure himself that he wasn't seeing things. The digits didn't change. The person who called Brad Hanson a half hour before he was attacked was Lisa Protus.

Depositing Brad at his apartment with instructions to call if the man needed anything, Cal stopped at *Back to the Fuschia* on Butler Street and ordered a sympathy bouquet sent to Vero at SIMON's with a note expressing his hope that the celebration of life went well. Then he hurried to the office. The afternoon brought no relief from worrying. After work, he had intended to go straight to the condo, but instead turned toward Culver. *I just want to see if she's all right,* he told himself. When he reached the Corner Café, he noticed movement across from SIMON's. A man and a woman stood at the edge of the parking lot. The woman raised a briefcase and swung it in the direction of the jewelry store. The man grabbed her arm and jerked it down. A car honked behind Cal, alerting the combatants, who looked his way. He ducked his head and turned the corner but not before he recognized the stony faces staring in his direction. Frank Holder and Elgin Barkley. Why were they together, engaged in an angry encounter, in the parking lot across from Verónica's store? Worries stacked up like cordwood.

Cal raced toward the alley and pulled to a stop along the curb. He checked his watch. An hour until closing, and the lights were still on. Should he check on Vero or give her space? His head said she didn't need him hovering. His heart begged to differ. What a cliché he had become. Didn't matter. Verónica Simon had wriggled her way past his defenses, damn her. Maybe she wasn't even there. He let the car idle as he pondered the choices. His phone rang. Norsuch.

"Detective? What is it now?"

"Did you drive Brad Hanson home from the hospital this morning?"

"I did. Is there a problem?"

"You tell me." Norsuch paused for effect. Cal rubbed his jaw. "Someone attacked him in his apartment. The man is dead."

Cal turned off the engine. "That's not possible. I left him alive an hour ago."

"Well, he's dead now. Thing is you're the last person to see him alive, so I have to ask you to come into the station."

"Now?"

"Now, unless you want us to bring you in."

"No, I'll see you in thirty." Cal bent over the steering wheel, inhaled sharply, and cursed the son of a bitch trying to ruin his life. A vibration in his pocket startled him. He looked at the phone in his hand. His phone. Then he realized he still had Brad's, the one with the call from Lisa the night of the first attack, the night Gisele Townsend turned up missing.

Vero

Vero loved to watch the light linger over the lake, loved how the thin bands of rose and violet stretched ribbon-like over the calm water. She stood by the window, looking past the lawn to the dock. The thumbnail of beach beckoned, reminding her of childhood days spent digging for treasure or making sandcastles. She rested her head against the glass, folded her arms around her waist, and allowed the day to settle over her. No matter how hard her brothers pushed, she would not be moved. The house belonged to her now, and she was staying.

Her phone chimed. She read her mother's invitation to come for dinner and stay the night. She declined. Grabbing a fleece throw from those stored in a cedar box beside the couch, she let herself out and walked to the beach. All the summer visitors had departed. The winter snowmobilers wouldn't arrive until after Thanksgiving. Goshorn was quiet, except for the occasional call of a dove or the distant rumble of traffic beyond the dunes. Nana Verna's letter crinkled in her pocket, a reminder of the final instruction from her. The hiding game. How had she forgotten the tradition, the almost sacred requirement to write a clue, then hide an object somewhere in the cabin? Sonny and Dave had never been very good at either part, but she and Nana had excelled at the activity, passed down from one generation to the next since the original house was built. Over the years, several items had never been found. If one year passed without discovery, another family member would be charged with starting a new round. How many summers had she and her grandmother spent trying to best each other? Kicking at pebbles, Vero recalled the year, her fourteenth, when Nana Verna had picked her up from school on a Friday in late May and driven out to the lake. Satisfied that they were alone, Nana unwrapped a small box and shook the contents until they rattled.

"You and I are going to play a special hiding game, just the two of us."

"Not Sonny and Dave or Mom and Dad?"

"Not this time. We'll hide something else for them. Now, pay attention. These are very special stones, Vero." She opened the box and poured ten gems into Vero's cupped palm. "If you find them before summer ends, you can use them in your jewelry making."

"Nana!" Enchanted by the way the stones caught the light, Vero reached for the box. "Where did you get them?"

Nana's eyes sparkled. "Let's just say finding gems is another old family tradition. One day I'll tell you all about it, but for now, this will be our secret. Now go down to the beach and stay there until I call, and no cheating!"

When her grandmother waved her in, Vero had searched everywhere, unable to find the hiding place. Then she'd started her freshmen year in high school and that special game had faded from her memory. Until now. Out on the lake, a goose honked, a straggler resting before continuing the journey south. She wanted to honk back, to say she understood its lonely flight, the perils in going forward when instinct warred against reason. She searched for a skipping stone and spun it out over the water, counting the bounces before it sank. When the ripples ceased, she turned west, scuffing along the narrow path that wound along the shore toward the spot where Lisa Protus had been found. Goosebumps rippled down her back. Had she made the right decision moving so far from town? Vero didn't think of herself as a foolish person, but the fact that a woman had been found dead at the edge of the property raised a huge red flag. A scrap of caution tape from the investigation rattled in the wind. Vero squinted into the growing darkness, wondering what the woman had been doing out here.

Headlights wavered down the lane. She shielded her eyes from the glare, stepped out of sight, and jogged back to the porch. Had she locked the front door? She scurried inside, pushed the bolt into place, and lifted the poker from the basket beside the fireplace. Footsteps crunched over the gravel. A fist pounded on the door. Vero's heartbeat ratcheted up faster than on any treadmill run. Thank goodness she hadn't turned on any lights.

"Vero?" Sonny called in stern, big-brother mode. "I know you're in there. We need to talk."

Propping the poker against the wall, Vero flipped the switch for the outside lights. Her brother's face popped into view, hair mussed, shirt and tie askew. He rested his hands on his hips and scowled into the half-moon of glass that decorated the door. She unlatched the lock and stepped aside. He strode in, wiping his face with his sleeve.

"Do we really need to do this now?" She stayed where she was instead of following him into the great room. He turned on a lamp before returning to tug her with him.

"Sit, Ironica." He shoved her into a leather armchair, then sat opposite her. "I know this is a difficult time, but you need to listen. Dave and I, we need your help. If you don't sell this land, I—" he wiped a hand over his face, "I'm going to lose my practice, and Dave, he'll lose his business, too."

"How is that possible, Sonny? Did you really gamble away all your assets?"

"It's not what you think. Dave's the gambler, not me. I lent him money, yes, but I invested mine."

"In what?"

"Bergeron's development scheme. If his plans for the properties out here fall through, I'll have to declare bankruptcy."

"I don't understand. How did you get involved with this land thing?"

Sonny dropped his head into his hands. "I met him during my residency in Chicago. He was a big donor to the hospital, and we connected. The development scheme was my idea. All of it. The Scottish. Goshorn. I told him he could make a killing in our community. And we will, if the deal goes through."

"And if it doesn't?'

Her brother looked up, his eyes shiny with unshed tears. "Something bad might happen, just like it did to Lisa Protus."

Stunned, Vero gripped the arms of the chair. She swallowed hard, licked her lips, and glanced at the alarm keypad, wishing she had armed the system after Sonny arrived. She sprang up, punched in the codes, waited until the light changed from green to red. "What do you know about Lisa's death?"

"Don't look at me like that." Her brother threw up his hands and scowled. "I didn't know her, but Dave did. I guess they dated a few times."

"They did?"

"Don't act like you don't know about our brother's wild side, V. He hangs with a rougher crowd. Always has."

Vero struggled to stitch the pieces of this patchwork quilt into place. Lisa Protus had the ring Cal bought. Lisa Protus worked for the Castro family. She had access to all kinds of information, including the possible acquisition of lake properties. Could she have been out here scouting with a potential buyer when things went wrong? Vero combed her fingers through her hair. All this speculation made her crazy, and Sonny's obvious discomfort didn't help. "What else haven't you told me?"

He rose to lean against the mantel, forehead braced in one hand. "Nana knew."

"Knew what?"

"About my financial difficulties. About Dave's gambling. About our parent's plan to retire south. She told me in the letter."

"Mom and Dad are moving from Saugatuck?"

"You didn't know?" He scrubbed at his chin. "I suppose they didn't want to upset you. Hell, maybe they thought you'd go, too. Nana encouraged them to buy a place in Florida. She even left them the money to complete the purchase."

"I can't even think about that. And I can't believe our grandmother left you without resources. Nana cared about all of us."

"That's the thing." He paced to the window to stare into the night. "I can have the money I need, but only if I agree not to make you sell the land or the shop."

Vero snorted. "Sounds like a solution to me. Thank you, Nana."

"You just don't get it, do you?" When she frowned, he gripped her shoulders. "I already promised Bergeron. If you don't sell, I'm a dead man."

Cal

A delivery van was parked behind the music store, blocking the exit from the alley. Cal checked his surroundings and reversed direction to park on the next street over. Skirting the truck, he walked only far enough to ascertain that Vero's car was not in its usual spot, then returned to his vehicle. Brad's phone buzzed again. He circled the block a third time. Barkley and Holder no longer stood arguing across from the shop. Cal tapped his driver's phone. The screen lit up immediately. He entered the passcode, navigated to the most recent call, and recognized the number immediately. Cerise Townsend. Cal thumbed the call button, then reconsidered. Why was Gisele's sister contacting Brad? He scrolled through the calls back to that last Friday night, startled to see that Gisele had indeed called while Cal was in SIMON's and again an hour later, which fit with Brad's fuzzy recollections of the night he was attacked. Her second call was followed by another from the Townsend Realty Office. A new puzzle, one which the detectives would be eager to explore, because there was no way he could hide Brad's phone from them. All he needed was one more weird coincidence and he'd find himself in a jail cell. He scanned through the list one more time, frowning at how many calls Brad received the night of Gigi's disappearance. Disturbed by this new puzzle, Cal headed for the meeting with Norsuch and Harry.

Traffic along the Blue Star stalled behind a semi pulling an oversized load of roof trusses. Before Cal reached the station, his personal phone chimed twenty times. He fielded several inquiries from buyers, soothed an anxious seller about the low number of showings, and spoke with Amy, the realtor who had taken Lisa's place. He parked in a visitor slot and was about to open the door when his father called.

"Papá, I'm late for a meeting."

"With whom, *mijo*?"

"The detectives investigating Gisele's disappearance."

"Calderón, this borders on harassment, and it has to stop. I'm going to call Canard."

"No, Papi, I have to do this. Brad is dead. Someone attacked him in his home."

"*No me digas...hijo de puta.*" Antonio hesitated, swore again, and went on. "That's horrible, but why do they need to speak with you?"

"Because I was the last person to see him before he died."

The silence stretched out until his father groaned. "I cannot believe this is happening. I'm contacting Glenn now. He is an expert at figuring out ways to protect this family. Do not talk to anyone until he arrives."

Cal pushed into the lobby. "I'm not afraid. I will tell them what I know, which is very little. I'll contact you when we're finished."

Over his father's protests, Cal ended the call. The duty officer greeted him by name, the significance of which did not escape him. He waited only a minute before Duane Harry came out. The detective merely nodded before leading him to the interrogation room they'd used before. Once inside, Cal placed Brad's phone on the table. Norsuch rose from his chair. Cal waved him down.

"One. I did not harm Brad Hanson. He was my employee and my friend. Two. I found his phone when I picked him up at the hospital. When I drove him home, I inadvertently stuck it in my pocket." He pointed at the cell. "That's his and, no, I haven't erased anything, but I did check his recent calls. They are disturbing. Three, someone is trying very hard to implicate me in all these crimes, and I'm sick of being the bad guy here. So, please, get your shit together, find Gisele, and find out who killed Brad."

Norsuch gestured for Cal to sit. "You finished? Cause if you are, we know you didn't kill your driver. His building has excellent video surveillance, which shows you leaving before Hanson goes downstairs for his mail, admits someone into the lobby, and returns to his apartment accompanied by the person he buzzed in."

Cal dropped his head in his hands. "This is a nightmare, and I'm worried that more people are in danger."

"Why do you say that?" Harry propped a foot on a chair and crossed his arms.

"There are calls on Brad's phone from Lisa Protus and from Townsend's realty office the night Gisele went missing, plus others from numbers I don't recognize. Brad always said he hated the twins, didn't know what I saw in Gisele, claimed when he had enough money saved, he was leaving Saugatuck for someplace warm and more laid back. So, why was he talking to either of them?"

Norsuch picked up the cell and scrolled through the numbers. "Looks like someone called him this afternoon, more than once. You answer?"

"No way. I'm trying to get out of trouble, Detective, not invite more in."

"Okay." Harry returned to the table to record the interview. "Tell us what you can about the morning with Hanson."

Cal recounted his actions from the moment he arrived at the hospital until he left Brad's apartment. He offered them his phone so they could check his calls and the times he'd made and received them. "He was acting nervous, not like himself."

"What does that mean?" Harry said.

"I think he knew something and was afraid to tell me what it was."

"Anything else?" After he copied the remaining details, Norsuch indicated Cal could leave. The door banged open. Glenn Canard rushed in, sweat marks under the arms of his sweatshirt. "My client has nothing to say," he sputtered.

Harry smirked. "Too late, counselor. Mr. Castro has spilled his guts, and he is free to go, for now." Dick Norsuch shouldered his way past Canard. Harry patted the man's shoulder as he strolled out. Cal laid an arm over the flustered lawyer's shoulders and steered him toward the exit.

"I told my father not to bother you, Glenn, but thank you for coming."

Glenn shuddered at Cal's tone. "You may not feel that way when I give you this." He pulled a business envelope from his back pocket.

"What is it?"

"The Townsends are suing you for the wrongful death of their daughter."

"But she isn't dead, not officially."

"Then you better hope the police find her soon. They may not win this suit, but they can drag it out long enough to destroy everything you and your family have built in Saugatuck."

Vero

Embers from the last log glimmered behind the grate. Vero pulled her knees to her chin, wrapped the blanket more tightly, and considered the dilemma Sonny had presented her. She should have known her brothers would complicate everything now that Nana Verna was gone. Of the three of them, she alone cared about the history of their family, the legacy, but it seemed like there was a lot she didn't know. Her father's revelation about Great-grandfather Simon and Jacob Holder had jarred her, and the photographs on the displays at the funeral reminded her of the photo albums stored in Nana's bedroom, where the lighting was dim. Fishing a flashlight from the junk drawer, she wandered down the hall to Nan's sanctuary. That's what she called it, her safe place. Maybe Vero would move into the room one day, but not yet. She glanced into her own bedroom, looked at the pictures of her and Nana fishing and her first clumsy attempts at jewelry making. Her grandmother had been so patient with her mistakes. Head bowed, heart aching, Vero stepped into the biggest bedroom in the house with the best view of the lake.

Standing by the window, she admired the slope of lawn and the sweep of water beyond the dock. Tonight, the moon was a sickle low in the after-midnight sky. The clouds that had plagued the day were gone, leaving the horizon aglitter with stars. Vero gazed west, tantalized by a fantasy of Cal Castro beside her, arms around her waist, breath tickling her ear. She felt safe with him, stronger and more confident, because he saw her that way. If only Nana were here to help sort through the tangled emotions the man caused every time she thought of him. She shrugged, set the flash on the bed, the beam directed at the storage chest, and released the dowel clasp. She propped the lid and inhaled the rich cedar smell emanating from the interior. The albums were wrapped in towels and arranged in chronological order dating back to the original years of the cabin. *Play the hiding game,* Nana Verna had urged. This is where it began.

It took longer than Vero thought to page through the relics of a hundred years of Simon family history. She started with the photos of summer campouts and her brothers' fishing. Beneath the last album, she spotted a rectangular wooden box, too small to contain a photo album. She ran her fingers over the cover, then yawned so fiercely her jaw cracked. Exhausted in spirit and body, she decided to postpone this trip down Simon memory lane until morning. Closing the chest, she reset the catch and tucked the box under her arm. Flashlight in hand, she returned to her room, pursued by flashbacks of her childhood at the lake.

Outside, the wind picked up, rustling the shutters and tossing the branches of the pines against the house. Vero had set the alarm after she convinced Sonny to leave. He had insisted she shouldn't be alone, but the lake itself didn't frighten her. It was everything else that set her on edge – the murder of Lisa Protus, Gisele's vanishing, the mysterious reappearance of the ring, the insertion of Cal Castro into her life. Fighting off another yawn, she smoored the ashes, set the fire screen, and changed into pjs before tucking the box beneath her mattress. She drifted off, thinking of Cal, then slipped deep into REM sleep, unaware that the system keypad recorded a front door tamper at 2:35 a.m.

Cal

The waning light cast deep shadows over the park as Cal walked the dogs to the end of the path. Amigo and Choco stood patiently while he unsnarled their leashes and unsnapped the collars. Finally free, the labs bounded toward the shoreline, paws kicking up sand as they nipped the foam at the water's edge. Cal zipped his jacket, shoved his hands in his pockets, and followed the dogs toward the chain ferry. How had his life gotten so fucked up? Back in the condo, the letter informing the Castro family of the Townsend lawsuit lay face down on the kitchen table. The call he'd placed to his father remained unanswered, although Cal was certain Glenn had informed the senior Castro of this recent turn in their fortunes. Securing the land at Goshorn for Bergeron seemed the only way forward. It wouldn't resolve Gisele's kidnapping, but it would provide a financial cushion to pay the mountain of looming legal bills. Which meant tomorrow he had to persuade Veronica to sell the property she loved. The wind whipped his hair over his face. He brushed it back, only to have a new gust rearrange it again. He couldn't do it, couldn't ask the woman he cared about to sacrifice her family heritage to save his own.

Amigo returned to sniff his jeans and raced away again in pursuit of driftwood near the waterline, while Choco nosed at trash along the beach. Cal kicked at clumps of sand. If only Gisele would surface. Dead or alive, preferably alive, and willing to explain what happened. Maybe she was as crazy as that character in the Gillian Flynn novel he'd read years ago, a woman who faked her own disappearance to screw over her husband. But he wasn't married to Gisele. They weren't even officially engaged, and now that he'd met Veronica Simon, Cal knew he'd never be happy with Gigi. He also questioned his commitment to real estate. True, he'd acquiesced to his father's demand seven years ago, but Cal's heart didn't beat for selling houses. What made him happy was coaxing melodies from his vintage Fender. His fingers twitched. He missed playing. He'd had so little opportunity to practice over the past week.

Cal picked up a stick and tossed it to Amigo, thinking about the gigs he'd agreed to play over the next two months. Keeping his musical efforts a secret had always been tricky, but Gisele never cared how many times he claimed to visit an out-of-town client. She always had her own thing going. Girls' nights out. Chamber of commerce outings. Meetings with the Rotary or the VFW. Maybe she'd been seeing other men. Cal didn't care. He only worried about disappointing his parents, but no one who frequented the bars where he played was likely to know his background or care who he was, especially since he used only his middle name when he performed.

Amigo, panting and ready for a treat, flopped down beside an abandoned sand pail. Cal pulled a biscuit from his pocket, then crouched to rub the dog's belly. The toe of his sneaker pried up a plastic shovel buried in the sand. Cal rescued the discarded toys, whistled for Choco, and he and the dogs headed back to the condo. He stopped by a recycle bin to deposit the trash and, hands in pockets, continued brooding. Amigo's low growl brought him back to the moment. From the shadow of the nearest building, a figure stepped out to block the path. The angle of the hood he wore made it impossible to see a face, but something about the slope of the shoulders looked familiar. Cal wound the leashes around his hand. Amigo growled again. Choco, whimpering, cowered behind him.

"Stay," Cal cautioned. The figure withdrew a hand from a pocket of the hoodie, the bracelet he wore catching a stray beam from the streetlight. Cal let out the breath he was holding. "Gisele."

"Hello, Cal. Miss me?"

"Like a sore tooth. Where have you been?"

Gisele laughed. "Here I thought you'd be pining away like a lost puppy. Hello, Amigo. Choco." She reached toward the male lab, who backed away, growling.

"Now that you're here, you can come with me to the police and clear the suspicions hanging over my head."

Gisele shook a finger. "Uh-uh. The play isn't over yet."

"What play is that, Gisele? Because I don't much care for the first act." He fumbled for his phone. She hissed at him.

"No, no, Cal. No audio. No video. Just you and me and my assistant." She gestured toward a car with tinted windows parked twenty yards away. Cal didn't recognize the vehicle. Gisele paced the grass. "Here's what's going to happen. You're going to deliver one million dollars in unmarked bills to the Mt. Baldy lookout that stupid pretender tried to co-opt two days ago. Of course, I know about that. I know everything, including the name of your new lover. Do you really think I'm going to let you go that easily? You will pay the fee, I'll return a little worse for wear but eager to resume my place at your side, and you will give me that goddamned ring you bought from Veronica Simon that clueless Brad showed Lisa, who stole it from him and tried to parlay it into a higher payout."

Brad? Lisa? A larger conspiracy or just more looney tunes from Gigi? Cal wondered if the crazy in her voice had always been there, or if this new, unhinged version was a product of the past week's chaos. He shrugged, stepping back to rest a hand on Amigo's head. "I can't do that, Gisele. The police have the ring, and they're not giving it back until they solve the murders of Lisa Protus and Brad Hanson."

"Wait." Gisele lifted a finger to her lips. "Lisa's dead? Brad's dead?"

"I thought you knew everything. How have two murders slipped your mind?"

"He didn't say—" She stopped herself. "Never mind. Get the money by Monday. I'm tired of waiting."

"I'll tell them about you."

Gisele laughed again. "And who will believe you? Look around. It's dark as mud out here. No one else is around. The dogs won't talk. You'll sound like a man trying to convince the police of his innocence."

"But when you show up, they'll know I told the truth."

"Will they?" She paused in front of him. "Or will they believe me when I tell them you took me, tied me up, kept me confined because you wanted the land deal for yourself?"

"C'mon, Gigi, this can't be about that damn development contract."

"You're right, Cal." She moved closer, poked his chest. "It's about you and me and the merger of our families and our fortunes."

"I don't want that. I never did."

"Oh, but you will. Or I can tell them about your mother's illegal immigrant status. And that," she poked him a final time, then backed away, glancing at Amigo as the dog continued to growl, "is why you're going to pay. I hold the winning hand here, Calderón. Once upon a time, I needed you to want me. Now all I need is your money. I found someone else to give me love."

Cal reached for her. She hopped back and broke into a run toward the idling car, which peeled away as soon as she climbed in.

Vero

Mist curled above the water, obscuring Vero's view of the spit of land where the Corbin cottage once stood. Looking toward the ruins of the burned home, Vero tried to imagine a multilevel resort in place of the legacy structures so many Michigan families had treasured for years. None had stood here as long as the Simon house.

She removed the tea bag from her mug to sip at the heady chai concoction Shea had gifted her on her last birthday. Today she would confront her parents and brothers about their desire to sell the land. Perhaps her decision would rupture the family unit for good, but she refused to be frightened or bullied into giving away their heritage. She glanced at the albums she had carried in from Nana Verna's bedroom this morning. The mystery box remained tucked into the deep pocket of the wool sweater she wore to ward off the chill. Time to turn up the heat. First, though, she should turn off the alarm.

Her bare feet made small slapping sounds on the wood as she crossed from the great room to the entrance alcove where the keypad resided. A red dot at the top right of the screen blinked. Vero frowned, entered the code, then swiped left to read the message on the screen. Front door tamper 2:35 a.m. Startled, she stared at the message, then rearmed the system. She lifted the curtain covering the window in the door and peered outside. Tendrils of fog danced lazy circles along the gravel drive. A doe stepped clear of the trees, ears flicking, and picked its way over the lawn. Two more soon followed. In the canopy of tall pines, a crow called to its mates. Vero scooted from window to window, squinting into shadows, anger overtaking the initial rush of fear. She rescued her phone from where it had fallen under the sofa and dialed Sonny's number.

"Veronica?"

She gave him no chance to speak further. "Did you come back here last night, Sonny?"

"No, but I wish I'd stayed with you. I've been worried—"

She cut him off with a curt thanks and dialed Dave. When he answered, she wasted no time confronting him. "Dave? Did you come by the lake house last night?"

"Why would I? Sonny said you refuse to consider selling the property, so I have no reason to talk to you."

"Don't go all ballistic on me." She wedged herself into a corner, her back protected by two walls. The fireplace poker dangled from one hand.

Dave exhaled heavily. "Look, despite your medical issues, you've always done exactly what you wanted to do, and Mom and Dad let you, but this decision, it affects all of us."

Disturbed by the defeat in his voice, Vero sank to the floor. "I don't want to hurt you, Dave, but this is our family's home. We can't let some out-of-town developer destroy what we've worked so hard to protect. Think, brother. Don't you have any good memories of being here?"

"Of course, I do." She listened to the scrape of chair legs as her brother sat down. "I don't want to let it go, either, but everyone says it's the best way to solve our financial problems."

"I didn't realize you had financial problems until Sonny told me. Why did you let things get so bad? And who's everyone? I mean, Nana left you and Sonny a sizeable inheritance."

"Yeah, she did, and it's all spoken for."

"Who do you owe money to, Dave?"

Her brother didn't speak for a minute. When he did, anger replaced his remorse and sadness. "Never mind that. Just think about what Sonny told you and try doing what's best for the family."

"I always do," Vero said. "Just like Nana taught us, or have you forgotten?" She ended the call. Head on knees, she ran through the possibilities for last night's intruder. Not her brothers. Could Cal have come over? No. He'd call first. Besides, he didn't know the code, did he? Maybe the person left footprints, but Vero didn't feel like going outside to look for them. Poker in hand, she retraced her steps to the master bedroom, checked the closets, and the downstairs storage. Nothing appeared to be missing. Had they come into her bedroom, watched her as she slept? She ought to contact the police, but all she had were speculations. She took out her phone, pulled up Detective Norsuch's number, then slipped the cell back in her pocket. There had been no alarm. Maybe there had been no intruder. Perhaps it was simply a battery glitch.

Leaning the poker next to the stove, she turned on the oven, then sat at the table, the albums spread around her, and set the box before her. The tarnished bronze clasp was locked. Banging her fists in frustration, she snatched a knife and attempted to wedge the top open. No use. Then she remembered the first envelope the funeral director had given her. She rescued her purse from a hook on the wall, unzipped the inner pocket, and retrieved the key she had stashed there. It slid easily into the keyhole but resisted turning. Afraid to break the slender metal key, she took it to the counter, oiled it lightly, and returned to the table. This time, the lock clicked open.

The lid creaked as she bent it back, exposing a four by five scrap of leather on top of yellowed papers. Etched onto the leather was an outline of Goshorn Lake. In the upper left corner, a date: June 1930, followed by the initials JAH. Vero recognized them, but her tired brain refused to recall the name. She lifted out the map. Small squares had been inked around the outline of the lake. She traced the shoreline to the location of the Simon cabin, but she didn't understand what the triangles represented. She set the scrap aside to examine the other items in the box. A paper folded into a tight square. Two black X's on a drawing of the house above the words *The Hiding Game*. How old was this sketch? The handwriting didn't look like Nana's.

The oven timer went off, prodding Vero to take out the cinnamon rolls. Her stomach growled, another reminder of the stress of the past twenty-four hours. Another rummage in the box revealed more trinkets, but she abandoned them to scramble eggs, glad she had stopped at the convenience mart after she left The Scottish for good. Wrapping the sweater more tightly around her, she shuffled through the first of the old photo albums while she ate.

Black and white images of people she didn't know stared up from the mounted photographs. Solemn looks and serious expressions dominated. Dates scribbled in the margins identified most from the late nineteen-twenties and early thirties. There was a photograph of the shop at its ten-year anniversary, the plain white façade bearing a sign reading JEWELERS. Multiple snapshots of weddings and births, followed by pictures of the original cabin followed by those of first one and then a second addition. It wasn't until the nineteen-thirties that she chanced upon a photo labeled Jacob Holder and Mary Carstairs in wedding clothes. The Simons were gathered off to the left, her grandfather Johan scowling at the couple. Vero closed the album and opened one labeled 1940-1950. Another decade of family outings. A cute picture of Nana Verna, veiled in lace and holding her sister's hand as they made their first communion together. More shots of lake outings, canoe rides, and cookouts, and one of Nana holding up a miniature trophy, the words Best printed across the bottom. Best at what?

When Vero started through the albums, the lake was just waking up. Now, bright morning sun angled across the water, gilding the ripples in a golden sheen. She glanced at the clock on the stove. Eight-thirty already. Surprised at how quickly the time had passed, Vero set her dishes in the sink and sighed. Then she sent texts to her parents and brothers, requesting they come to the house for a meeting. She also sent a message to Shea, asking her to work today, unable to leave until she understood the mystery of the wooden box. She fingered the leather illustration of Goshorn Lake. Who had drawn it? Why was it important enough to save? She picked up the square of paper and, mindful of the brittle edges, unfolded it with care. The note contained a second list, older than the first, with a poem titled The Simon Legacy, penned in Edwardian script, but in a firm, more masculine hand than the cabin drawing.

Seek that which is hidden
find that which is lost
take only what's offered
but consider the cost
remember the family's fortune

depends on your clever clue
when you find the treasure
take only what's needed
give back only what's due

This was underlined and separated from four numbered instructions and a new title: *The Hiding Game,* printed in a completely different hand.

Rule one: When it's your turn, hide the map.
Rule two: Craft a clue.
Rule three: The first person to find the map hides it next.
Rule four: One winner each summer
Remember: Real treasure hides/where angels gather/To find it first/makes you a gem

Vero stared at the instructions. Two different games, one leading to some kind of family treasure, the second a whimsical pastime invented by Simon family members. Maybe the games had another purpose? If so, she couldn't find the logic. Perhaps the initial reason had been forgotten or the purpose subverted. She, Sonny, and Dave had played the hiding game all the years they'd been coming to the lake. Nana Verna had explained the rules, but the things they had hidden were nothing like the ones hinted at on the list. Could Frank Holder's tale of stolen jewels contain a kernel of truth in a past that was becoming more convoluted by the moment? She reached for the final document at the bottom of the box when her phone rang. Unidentified caller. Vero answered.

"Miss Simon?" The voice, deep, sensual, and female, oozed at her. "This is Cerise Townsend. I apologize for the early call, but—"

Vero cut the woman off. "I have no reason to speak with you, Miss Townsend, and if you're calling about my family's land, you're wasting your time. Our property is not for sale."

"Oh, I think it is," Cerise said. "Your loan on the jewelry store is due at the end of the month. You need cash, Miss Simon, and I can get that for you."

The woman's arrogance provoked Vero. "How could you possibly know about my personal business?"

"I'm a lawyer, Miss Simon. I have contacts throughout the region."

"Why don't you use them to find your sister and leave me alone?" Vero hung up before Cerise Townsend could rile her further. Fury rolled through her, and embarrassment. Was the bank leaking information, or had the woman found out from one of Vero's brothers or the store employees? No, neither Agatha nor Shea would be that disloyal. Whatever was going on, she couldn't face it wearing flannel pants and an old sweater. Finishing the last of her tea, she hurried to shower, then pulled on leggings and a long-sleeved top. She gathered her hair into a scrunchie and inspected herself in the mirror. The toll of the last week showed in the dark circles beneath her eyes. She tried a smile but failed to sustain it. She had nothing to feel joyful about. Her world was crashing. She had no one in her corner. *You have Cal*, a small voice whispered. She shoved it down. *Toughen up, missy*. Nana Verna's voice sounded louder and clearer than ever here at the lake house. *Play the hiding game, Vero. Play to win.*

She pushed her shoulders back and headed for the fireplace. She removed the basket on the mantel to fish out the clue lying unread within. She remembered Nana writing it over the Labor Day weekend, her cancer diagnosis a mere two weeks away. As she reached for the paper, the doorbell rang. Her hand shook, knocking the basket to the floor. The clue fluttered free and drifted behind the fireplace screen.

"Hello?" Link Storey called. "Veronica? It's me, Link."

Clenching her fists, Vero debated whether to open the door, then relented. She shut off the alarm, undid the bolt, and yanked the handle. "What are you doing here?"

Link shifted a clutch of papers from one hand to the other. "It's true, then? You moved all the way out here just to get away from me?"

The plaintive tone teased a small smile. "You had nothing to offer me, so I took the best option."

"That's not quite accurate, is it, Veronica?" When she ignored his innuendo, he frowned. "Can I come in?"

"What do you want, Link?"

He bulled past her into the great room, looking around as he did so. "Beautiful place. A bit much for one person, huh?"

"Link?"

"All business today? Fine. Here's the deal, Veronica. You need a place close to town, but you can't afford the ones currently available. What if I told you there was a way to buy a place and save the shop?"

Vero threw up her hands. "First Cerise, and now you. How is it that everyone in Saugatuck knows my business?"

Link frowned. "What about Cerise Townsend?"

"She called this morning with an offer to buy my property, and I'll tell you what I told her. I'm not selling. This is Simon land. It's staying in the family. End of discussion. And you haven't answered my question. I didn't submit any forms requesting credit checks, so how do you know about my financial situation?"

Storey ran a hand over the mantel. "Your brother owes me, Vero, big time. There's an easy way out of all our money problems. Think about it. Bergeron wants your land. You let me broker the deal, everyone gets what they need."

"Dave owes you money?"

He tossed the papers on the table. "Read this. It's a more-than-fair offer. One quick signature, and everyone gets what they want."

"And if I don't?"

"Don't go there, Veronica. It's not a pleasant consequence." Link headed to the door. "Another piece of advice, sweetheart. Cerise Townsend is a viper. Stay as far away from her as possible."

"Time for you to leave." Vero practically pushed him out. He turned, gripped her wrist, and dragged her closer.

"This isn't finished. Call me when you realize that. My number's on the top page." He wrapped his other hand around her neck, his thumb resting over the pulse point. "No one's going to help you, and out here, no one will hear you if you scream."

Vero dug her elbow into his ribs and pushed away. "Don't you threaten me."

"I don't threaten, I promise. What'll it be, Veronica. The devil you see? Or the one that arrives unseen in the night?" Storey winked, jumping back as she slammed the door in his face. Then he headed down the path, his loafers crunching over the gravel, menace trailing behind him.

Cal

The realty office buzzed with typical Sunday bustle. Although sales generally slowed in the fall, this year, post-pandemic and with interest rates scheduled to rise, the market was hotter than ever. Cal took a deep breath. His next moves were crucial. Nervous, he waited for his father to get off the phone.

"Calderón." Antonio patted his son's chest. "You need to speak with me?"

Glancing around the busy anteroom, Cal gestured down the hall. "Can we go into your office?" He remained standing while his father settled behind the desk.

"So, you are going to speak to the Simon woman today?"

"I am, Papi, but not about her selling the property."

"Calderón."

Cal lifted a hand. "Hear me out. I have a request to make, a proposition, and an ultimatum. But first, you need to know something. Gisele is alive. She came to me last night with a demand and two threats, one that concerns you and Mamá and one that threatens the firm."

"Close the door, *mijo*." Antonio folded his hands over the desk calendar and waited for his son to begin. An hour later, Cal and his father followed the gravel drive down the lane toward the Simon lake house. Cal accepted the contract from his father and waited for Antonio to join him before stepping onto the porch. Choco and Amigo bounded in circles over the wet grass. Cal knocked three times, each rap louder than the one before. When Vero didn't answer, he paced the length of the porch before trying again.

"Perhaps Miss Simon is not at home."

"She's here, Papá, but she may not want to see me." Just as he said the words, the door creaked open. Vero peeked out. She glanced at the paperwork he carried, noted the briefcase his father held, and shook her head.

"Go away, Cal. I told Cerise and Link the same thing I'm telling you. I'm not selling." She tried to slam the door. Cal inserted his boot, pushed against the wood, and shoved it open. Panicked, Vero turned to run, her hair escaping the band that held it in place to tumble down her back as she raced toward the back of the house. Cal grabbed for her and missed. Handing the contract to his father, he followed her onto the deck that faced the lake. Vero stumbled down the bank to the sandy beach and stopped at the water's edge. Hands on knees, she gasped for air. Cal came up behind her, placed his hands on her shoulders, and turned her to face him.

"Verónica, *querida*, I, we, don't want you to sell your home or the shop. My father has a business proposition for you."

"You...what?" Vero tried to push away. Cal refused to let her go.

"Listen to me, you stubborn, beautiful woman. We understand family, what it means, why it matters. Come back to the house. Let us explain the offer."

Vero narrowed her eyes. Fists clenched, she stared at him. "You're serious?"

"I am, *mi amor*. I believe I have found a way to help us all." He traced his fingers down her cheek, then looked around, noting the isolation of the cabin in relation to the other homes on the lake. "And there's more. But I need you to come inside and listen. You're not safe out here alone, not yet."

Vero dug her toes into the sand, shivered, then strode toward the cabin. "I think someone tried to break in last night."

He caught her elbow, forcing her to stop. "Tell me."

On their way to the porch, she recounted all that had happened since the celebration of life for Nana Verna, including the discovery of the instructions for a game she thought she knew how to play. Once inside, Cal stoked a fire while Vero fetched socks for her cold feet. Antonio Castro busied himself in the kitchen preparing a pot of coffee, then spread the contents of his briefcase on the table next to the photo albums and the mystery box.

"You appear to be visiting your ancestors, Miss Simon." He set three mugs next to the paperwork and settled at the head of the table. "Find anything interesting among these old photos?"

Vero joined him. Cal followed. "Did you know my grandmother, Mr. Castro?"

"Only to exchange pleasantries. Our family has only lived in Saugatuck for a single generation, long enough to establish a business, not long enough to sink deep roots. There is a story there yet to tell, but right now, the focus is on you. I have read a little about this area. Fascinating, the contributions of the Holders and the Simons, no? City records indicate a significant number of artists and artisans came here in the early 1900s. That is when your people, the Simons arrived, I believe. This," he waved a hand around the room, "was built in the 1920s and expanded as the family grew."

"How do you know this?"

"When you buy and sell properties, Miss Simon, you do a great deal of investigating origins." Mr. Castro shrugged. "I'm surprised you're surprised."

"It's Vero or Veronica, please, and I'm not so much surprised as intrigued." She sipped from her mug before confronting him. "However, if you're here to buy my land, the answer is no."

Antonio spread his hands over the papers in front of him. "Hear me out, Miss Simon. First, I need to explain something to you. My son has never been in love with real estate. His heart lies," Mr. Castro turned a keen eye on her, "in another direction. I've worked hard to keep him by my side, but today he informed me he intends to pursue a different path."

Vero turned to look at Cal. "He does?"

Cal nodded. His father sighed. "Yes. I wish I could dissuade him, but it's time Calderón followed his own passion. You, however, seem to know exactly what you want. You have done well to keep the jewelry business going, but you need help or you're going to fail."

"How is it the entire world thinks I'm not competent to succeed?"

"It's not that you're incompetent. If my hunch is correct, your strength lies in creating, not marketing. You need capital and a marketing strategy. That where the Castros come in. We have the money and the expertise to salvage your business."

"What are you saying?"

"If you agree to our proposal, Castro Realty will cover your loan at the bank, and Calderón will manage the marketing for Simon's."

"The jewelry store? But—" Vero wandered to the fire. "What about the house? The land?"

Cal started to speak. His father held up a hand to forestall him. "This developer, Bergeron, he won't stop until he has devoured as much of Saugatuck as he can. But there is a way to tame him. How much land do you own here at Goshorn?"

"Forty acres, but they are not contiguous."

Castro hummed. "And how much land is connected to this cabin?"

"About a third of that. The rest consists of separate parcels around the lake."

"Good." He exchanged a look with his son and held up a finger. "I propose you allow me to negotiate with Mr. Bergeron to sell only the unconnected parcels, with the stipulation that they be developed into single family homesteads, and that your land here," he jabbed a finger at the map from the mystery box, "remains intact and in the hands of the Simon family in perpetuity."

"You can do that?"

Mr. Castro blinked slowly. "The man sees only dollar signs. If he can get half the land, he'll still make a great deal of money, and you can tell all the vultures circling around you to go to hell."

Vero sat down, stunned. "Why would you do that?"

"Look over the paperwork. Sleep on it, if you wish. When you decide this works for you, sign these." Antonio tapped the papers. "As for why, you'll have to ask my son. Now, I'm going back to the office. Call me, *mijo*, when you're ready to come home."

Vero looked at Cal, who checked his watch. "The detectives should be here soon. Send a car for me at three." Cal paused at the thought of someone besides Brad chauffeuring him around. Vero moved to Cal's father and hugged him, startling the man.

"Thank you, Mr. Castro. No need to send a car. I'll drive Cal back to Saugatuck, or someone from my family will. I've already asked them here this afternoon. And, thank you. You've given me much to think about."

Mr. Castro smiled. "It's going to be an interesting gathering, I suspect. You'd better put on more coffee."

Vero and Cal stood in the doorway, watching the senior Castro make his way to the car. When the sound of tires on gravel faded, Vero confronted Cal.

"What's going on?"

"I'll explain everything," Cal said, wrapping his arms around her. "What time is your family meeting?"

"I asked them to be here by two. Before they get here, you have some explaining to do."

"I do, and I will. But first, there's this." He leaned in and pressed his lips to hers.

Vero

Cal's kiss alerted every nerve in Vero's body. She surrendered to his silent command, wanting, needing the contact, the proof that the spark between them burned true. What started as affirmation escalated to a frantic skimming of hands across tender flesh. Cal drew back enough to whisper, "I want you, Verónica."

"Yes." She drew his head down, ran her tongue along the seam of his mouth. "I want you, too. So much it scares me. But not yet here. Not yet now. Can you just hold me, Cal?"

"*Sí, mi amor*, I can, and I will." He walked her to the sofa, bundled her in the quilt, and lay down with her tucked against him. The logs crackled, the fire hissed. Vero sighed into his chest, surrendering to sorrow and uncertainty as his arms tightened, keeping her safe. They slept until one. She woke to the solid press of his chest against her back. A glance at the clock got her moving. She shook Cal until he roused, his sleepy grin enough to make her tremble with longing. Why did this man send her spiraling into thoughts of what might be?

"Cal, get up." She shook his shoulder, allowed her hand to slip over his chest. "My parents. They'll be here soon, and I have to tell you some things."

"Way to kill the moment, Simon," he chuckled, wrestling her down for a kiss. He rubbed her nose with his and sighed. "I'd rather stay right here with you, but I have things to tell you, too. Primarily, Gisele's alive and trying to frame me for her murder. Also, the blackmail threat she used to trap me is as empty as her heart."

"Gisele was blackmailing you? How? Why?"

"The tale is long and winding. It starts with Glenn Canard serving with the Peace Corps in Colombia until the unrest there forced the government to suspend operations. He worked with my grandfather, who was assassinated. Don't ask now. Long story short, my father and the rest of the Castros were in danger. Glenn worked for years through the Friends of Colombia to get my father and the rest of the *familia* sanctuary in the States. Since my parents were not yet married, my mother's journey was more complicated. Anyway, Gisele found out and assumed that my mother was here illegally."

"You didn't know any of this?"

"No. My parents prefer to keep the past in the past. I finally told my father that Gisele was blackmailing me and why. That's when he told me the truth. If I had known about their escape before, Gisele could never have pulled this con."

Vero sat down, her knees shaking at the fear he must have felt for his family. "Tell me." She listened to Cal relate the events of yesterday, including the discovery of the calls on Brad's phone.

"Norsuch and Harry are checking call logs. We should find out who he contacted. I don't understand why Brad would be talking to a woman he repeatedly said he had no use for."

Vero reached for Cal's hand. "Strange bedfellows."

"You think we're strange, *mujer*?" He tickled her with his morning beard. She pushed him off, then rose and headed for the bathroom.

"I think you're perfect, Calderón Castro, perfectly strange and puzzling and inscrutable."

"Inscrutable?" He stood outside the door to the bath as she brushed her teeth. His eyes lingered on her face in the mirror, his expression unreadable. "What do you think is happening here, Vero?"

"I honestly don't know, Cal, and that scares me more than the person who tried to break in last night."

That caught his attention. He asked her to tell him again what happened, then helped her tidy up the cabin. Back in the kitchen, Vero prepared another pot of coffee. Cal moved onto the deck to stare at the water. When she stepped beside him, he gathered her close. "Okay. Here's what we're going to do. First, offer your family the Castro investment plan. It's solid and a good solution. The question is can you live with it?"

Vero sighed. "I think I can. Was that your idea, to split the land?"

When he nodded, she kissed his cheek. Cal growled and nuzzled her ear, then spoke again. "Okay, let's find out what the detectives have planned for the ransom effort tomorrow. Then, when you're ready, we're going to make love."

"We already did that a few days ago."

He settled her closer against him. "And I plan to do it again and again until you tell me to stop."

Vero closed her eyes. "I don't want you to stop."

"I don't plan to." Cal kissed the top of her head. "But first, we're going to solve the damn hiding game. If your grandmother wanted you to play, we'll play."

"I can live with that plan, too," Vero said. "Come see what I found in Nana's cedar chest."

When the doorbell chimed, Cal closed the lid on the box and tucked it under the sofa. Angela Simon entered first, carrying a tray from the Café, followed by Vero's brothers and her dad. Her parents settled at the table. Sonny propped his elbows on the counter, solemn and frowning. Dave paced, hair rumpled and shirt misbuttoned. Vero's father began by addressing the loss of Nana Verna, then quickly turned to the debate about selling the lake properties and the jewelry store. "Veronica, you must know it's the best solution for all concerned."

Arms crossed, frowning, Vero heard him out. When he finished, she exchanged a look with Cal and brought out the paperwork Antonio Castro had left her. "Actually, Dad, it's not the best solution. I'm not closing SIMON's. The shop has been in the family for one hundred years, and since childhood, it's been my dream to run it."

"But, Vero," Dave interrupted, "you have a balloon payment on a loan that's due soon, and you can't meet it."

"I wonder how you know that, Dave, since Nana and I told no one about it. Oh, wait, could it be because you owe money to Lincoln Storey? And he used that fact to threaten me unless I sold the land to him? No," she held up a hand, "you don't have to answer that. The fact is I have an investor who will cover the loan when it comes due at the end of the month. As for the properties here at Goshorn Lake, I have a solution to that problem as well. If you all agree and sign today, we'll allow that developer Bergeron to buy the noncontiguous—"

"The what?" Dave scratched his bed hair.

"The acreage not attached to this plot, but only if he agrees to abandon any designs on the main house and grounds and to certain other conditions regarding the development of each parcel. The family home remains with me now and forever. You're all welcome to visit, but this house is mine, and I get to say who comes here."

"Is that why Cal Castro is here? Did he talk his way into your bed to get your business?" Sonny glared at the realtor.

"My relationship with Cal is none of your concern, Sonny." Vero looked around the table. "Each of you will benefit from these transactions. The shop and the property here will remain in Simon hands, which is what Nana wanted all along."

"But, honey," her mother grasped Vero by the wrist, "you barely know these people. How can you think of going into business with them? And he has a fiancée and has been, um, accused of harming her."

When her mother sputtered to a stop, Vero shook her head. "I know you're only saying these things because you care about me, Mom, but the truth is none of you have ever thought me capable of running my own life. I'm here to tell you you're wrong. I want you on my side, but I don't need your permission. According to the law and Nana's will, the shop and the land belong to me."

In the silence that followed, the coffee pot gurgled. Vero's mother uncovered the pastries and set them next to the cinnamon rolls. Dave and Sonny helped themselves, then wandered into the great room. Her father scrubbed his lips and started toward her when a knock caused them all to look up. Cal reached the door before Vero.

"Detectives." He motioned Norsuch and Harry inside. "You're just in time."

Cal

A stiff breeze accompanied the detectives into the house, stirring the papers on the table. Goosebumps raced up Vero's arms. She gathered up the errant pages and set them aside while her mother bustled to offer drinks. Norsuch declined. Harry helped himself to an apple fritter. After the requisite pleasantries, the older detective glanced around the Simon family and raised his brows.

"We appear to be interrupting a family meeting."

Vero spoke up. "My parents and brothers were just leaving, after they sign some paperwork."

Harry narrowed his gaze on her. "Doing business on a Sunday?"

Vero returned his look with one of her own. "My grandmother just passed, Detective. We have many details to settle regarding her estate. Mom? Dad?"

Her father accepted the pen she offered and signed the document Antonio Castro's lawyer had prepared. "I hope you know what you're doing, daughter."

Shrugging into her coat, her mother hugged Vero. Her father sent one measured glance Cal's way, then headed out. Sonny also signed, thrusting the document toward her without making eye contact. He nodded at the detectives and hurried after his parents. Dave drummed his fingers on the counter, then pocketed his copy of the agreement and edged toward the door.

"I'll think about it," he said, sneering at Cal as he passed in front of the realtor. He scowled at Vero, then turned to Harry. "Hope you find out what happened to Mr. Castro's girlfriend before my sister ends up hurt."

Before Duane Harry could ask what he meant, Vero's brother rushed out, the slam of the door one more sign of his anger. The detective raised his brows even higher. "What's got Dave in such a snit?"

Vero began to tidy up the breakfast remnants. "My brother doesn't appreciate the actions I've taken to preserve my grandmother's legacy. Typical family squabbling. I can make myself scarce while you talk with Cal."

"Not necessary," Norsuch said. "We came here, Miss Simon, because Mr. Castro indicated a desire to include you in our plans to resolve the issue of Miss Townsend's disappearance. Now, we'd like to know why."

Cal spoke up. "Vero has been threatened herself, by whom we don't know. Last night someone broke into the cabin."

"You have proof of that, Miss Simon? Was Mr. Castro with you at the time of the alleged break-in?"

Vero blushed, straightened her shoulders, and prepared to speak. Cal stopped her. "I wasn't here, or we might have caught the intruder. This isn't the first time she's been threatened, you know."

Harry dusted the crumbs from his hands and took out his notebook. "Refresh my memory, Castro."

"Verónica?" Cal said. Vero clenched her fists and took a deep breath, then recounted the story of her near run-down by a mystery car. She told them about the suspicious loiterer across from the shop, and the way Frank Holder showed up, claiming to be a long-lost cousin and demanding a share of an inheritance she knew nothing about. When she finished, she rested her chin on her hands and sighed. "Cal, go over what happened to you last night. Then tell them about Bergeron's demand."

Cal repeated his encounter with Gisele, the threat she issued if he didn't bring the money. Then he explained the warning the developer had issued. Harry pursed his lips as Cal finished his story.

"Sounds convoluted to the max," Harry said. "Let's concentrate on Miss Townsend first, sort the rest as we go."

"I assume Gisele told you not to involve the police," Norsuch said.

"She did."

"So, she warned you against bringing us in. Why did you?" Harry straddled a chair, sipping coffee from a mug bearing a smiley face.

"Because I've realized something these past few days. Gisele Townsend and whoever she's working with have tried to fuck up my life. She wants to destroy everything my family has accomplished, and I want it to stop." Cal looked at Vero. "I care about Miss Simon's safety, and I cared about Lisa Protus and Brad Hanson. I'm sick of being played, and I don't want anyone else to get hurt. Can you please find out who's behind these crimes, and let me, let us, get our lives back?"

Norsuch shuffled his feet, then pulled out a tablet and laid it on the table. "We can try. Here's the plan, Castro."

Cal leaned in to read through the proposed action. It was clear, precise, and dangerous. If Gisele and her accomplice had murdered Lisa and Brad, they wouldn't balk at killing someone else.

"It's risky," Cal said. "If they sense you're with me, they won't hesitate to take me out."

"That's why the team is setting up tonight," Duane Harry said. "And why you're going to carry a weapon."

"I'm not a gun guy, Duane."

The detective shook his head. "You will be tomorrow."

Vero fisted her hands on her hips and glowered at him. "Seems like Cal takes all the risks, and you reap all the rewards, Detective." She grabbed the screen from him, settled in a chair, and pored over each line of the plan. Norsuch wandered around the room, stopping to stare at the quiet lake.

"Castro," he said, without turning, "keep your phone on tonight. Duane and I will call with the final timeline once we've squared it with the SWAT team. Do you understand me? No sudden moves. If Townsend contacts you again you dial us in ASAP. Understand?"

"I hear you, but I'm concerned for Veronica. This place is so remote, and there's already been one attempted break in."

Harry agreed. "But we don't have the manpower to station a cop out here overnight. Any chance the Townsend woman knows where you are?"

"Maybe. She threatened to harm Vero if I didn't comply."

The detectives debated the pros and cons of Cal and Vero staying at the lake house. In the end, Norsuch made the call. The two would remain in place until tomorrow. When the detectives finally said goodbye, Vero drew on boots and a jacket and left the cabin. Cal followed, his tennis shoes dragging at the sand on the beach.

"What's wrong?"

She sighed. "They've already killed twice, Cal. You'll be in danger the entire time."

Cal draped an arm over her shoulders. "Don't fret, *mi amor*. I've already done this once."

"Yeah, well, that guy was a cuckoo bird."

"Have faith, Verónica. Tomorrow, one way or the other, this will all be over."

"Not if we don't figure out that damn hiding game my grandmother cooked up."

"I thought you said it was a family tradition."

"It was. It is. But I'm pretty sure Nana Verna put her own stamp on it, and she was, hands down, the best at the game."

"We'd better get to it, then. I may have plans for you later."

Vero

Vero surveyed the contents of the refrigerator, wrinkled her nose at the choices, and sighed. The pickings were slim indeed. In the freezer, she found a package of frozen fish sticks, a container of homemade applesauce, and two steaks that didn't look like they'd been in there long enough to suffer frostbite.

"We may not have to go to the store," she told Cal, "if you don't mind the Goshorn Lake version of surf and turf." Hunched over the contents of the mystery box, he barely acknowledged her until she tapped his shoulder. "Calderón Castro, are you listening to me?"

"Sorry. I'm trying to figure out this damn list." Picking up the instructions, he read the rules aloud. "*One: When it's your turn, hide the map in the cabin. Two: Write a clue. Three: The person who finds the map must hide it next. Four: only one winner each summer.* This is hardly mysterious."

She jiggled his arm. When he looked up, she pulled out the oldest note from the collection. "This is the important clue. *Real treasure hides/where angels pray/To find it first/makes you a gem.* And there's something else." She handed Cal the oldest journal, then sat back as he read the story of her family's criminal past. When he finished, he set the journal down and scrubbed at his chin.

"So, you think what? That the stolen gems are part of the Simon legacy?"

"I don't know what to think yet, but it looks like my great-great-grandfather was a crook, and Nana Verna knew it."

Cal noticed her hesitation, the shadow of doubt and despair hovering over her. He pulled her onto his lap. "Explain the game again," he said.

Vero leaned into his kiss, then pushed free of his embrace and returned to prepping the dinner. "Every summer, Nana appointed one of us to hide a silver dollar, one supposedly passed down from the original Simon ancestor, somewhere in the cabin. She claimed it required skill, deception, and the ability to craft a clue that would lead the seekers to the coin, but not right away. The intent was to keep us looking all summer."

"But you think there's more to it."

"Nana's final words to me were to play the hiding game. Now, it's not summer, and there's no coin to hide. Dave found the one I hid last summer, but instead of hiding it again, he kept it."

"Not into sharing, huh?"

"Dave's my brother, and I love him, but he's not family oriented. He only cares about himself."

"So, if he didn't hide the coin again, what are you thinking?'

Vero considered his question. "I keep thinking about my grandmother going out of town several times a year to purchase gems for the store, or so she claimed. She never stayed away for long, and she never spent much money. I've kept the books the past five years, so I know. It seemed odd, but whenever I asked, she claimed to have a special travel account. I had no reason to doubt her. Anyway, each time she returned, she brought back a quantity of diamonds and other gems, including rubies like the one in the ring you bought."

"The ring you created."

She glanced at Cal, blushed, and went on. "Frank Holder's story about our twice great-grandfathers got me thinking. What if she never left Saugatuck? What if there are gems hidden somewhere at the lake? That would explain how she returned with them without spending any capital. And there are so many hiding places out here."

"It would validate your suspicions about your ancestor being a thief." Cal flipped through the pages relating the story of the Simon-Holder caper. Was it truth or family myth? "That's a lot of speculating, Vero."

"I know." She looked around the cabin. When the original kitchen was updated, the wall separating it and the great room was removed. Contemporary furniture pieces shared space with antique tables wearing the patina of age, providing multiple places to hide gems.

Cal took the list from her. "The fifth rule isn't like the others. *Real treasure hides/where angels gather/To find it first/makes you a gem.* Have you been searching?"

"Last night I checked every hiding spot my brothers and I ever used. Nothing. But the reference to angels got me thinking about Nana's collection."

"What collection?"

Vero dried her hands and headed toward an armoire in the corner near the fireplace. She pulled the doors wide and rooted through the games, puzzles, and accumulated detritus of Simon cabin days. On the bottom shelf, she located a box bearing the words **Verna's Angels** in black marker. She toted it to the table and, sliding the items from the mystery box to the side, set it down. "My grandmother was not a sentimental person, yet she kept these on the mantel and forbade us to touch them. One year, I must have been three or four, I don't remember, my mother says I dragged a chair over, picked up the tallest statue, and shouted, 'Look, Mommy, angels can fly.' I hurled it into the air. Of course, it crashed and cracked its halo. My dad glued it back together, but Nana decided to put her collection away until I grew older. Thing is, she never did bring them back out."

Vero tugged at the tape sealing the box. It refused to pull free. Cal retrieved a knife from the kitchen to pry the fibers loose until the flap sprang open, revealing the statues nestled inside. "Show me how they were displayed."

Vero arranged the angels as she remembered them. When she had them lined up, she stood back, hands on hips, and frowned. "I can't be sure of their placement, but that's close."

"So, angels gathered, but not all are praying."

"The one I tried to fly isn't, but most of the others are." Vero shuffled the pieces until all the praying angels stood together, while Cal inspected the mantel itself. "I've never seen carvings like these. Did someone in your family make this?"

Vero ran her fingers over the etchings in the wood and stone. "Feels like fingerprints." She fit her fingertips into the indentations and pressed. The end caps creaked, accompanied by a grinding that grew louder, as though the mechanism that powered the devices needed oiling. After a loud click, a drawer slid out from each end of the beam. Vero stood on tiptoe to look inside.

"What is it, Vero?"

"Oh my God, Cal, Frank Holder's claim might be true." Reaching into the left-hand drawer, she drew out a small, velvet bag, the fabric worn from handling. Plopping down, she cradled the bag in her lap, undid the drawstrings, and slipped a hand inside. When she opened her fingers, six large rubies sparkled in her palm. Cal counted the bags in the left drawer, then moved to the right. "There are twenty bags, Vero. If each one holds more gems, there are probably enough to keep your shop going for another hundred years."

Vero returned the rubies to the pouch and set it on the sofa. Rising, she touched the indentations again and the drawers slid back into place. The end caps returned to their original position. "Oh my god, if you didn't know they were there, you'd never find them." She joined Cal, who stood, hands in pockets, gazing into the dying afternoon light. Slipping into his arms, she leaned against him, felt his tension.

"Looks like you don't need the Castros after all."

"I'm afraid that statement isn't quite true, Cal. I don't know how it happened, but you have become a very important person in my life."

His hands tightened on her waist, then relaxed as he stared at the lake. "Hold that thought, *mi amor*, and tell me something. Did you set the alarm?"

Amigo and Choco raced out from the bedroom, barking a warning. Vero looked where Cal pointed. A small boat cut diagonally out from the public beach and headed toward the lake house. As it drew closer, she spotted two figures, one steering, the other clutching a hat to his head as the wind whipped around them. She raced to the alarm pad, punched in the code. Cal quieted the dogs before checking the locks on the doors. Along the far horizon, dark clouds boiled toward them, churning like suds in a washer. "Could we get any unluckier?" Vero muttered as she scurried down the hall to close the shutters in the bedroom.

Cal followed behind, helped her secure the windows, and hurried her back to the great room. "Hide the rubies."

She snatched up the middle cushion, unzipped the cover, and thrust the bag deep into the thick foam padding. Replacing the cushion, she looked around for something to use as a weapon. If she were starting a fire, it made sense she'd be holding a poker. Intent on doing just that, she moved the screen aside and added two logs to the sputtering flames. Cal kept an eye on the approaching visitors.

"I know who's coming," he finally said. He gave a thumbs up to Vero's efforts to build the fire. "Barkley and Holder. I haven't figured out how they're connected to each other, but they're here together." The boat drew up to the Simon dock. Holder jumped out to secure a line, extended a hand to the insurance investigator, and glanced at the sky. They scanned the water and the land to either side of the beach. Argued about something. The insurance investigator turned back to the boat. Holder grabbed Barkley's arm and tugged her behind him toward the house. Meanwhile, the fresh wood caught fire. Vero used a bellows to coax it along as footsteps clomped across the deck. Now that she could see them, Vero recognized the determination in their approach.

"I don't see any weapons," Cal said. "You want to let them in?"

Vero hesitated. "They can see us well enough, so it's no use pretending we aren't here. But keep your phone handy. Norsuch said he was going to call with the specifics of tomorrow's drop. If we need help, he and Harry are the ones to call."

Cal nodded. "Two pit bulls, for sure."

"Walk softly," Vero said, holding up the iron poker, "and carry a big stick. Can you get the alarm?" She whispered the code. After Cal unlocked the system, she opened the door. Frank Simon and Elgin Barkley scurried into the cabin, the wind from the approaching storm pushing at their backs. They stood, uncertain and wary, and looked around. Holder rubbed his hands together, glared at Cal, and walked over to the hearth. Barkley swept her bird eyes from Vero to Cal and back, then shrugged out of her coat.

"Well, isn't this cozy. Tell me, Castro, what are you doing here?"

"Not your concern, is it, Barkley? Although I'd sure as hell like to know why you are." Cal cocked his thumb at Frank. "We know why Holder's here."

Frank looked stricken. "Elgin has every right to be here. She's my wife, and we just want what's coming to us. What my father swore belonged to me."

257

Vero picked up a journal from the stack on the table. "The thing is, Frank, Jacob Holder may be your great-grandfather, and maybe he was adopted by the Simons, but he was never a blood relative. He married a woman named Mary Carstairs and later abandoned her. My grandfather, Stan Holder, was their son. But there is no record of Jacob after he left Saugatuck, and no way of knowing if he had any other children. Unless you have formal records establishing your connection to him, you have no legal right to anything from the Simons."

Frank and Elgin looked at each other. She blinked twice and nodded. Holder extracted a document from the inside pocket of his coat. "My grandfather had an affair with a much younger woman, my grandmother Regina. Although they never married, he did acknowledge my mother as his daughter and made it clear, by the terms of Johan Simon's will, that the Holder branch was entitled to share in the Simon wealth, which all stems from the story of our great-great-grandfathers' crime."

"That's a lot of greats." Vero lowered the poker. "What crime are you talking about?"

"One I have no interest in bringing to light, unless you force me to do so."

"What is it you really want, Holder?" Cal stepped forward. "How much do you want to go away and leave Veronica alone?"

Frank crossed his arms. Before he could speak, Elgin slipped between them. She placed a hand on Cal's chest and shoved him back. "Enough to make our lives comfortable, like yours."

"In case you haven't noticed, Barkley, or whatever the hell your name is, my life isn't exactly smooth sailing at the moment."

"Yeah." She passed a hand over her windblown bob and smiled. "I have a bit of information to sweeten your pot. Miss Simon gives us what we deserve, and you get the name of the person who forged your name on the insurance papers."

"Blackmail, Barkley?" Cal rubbed his chest. Three people trying to force him to do their bidding by threatening to expose secrets. What were the odds? The whole mess was giving him heartburn. "I'm smart enough to know that never goes away."

"Cal." Vero interrupted the staring contest. "We have a few cards of our own to play. Breaking and entering. Menacing. My shop has excellent surveillance cameras, cousin. So does the cabin."

Cal swung around. "What are you talking about, Vero?"

She motioned toward the smoke detectors mounted around the room. "Not all of these are for fire, and the videos feed directly into the monitoring company. I checked this morning. You two are on camera disarming the system, looking around, then darting away when a raccoon showed up in the entryway."

Elgin reached for Frank, and they sank onto the couch, hands linked and looking sheepish. Some wordless communication passed between them. When the woman looked up, she sighed. "It seems we're at an impasse. We all have secrets to reveal, and we all have a reason to keep them hidden. I'll tell you one of ours. We've been trying to have a baby for a long time, and now we are. But, Veronica, we need money. Frank's inheritance will pay our debts for all the fertility treatments and allow us to finally buy a house, even expand Frank's investigation business."

Vero heard desperation in the woman's voice and fear, two volatile emotions that could easily turn dangerous. Cal slipped an arm around her waist. "Vero?" he said. "I've seen that frown before. What are you thinking?"

She patted Choco, who had edged into the gathering to rest her muzzle against Vero's leg. Amigo crouched by Cal, waiting for a signal to advance or retreat. Vero squeezed down on the sofa next to Elgin. "I have a solution, but if you agree, you have to tell what you know about the insurance scheme. You play all your cards. No holding back."

Frank rubbed his neck. "No police?"

"Not for you or us."

Elgin leaned forward. "What do you have in mind?"

Vero held up a finger. "First, Frank agrees to a DNA test, to prove he is who he claims to be. Second, Cal's lawyer draws up an NDA for each of us to curb any impulse to renege on the agreement."

"What is the agreement?" Frank said.

"You need an income stream. I need a working partner to help SIMON's survive. Cal and his father have agreed to provide the capital required to pay off an upcoming loan, and he has reluctantly agreed to be my marketing guy, but that's a job he will come to hate. I don't want that for him. So, Calderón Castro is going to pursue his music dreams." She met Cal's eyes, saw the light in his gaze, the warmth in his smile. She owed him a gift equal to what he was giving her. "Once you prove you're a

Holder, you and Elgin partner with me in the jewelry shop. If, and that's a big if, there's really a treasure and we find it, we will share equally in the profits."

"You said all cards on the table." Frank got up to pace in front of the fire. "You're holding something back, aren't you?"

Vero stood to face him. "Do you agree to the terms?"

"Elgin and I are in this together."

Vero turned to the insurance agent and gripped her elbow. "The only way this works is if no one keeps any more secrets. You tell Cal who forged his name on the documents, and you tell the police."

The woman shifted in her seat. Vero gnawed her lip. What if, like that old princess and the pea story, Barkley detected gems hidden in the seat cushion? Choco yawned, her doggy whine loud in the tense silence. Amigo wandered the room, sniffed Cal's pockets, and plopped down by the back door. "Elgin?"

"It was the secretary, Lisa Protus. I have the proof in my briefcase back at the hotel."

"Lisa?" Cal said. "What would she have to gain by such a maneuver?" He looked at Vero, the realization hitting them at the same time.

"Oh, my God," Vero said. "They planned this together."

Frank raised a hand. "Planned what?"

"Gisele Townsend's disappearance. Framing Cal. Maybe Lisa got cold feet and threatened to tell. But how was Brad Hanson involved?"

Cal shook his head, thinking through the last time he saw Gigi and Cerise together, the argument they had. "We're missing something important. When Gisele cornered me, she had someone else with her. I'm betting that someone helped kill Lisa and Brad."

At the mention of the murders, Elgin gagged and, hand over her mouth, clutched her stomach. Vero rushed her down the hall to the bathroom. The men looked at each other. "Who's Brad Hanson?" Frank said.

Cal explained his connection to Brad, noting Holder's attention to the details he shared. Not surprising, since the man was a private investigator but perhaps not a very good one if he had overlooked Brad. Vero and the insurance woman returned, Elgin white-faced and holding a fistful of tissues. Frank pulled her down beside him. "Don't judge us by the past few days, Veronica. We just want to provide for our family."

"Then let's get started." Vero joined Cal at the table. "Cal."

"I sent a message to the police. Meanwhile, why don't you and Frank talk about your great-great-grandfathers, Carl Holder and Sebastian Simon, and their connection to the 1893 World's Fair?"

Barkley stared at him, her expression proof that she, at least, didn't know the full story. Vero retrieved the oldest journal and held it up. "This explains everything, at least I think so. Frank, what do you know about an exhibition of gems at that Fair, one sponsored by a man named Higinbotham?"

Frank helped Elgin recline, covered her with a blanket, and came to the table. Vero handed him a sheaf of yellowed newspaper clippings stuffed into a plastic holder. "It's true that our great-great-grandfathers worked in the logging industry," Holder said as he sifted through the clippings. "This man, Higinbotham, must have, too."

"That must be how they met. They were doing transport work, delivering materials from the Saugatuck area to Chicago builders. Although there's no account of their initial meeting, Cal and I believe Higinbotham recruited Carl and Sebastian to help with the gem exposition, to deliver and set up the exhibits and perhaps even guard the collection. There were extra gems intended for display and sale during the Fair. A quantity of them went missing."

"I'm a pretty good student of history," Frank said. "I don't remember reading about any theft of gemstones."

"Higinbotham had insurance, and he would have hated the scandal, thinking two nineteen-year-olds from the country had absconded with a king's ransom in gems."

Holder shook his head. "You think that's how they got the funds to start the jewelry shop?"

"I do." Vero scooted beside him. "As much as I hate to admit it, our forebears were thieves. Nana Verna knew it, too."

Cal squeezed her shoulder. "Explain why you think that."

"Every year she left town in the fall, ostensibly to purchase new stock, but she never went anywhere. I found receipts in among the old clippings. The farthest she ever traveled was Chicago, where she stayed at the The Sauganash Hotel for two weeks, then came back to Saugatuck."

"Are you saying she lied about buying gems abroad?"

"Yes. Wherever she got the jewels for the shop, she didn't buy them. The books show no expenditures for gemstones since Nana took over the shop."

"Then my grandfather's stories must be true," Frank said, "and you know where the stolen gems are."

Vero clasped Cal's hand and stared out at the lake, the lie heavy in her mouth. "I don't know, but I have an idea. Once you prove you're family, I'll share my suspicion with you. But, Frank, no one except the four of us must ever know. Imagine the shit show if the Holder and Simon families were outed as thieves. Both our reputations would disappear for good."

Frank glanced at Elgin, who had fallen asleep on the sofa, turned back. "You have my word, cousin."

Cal's phone lit up with an incoming call. He rose to take it on the deck, his voice inaudible. Vero watched him pace. When the call ended, he looked at her, nodded, and slipped the phone in his pocket. Back inside, he helped himself to a beer and leaned against the counter. "Drop is set for tomorrow."

Frank moved to the table to examine the contents of Nana's mystery box. Vero glanced at the fireplace mantel, thinking about the wealth hidden there, the secrets her family had hidden for so many years. Was it right to continue the silence?

Cal

Wind whipped the waves against the shoreline, snapped the flags on the poles along the docks. Errant flurries swirled along the walkway. Cal glanced back at Vero, hunched into her coat, the worried look she'd worn since sunrise evident even at this distance. He raised a hand, motioning her to head for the shop, then squared his shoulders, made his way to the chain ferry, and stepped onboard. Norsuch and Harry had gone with the swat team and lay hidden among the pines on Mt. Baldy. For all any observer knew, Cal was alone. He clutched the money case close and waited for the cop working the ferry to close the gate. Normal operations ceased on Labor Day, but Norsuch had prevailed upon the city to grant access for this, their second, operation.

Once deposited on the other side, Cal trudged up the hill, shivering at the chill air that found a way inside the collar of his jacket. By the time he reached the stairway to the top of Baldy, sweat trickled down his back. He scanned the area, but even the regulars had judged the day too blustery for the climb. Setting aside the worry about all the ways this go wrong, Cal clutched the handrail and concentrated. Thin layers of ice coated each tread, making the ascent treacherous. He struggled to keep an eye on the woods to either side and maintain his footing. When he reached the halfway point, he paused to drink from the water bottle at his belt and check the time. The climb was taking too long. If he didn't move faster, he'd miss the handoff. Rage claimed him, anger at Gisele and Lisa for their attempt to frame him, to ruin his family business, to destroy everything he'd given up his dream to secure. What if Gigi and company were still screwing with him? A flash of blue ahead caught his attention. Cal crouched, wary, waiting for more movement. When nothing happened, he pressed on.

The last flights were the most difficult. His legs protested each step. The money case dragged at his arm. He steadied himself and, breathing heavily, surmounted the final flight. A figure in a hooded trench coat gazed out toward the waters of Lake Michigan, shoulders broad and straining at the material. It wasn't a woman. Cal hesitated, then set the case down and backed away. "Where's is she?"

Without turning, the man waved at the slope beyond the stairs. A minute passed. Two. Ten. A head appeared, hair covered by a ski cap, scarf blowing in the gusty wind. She looked up, smirked, and climbed on. Gisele. She extended a hand to the mystery man, who tugged her onto the boards and slipped a hand around her waist. They faced him together, Gisele Townsend and Link Storey. *Fuck*. Storey pulled a gun from his pocket and pointed it at Cal. "Get the money, Gisele."

Cal darted forward, grabbed the case, and hauled it back to his side. "Not yet. Where's your other partner, Cerise?"

Link and Gisele looked at each other, looked back at Cal. "Well, see," Gisele gestured at the woods, "I knew you wouldn't come alone. You don't like being told what to do, so we have a little insurance policy in place."

At the mention of insurance, Link snickered.

"Where is she?" Cal eased toward the first step down. Gisele preened.

"My sister and I had a disagreement about this whole scheme. She was opposed from the beginning." Gigi smirked. "We couldn't let her jeopardize everything."

"Where is she?"

"Remember the video we shot in that secret hideaway? She's there, waiting. As soon as Link and I are far enough away from you and Saugatuck, I'll text you the location."

"So, this is all about the money? You thought you'd get a million dollars from the insurance scam, and she helped you do that?"

Link scuffed a booted foot over the ice-covered floor, but he didn't lower the weapon. "No, Cerise protested, but after we proved how serious we were with Protus and Hanson, she shut up. But, hey, what do you care? Hand over the case, Cal, and we'll be on our way." Link raised his voice. "Officers, we have a hostage in a secure location. Stop us, and Cerise Townsend dies."

"Always thought you were a bastard, Storey. Good to know I wasn't wrong." Cal eased down one step, lifted the case, and heaved it over the railing. It sailed high and crashed into the brush, rattling and banging as it slipped and rolled down the mountain. Storey pulled the trigger. Cal dove sideways and slid, feet first, down the slick stairway. Gisele turned and ran onto the sandy western path. The SWAT team erupted from their hiding spots, weapons trained on Lincoln. Several broke off to follow Townsend. Storey edged toward the downside of the stairway and fired two more times. Wood splintered above Cal's head, but he kept slipping down the hill until he reached the first rest stop. Looking up, he watched a bullet strike the realtor. Storey faltered, fell to one knee, then toppled forward. Norsuch labored toward Cal, who lay on his side on the icy platform.

"Hey, Castro, you hit?"

Cal groaned and sat up. "No, just embarrassed."

"Man, you're a damn hero." Harry staggered up to clap Cal's shoulder. "What made you throw away the case?"

"Reflex, man." Cal dropped his head in his hands. "I couldn't let Gigi win."

Harry extended a hand to haul him up. "Storey's history. We've got Gisele. She'll tell us where her sister is."

"Don't be so sure, Duane." Clutching the handrail, Cal started down. "She only cares about herself."

A shout from the woods brought their conversation to a halt. "Found it," one of the SWAT guys called, emerging from the trees with the case in hand.

"Great," Cal muttered. "At least we didn't lose the money."

Vero

Lacey flakes of snow drifted over the pines that fronted the Country Club, turning the December landscape into a postcard of winter in Michigan. Vero surrendered her keys to the valet. Shuddering at the memory of what had happened to Brad Hanson at this very place six weeks ago, she drew her coat tighter, straightened her shoulders, and marched toward the entrance. The annual Chamber of Commerce holiday celebration was already half an hour old when she approached the sign-in table. A woman crossed her name off a list, offered her a nametag, and directed her toward one of the banquet rooms. Vero repressed the urge to turn and run. This was her first foray into the networking arena as the owner of a Saugatuck small business, and she was nervous. Last night Cal had left a cryptic message, something about unexpected surprises tonight. What was he hiding?

Vero handed her coat to the woman checking them, stuffed the ticket in her purse, and headed toward the party. She noted the clusters of professionals in the entry hall. Shopkeepers congregated in one corner. Restauranteurs gathered around the serving carts. Real estate people, minus Gisele, who was currently engaged in plea dealing while Cerise faced disbarment. Vero still found it hard to believe that Gigi and Storey had chased her that snowy night and that they had invaded her apartment hoping to find the ring Lisa Protus stole. Thinking of the robbery, Vero recalled Ellie's text from earlier that afternoon: `You got this girl strut your stuff in that hot new dress and have fun`

She ran a hand over the green velvet that matched her eyes and thanked God Ray had recovered from the knife attack. Everything could have been so much worse.

Shrugging off those memories, Vero scanned the crowded foyer. She spotted the Castros, but Cal wasn't among them. She had seen him less frequently since the capture of Gisele Townsend and the rescue of Cerise, their individual responsibilities forcing them in separate directions. But Antonio Castro had followed through with his commitment to invest in the shop. Frank and Elgin had signed the non-disclosure documents Glenn Canard drew up and were in the process of moving to the area. Elgin was eager to open her own insurance agency, and Frank planned to assist Vero in the jewelry store as well as continue his P.I. business.

The Castro community ties and reputation, cleared now of all suspicion, had stabilized the shop's financial situation, for which she was very grateful, but she missed Cal. Now that he was concentrating his efforts on his music career and recording an album, he spent most of his time out of town. Phone flirting and sexy innuendos weren't the same as being naked, warm, and satisfied in his bed. She blushed at the memory of their weekend in Chi-town right after the arrests. But prior to the mysterious text, Cal had been unusually distant. Of course, their relationship was probably built on nothing more than circumstance and mutual danger, a fleeting attraction due to close quarters and lust. Was that all it was? Vero swiped tears from her eyes and stepped into the banquet room.

Fairy lights hung suspended from the ceiling. Decorated pine trees graced each corner, gifts for needy families stacked beneath the boughs. Bartenders manned three stations as waiters circulated with trays of hors d'oeuvres. Drinks in hand, the Holland-Saugatuck business elite mingled or claimed seats at tables for eight, each decorated with a hurricane lamp holding a red candle, greenery artfully placed around each one. She glanced at the place cards, found her name at the table marked Castro Realty. She set her purse on the chair and looked up in time to catch Cal weaving his way through the crowd. She hated the way her heart leaped. She needed a moment to prepare herself. Pretending not to see him, she headed for the closest bar or the nearest exit, whichever appeared first. A hand on her elbow tugged her to a stop, and a voice she'd heard mostly on the phone over the past month whispered in her ear.

"Going somewhere, Miss Simon?"

She stuttered out an inane reply about the restroom. Cal steered her toward the French doors that exited onto the terrace. "We aren't going outside," she sputtered. "It's snowing."

"You'll look good with snowflakes in your hair. Por favor, Verónica." When she nodded, he hustled her through the doors, where the magic of winter rivaled the indoor splendor. In an alcove off to the right, a gas fireplace roared, benches and throw pillows arranged in a semicircle around it. Cal settled her beside him on a bench, pulled a blanket over their knees, and sighed. "Finally, I have you back where you belong."

"You—what? I've barely seen you since Gisele's arrest." She sounded strident, swallowed the hurt, managed a smile. "But I am glad you're playing music again."

Cal placed a finger on her lips and shook his head. "I know I haven't been in touch. It's unforgiveable, but it's part of the plan."

"What plan is that?"

"The one where I make you miss me so much you won't say no."

Vero wanted to put her hands on her hips and scowl, but Cal's arm tightened around her while he rooted in his pants pocket. He pinned her with a stare. "I want to kiss you, Vero. Do you want to kiss me?"

The yes slipped out before she could squelch it. He pressed his lips against hers, eliciting a throaty moan. "Calderón Castro, what are you up to?"

"I know we barely know each other, and I know I've been away way too much these past weeks, and I know it's too soon to say yes, but I hope you'll say maybe." He opened his hand and held out the ring she'd crafted, the one he'd purchased from her in what now seemed a lifetime ago. "This belongs to you. It's always been yours. I finally got it back from the police, and I want you to take it, but only if you say maybe."

"What am I saying maybe to?"

"Loving me. Being my wife. Sharing this wild, crazy new journey with me. We can date. Take your time. But you can't have the ring back unless you say maybe."

Vero didn't need time. She had accepted her feelings for him long ago, when shared danger had accelerated a bond that formed the moment he burst into SIMON's. She touched his cheek, then rolled her eyes and snatched the ring from his hand. No more hiding games for her. She slipped the ring on and smiled.

"Maybe yes."

The End

Acknowledgments

The first time I visited Saugatuck, Michigan, and climbed Mount Baldy, I knew I had to set a story there. This novel is the result of falling in love with a very special destination and finding characters who feel the same. The Chicago World's Fair of 1893 was only a distant footnote until a brainstorming session with members of the Central Ohio Fiction Writers organization to which I belong told me I need a jewel thief in the plot. And so I added two! Higinbotham really existed and he did host an exhibition at the Fair. The jewel theft I created as part of the plot, but it was fun to write! I also added or rearranged parts of the landscape, especially around Goshorn Lake. I hope the locals will forgive my liberties.

The novel benefitted greatly from my beta readers, so I extend my deepest gratitude to Linda Garcés, Leah Lore, Rebecca Case, and Jeannie Smith. Each read the manuscript, contributed their unique observations, and helped me polish the novel. I offer special thanks to my husband Gregg, who, through the years, has grown into the role of first reader and chief critic. He never disappoints in his close reading and catches all the car, gun, and outdoor details that escape me. Any errors of commission or omission are mine alone.

Dear Reader, if you like a book, please consider recommending it to your friends and posting a review on any social platform. Interested in future Byrd & Crowe mysteries or more novels by this author? Sign up for J.E. Irvin's newsletter at www.janetirvin.com for exclusive information, details on forthcoming books, and giveaways!

===

For sales, editorial information, subsidiary rights information
or a catalog, please write or phone or e-mail

New Atlantian Library
Manhanset House
Shelter Island Hts., New York 11965, US
Tel: 212-427-7139
www.AbsolutelyAmazingEbooks.com
bricktower@aol.com
www.IngramContent.com